Also by Andrea Kon

This Is My Song: A Biography of Petula Clark - WH Allen and Comet Books 1983
How to Survive Bereavement - Hodder and Stoughton - 2002
How to Find Love in Miid-Life - Hodder and Stoughton - 2003

The Amber Tablets

Andrea Kon

ISBN: 978-1-6847-0488-0 (sc)
ISBN: 978-1-6847-0487-3 (e)

Library of Congress Control Number: 2019906248

Lulu Publishing Services rev. date: 10/02/2019

Contents

Preface

On a visit to Israel many years ago, I met a cousin of my mother's who was born in Russia and who had survived part of the nine-hundred-day Siege of Leningrad that began in September 1941. Unlike the estimated one million souls who died of starvation, he escaped Russia's second city by braving the Ice Road across Lake Ladoga. As a journalist, I longed to hear more of his stories of survival in the face of apparently impossible odds. Sadly, the barriers of language, of miles, and of passing years prevented the conversations I longed to have with him. In 2007, I went on a trip to St Petersburg, formerly Leningrad, and took a tour of the Catherine Palace and visited its legendary reconstructed Amber Room. Standing in the magnificent fifty-five square metres (590 square feet) room and listening to the guide tell of how seven unskilled German officers had dismantled the room and packed it for shipping to Königsberg Castle in the Baltic in a mere thirty-six hours, I found the story unbelievable. Surely it was impossible for even the strongest skilled soldiers to complete such a herculean task of packing the vast panels of priceless amber mosaics, mirrors, and candelabra, to transport them, intact, in wartime quickly. I was fascinated. I started to research and read all I could about the disappearance of the original Amber Room that had been on display when the Russians entered Königsberg Castle in April 1945, and then dramatically disappeared without trace. I read all the possible explanations and rumours as to the fate of this priceless treasure. None has ever been confirmed. Despite rumours to the contrary, not a piece of the original Amber Room has ever been found.

I started to think about the logistics of how it had been moved from Leningrad (now St Petersburg) in 1941. My imagination took over. Supposing the Amber Room had been dismantled, not by seven burly German officers as the guide inside the reproduced Room now on show in the Catherine Palace told us, but by a Jewish slave labour gang of 150 men under orders (and the whips) of the Nazi authorities. The amber pieces themselves that comprised the mosaic panels that covered the room would have become very fragile, They had been covered by anxious Russian curators with a "skin" of flour-and-water paste and cigarette papers, hidden under hessian in an effort to hide it from the marauding Germans. Supposing some of the pieces of mosaic had fallen off the panels as they were removed, and what if one labourer had swallowed three pieces of amber mosaic no bigger than medicinal tablets. Supposing many years later, it was discovered that those three little pieces of amber were the only morsels of these mosaics to have survived?

This fictional story grew in my head and slowly became melded with so many other stories of the Jewish people at that time in history—stories from my own family and those I have read about or have been told by others.

During the Second World War, the Holocaust devastated the Jewish community in Europe and beyond, and my family, like most Jewish families worldwide, lost beloved members to the horrors of the Nazi war machine. Others incredibly, amazingly, miraculously and thankfully lived to tell the tales to their descendants. I don't know the names of all those in my own family who died, nor do I know exactly how we were related, only that they were once respected and once loved and that I, like many others, think of them as well as six million others who perished in the Holocaust. Every one of them deserves to be remembered as individuals, as mothers and fathers, sisters and brothers, children, grandparents, and grandchildren, and not only as victims. They were people just like us who lived and loved and fought and laughed and then succumbed to one of the cruellest mass murders in history.

I have altered the ways in which the Ghettos were run and the titles of those who were in charge to suit my plot line. I hope that readers will understand why.

I hope readers will understand why I used the real names of some off the Ghetto heroes, such as David Brawer in the Grodno Ghetto, and young Joseph Gavi in Minsk. I have used the real names of some who perished in their memory; the list "Hanna" is forced to type in Ghetto comes from a real list of those who perished in that terrible place. I have woven other heroes in where I can such as; Aaron Fiterson, Rosa Zuckerman in Minsk; Bergen-Belsen heroine Dr Hadassah (Ada) Bimkow Rosensaft in the DP Camp at Bergen Belsen; the late Reverend Leslie Hardman from Hendon in London, the first Jewish chaplain to go into that place of death, and 'Ada' Bimkow-Rosensaft's husband Joseph Rosensaft. Joseph Rosensaft, also a survivor, led the community of Jewish displaced persons at the camp where he stood firm for the rights of those who were beginning to rebuild their lives there. The couple married at the synagogue in Celle in 1945.

During the last century, politics, religion, and racism have torn millions of families and friends apart all over the world. Although *The Amber Tablets* is based on historical events between 1941 and 1950, and although some of the events described herein did happen, this story is entirely fictitious. Any resemblance to any persons living or dead is, with the exception of some amazing heroes and certain Nazi officers and politicians of the time, entirely coincidental. I offer my tale in memory of millions world-wide who die for their religious heritage and beliefs.

Acknowledgements

My grateful thanks to all those who have helped me with historical background and detailed information of how it really was. I hope those I don't name personally will forgive me and understand, but without them all, this book could never have been written.

My thanks to Nitza Spiro, founder of Spiro Ark, who led me to Amnon Weinstein, violin restorer extraordinaire, keeper and restorer of violins of the Holocaust. She told me many stories of survivors, but particularly the heroic story of the young violinist Motele Schlein. Motele was older than Arieh Weinstein and sadly didn't survive the war, but the young partisan was the inspiration for Arieh Weinstein's story. My thanks to the International Tracing Service, who kindly led me through the machinations of the service they offered to victims of the Holocaust in conjunction with UNRRA and the Red Cross after 1946. My thanks, too, to Clarks Shoes, who told me how to make possible the hiding of pieces of amber inside the heels of a pair of old boots.

My thanks also to Sir Ben and Lady Arza Helfgott and Ben's sister Mala Tribich, MBE, whose hospitality led to introductions to such amazing people as Lili Pohlmann of the 45's and Anita Lasker-Wallfisch, who played the cello in the Auschwitz Women's Orchestra. I thank Rita Eker and Doreen Gainsford (on behalf to the 35's Campaign for Soviet Jewry) for opening old files and enabling me to discover background information of the lives lived by so many Russian Jews from the period 1945 through to the early 1960s.

My grateful thanks, too, to Shimon Vapne, who sadly passed away in 2000 but who welcomed me back very warmly into our family in 1984 after so many wasted years; Simeon Karminsky is loosely based on him. His daughter Paya Yussim, a former first violinist with the Israeli Philharmonic Orchestra, filled in so many details of real life in Russia in the 1940's and 1950's. She confirmed most of the story of the tablecloth.

I would like to thank my writing tutors and fellow students at the Mary Ward Centre in Central London, at the Hampstead Scientific and Literary Society and the City Lit, all of whom listened with such patience and gave me to much practical advice, encouragement and feedback to help me write and finish this book and gave so much valuable feedback.

I would like to thank my amazing agent, Fiona Lindsay at Limelight Management, for all her patience and assistance. Most of all, I want to thank my long-suffering husband, Peter Gordon, for encouraging me to finally finish this eleven-year-long journey—and for tolerating being awakened at night as I relived scenes from this book out loud, in dreams and in nightmares.

Prologue: November, 1941

It was bitterly cold. Snow was blowing in through the frames of the glassless windows, laying a hem of delicate white lace to melt on the intricate wooden parquet floor beneath. His painfully dry mouth began to salivate. If only he could lick it, run to the other side of the room, and scoop up one huge handful to assuage his thirst and perhaps even ease this dreadful hunger that was gnawing at his stomach like the sharp claws of a rat. For him and the other 150 shivering slave labourers working to dismantle the vast amber mosaics in this place, starvation was a constant partner, teasing them with the knowledge that they were still alive, threatening to overpower them with sudden death. All the labourers were clad in nothing more than thin cotton blue-striped pyjamas. By contrast, seven well-fed, whip-wielding soldiers warm in heavy grey greatcoats, their throats muffled with thick woollen scarves, their hands warmed by lined leather gloves, were stationed round the room, thrashing their arms back and forth around their bodies to retain heat. All of them wore the black peaked caps of the Gestapo.

Simeon Karminsky was about to lay a small piece of the fragile amber mosaic that had fallen from its panel into the gauze cradle attached to the "coffin", where it was to rest, when he became acutely aware of the tiny honey-coloured piece in his hand. A screech of terror from the right-hand side of the room suddenly shattered the eerie silence. Until that moment, and although there were around 150 men in the room, the only noise had been caused by their movements. But this was an animal scream. Simeon looked across. The sound lowered to the howl of pure animal anguish, like a wolf caught in a forest trap, as steel-tipped whips lashed out, scoring into the skeletal frame of the man being beaten.

The SS officer in charge blew a whistle. Work around the room stopped.

"I warned you. Did you think we wouldn't notice little pieces of amber sticking out of your ugly earholes, you Jew fool?"

Simeon and his workmate had lowered the huge panel into the crate before standing straight in obedience to the whistle. Simeon looked down at the tiny piece of resin with a single insect at its centre still in the palm of his hand, no bigger than a headache tablet, and suddenly, inexplicably, he was obsessed by an urge to swallow it now, while everyone's attention was diverted. He focused hard, his thoughts recalling the delicious taste of his mother's warm chicken soup, thick with chopped vegetables and golden fat floating over the tiny pieces of chicken that hovered just below the surface. The little morsel of amber was similar in colour to Mama's soup, that deep appetising golden liquid that washed down his throat, leaving behind the taste of deliciousness. He could smell the soup, and his mouth filled with saliva. He pretended to wipe his mouth, but instead he placed the amber "tablet" on his tongue and swallowed hard. It was gone almost before he realised it, leaving a bitter, sticky, floury taste. Although the tiny insect had been petrified inside the piece of amber millions of years ago, he wondered vaguely whether it might have retained any nutritional value. He was so desperately, terribly hungry.

The man continued to scream as a steel-tipped whip played agonisingly around his thighs, calves, and feet, cutting into the frail skin so that everyone could see the thin streams of blood that dripped down his bony legs. He appeared to be doing a bizarre dance. All eyes were on him, even those of the SS officer in charge, who stood smirking, a cigarette in a tortoiseshell holder balancing on his bottom lip. The whips cracked again. The screams had quietened to a low, continual guttural whine until the next whip crack, when they intensified again. The man's arms and legs were flailing as he tried to hit back at his attackers with almost superhuman strength. It looked as though even the two large soldiers who were trying to contain him had failed to quell the ferocity of their frail victim's response to their beatings. Now there were four well-built, well-nourished soldiers grappling at the victim's hands and feet. At any moment, Simeon thought, the man's manic agony would surely be ended by a single shot. Humans didn't treat rats like this.

Simeon leant forward towards the cradle, pretending to put another piece of mosaic into it, but instead he lifted one out. It was a small, many-sided piece. He could feel carving on its exterior. It was dark as a treacle toffee. The remembered sweetness of toffee filled his mouth in place of the savoury chicken soup. He thought he would kill for a real taste of toffee. He swallowed the second piece just as the man's screeches rose to a crescendo. All attention was glued on the madman now. No one was taking any notice of Simeon Karminsky.

It was a private challenge: Simeon Karminsky against the pure evil of the entire Nazi regime. He stretched his arm into the cradle for a third time and picked another piece out by touch alone. He managed to glance at it briefly before putting it into his mouth. It was a darker gold than the first piece, but whereas the other two had been unconventional shapes, this one was long and thin. Its surface was etched with fine deep ridges ending in a tiny smooth, curved, claw-like end. It might have represented an eagle's claw, its talon. Only as he swallowed it did he realise he'd misjudged the length of the thing. It stuck in his throat, causing him to choke.

The sound of whips beating against the wooden floor, the poor man's high-pitched yelps, and a shot fired across the room all echoed loudly, masking Simeon's cough. He watched the victim fall to the floor like a marionette whose puppeteer had suddenly dropped its strings. A second shot was fired into the prone body. Simeon had to stop coughing. He drew on all his willpower, knowing that if he didn't control himself, the gun would be aimed at him. He swallowed again, hard. The thing was moving down his throat, the natural, unconscious action of swallowing taking over his gullet.

The man he'd spoken to earlier sidled close. "Did you do what I think I saw you do?" he whispered.

"Depends what you think you saw," Simeon Karminsky replied in a hoarse whisper.

Chapter 1

Simeon, late August 1941

THE LAST TIME SIMEON KARMINSKY HAD BEEN HOME WAS IN LATE JANUARY. He remembered so clearly how he'd dressed himself in the uniform the Russian Army had sent for him. He'd pulled on the heavy cotton underwear designed "to keep out the Russian winter", drawn the uniform *gymnasterka* M41 over his short, curly red hair, tucked his khaki breeches into heavy, black knee-high boots, and shrugged into the sheepskin they'd sent him. He had a grey woollen hat as well. Then he'd kissed his mama and tearful pregnant wife, Dora, goodbye and marched proudly down Rigas Street in a blizzard.

Now as Engineer Third Class Simeon Karminsky, late of the Twelfth Mechanised Corps of the Forty-Second Brigade, he retraced his steps. All that remained of that uniform were the torn shirt, heavily soiled breeches, and tall black boots. Sweat dripped down his filthy neck. He itched all over and couldn't help scratching as the hot sun burnt his scalp and his neck through the hatless bush of his fiery red hair. It had taken Simeon fifty-six long days and as many sleepless nights to walk and hitch his way back from the battlefield at Raseiniai to his home village of Krustpils in Latvia.

He'd slept in ditches and alongside cattle and pigs in barns when it rained. Every village he'd walked through had been crawling with the Nazi bastards. Messages of hate towards the Jews had been scrawled on walls and fences everywhere. He'd read the notices forbidding Jews to enter cinemas or schools and requiring them to sit on certain benches in parks. They could enter only certain shops. He still had a couple of roubles left in his pocket and had been able to buy bread, cheese, and bits of fruit in a few markets. When he couldn't buy food, he stole it.

"No, I'm sorry. I don't have coupons," he'd explained to one stall holder who demanded coupons for two hundred grams of bread. "I've just come off the battlefield. People's Volunteers. The Red Army. Can't you see?"

He skittered through the forest, keeping low behind bushes, until he reached Krustpils Castle on the outskirts of town. It looked the same as it always had: a large, imposing yellow structure. He'd lived here all his life, yet he realised suddenly he didn't know anything at all about the famous castle.

As he walked farther towards town, he sniffed. The foul odour of burnt and charred wood filled his nose. His eyes watered, and he could feel rivers of dirt running down his freckled face. He looked up and realised he was standing right beside the place where the Olmsher Bet Midrash, the exquisite three-hundred-year-old wooden synagogue decorated with carvings of flowers and eagles and renowned for its beauty throughout Latvia, had stood. But it wasn't there anymore. All that remained were charred sticks of wood and an outline where rooms had been. He'd celebrated his bar mitzvah, his congregation's acknowledgement that he had reached Jewish manhood, here. It was where he and his seventeen-year-old Dora had stood beneath the wedding canopy exactly one year ago and heard Rebbe Yitzhak Guartin sanctify their marriage. His beautiful Dora had flowers in her long, dark hair, her face was covered with a white veil, and her big brown eyes had sparkled. She was so petite—elfin—and only a child, yet now she was expecting a baby herself. He wondered whether she'd grown round and fat or if she had possibly even given birth already.

Two German soldiers in grey Wehrmacht uniforms emerged from a doorway, and Simeon instinctively drew back into a gap between buildings. The bloody Germans were swarming everywhere else. Why had he told himself they wouldn't be here? He'd spent the last two months dodging them at every corner.

He'd known the Molotov–Ribbentrop pact of 1938 couldn't last. When the Germans overran Poland in 1939, it was obvious that Russia would be next. The powers that be had known it would come to this. Why else would Simeon or any of the other People's Volunteers have been called up for basic training last December?

The call to arms had come at work. A qualified mechanical engineer with a degree from Riga University, Simeon had been working at Tank

Factory 174 in nearby Jekabpils. Tanks had fascinated him since childhood, and his specialist knowledge of the now almost obsolete T-24s and the newer T-26s that made up the bulk of the Red Army's war machines meant he was an invaluable asset.

He'd been working on modifications to the secret T-34s and KVs, the Soviets' latest and most innovative field tanks, when he'd been summoned to his boss's office. "You are to stop what you're doing and go directly to Chief Engineer Preditis's office," the secretary said to him. He wondered which ambiguous rule he'd flouted. They were always changing the rules. This was Stalin's Russia.

He knocked somewhat tenuously, and Preditis himself answered the door. To Simeon's amazement, he extended his hand warmly. Simeon blinked, not sure what to expect next. Then he saw a man in military uniform occupying one of the two chairs in front of Preditis's desk.

"A drink, Karminsky?" his boss said.

"Thank you, but no, sir. Not while I'm working."

"May I introduce you to Lieutenant Colonel Leonid Berlovsky? Colonel Berlovsky is in command of the Mechanised Corps of the entire Soviet Army." He turned to the officer and said, "Sir, may I present our star worker in this factory, Comrade Simeon Karminsky?"

Simeon blushed scarlet. The lieutenant colonel took a gold case from his pocket and offered cigarettes to both Preditis and Simeon. Simeon took one and puffed anxiously, wondering what might come next.

"You know these tanks, especially the newer tanks, better than any man in the factory, I understand," the lieutenant colonel said. "I hear excellent reports of you. We need a man with knowledge like yours to carry out running repairs on these tanks in trials they are doing in Lithuania. We thought you are the man to take charge of these trials, modify the tanks if they are found to be lacking in any way, advise the soldiers in the field on maintenance, and so on. You would be in a position of vital importance with the Twelfth Soviet Mechanised Corps, Comrade Karminsky. You will go through basic training of course, but you will soon learn the army ways. From henceforth, you are to be known as Lieutenant Engineer Third Rank, the Forty-Second Brigade, the People's Volunteers. You will answer directly to Major General Shestopalov—as indeed do I."

"I'm going as a working engineer, not a fighting soldier," Simeon later tried to reassure his doubting mother and wife.

He'd initially been billeted in Riga and was able to commute the 140 kilometres home for weekends when he wasn't working. In March, however, news came regarding the Germans' progress into Poland, and it certainly wasn't good news for Jews. Many, they heard, were being herded into ghettos in both Austria and Germany. He felt compelled to write home, although he knew it was dangerous for them all. He must try to ensure his wife and mother moved somewhere safe. Leningrad. That was it. Surely the Germans could never get into Leningrad. He'd write to them, telling them to go on "holiday" to stay with his cousin Ivan until the baby was born.

> Dearest Dora and Mama,
>
> (Please, Dora, read this to Mama, won't you?)
>
> I may be away a little longer than I anticipated and wonder if you two should take a trip to Leningrad, where you can stay with our cousin Ivan and his wife, Gilda. The sea air in Leningrad will do you both good, and should the baby arrive early, perhaps Gilda could give you a helping hand. I will join you both there as soon as I can. I love you.
>
> Your adoring husband and son,
>
> Simeon

The Germans crossed the border on 22 June in what became known as Operation Barbarossa. Simeon had been working underneath a tank when the end came for him on the fourth day of what was later to be known as the Battle of Raseiniai. The Russians, most of them ill trained and poorly armed, held out for three days against the German bombardment both on land and from the air. On the fourth day, three of his comrades were huddled in the cabin of a T-24 tank. They were without food, without water, without ammunition, and with little fuel. They needed a miracle to save them, and all their hope for that miracle lay with Simeon Karminsky.

Simeon was conscious of the impact as the Panzer struck. He immediately braced and then rolled as far and as fast as he could away from the burning vehicle. He felt himself lifted into the air by the up-blast, knowing the men inside the tank stood no chance.

He awoke to find himself face down in a muddy ditch, the taste of wet earth sour in his mouth. He felt his limbs. They all appeared to work, but as he attempted to turn over, a sharp wave of intense pain gripped his ribcage and overwhelmed him. He managed to pull himself up very slowly, every intake of breath an agony.

He looked around and rubbed his eyes, making them smart. Everything was quiet now. Everything was still. He saw loose limbs littering the ground—here an arm, the palm of its hand outstretched as though waiting to receive a gift; there a leg in its high leather boot torn off from the thigh; a headless torso spreadeagled in the mud. The remnants of his precious tanks were now burnt-out shells, some lying on their sides like discarded toys.

He listened but heard nothing. He coughed, and even the sound of his own cough was silent. The noise of the explosions had deafened him. He prayed it was only temporary.

Simeon lay still for hours until the sky began to darken. Still nothing moved. He shook his head and stared at the horizon, believing he could see smoke in the distance. Around him, the land looked deserted. Had he alone of the Twelfth Mechanised Corps survived this battle? There was no one left to ask permission as far as he could see. There was only one thing left for him to do: go home.

He was now outside his old home at 81 Rigas Street. To his horror, the door of the little wooden one-storey building that was his parents' hardware shop and the place where he'd been born was hanging loose on one hinge. As he put his head inside, he realised he was too late. He cried out in dismay. "Mama, Dora! Dora, where are you?" Then he stopped himself. Saucepans, buckets, cleaning mops, brooms, watering cans, and colanders lay scattered and broken alongside knives, nails, screws, and wood saws caught with tangled string. He walked through to the living quarters at the back. The mattress that had been on the bed he and Dora shared, the same mattress on which he and his twin sister, Hanna, had been born, lay on its side, slashed through. "So," he whispered to himself, "they were looking for hidden money." On the large scrubbed pine table that also served as a work surface, the remains of a meal stood, mouldy and blue. *How long has it been sitting there?* he wondered. His foot crunched, and he heard the tinkle of a little bell. He picked up his foot to see he'd crushed a wooden rattle tied round with a pink ribbon. It held a tiny silver bell at its heart. He cradled it gently. A pink ribbon. So, it was a girl. He had a daughter. His mother had had two such rattles, one tied with a pink bow and one with a blue one. Hanna's and Simeon's. His mother had preserved them as keepsakes "To remind me how you two were once sweet babies," she'd told them. When Hanna had announced she was pregnant, his mama had been so excited at the idea of a grandchild that she had retrieved them from the drawer in which she kept all her precious keepsakes. On hearing of the birth of her first grandchild, Max, named for his grandfather Moshe, she'd given him the blue-beribboned rattle.

"Such a blessing to have a grandson," she'd told Simeon. "I will stay with Hanna and help her husband's mother, Rachel, tend the baby, at least until after the circumcision. Such a shame your papa didn't live to share such joy. The other rattle is for the first granddaughter. It will be your daughter, I hope."

So, she'd kept her word. Dora had had a girl and Mama had given her the rattle. He stroked the mess of wooden splinters, its silver bell silenced by crushing but with its little pink ribbon intact.

"I wonder what Dora has called her?" he whispered to himself. A tear slid down his face as he realised he hadn't even had enough time together to discuss baby names with his young wife. He slipped the broken rattle into his pocket.

Perhaps they'd gone to Leningrad as he'd suggested, although by the look of things, they'd left in a great hurry. Would his meticulous mama have left a half-eaten meal on the table if she'd run to catch a train? No. She would have insisted the house was tidy "for when we get back". He knew his mother so well. Dora was very much the same. But whom could he ask? The place was overrun with the enemy.

There was only one person in this town who might know where they were: Anna Berzin, his mother's non-Jewish friend. They had become friends after her frequent visits to his parents' little hardware shop. They had so much in common, Anna Berzin and his mother. He remembered how, in summer, they would often sit, embroidering tablecloths for their daughters' and future daughters-in-laws' bottom drawers, together. He could see them now, his mother's cloth a triumph of brilliant colours, bright red poppies, yellow roses, blue irises and purple lavender set amid glorious shades of green leaves. Anna's cloth was a pretty collection of blues, whites, and greys. Pulling threads in and out together, sipping black tea through sugar cut from the lump held in their teeth as the sun faded to a golden glow, they appeared to be in total harmony in both mind and spirit.

It took Simeon another quarter of an hour to reach Anna Berzin's red front door. As he passed the old kosher abattoir, he could hear the pathetic sounds of animals trapped inside, crying and banging helplessly against the corrugated iron walls. Their cries sounded almost human.

He knocked at the Berzins' door. Even as Anna opened the door a slit, he could see his mama's tablecloth on Anna's table and breathed a sigh of relief. No one else had a cloth like that embroidered with such glorious bouquets of hand-stitched flowers.

"Thank God," he murmured softly. "They're here. Anna, I knew you wouldn't let them down." He almost fell into her arms. The balloon of hope burst as she stared at him, her blue eyes narrowing to slits in her thin, drawn face. For a moment, the two of them stood, simply staring at one another. It was hardly the welcome he'd hoped for.

"So what does the brave Jew soldier Karminsky want?" She drew her cheeks in, gathering spittle, pursed her lips, and spat at him. He shook his head in disbelief. Had she done that for effect? Did she think she was being watched?

"Anna, dear Anna. Quickly, please, let me in. Did Mama and Dora go to Leningrad? Or did they go to Hanna in Vidzy? Or are they here, Anna? Are you hiding them? If you know, Anna Berzin, tell me, please? Tell me and I'll go."

He had put his foot forward on her doorstep in the expectation she would drag him inside as quickly as she could to avoid being seen by the Germans. Instead, she tried to slam the door against his foot. "Get out, filthy Jew. You stink."

He pushed his shoulder against the door. He had lost much weight since the Battle of Raseiniai, but even so he was taller, stronger, and heavier than Anna. The door gave slightly. There was still no doubt in his mind. If Mama's cloth was on her table, then Anna had helped them escape. She must have feared she was being watched. They were hiding in her cellar. That was it. Mama had given her the cloth in payment for hiding them.

"May God bless you, Anna Berzin," he whispered. "The cloth."

Anna's lips were drawn tight the little ridges on her upper lip stretched over pale pink gums. He could see every one of the wispy grey hairs sprouting from her pointed chin. She was very bent. He had a vague memory of Mama mentioning that she had some kind of rheumatoid disease that made movement difficult for her.

"Go join the rest of them in the abattoir, Jew!" she shrieked.

Hanna, the voice inside him pleaded to his big sister. He and his twin had been able to communicate without words almost since the day they were born in February 1919. She was thirty-five minutes older than he and would always be his "big sister".

Help me, Hanna. Tell me what to do.

Anna Berzin called over her shoulder, "Valdis, run for the police."

Valdis Berzin's stubbled face appeared over his mother's shoulder, his brown hair hanging lank and greasy. Simeon knew he himself stank, but Valdis's stench was worse. He pushed himself in front of his mother, and it was then that Simeon saw the glint from the blade of the kitchen knife reflected by the candle on the table. "You heard her. Get out, Jew," Valdis roared at him.

"I'm not leaving here without my mama's cloth!"

Valdis Berzin was facing Simeon now, the knife pointing straight at Simeon's chest. Fear pumped his adrenaline, fuelling him with fight. Without thinking, he wrestled with the weaker man and pushed his arm behind his back. They both heard the bone snap. Valdis screeched. Simeon had the knife. "You bastard!" he yelled. "You'd stand by and watch friends shipped to their death and do nothing." He thrust the knife into Berzin's chest and yanked it out. The man sank to his knees. Blood spurted from the gaping hole and began dribbling from Valdis's nose and mouth. His eyes flickered.

Simeon was inside the house now. He slammed the front door with his foot. Anna Berzin tried jumping onto his back. She was screaming and scratching at him like an alley cat. "Filthy Jew. I'll see you hang for this."

Simeon turned on her, the knife still in his hand, and caught her shoulder. She yelped with surprised pain, fell off his back, and sank on the floor. He thrust the knife again, this time into her back. Too shocked and weak to scream or cry out, she whimpered. Blood was everywhere, the blood of mother and son pooled together. Valdis was quiet. Simeon knelt beside him and put his finger to his neck. There was no pulse.

He could hear Anna fighting for breath in noisy hollow gasps. He stood back, surveying what he'd done, in horror. He hadn't killed a single soul in battle. Now he'd murdered one, if not two, of the people he'd known all his life. Valdis was dead. Anna would soon join him. How much longer would it be until a suspicious neighbour came to investigate the noises?

He picked up Anna Berzin and realised there was no weight to her. Her face was chalk white, and she was still gasping and coughing blood. He laid her in a corner, and she started to gibber senselessly in a high-pitched tone.

Simeon's own clothes were soaked in their blood. He went to the kitchen sink, stripped naked, and pumped cold water into the bowl in the sink. As he sluiced his body down, he watched it turning from pale pink swirls to a watery blood red. He emptied the sink, refilled it, and soaped himself with the sliver of green household soap he found on the side, afterwards drying himself as best he could on the filthy rag Anna Berzin had used as a dishcloth. Suddenly he recalled what she had said: the Jews were in the abattoir. He had heard people. People, not animals. Fear struck at him. Supposing his mama, Dora, and the baby were in there? Supposing they were among those he'd heard fighting and scratching and banging for freedom? He must go and rescue them. He must do it now.

He needed clothes. If only he could speak to Hanna; Hanna would know what to do. She was the practical twin. He ran into Valdis Berzin's bedroom and pulled two blankets off the bed. Back in the living room, he rolled Valdis in one blanket and Anna in the other. She was barely breathing now.

He picked up the rattle and put it in pocket of the borrowed trousers and threw the blood-soaked garments that had once been his clothes, along with his identity card, onto the fire with an extra log. He watched it all catch. The blood sizzled. The room stank. Back in Valdis's bedroom, he picked up the clothing that had been strewn around the floor. He found a rough woven shirt, some bib-fronted workman's overalls, and some heavy, muddied boots built up on one side to minimise the man's limp. Valdis had suffered from polio as a child, Simeon recalled. The boots were almost the same size as his own. He pulled them on and stood up. The acquired limp felt very strange. He walked across the living room and added another couple of logs from the bucket in the hearth to the fire so it flared vigorously. He picked up the rattle and put it in pocket of the borrowed trousers. He tapped the trousers and realised he'd thrown his cigarettes away with his uniform trousers. He was dying for a cigarette. Back in the bedroom, he opened the drawer at the side of Valdis Berzin's bed and found three unopened packs. He opened one of them and lit a cigarette. A fourth pack, tucked right at the back, contained a fat roll of rouble notes. He stuffed the cigarettes and the money into the front pocket of the workman's bib trousers. Then he saw the real treasure: Valdis Berzin's identity papers were lying on top of the bedside table.

He let himself out through the back. Looking back, he saw his mama's tablecloth. It had been splashed with droplets of the Berzins' blood, but he couldn't leave it there. He stuffed it into a rucksack he'd noticed in the little bedroom. As he went back to the kitchen, he grabbed at a loaf of black bread and some cheese. Only as he saw it had he realised how hungry he was. He hadn't eaten for more than twenty-four hours. He drank some water from the pump.

He had to get back to the abattoir. According to his watch, it was now nearly five in the morning. In the half-light of predawn, he crept round the familiar backstreets to the abattoir, keeping as close as he could to the shadows of buildings. He stopped to listen. Silence hung heavily over the corrugated iron shed now. Maybe they were all asleep in there. He dared not make a noise for fear of waking any light sleepers amongst the guards. He heard Hanna's voice in his head: *Get out. Run—as fast and as far as you can. You are a murderer now, a wanted man.*

A metal waste bin rattled against the tin shed. Probably rats. The dustbin rolled and hit the iron shed again. He walked cautiously round the building. At the back, the corrugated iron stood proud of the ground. He lay on his belly and looked through the crack. The place appeared empty. It had been vacated, almost certainly by force, in the few short hours since he'd entered the Berzin house. All that remained was a vile stench which the occupants, whether man or beast, had left behind. Again, he wondered where Hanna was. Had the Germans reached Vidzy? Byelorussia was right on the Polish border. He heard the clang of the dustbin against the corrugated iron again. The bin was moving as if possessed. Had Anna Berzin told him the truth? Had there been people in there, his people? His own family, perhaps? He caught a flash of what he thought must be a rat's brown tail scuttling from the dustbin and out into the forest. Whatever had been inside that bin was now running free.

He stood still for a moment longer, trying to hear his twin sister Hanna's voice the way he used to when they were small and bullies in the playground teased him about his red hair. All he could hear, however, were the old familiar forest sounds. He knew he must go to Leningrad to look for his mother and sister.

Chapter 2

Hanna, Vidzy, Latvia, 22 June 1941

"MAX, SHMUELY. QUICK. UNDER THE TABLE. SHH. VERY QUIET." HANNA bent low to reassure her little sons, her finger to her lips. She heard four-year-old Max trying to muffle his two-year-old brother's fear-filled whimpers and put her finger to her lips as she saw the older brother stiffening his lips and drawing the terrified toddler into his shoulder. "Shh," she whispered. "Stay there. Mama's here." She watched Max bravely swallow a sob as he responded to the urgency in her voice. She stood quickly, adjusting the fall of the long white tablecloth to conceal the children. Standing back, she could still see a tiny sandy curl of her youngest son Shmuely's hair. The tablecloth wasn't quite long enough to totally conceal them.

"Back darling, back, quickly," she begged him. "Max, you're a big boy. Look after him. Keep him away from the edge. That's it. Right back against the wall. Quiet. No. No, don't try to look out of the window."

"Links, stamp. Recht, stamp. Links, stamp. Recht, stamp. Halt." The synchronised clatter of hundreds of steel-tipped jackboots pounding on the sun-baked muddy main street of Vidzy stopped right outside the old single-storey wooden house that was their home. Hanna knew her neighbours would be as scared as she was.

For a few moments, everything was ominously quiet. A bellowed order broke the silence. Hanna braced herself. She heard little Shmuely whimpering again and Max trying to quieten his sobs. "Mama says shh,

11

shush," he whispered. She leant down on her haunches with her finger to her mouth, praying for just a minute more.

"Remember, I told you this is a very special game of hide-and-seek. Nobody must find you, especially not the soldiers. Shh, darling boys. Not a sound."

The silence was shattered as the heavy leather Wehrmacht boots collided with their neighbours' weak wooden doors. The sounds of the wood splintering, the screams and cries of terror as the soldiers entered the neighbouring houses further up the street, overwhelmed by the roaring guttural orders, shredded the once peaceful little village.

They had prayed so hard this wouldn't happen. Nevertheless, Hannah's clever husband, Nat, was ready. He'd heard the news of the anguish the Nazis were inflicting on the Jews just across the border in Poland. He was a tall, dark man with dark curly hair and well-developed muscles. As a carpenter and furniture maker, he was used to hauling heavy blocks of wood. He was in the forest right now, making the little boathouse on the edge of the lake as habitable as possible for the five of them, Hanna; his mama, Rachel, who lived with them; their two little boys; and, of course, himself. The disused boathouse was a special place. They had no idea to whom it belonged, only that it was on the shallowest reach of the lake, where it had apparently remained empty for years. The padlock on the front was rusty with damp and age. At the back, however, a few of the boards had loosened. Inside it housed two old rowing boats, covered in a tarpaulin, as well as other boating junk. The children both loved this place. It was their favourite picnic spot. They could paddle safely in the shallows of the lake while their parents relaxed and enjoyed lazy summer afternoons, shaded by a large oak and a number of pines and willows that hemmed the edge of the thick forest.

Little Max, having discovered the loose board at the back when the family had been playing hide-and-seek with him, disappeared through it. They were used to Max "hiding" where they could spot him easily. A sturdy child, tall for his age, with thick, curly dark brown hair just like Nat's and eyes even darker than his father's, he had his usual hiding places just behind a tree or in the long grass, where he'd lie flat. They would carry out a pretend search, watching him all the time. "Maxi, where are you?" they would call. Suddenly, the toddler would jump up, laughing and shouting: "Here I am." He would jump on his mother's back, pulling at her long red curls, or spring onto his papa's lap, giggling: "You didn't look hard enough." But this one time, there'd been no giveaway giggle, no easy sighting. They both began to panic when a meticulous search of his pet hiding places had failed to reveal him.

"That little monkey. He's run off into the forest," Nat said, trying to allay Hanna's obvious fears. "But you know him. He won't stay hidden too long. Any minute now he'll start giggling. You stay with the baby while I go searching." He had given her a reassuring hug. "Don't worry. He'll soon be back." She was a slight woman but tall like her twin brother, Simeon. They shared the same carrot-coloured hair and physical strength, but at that moment, she had been rendered rigid with fear. She and her husband both began to shout loudly: "Max. Maxeee. Where are you? Come out. You won!" Nat had already begun to run around the outside of the little shack, looking for clues, when they heard the inevitable giggle. It came from inside the old boathouse. How had he gotten in there? Hanna had been twisting her red-gold hair anxiously around her forefinger and clenching her teeth. Nat had discovered the loose board. Unable to squeeze his large frame through, he'd tugged at the plank with his bare hands until it gave enough for him to clamber inside. There he found his naughty little son crouching beside one of two rowing boats, both covered in the tarpaulin. "Here I am. I won. I'm the winner." Max chortled.

They'd both tried to scold him, but they couldn't help laughing at their small son's ingenuity.

It was that game that had given Nat the idea of turning the boathouse into a safe hiding place as early as May, as the news from Poland became darker and more ominous. There was talk of death camps the Nazis were building in and around Germany, Poland, and Austria, and of Jews being rounded up into ghettos and slaughtered in their droves. It was too close for comfort. They'd furnished the boat hut by degrees, transporting tins of food and other essentials there in the horse cart Nat normally used to carry raw wood from the forest to his carpentry shop or to deliver the beautiful furniture he had made in the yard of their home to the nearby towns and villages. He was at the boathouse now, having delivered a new table to the Tarasevich family in Polatsk. He'd gone on from there to the boathouse as far as Hanna knew, this time to take kerosene, a second stove to keep them warm if they were forced to stay there all winter, and clothing, bedding, and blankets. Listening to the chaos outside her own front door now, Hanna wondered if they'd left the move to the boathouse one day too late.

"If they come when I'm out, don't show them fear," Nat had repeatedly told her. "Bullies become bigger bullies when they see they're winning." It was easier said than done. She motioned to her mother-in-law, a tiny round woman in her late fifties whose fine white hair was tied behind her head in a black scarf, babushka style, to sit in her rocking chair.

"Remember what we discussed, Mama," she said, placing a supportive hand on the older woman's shoulder as she passed her and walked towards the door. She peeked briefly under the tablecloth one last time. The two children were huddled together, clutching one another tight with fear. Then, pulling herself up to her full height, as tall and straight as she could, she opened the door, catching a young Gestapo boy with his leg poised to kick it down. Despite her fear, she couldn't help but smile at the look of amazement on the youngster's face.

"Can I help you?" She spoke in perfect German, making it sound as though she were greeting a peddler rather than a man who was threatening her family's very existence. She would show these evil men that not every Jewish woman cowered at the sight of Nazi bullies. She wouldn't let them smell the fear that even now was gnawing at her guts. They wouldn't read terror in her eyes or hear her heart thumping in her chest. She had heard about the tactics of these men. She knew they might eventually find the boys. There was no other place in this little house to hide them. All of them might be kicked, beaten, or even killed if they were found, but it was a risk she had to take. She'd do anything and everything required of her to keep her precious babies safe.

"Heil Hitler." A tall blond Gestapo officer stood behind the youth she'd caught with his foot in the air. He doffed his cap as though they were playing the same game. "SS-Hauptsturmführer Frederick Schlossberg at your service, ma'am." The two young soldiers who looked barely old enough to shave stood behind him, giggling. One was shorter and even slighter than Hanna.

"So, a Jewess who welcomes us. Unlike your pig ignorant neighbours, you have the sense to open the door before we kick it to splinters. Is this a welcoming committee?"

He strode inside as if an invited guest and gestured at the old woman sitting motionless in her rocking chair. He turned to Hanna. "Your mother? A clever Jewess? Or an arrogant old bitch?" He looked Rachel up and down, then turned his attention back to Hanna. "With that red hair, maybe you are not a 100 per cent Jewess after all," he sneered. "Did some naughty Cossack have his wilful way with your mother? Go on, Mama, tell her the truth now. Who's her real papa?"

He spoke in German. Her father had originated in Germany, and it had been her second language in school. She was almost as fluent as he was. She answered him in perfect High German, without a trace of an accent. "What do you want with us?"

"Huh." He was looking around him. She saw he'd noted the black pot on the range in which Rachel had been cooking a thick meat and vegetable stew since early that morning. He sniffed. "Even Jews cook, then," he remarked, looking surprised. "It's all too neat and tidy. We can't have that, can we, boys?" He looked behind him at the two youths who were in attendance on him. "So you speak our language and without even a hint of that common Yiddish. Very useful, I must say, in these troubled times."

The officer pushed Hanna to one side and stood beside her, arrogantly picking up a loose lock of her hair that had fallen from her bun and letting it run through his fingers. She fought the instinct to step back and remained totally still. He moved across the room, to where an ancient painted violin that had belonged to Nat's father hung on the wall. It was a Klezmer violin, exquisitely decorated on the back with painted flowers. There had been no money for such luxuries as pictures when Nat's parents were young. The violin had served a dual purpose as both decoration during the day and amusement in their home, especially when a celebration was called for. Often, Nat would play it during the long winter evenings when it was too dark to continue carving in his workshop in the yard, and Hanna and their babies had danced to his music.

The officer Schlossberg lifted it from its nail and tapped it so that it made a hollow sound. "No jewels hidden in that then. You!" He pointed at one of the boys. "Stand on it. Give it a good bashing. That's it. Make sure there's nothing inside."

Rachel started to protest. Tears were coming to Hanna's eyes despite herself. The SS-Hauptsturmführer turned and hit the old woman across the face. "Shut up, Jew bitch. You'd be surprised at how many of these cheap instruments contain a cache of money and precious jewels." He moved over to the stove and allowed his hands to stroke the row of copper pots and pans, gleaming on their hooks beside the range. With a single movement of his arm, he struck them all so they crashed to the grey slate floor, denting them in the process. The two German boys watched silently as he fingered the delicate china, arranged attractively on the dresser next to Rachel's silver candlesticks in which she lit the Sabbath candles every Friday night. Again with a single movement, he pushed against them, smiling as the china clattered and smashed into smithereens. At that moment, Rachel sneezed. Frozen with fear, she dared not pull out her handkerchief to wipe her nose, and sniffed helplessly.

"Snotty bitch there. Your mother?"

"My mother-in-law."

"Your husband?"

She looked up at him. "Out," she said, "as you can well see." She sounded arrogant in the face of such danger, even to her own ears.

The SS-Hauptsturmführer stood still for a moment, again rubbing his clean-shaven chin, surveying the two women. Hanna noticed that a long, blond lock of hair had fallen out of the uniform cap and was playing on his forehead. One of the boys took his inactivity as his cue to trash the cupboards, smashing everything in sight. The other one suddenly bent low against the table, pointing at the floor, where a small rivulet of yellow liquid was trickling along the cracks between the tiles and under the square of carpet. Hanna knew instantly. The children had been as quiet as mice, but one of them had wet himself in fear. The tallest, and obviously oldest, of the young men, a blue-eyed, fair-haired Aryan youth, leant down, reached a long arm under the table, and grabbed both boys simultaneously by their collars, hauling them out from their hiding place like puppies.

"So what have we here, then?" It was the SS-Hauptsturmführer speaking. "Both pups are yours, I presume? Two filthy little yid kids who can't control their bladders." Turning his attention back to the young man holding them, he said, "Put them down, Lieutenant." To Hanna he asked, "The dark one is like his papa, I presume?" He nodded at Shmuel, the baby. "With that red hair, I presume that little one's yours."

Max was staring straight ahead, embarrassed, bewildered. The dark stain on his grey shorts was evidence that he was the one who'd had the "accident".

Hanna attempted to speak. "He is only four. He is ..." She didn't finish the sentence. The leather-gloved hand whipped across her face, and she could feel a welt rising on her usually white, freckled cheek.

"So, let's see. We have here an old Jewess hag who sits shaking in fear and cries but won't speak; a child who pees his pants; an even smaller Jew bastard who stands glaring; and you, an arrogant half-Jewess who thinks it's clever to backchat an officer of the Third Reich in his own language."

Hanna felt the bile rising in her throat. He moved towards her. Expecting him to smack her face again, she turned her head sideways. However, instead of hitting her, he began playing with her hair again, removing the tortoiseshell comb she wore to keep it in place. Her heavy hanks of orange-red curls fell onto her shoulders. Her face stung and she longed to rub it, but she wouldn't afford him the satisfaction of seeing her pain. He picked up a curly strand again, then dropped it again. Her hair was fascinating him.

"A tall, blue-eyed Jewess with bright red hair," he muttered, almost to himself.

One of the youths had spotted the bean and barley soup bubbling on the range. Nodding at his superior, he approached the steaming pot, picked up the pan in his gloved hands, and threw the bubbling mess across the floor. It splattered as it fell, showering Hanna and the boys with droplets of boiling liquid. Hanna clenched her teeth to stop herself yelping. Both children squealed with pain, as did Rachel. Without warning, one of the boy soldiers kicked at Rachel's rocking chair from behind. She fell heavily, face forward, into the scalding mess that had begun snaking across the tiles.

"You'd better eat it now, hadn't you? Can't waste good food in these difficult times. It could be the last hot meal you all get for quite a while."

Hanna stood staring, not daring to move to help her mother-in-law.

"That means you too, Jew bitch. Get down. Or do I have to push?" The officer pushed Hanna anyway. The hot soup was scalding her knees. The children were perching on their heels, understanding what they had to do, and trying to scoop the boiling solid vegetables into their mouths with their hands. One of the younger men hit them both across the back with his stick so they fell flat into the bubbling mess. "That's right. Down, like the animals you are. On all fours. Now let's see if you'd make good little pigs." He was mocking them. "Go on. Lick it up. Use your tongues. That's what tongues are for. Lick, lick, lick."

Hanna tried to look up. A boot trampled the back of her head, pushing her face down again. The liquid on the slate floor was scalding her nose. "You Jews—you are no better than animals, so it won't make a difference to you eating like this. You're used to it." Although they couldn't understand him, he'd made his intentions totally clear. "I'll see you later. You will be in the market square at six tonight with all the other dirty Yidden. One suitcase each. Enough food for one day. All of you. Including this mysterious missing husband of yours. Is that clear? You are to be relocated east, for work."

He turned to face Hanna directly again. "Hoch Deutsch, eh! Bet you didn't learn that in the Jew school." He was giggling to himself as he left, slamming the door behind him. "Bloody Jews," Hanna heard him remark.

"Come on, Mama Rachel. We have work to do. We must pack."

"You pack, Hanna. I'll get the children cleaned up." They stood together for a moment, the older woman and the younger one, and looked at the frightened, confused little boys. The two children sat, white-faced and completely still, in the now congealing mess on the floor. As Hanna put a few essential clothes into a bag and cut some sandwiches for the long walk, Rachel took the boys into the kitchen, heated water, and washed them before changing their clothes. Then she walked to the bureau, took out the drawer, and fumbled behind it. She found what she was looking for, a small black velvet bag. She emptied the contents onto the table.

"Hanna, I'm stitching this into the waistband of your brown skirt. This is my engagement ring and the little bits of jewellery Nat's father, Jacob, bought me. Take them. Keep them safe. There's a little money too. You might need it."

"What about you? You'll need it. You're coming, Mama Rachel."

"Not now. I'll wait. Nat will come back for me with the buggy. You go ahead, but take this."

Hanna started to protest.

"Not for you, my darling. For the boys. To keep my precious boys safe. Quick. Get ready. Now, go."

They embraced. Then Hanna called to the boys. "Come on now. Give Grandma a kiss. Come. Let's go play in the forest and forget about what just happened. But you must stay close to me. If you see any of the horrible men with those grey uniforms and black hats, you mustn't shout out. Just pull my skirt and tell me. We're going to the hut where we have picnics. Remember the lake? Where we used to have picnics. Hurrah!" Later Hanna was to recall this as the very last time she'd ever heard her children being their normal, happy little boy selves.

She wondered where her twin brother was at this moment. Usually one of them knew when the other was in trouble, but she had none of the feelings she sometimes experienced when he was in trouble. Was he still on a battlefield? He'd joined up, she knew that. Her sister-in-law, Dora, had written to her in March, hinting that Simeon was "serving his country" without actually spelling out how. The troops had been mobilised this morning according to the radio. Hanna usually thought about her brother, her "other half" as she referred to him, almost every day. She thought about whether the family in Krustpils were receiving the same bullying tactics from Nazi hands as they were here. Recently, with the worry of the Germans coming and their frantic plans to prepare an escape if the worst should happen, she had barely had time to think about everyone back home. She wondered whether Simeon might have suggested to them that they go to Leningrad for a little holiday to stay with their cousin Ivan's family, as he had written to her. Ivan and his wife, Gilda, had a big apartment all to themselves. Hanna and her family knew this from the letters they'd received sporadically. That's what Hanna should have done, taken the boys and Nat's mother and run to Leningrad; she and Simeon had always been so close to Ivan. But no. Nat had insisted he could look after them here, whatever happened. They were better staying here together. She wondered whether Simeon's new young bride had had more sense than she'd had.

Hanna and her boys had to get ready to go into hiding, and they needed to hurry, but, thank God, they had a little time. Hanna looked at the clock on the wall. It was midday. In two hours' time, whether Nat was back or not, they must be gone. Hopefully he'd realise what was happening and would meet them in the boathouse. She prayed he would come back, collect his mama. *Simeon, please help me!* she cried inside her head. *Simeon, please show me a sign so I can see you are there.*

Chapter 3

Simeon

I N LENINGRAD ONE COULD NEVER BE SURE OF THE WEATHER, EVEN IN LATE
August. On a balmy night like this, the city's lovers would usually
take advantage of the rare evening warmth and stroll along the Neva
embankment, making the most of almost sixteen hours of daylight every
day, the last of the white nights, which would be gone almost as suddenly as
they had arrived and lead to freezing nights of winter.

As Simeon left Vitebsk station, he realised that the Leningrad of today
was not the Leningrad he'd known all his life.

"They've just bombed the line at Mga," he heard someone whisper to
a companion as he left the station. He looked at his watch. It was almost
10.30 p.m. He had left behind the horror of the Rigas Street murders by
slipping out into the forest behind the house in the early hours. Dressed in
Valdis Berzin's filthy old farm clothes, he looked unremarkable. The built-up
boots gave him a limp that avoided awkward questions as to why he was not
away serving his country like most other able-bodied men. He would say he
was Valdis Berzin, a crippled farmer going to visit his friend's family, if he
were asked. He was relieved to meet no one.

By the time he reached Krustpils station, it was 5.30 a.m. If the train
was running to time, it would arrive soon after six. To his amazement, it
arrived soon at 6.15 a.m. He was relieved no one else was waiting for the
same train. The so-called station was little more than a "Halt" marked by a
large white X sign with a red cross inside the white. The roubles he had taken

from Valdis Berzin were more than enough to buy a third-class ticket from the conductor on board. He had plenty of money left over to feed himself, when the train pulled in to its second stop, persuaded a man selling stale rolls on the platform to sell him two. He ate half of the first one and willed himself to save the other one-and-a-half. His hunger was exacerbated by the fact the journey that should have taken thirteen hours ended up taking almost sixteen.

He must have caught one of the last trains into Leningrad. He had managed to secure a seat and had dozed a little, but he was still tired. It was just after 10.45 when he disembarked, yet despite the hour, people were working everywhere. He heard the chink of shovel against stone, grating and frantic, from every direction. He was aware of low chatter between comrades as they stopped to catch their breath and rub their sore hands before following more orders. An old woman sat on a wooden bench, her fingers working knitting needles, the khaki-coloured wool flying in, out, and around the needles. He wondered what she was creating. The sight made him think of his own mama again, whose work-worn hands were never idle. She was always either cooking and cleaning in the house; working full time in the shop; or sewing, knitting, or embroidering if she had nothing more to do. He thought of the once beautiful tablecloth she'd made, now a rag stained with the Berzins' blood and crumpled into the knapsack on his back. He approached the woman politely. "Excuse me, Madame, but what's going on?"

She ignored the question to pose one of her own. "Why aren't you digging? Everyone's digging. A fit young man like you just walking around like tomorrow will do. Why are you wearing that stupid boot? It's making you limp. Everyone's working building shelters, planting vegetables, digging ditches—anyone older than ten and younger than sixty. Me? I'm too old to dig ditches, so I'm knitting socks for soldiers. We're working to save Leningrad." He'd eaten the second half of the first roll on the train. No longer able to stave off his hunger pangs, he was eating the second now as he walked, cramming it into his mouth too fast then choking.

Dry ditches threw up their dust along the sidewalks. Simeon had only three thoughts in his head: Dora, his mama, and the new baby. He made up a walking chant. "Dora and the baby must be here. They must be here. Of course they are here." He repeated the mantra over and over, his lips moving in time to his feet. With every step, his belief that Dora had gotten the message and acted on it grew stronger. A light breeze enfolded him like a gossamer blanket, comforting him. Only another fifteen or twenty minutes—half an hour at most—and they'd be reunited. He'd arrive just in time to share breakfast with them, if he was lucky.

Suddenly, lemon-hued searchlights rent the sky, throwing their dancing beams across the water as they scanned left to right, right to left in the grey dawn light. Simeon could hear shells blasting on distant targets. It was too close for comfort. Surely Stalin would protect Leningrad, with its amazing art treasures, as he would protect no other city in Russia. Simeon could see with his own eyes how determined the people of Leningrad were to preserve their home. Whatever tragedies were to befall Moscow or Stalingrad or the rest of Russia, Leningrad would stay safe for as long as gentle waves continued to lap the shores of the Neva. As long as Leningrad dug its bomb shelters and tended its vegetable gardens and dug its bunkers and air-raid shelters, Leningradyans would carry on with the rest of their business as usual. The preparations for the war that was raging around them were precautionary. The Germans would never take this city.

Anna Berzin had taunted him with her ridiculous abattoir story. She had set out to hurt him, injure him, scare him. That was idle gossip magnified in triplicate, the way gossip tends to grow. People incarcerated in an abattoir. Even the Nazis couldn't stoop so low. As he walked, he even managed to smile to himself.

He knew the route by heart, but he kept thinking he'd lost his way. The landscape changed at every street corner. He was conscious of an itch that started at his head and continued down his neck and went under his clothes. He'd thought he'd scrubbed himself clean of vermin in the Berzins' kitchen sink. He figured he'd caught something from either Berzin's clothes or on the train. From Berzin's clothes more than likely.

Exhaustion was catching up with Simeon. It was a real effort to put one foot in front of the other. Finally, he arrived at the grand government-owned apartment building near the Academy of Sciences where Ivan's wife, Gilda, worked. He crossed the wide avenue one street behind the Universitetskaya Embankment and hauled himself up the stone steps of the grand old three-storey apartment building. He'd made it. Now Dora, his mother, and the baby were only a bell pull away. Anna Berzin's words were haunting him. The abattoir? Stupid cow! He grimaced to himself. Stupid, and now very dead, cow. To his relief he saw the name Solomon on the bell push. It had been at least two years since he'd visited Ivan. Their little girl had been just a month or two old. He remembered the first time he'd seen the gorgeous three-room apartment where they lived, thanks to Gilda's position. They had their own bathroom, a sitting room and, he remembered, a huge kitchen with an enormous pine dining table—the sort of accommodation reserved only for high-ranking, party card–holding officials and academics.

"You lucky devil," he'd said. "All this for the two of you and a baby. We could fit your mama's house and my mama's house into this apartment and still have room to spare."

"The reward for Gilda's academic service to the Ministry of Food Science," Ivan had told him proudly. "She is almost a professor now, you know. And of course, my contribution to the writers' union helps."

Simeon contrasted Gilda's and Ivan's rewards for success in their chosen professions with his own. Ivan, three years his senior with a degree in Russian literature from the University of Leningrad, had met Gilda, a food science engineer, at a student debating society. Simeon's degree was in mechanical engineering from Riga University. What had that earned him aside from a job in a tank factory? His family still lived in the tiny wooden cottage at the back of a shop, the same home he'd grown up in. His cousin and his wife not only had a spacious city apartment all to themselves, but they also had an inside bathroom and toilet, running hot and cold water, electric lights, and in winter the ultimate luxury, central heating. The home behind the shop had a cold water pump in the kitchen, a vast boiling pan to heat water for bathing and cooking, and a lavatory in the yard.

As he stared up at the third-floor windows that he remembered as those of apartment, he allowed himself a moment's pleasant anticipation at their reunion. The windows were all slightly open despite the blackout, in deference to the heat. His ears pricked. Could he hear his own baby's soft mewling? A mangy-looking cat jumped across his feet, and he realised the sound he'd heard was that of the cat, not the baby. They were all asleep of course. It was going on four in the morning. All safe up there inside the beautiful apartment. He lit a cigarette, took a single puff, then threw it on the step and stamped the glow out, suddenly impatient. The river filled his nostrils: damp mould, seaweed, engine oil, the smell of a city riverside. He pushed the bell. No answer. He pushed again. Couldn't they feel the urgency in his ring? He left his finger on the button. The ringing echoed in the empty hallway. Feet clattered on the marble staircase. His cousin Ivan's voice asked, "Who is it? What do you want?"

"It's me, your cousin. Simeon Karminsky. I've come for my wife and mama, your Tante Rosa."

A chain clattered. A bolt shot. The door opened slightly. Simeon could see Ivan's unshaven face and sleep-filled blue eyes peering at him. "Simeon Karminsky. What the ...?"

"They are safe. Here, with you? Not in an abattoir? Not shipped to work out east?"

Ivan had opened the door far enough to admit Simeon, then hastily closed it again, his fingers to his lips as he led him up three flights of stairs. On the second landing Simeon reached out a hand and felt for Ivan's shoulder.

"For God's sake, Ivan. Tell me they are here, yes?"

Ivan returned the question by tapping his finger rapidly against fast-closed lips again and shaking his head.

They reached the heavy oak front door to the apartment. Ivan tapped in a pattern, obviously a code. The door opened. Ivan's wife stood there in the hallway, a light pink cotton housecoat covering her night attire. A tiny girl was resting sleepily on her right hip. The apartment was in darkness apart from the glow of a single candle, flickering faintly in a room to the right. It was then that Simeon realised that they were the only other people inside the flat. All the doors were open. There was no sign of Dora or his mama. They were four people in the apartment, including himself and the sleepy toddler.

"What are you talking about?"

"I told Dora to bring Mama here. I wrote to her way back in March. I had to get them out of Krustpils, you see." Suddenly, he became aggressive. "They're not here. You sent them away. You must have sent them away." Simeon's voice was frantic. "Or was it that you never let them in? Your own aunt! I can't believe you did that. Your favourite aunt. And my wife. Why did you turn them away!" Simeon felt himself starting to panic, his voice rising. "Where are they, Ivan?"

"They've never been here."

"I don't believe you. I was away fighting. I heard the pact was breaking down. Dora. Mama. I told them: 'Go to Ivan and Gilda's for a holiday.' That was in March. I thought they'd come in April perhaps. Dora is pregnant, you see. Was pregnant. The baby must be born by now. I knew the Germans wouldn't make it to here. That's why I told them to come." Simeon thought back to the thousands of people he'd seen pouring out of Vitebsk station.

Gilda, who had been standing beside Ivan, laid the blonde child, who had fallen asleep again in her arms, down on a green settee and tried to place herself between Ivan and Simeon.

"No one's been here, Simeon. Not Dora. Not your mother. No one."

"They must have gone to Vidzy then. Sorry I troubled you." The sounds he'd heard as he passed the abattoir echoed in his mind. Had there really been *people* in there? Had he walked away from his own beloved wife and mother, from other family and from friends, people he'd known all his life? Impossible, surely. Anna Berzin had only said it to upset him. He'd been wrong to come here. Of course they would have gone to Vidzy. His mother would have wanted to be with her daughter and grandchildren, naturally, and who better to help Dora than her sister-in-law?

"Don't worry, Ivan. Gilda. Sorry to have troubled you. I'll go now. I'll go to Vidzy. I should have gone there first."

"Shut up, Simeon. You're hysterical. Ivan, this is too much! You'll wake the whole bloody building. We've already got enough troubles of our own."

"I have to find them. You don't seem to understand what's happening to the Jews all over Europe. You're protected here, away from the German invasion."

Ivan's voice was stern. "I give you my word that neither has your mama been in touch with us nor have they been here. We haven't heard from them for almost a year, since we received a card last Jewish New Year. You can't go out again now. Not without papers. You'll be arrested. If you intend to travel to Vidzy, you'll have to wait until tomorrow morning."

Ivan led the way into the room with the flickering candle. Gilda picked up the sleeping child and followed, perching her daughter on her right hip. The child's face was tucked against her mother's shoulder, but Simeon could see the top of her little head, covered with a down of thin, sandy-coloured hair. She lifted her head, and her big green eyes stared at him.

"Poo," she said. "Man, you stink." She held her nose between two small fingers.

"Excuse Lena," Ivan said, obviously embarrassed. "She's not yet three."

"Soon I'll be three. Go wash, you man."

"Shh, Lena. That's rude."

"She may be rude." Simeon allowed himself to smile despite his dreadful feelings of disappointment and foreboding. "But she is absolutely right."

"Come on, Lena. You've got to get up early tomorrow for your nursery outing. Remember, you're going on a holiday like a big girl, without Mama and Tatti. The man won't be here when you wake up."

Simeon looked to the floor, his face flaming with shame. Ivan was glaring at him in the shadowy candlelight. Simeon's empty stomach was churning with hunger. Eventually, starvation overruled pride. He mumbled the words shyly. "Please, Cousin, give me something to eat before I leave? I'll pay you, of course. I'm not a beggar yet."

It was Ivan's turn to blush. "It's not a question of money. Food is already rationed here. Don't take any notice of Gilda. She's worried about Lena. They're evacuating all the children of essential workers tomorrow. They say tomorrow. It's the third time we've prepared for her evacuation. Twice before it's been cancelled at the last moment. We don't know where they're taking them. They won't tell us."

He cut the heel off a hunk of black bread and put it on a plate with a small piece of cheese.

"That's my cheese ration for this week," he said, handing it to Simeon. "You'll need a local ration book if you intend to stay in this city for more than a day or two. You'll have to register later, of course. We can't risk the smallest infringement of the rules. Gilda's job, you see. And my work at the writers' union. If anyone connects us and you're not registered ..."

Simeon swallowed hard, wishing he could spit the mouthful of bread he was chewing back in his cousin's face. This wasn't the Ivan he remembered. "A drink? Or is water also on ration?" Ivan reached for a glass, turned on the tap, and handed him the glass. "Don't worry. I'll leave first thing tomorrow. Of course they must be in Vidzy. Where else would a mother run, if not to her daughter?"

"I'm sorry if we don't appear to have offered you the warm welcome you expected. No one told you to turn up in the middle of the night, Comrade Cousin, disturbing other comrades' peaceful sleep before a traumatic day."

The voice from the doorway was Gilda's. Simeon wondered how long she'd been standing there. "For pity's sake, Ivan, get him into the bathroom before he infests us all with his lice and fleas. Lena's right: he does stink. The last thing we need is for one of us to catch his vermin. Can you imagine what they'd say at Nursery 21 if Lena arrives tomorrow scratching like crazy and filthy with vermin?" She was speaking directly to Ivan as though Simeon didn't exist.

"I'll go now."

Gilda shook her head. "Just get him into the bathroom and out of those flea-ridden rags."

Simeon licked his fingers and ran them around the rim of the plate, anxious not to waste a crumb. He put the plate on the pine table and followed Ivan down the corridor into the bathroom. As he turned on the gas geyser above the chipped white enamel bath, the ancient water heater banged and groaned in protest. A dribble of steaming water started to trickle reluctantly from the tap. Seemingly oblivious of the noise, Ivan motioned Simeon closer. "Be careful what you say," he whispered. "We're bugged. Another little perk of Gilda's lofty position at the Ministry of Food Sciences. The party are always keen to know what we're eating for breakfast."

Simeon started to undress, dropping Valdis Berzin's old workingman's clothes into a heap on the floor. They could both see that the white freckled skin on his legs, thighs, and torso was pockmarked with angry red bites.

Ivan picked up the bundle. "I'm going to burn these. You can't wear them again," he said. Suddenly Simeon remembered.

"Wait," he shouted. "Give them here. He grabbed the filthy rags and extricated Valdis Berzin's precious identity papers.

Ivan's eyes widened. "Not yours? Valdis Berzin, eh? Isn't his mother the non-Jewish woman who comes into your home to light the fires and who keeps the oil lamps burning on the Sabbath? The widow Berzina? I remember her. Why are you travelling with his documents? Where are your own papers?"

Simeon's eyes travelled around the bathroom, wondering where the bug could be hidden. A single light bulb hung from the ceiling. Ivan had not turned on the electric light. The only light in the room came from the two candles he'd lit on either side of the large ceramic washbasin.

"Suffice it to say Valdis Berzin has no further need of his papers."

Ivan held the towel above both their heads. "He's dead? You stole them?" Simeon shrugged. 'He stepped into the shallow bath and scrubbed himself all over with the hard green soap he'd been given. Just as he lowered himself into the shallow water, Gilda knocked on the door. She handed Ivan a pile of clothes and a bundle of old newspapers. As he stepped out of the bath, he saw Ivan laying the papers across the enamel sink. He was wielding an old cut-throat razor.

"Bend your head over the newspaper," he ordered and began to shave his cousin's head from the nape of his neck to his forehead using long strokes. As hanks of Simeon's matted hair fell onto the paper. He was astonished to read the headlines. *Victory at Raseiniai.* Russian troops beat back German onslaught. He wondered how much more misinformation was finding its way into the public domain. He lifted his head and pointed at the story. "Lies," he mouthed. "Propaganda. I was there. I know,"

Ivan mouthed back, "We all know. At the writers' union, you write what you are told to write. You report what you are told to report. No arguments if you value your life."

The clean clothes Gilda had sorted for Simeon were a bit too short. He was several inches taller than Ivan. However, they hung down on his spare frame. It had been months since he'd eaten a decent meal. Ivan led him back down the dark hallway to the grand salon with an oriel window. The walls were covered in red flock and gold paper. The furniture was French, adorned with pearl inlay and fine gold ormolu. Simeon gasped at the luxury of it.

"I've only ever seen such a room portraying Western materialism in the cinema," he said, breathing out sharply as he spoke.

In one corner a display cabinet stood on slender carved legs, silver ornaments gleaming from behind its bevelled glass doors. The sofa, on which bedding was folded, had gilded legs and an ornate red velvet button-back in the Louis XVI style. An ormolu clock ticked on top of a walnut chiffonier. "You will sleep here for tonight. Be careful. The room is Gilda's pride and joy," Ivan said, amused at Simeon's obvious reactions to its grandeur. "She was going to put you on the old green settee in the kitchen, but we have to give Lena a very early breakfast. We are meeting at the bus station at eight in the morning." He looked at his watch. "Today. You can rest for two hours.

"I'll leave you."

Ivan closed the door, leaving Simeon to make up a bed on the hard horsehair sofa. Eventually, in search of a comfortable position, he rolled on to the floor, enveloping himself in the blanket and tucking the pillow under his cold and unexpectedly bald head. He was dozing, but through the thin wall he could hear Ivan and Gilda talking. He heard her giggle. Then he heard a rhythmic banging. *They must be making love,* he thought. He hadn't thought of sex for months. Occasionally, he'd awakened to discover he'd had a wet dream. As he listened now, he thought of Dora and felt his erection grow. His beautiful, petite wife with her full round breasts and button nipples. He turned his hand and could feel the bush of dark curly hair that adorned that secret place of hers in the palm of his hand. He was massaging himself when he heard Gilda cry out and, to his despair, discovered he'd come in his own hand. Too scared to get up and walk to the bathroom for fear of causing another scene, he found himself crying. He missed Dora more than he'd ever thought possible. He loved his wife and wanted to protect her—protect her and the baby they had made together. He wondered, would he ever hold them in his arms again?

Slivers of light were peeping round the blackout tape, signalling another glorious late summer's day in Leningrad. Simeon dressed quickly in Ivan's clothes. As he walked into the kitchen, he saw that the child, Lena, was sitting in a high chair at the kitchen table. Her sandy blonde hair had been neatly tied into a fine ponytail with emerald-coloured ribbons. Gilda, clearly edgy, was trying to feed her, but the child was obstinately closing her mouth as the spoon approached so that sticky porridge was smeared on her cheeks.

"Want To-To. To-To hungry," she was shrieking.

"Not now, Lena. To-To is already in your bag with Ton-Ton, waiting to go with you on your holiday." She turned to Simeon. "Did you know Lena's going on a holiday with all her friends from Nursery 21?" she said, trying to keep her voice bright. "What a lucky little girl."

"Can I come too, Lena?"

"No." The child shook her head vehemently, quickly sealing her mouth again. "Dirty man," she spat at him through gritted teeth.

Gilda's eyes were watering as she tried to coax the child. "You'll be hungry later. Don't make this more difficult than it already is, sweetie."

"To-To will be hungry later," the child said, mimicking her mother. "To-To wants porridge. I heard him say so."

"But he's already in your bag, Lena."

Simeon stood himself behind Gilda, trying to make funny faces to distract the child. "To-To. I want my To-To. I want To-To *now*."

Ivan came into the room, a shaving brush in one hand, his cut-throat in the other, half his face covered in soapy lather.

"For God's sake, Gilda, give her the bloody toy or we'll be late. Be a good girl, Lena? Eat the lovely porridge Mama made. You don't have children yet, do you, Simeon?"

"I already told you. Dora is pregnant. The baby's due any day."

Ivan wiped the remains of the now chilled shaving soap off his face with a towel. The child was still howling for her toy. They all heard the click as Ivan opened the child's case and then returned to the kitchen carrying a pocket-size white toy poodle. He handed it to the triumphant child, who grabbed it by its ear and obligingly opened her mouth.

"You shouldn't give in to her like that, Ivan," Gilda remarked sharply, looking at Simeon as though for backup. "She won't go anywhere without Ton-Ton and To-To." She was spooning the last of the porridge into the child's mouth.

"She won't be here for you to fight with her tomorrow," Ivan remarked quietly. "What does it matter?"

Gilda wiped the child's sticky face and lifted her out of her chair. "Bathroom, now. There's a good girl."

"I go wash To-To now," Lena said as her mother placed her on the green linoleum floor and folded the porridge-spattered cloth.

29

Gilda spoke to Simeon. "If you want something to eat, help yourself. I haven't got time to wait on you. There's leftover porridge in the pot. We've eaten."

"Don't worry. I understand."

"If you'd understood, you wouldn't have come here at all."

"Simeon, can I have a word?" Ivan led him out of the kitchen and back into the hallway.

"I've been thinking a lot about what you said last night. About war coming here to Leningrad. It looks as though it could. The thing is, if something happens to me, will you come back and keep an eye on Gilda and Lena for me?"

"If that's what you want. But such a promise must work two ways. If you survive and I don't, which is much more likely, will you look out for Dora and my baby?"

"Can we shake on it, Simeon?"

They hugged one another for a moment. "Remember how, when we were kids, we pricked our thumbs and swore we'd be blood brothers? That still holds true for me, Simeon."

"Me too."

They walked back into the kitchen, where Lena stood, looking much fatter than she had seemed ten minutes earlier, her face almost as red as the scarlet coat she had on.

"They said only one change of clothes in the bag, so I dressed her in two of everything," Gilda explained. "She'll need the coat in winter."

As they walked into the hall, Simeon saw Valdis Berzin's knapsack. He walked over to it, removed the soiled tablecloth that his mother had embroidered, and threw it into the kitchen sink. "It was my mother's," he announced. "It's stained with blood, but I'm sure you can get the stains out. My mother stitched every stitch herself. Keep it as thanks for your hospitality. It must stay in the family and keep this safe as well." Ivan looked and saw a baby's broken rattle.

Gilda started to protest, but Ivan interrupted. "We don't have time for an argument now. Thank you, Simeon. We'll take care of it until you get back." The three adults and the child walked out of the door together, Ivan and Gilda each holding one of their daughter's hands. As the door closed, Simeon looked back. On the floor, he saw the child's precious toy poodle dog abandoned in the hall, but he said nothing.

Chapter 4

Hanna

HANNA WAITED UNTIL SHE WAS SURE THE BOYS WERE FAST ASLEEP BEFORE she left them. The journey into the forest on her own with the two children had been hard work. Rachel had refused to come with them, saying she would wait for Nat. "I'll only slow you down even more if I try to walk. I'll ride with Nat on the wagon."

It had taken Hanna five hours to reach her destination because the children tired quickly. The hardest part was keeping out of sight. Mostly, they followed the path of the main road. However, each time she had heard a vehicle approaching, she stopped and hid in bushes. At first, the boys had thought it fun, but soon they tired of the game. She had bribed them with sandwiches and with chocolate. She'd managed to save a single bar for a special occasion. This was undoubtedly it.

It was immediately clear that Nat wasn't here yet. There was no sign of the horse and cart. The three of them had eaten some bread and cheese and drunk fresh water from the lake. Then she'd tucked the boys into the bed she'd made up for them in one of the old boats, side by side, praying that Nat would arrive very soon. The children were exhausted and had fallen asleep immediately. When it got dark and there was still no sign of him or his mother, Hanna decided Nat must have been held up by all the German traffic on the road. She crawled into the same boat, snuggling up to Max, who murmured softly and snuffled in his sleep.

One day passed with no sign of Nat and Rachel, then another. Hanna insisted on keeping the children inside the boathouse during daylight hours for fear that they would be seen or heard. They became bored and fractious. She tried to ration the food, but at the end of the sixth day, she was running low on basic foodstuffs. She opened several tins and cut down on what she was eating, but she realised she would have to go and get some fresh food if they were to survive.

However, she had to admit, even to herself, that taking the boys would slow her down. The best thing she could do, she reasoned, was to go back to the village when they were asleep. She could travel back in half the time and be back in the boathouse before they awoke. She was sure the roads would be empty now the Gestapo had done their job—removed all the Jews—and that now they were gone.

She crept along the familiar dirt road to her home and walked into her own back yard. There was no sign of Rachel or Nat. She heard the horse neighing in the small stable. So Nat had come back and stabled the horses. Perhaps he was hiding somewhere nearby. He would see her, and they could run back to the boys together.

Hanna prayed the children wouldn't awake while she was gone. She opened the cupboards. The bread was stale and the cheese laced with blue. There were a couple of tins. She tipped those into a shopping basket together with some biscuits. Anything was better than nothing. She gathered a couple of the children's books from the shelf. She intended to buy bread and fresh fruit on the way back. She must be quick. As she opened her door, she saw to her dismay that Vladimir Zhurzavle, a dirty old peasant, his chin unshaven, his grey shirt unwashed and unbuttoned, stood waiting for her.

"Good Lord, Mrs Abramskya. Our little carrot-top Hanna. You've come home. And I thought the nice Germans had gotten the lot of you and washed you all down some sewer."

Hanna thought quickly. She tucked her hand inside her shawl and rummaged for one of the jewels in the bag Rachel had sewn into her waistband. "What do you know, Zhurzavle? Where did they take them?"

"Why would I give a Jewess such information when my good friend the mayor will pay me plenty for finding you?"

"Rachel is an old lady. Nat only ever did good things for everyone in the village, including you."

"And robbed us clean for his clumsy furniture. You're a lot of lying, money-grabbing thieves, you Jews. Where do you hide your horns, eh, madam?"

She held out the little diamond so she could see it glinting in her palm. He reached for it, but she snatched it back. He tried to wrestle her for it, but she was stronger than he expected. "First tell me where my husband and mother-in-law are?"

"I watched you run away with those brats of yours. I'll bet the old Hauptsturmführer, or whatever he called himself, would pay me handsomely to turn you in. So would our mayor. They'd pay much more than this is worth."

For a moment or two, they stared at one another in silence. Finally, Vladimir had to speak. "You really want to know? Your old man got back just in time for the round-up. They herded them together—your man, the old woman, and all the rest—counted them, and shot half a dozen just to show they meant business. The rest went into lorries. Don't know where they were heading, and don't care as long as they're away from here.

"The diamond?"

"The trouble with you lot," Hanna said, imitating his tone, "is that you don't know the difference between a diamond and a worthless glass chip I keep in my pocket just to fool idiots like you." She threw a small rouble note at him, turned her back on him, and went back into her house. She wouldn't give him the satisfaction of seeing her cry. At least now she knew what had happened. She must get back to the boys before they awoke. At first, she thought of taking the horse to get back to the boys as fast as she could. But the horse would be another mouth to feed, and its presence by the hut would give them away. She would make her way to the village of Lovchnskiye and use the little diamond to buy some proper food. She could still make it back to her boys before dawn. How would she tell them that their dear Booba and much loved Tatti weren't coming after all? She'd find a way.

Hanna managed to buy two loaves of newly baked bread from the baker, who was just taking the first batch from the oven as she reached him. The smell teased at her nostrils. She was starving, but she wouldn't touch them until the boys had eaten their fill. She managed to get some cheese, some salt herring, and some eggs from the general store, and some apples and pears from a market stall. It was enough for a couple of days if she herself ate sparingly. It would give her just enough time to formulate a plan. She paid for the food with the rest of her roubles. Currency was far less likely to cause comment than diamonds. Now that she knew the Germans had gone, she could begin to plan what to do next. They would survive.

Hanna reached the boathouse much later than she had intended and was relieved to hear no noise.

The boys hadn't awakened. They wouldn't even know she'd been gone. She'd let them out today for a little paddle. They would go for a walk, perhaps. She let herself in through the broken slats. Suddenly, it felt too quiet. She tiptoed across to the bed in a boat and, for a moment, thought her eyes were deceiving her. The bedclothes were ruffled as though the children had just jumped out of them. The bed was empty. Maybe they had heard her coming. They were hiding from her in the other boat. *Come on, Hanna,* she told herself. *Life is hard enough for them. You have bad news. Lighten up for their sake, just for a minute or two. Play their game.*

"Come on, you two. I have a wonderful breakfast for you." Perched on the side of the other boat, she realised they weren't in there either. "OK. Come on out. You win. I've got a special prize for the first one to reach me. I'm shutting my eyes so I won't see your hiding place." She held out her arms for the boys to run into. There was no rushing of small feet. Her arms remained empty.

She grabbed for the torch she kept hidden at the top of her sleeping space and turned it on. It was obvious now that they weren't in the hut. If they were, she'd have heard Shmuely giggle. He could never stay quiet for long. They must have gone out. That was it. They were so frustrated at being kept indoors twenty-four hours a day for all this time that they'd awakened early and decided to go outside. She couldn't blame them.

"Max. Shmuely. Shmuely. Max!" She pushed back the loose boards without thinking to replace them and ran into the forest. Her calls echoed back at her. There was still no sign of them. She stood quite still. Hearing nothing, she ran to the front of the hut, her eyes scanning the shoreline. Perhaps they had run into the water. Maybe they'd drowned. Shmuely couldn't swim! How could she have left them alone in a place so full of danger? The sky was growing pink now as the sun rose. Then she spotted them, two tiny figures, clothed in just the vests they'd gone to sleep in, lying side by side on the muddy shore. Their underpants were missing. At first she thought they were asleep. Two normal naughty little boys, desperate for fresh air, disobeying their mother as boys will do. And then being so tired, they didn't even awake when she called them. She looked at her sleeping sons, admonishing herself for her panic. "Silly fool," she said. And then she looked again. There was something strange about their sleep. Why weren't they wearing pants? Why were they so still? She knelt down and pushed the quiff of curly brown hair gently off Max's forehead, thinking how like Nat he was. When she drew her hand away, it felt sticky. It was blood. Her son's blood. She knelt closer to hear him, but he wasn't breathing. There was no rise and fall to his chest. She felt for his pulse. His skin was cold; his limbs, stiff. One arm lay across his chest. She tried to lift it. It was rigid and heavy. This was a nightmare. In a moment she would wake up in bed with Nat in the warm hollow next to her. She would go into the room next to theirs, the one that the boys shared, and they would both be asleep in the large old bed. Max would be hidden, snuggled right under the huge down quilt, while Shmuely would be half on top of the bedclothes, one arm flung right out, his straight red-blond hair a tousled mop.

Hanna rubbed her eyes, but still the scene before her hadn't changed. Shmuely was on his stomach next to his brother. She rolled him over. There was a trickle of blood on his forehead, too. She ran her hand gently across his forehead and felt the tiny hole where the bullet had entered his skull. The bullets had penetrated each boy's head at roughly the same angle. Both had been dead some time.

Who would shoot children in cold blood in such a way? Two innocent children. What harm had they ever done anyone? Their discarded shorts were lying in a heap just beyond the boathouse door. Looking behind her, Hanna saw that the rusty old lock had been wrenched from its hook. Whoever had shot her sons had pulled their pants down, seen that they had been circumcised, and known they were Jews.

She sat still, too shocked for tears. Nat would never forgive her for neglecting his sons, for leaving them alone. This was all her fault. They may all have been hungry, but the children would both have been alive. Perhaps she could have caught fresh fish in the lake with her bare hand, and they could have cooked over the little fire and eaten it with forest berries. They would all have survived. She should never have left them. Not for a moment. She made a space between her sons and lay beside them, drawing their unfamiliarly stiff little heads onto her shoulders. "Come back, my darlings. Don't go. Come back. I'm so sorry. I love you."

The sun rose high, bathing them in the warmth they'd craved. "The sun put his hat on today, especially for you. Shall we take a paddle after breakfast like we used to with Tatti?" But their faces were cold now, their little limbs so stiff that it was hard to disentangle herself from them.

Hanna made her way back inside the hut and took out a spade and two blankets from the bed. The earth was soft where it was lapped by the lake. She dug two small shallow hollows, wrapped each boy gently in a blanket, and laid them down. She held each stiff body tenderly in her arms, nuzzling them against her breast for a moment before she kissed each goodbye. She covered the holes with mud from the shore and then collected pebbles, from which she created a six-pointed Star of David on each mound. She tried to remember the prayer Simeon had recited when their father had died. "Yiskadal, veyiskadat, shemay rabbo …" They were the only words she could recall. "God keep your darling souls safe." She wept, looking at the small piles of wet earth that were her sons' graves. She heard a scream, a terrible scream, and stopped to listen. Suddenly she realised the scream was hers. She hoped someone would hear and come and kill her too. That way she could be with her boys. She sat beside them for a while, stroking and kissing the mounds of earth where she had buried their little heads, wiping roughly at the mud that clung to her lips. Finally, when her tears were all spent, she stood, brushed at her skirt, and walked away.

Chapter 5

Simeon

As he retraced his steps to Vitebsk station, Simeon was aware of the frenetic energy he'd seen and felt all around him when he arrived last night. He'd almost reached the square in front of St Isaac's Cathedral, now a vast allotment, when he heard an announcement over loudspeakers that boomed across the city. All routes in and out of Leningrad were closed as a result of enemy raids.

He must get to Vidzy, even if he had to walk there. He began turning in circles in the street, unsure of which way to go. He had no official permit to be in Leningrad. There was no point returning to Ivan and Gilda's. He couldn't stay under the same roof as that bitch. She'd made that clear.

He had crossed the Schmidta Bridge again and hoped he was walking in the direction of Ladoga when he came across the same old woman he'd seen the night before, still knitting her socks as people toiled around her. "Didn't I see you here last night? What's the matter? A problem?" A stupid question. Today everyone had a problem. Some had bigger problems than others.

"I have to get to Byelorussia to find my wife," he said.

The old woman shrugged. "I wish you luck. No transport in or out of the city now. Nothing at all. The trains are stopped. The trams won't last much longer. They're saying the Germans are only about thirty kilometres away. Do you drive?"

The question was so unexpected. "Yes, but what good will that do me? I don't have a vehicle."

"You don't have a place to stay, either. Go to the military hospital on Suvarovo Street. They're desperate for ambulance drivers. They won't ask too many questions."

It had been easy enough to find the hospital, and far less of a problem than he expected to "sign on". He limped heavily as he moved towards the registration desk, clutching Valdis Berzin's papers proclaiming him a victim of poliomyelitis. The papers received little more than a cursory glance. After the briefest of explanations, he was handed a registration document and a ration book entitling him to a volunteer worker's allowance of three hundred grams of bread a week and half a litre of vodka. He could eat in the canteen, sleep in the dormitory in a bed shared with another man, and ferry the worst of the injured patients – mostly survivors from the Western Front – between this hospital and the grander Erissmann six kilometres away on Apertesky Island. He was teamed with another "cripple", Anatoly Bogaevlov, who'd lost his toes from frostbite while serving at the front last winter. Bogaevlov walked with sticks and acted as their driver. Gregory Konstantinov – who suffered from poor eyesight - was the second stretcher -bearer. The three men found themselves crossing the Schmidta Bridge a dozen or more times a day while bombs exploded around them and Leningrad's citizens ran for cover.

They were on Schmidta Bridge the night the Badayev warehouses were bombed. Simeon and Anatoly were used to sharing driving the six kilometres between the Suvarovo and Erissmann hospitals while the sirens wailed. Until now, they'd mostly been false alerts, but every siren on 8 September 1941 was warning of renewed disaster. It was a night no one in Leningrad would ever forget.

It was a clear night, the whole city illuminated by a moon so bright that it seemed to have taken sides with the enemy. Wave after wave of black aircraft crossed the city at a low altitude. "They look like a flock of hungry crows," Anatoly Bogaevlov shouted above the din of war as Gregory Konstantinov drove across the city like a dervish while Simeon and Anatoly fought to stop their patients falling from their bunks. The Luftwaffe planes rained bombs directly onto the wooden warehouses containing 99 per cent of Leningrad's food stores. Tongues of orange flame leapt upwards. People choked and struggled for breath. Heavy black smoke began choking Leningrad's weakened lungs; as the meat stocks burnt, the aroma of barbecuing meat mocked its citizens' starving stomachs, and as sugar, fat, and oil caramelised, the sickly sweet smell of fresh toffee apples caused their mouths to slobber helplessly. "I feel like a dribbling baby." Simeon laughed, but it was no laughing matter.

"I didn't realise how hungry I am," Bogaevlov said as they drove on to deliver a pair of soldiers, each of whom had lost a leg in the battles that had been raging on the outskirts of the city, to the Erissmann.

"Last night, the glorious Russian army recaptured Kingisepp after a brief spell in the hands of the invaders," radio speakers boomed across the city. "Smolensk and Staraya are back in Soviet hands. A powerful relief force is on its way to ease the city's pain."

The wards in Suvarovo Military Hospital were so overcrowded that sick men lay on the floor, one groaning body almost stacked on top of another.

"These are no longer men, no longer individuals with names, or homes, or fathers or brothers," Anatoly Bogaevlov said as they took a rare break, smoking to assuage the hunger pangs that gripped their stomachs. "They're just numbers. Thousands of nameless, faceless bodies."

A week later, the smell had abated, but the situation had worsened. "Did you hear? Betty, the elephant in the zoo, copped it!" Simeon stubbed his cigarette out on the ground and crushed it underfoot irritably. "There's no food left in the city. The bread we eat tastes of ash and sawdust. Someone told me they're actually using the sweepings from the flour store, mixed with ash, to make bread so not a grain is lost. And what's the local gossip as people's bellies swell? They're not chattering about Leningrad in a state of siege or the dead who are littering our streets or piling up at the cemetery gates. It's the death of a bloody elephant."

It grew colder. The casualty lists mounted. Medicine was in short supply. In early November, when the siege had been in place for almost eight weeks and just as the first snows were falling, Simeon was at the head of a stretcher carrying a badly burnt patient into the Erissmann when he thought he heard someone calling his own surname. It had been so long since he'd heard himself referred to as anything other than Berzin that at first he thought he was dreaming. The only part of the patient's face that could be seen were a pair of brown eyes. The eyebrows had been singed away. The eyes rolled backwards in sunken sockets and fixed themselves on Simeon's face. They were begging wordlessly for pain relief. Blood was seeping through the bandages from the man's head wounds. Simeon leant forward, attempting to hear what the poor bugger was saying. His voice was becoming more agitated as he tried to make himself understood but failed, and then his voice weakened. Simeon must have misheard. This was a feverish call for a wife or a plea for water relief from pain. Simeon bent closer. The body stank of burnt and rotting flesh. Suddenly, to his horror, he realised he had heard correctly first time. "Ka … ains … key? 'Omrad Ka … ins … skeee." The wounded man was trying to lift an arm, to point. "Ooh. Ka … kin … sky."

Simeon felt obliged to glance at the brown card label attached to the tattered remains of the soldier's trousers, identifying him by name, rank, and number. Dear God! It was Lieutenant Colonel Leonid Berlovsky, his old CO. He'd been so sure the man had perished on the battlefield at Raseiniai. Everyone had died there, hadn't they? If Berlovsky had survived, who else from the Forty-Second might turn up here? Perhaps now, even as Simeon was ferrying unidentified men back and forth, he'd been identified by others as Engineer Third Class Comrade Simeon Karminsky, masquerading as peasant polio victim Valdis Berzin.

"Do you know which unit they come from?" he asked Anatoly as they limped side by side into the Erissmann, hauling bodies in return for signatures to confirm delivery of another batch of the injured.

"They're under the command of Marshal Grigori Kulik now. They merged the Forty-Second with his own regiment to form the Fifty-Fourth," he said. He pulled Simeon to one side, putting his arm around his shoulder. "They say he's a great friend of Stalin's. That's why he's gotten away with total incompetence for so long. Personally, I don't think Kulik is capable of breaking a china cup, let alone a front line."

Simeon nodded, noncommittal. Anatoly Bogaevlov was a relatively new acquaintance. Ostensibly, ambulance team no. 691 had truly become a team. But for all Simeon knew, either one of them might have been planted to learn more about him. To disagree with his new friend might cause him to be labelled a troublemaker. To agree could be seen as treasonable. He knew that no matter what, he must escape before he was recognised for himself. He'd almost certainly be court-martialled and shot. He had to get to Vidzy and the safety of Hanna's home. He couldn't wait any longer. He had to leave right now if they were bringing in patients from the field who'd been serving in the Fifty-Fourth.

Simeon was waiting by the ambulance when the air-raid sirens whined for the third time in two hours. Anatoly had gone inside to collect some paperwork and Gregory had gone for a pee behind the bushes at the back. For Simeon, it was now or never.

Outside the hospital gates, Simeon could see people fleeing to the shelters as the warning rose to an ear-splitting pitch before fading to a long, low whine and then screaming again. A flock of black bombers with swastikas on their tails flew low overhead. He saw them release their deathly cargos and threw himself down as explosions rocked the ground around him. A second wave of enemy planes filled the skies. Buildings flared. Only when he stood up as a third wave dispatched their evil cargo over the city did he realise he was now entirely alone in the street.

Masonry was tumbling as the aftershock of the bombs loosened foundations. Buildings sheared, opening bedrooms and living rooms to the wide world, the detritus of ordinary life revealed as tables rocked on the edge of scarred dining rooms. Simeon watched a whole bed crashing towards him from a gaping third- or fourth-floor room and explode into a million splinters. He had been keeping to the centre of the wide avenues, but now he realised he had reached the Neva embankment. More planes rose across the Gulf of Finland and flew towards him, while blinding searchlights cut through the darkness, performing an eerie dance across the water. There was only one way out of Leningrad, across Lake Ladoga to the north-east. If only he could get out of central Leningrad, he would find a way to get to Vidzy. He'd walk a million miles if necessary, to find Dora and their baby.

The night was cloudy, threatening snow. He had no moon to guide him. Left or right? He decided on right. He pulled up the collar of his jacket against the icy air. He had no hat, and not for the first time, he cursed his bright red hair. It had grown since Ivan had shaved it nearly two months ago, and now, he figured, it must have been shining like a beacon to the fliers who strafed the ground. His eyes were fixed forward, searching for clues that might help him identify where he was, when he tripped. At first, he thought he'd tumbled over a bag of rags, but the rag bag was solid. He looked down to see a body curled in the foetal position. He stooped and turned it over, ready to help it to its feet.

"Sorry, mate." The words were automatic. It was a man, his eyes open, gleaming like a cat's. He was dead. Simeon tried to afford him the dignity of closing his eyelids, only to find they were frozen solid, the eyelashes sparkling with frost. No doubt the body cleaners would pick him up and take him to Piscaryovka for communal burial when the cart came along tomorrow morning.

Simeon had reached an area of ice-spangled grass and skeletal trees. The black sky was beginning to lighten into a blue-grey dawn. He must have walked farther than he'd thought. He looked back, and behind him he could see the features of Leningrad, the bones of its bombed buildings standing black and stark against the sky, rafts of twisted metal joists standing as proud and as skeletal as its citizens. The road had bent away from the riverbank, and the frosted greenery and clumps of bare trees thinned. He was in an industrial area. Angular concrete apartments rose on either side of the road, built to house the workers from vast factories that were set back in their own grounds, their gates guarded by uniformed men.

Concentrating was becoming harder. Simeon had expected to cross a physical barrier beyond hunger, but the intensity of his stomach's gripes had only worsened. He felt weak and exhausted. Once or twice he'd been passed by German lorries and once by a car with a red flag emblazoned with a black swastika flying from its bonnet. Somehow he had escaped the besieged city with far less opposition than he'd expected.

He had four cigarettes left but only three matches. He had rationed himself to two puffs of a cigarette when the hunger became too much to bear. He lit one of them now and drew the smoke down. As it entered his lungs, he felt dizzy and light-headed. He treated himself to the luxury of a second deep inhalation before pinching the glowing end. There was still one good long draw left in it. He would keep it with the dog-ends of the three remaining cigarettes. If necessary, he could wrap the leftover tobacco in a leaf. He needed to find more matches.

Simeon looked down. Small vegetable patches lined the roadside. The patch next to him was full of winter cabbages, their thick heavy leaves curling under the weight of morning ice. He remembered how his mother used to make delicious white cabbage soup at this time of year and store it in large bottles for the rest of the winter. The memory set his salivary glands flowing.

His stomach was hurting again, and the cabbages were tempting. He tried to pull the first one from the frozen ground, but its roots remained glued in the solid earth. Only a single leaf tore away in his hand. He stuffed it greedily into his mouth. It was gritty and bitter. He swallowed. Bugger! If only he had a penknife. He sacrificed one of his precious matches to melt the ice, hoping the worst of the dirt and grit would run off in the melted water, but the match wasn't hot for long enough to leave the cabbage leaf any cleaner. He heard the lorry rumbling behind him but took no notice. He must eat the cabbage leaf. So absorbed in his task was he that he didn't hear the lorry grind to a halt.

"Papers?" The man in brown leather coat, a black SS uniform hat covering his head, held out his hand.

Simeon shook the bag from his shoulder and reached into the front pocket, his frozen fingers fumbling as he handed over Valdis Berzin's papers.

"You have no permit?"

"I have a permit."

The man waited while Simeon again fumbled in his rucksack.

"You're not a factory worker from Kalpino?" The man lifted his hand and passed Simeon's papers to a man standing beside him, pointing with a gloved finger. "Here it says porter at a military hospital, Leningrad. Run away, have you? Work too hard? Were we making life too difficult for you, *Berzin?*"

Simeon pretended he didn't understand. A gloved hand smashed him across the face. Six other men had come to join his antagonist.

"What do you think we should do with this shirker, Brigadeführer, sir?" The speaker turned to the man standing next to him, heavy black eyebrows forming ledges over small, slit eyes, his jowls, the colour of a jaundiced peach, hanging over his collar.

"I think, Brigadeführer, that he might like to take a little ride with us."

The Brigadeführer lifted the leather gloved hand again and smashed it into Simeon's nose. "Just to let you know who's the boss."

The second blow caught Simeon off guard. He fell to his knees, pain exploding, blood spurting from his nostrils. He felt his bladder voiding, the urine hot against his leg. His face reddened, flaming against the stinging cold. As he pulled himself back to his feet, the men began laughing, pointing at the steaming stain on his left trouser leg.

"You'll find it easier to eat the cabbage half cooked," the Brigadeführer remarked. "Go on, eat it."

Simeon bent down and pulled the cabbage. It came up quite easily now. Blood was still dribbling from his nose. He wiped the wet mess with his filthy sleeve. The thought of eating the urine-soaked cabbage made him retch. He tried pull the wet trouser leg away from his skin.

"Take them off. Off! Filthy incontinent bastard."

The first officer placed himself in front of Simeon and began to tug at the string holding up his trousers. The trousers fell to his knee. The other men laughed as they stared at his circumcised penis, withered and shrivelled with cold.

"Well, well, well. A better prize than we thought. A Jew in Kolpino! They get bloody everywhere, don't they, these bloody Jews."

They picked him up bodily, his trousers still round his ankles, and threw him through the tailgate of the covered lorry, where he lay on the floor. He counted the boots. There were ten feet in total: five other soldiers in the lorry, three sitting on the bench to one side of him, and two on the other. Each time Simeon tried to lift his head, one of the soldiers kicked it down again.

Simeon heard the tyres crunch on gravel. The truck stopped. "We're here."

One of the soldiers jumped up, let down the flap, and pulled Simeon out by his feet. As he landed, he felt his tooth go through his lip. He looked up to see a vast building, a turquoise palace, embellished with white and gold, like an iced birthday cake. A group of men wearing striped pyjamas stood in formal lines in front of him. He felt a gun in his back as he was pushed towards them.

"Welcome to the Catherine Palace, Jew," the Brigadeführer said.

Every breath stung Simeon's throat. He was shivering uncontrollably, partly from cold, partly with fear. He managed to struggle to his feet, grateful for Valdis Berzin's sturdy boots. Their weight alone enabled him to stand upright. In front of him, he saw a pitiful group of skeletons dressed in a strange uniform of blue berets and blue and white striped pyjamas. Other men in similar uniforms but with red armbands over their sleeves stood behind trestle tables to one side, huddling beside giant black cauldrons that were precariously balanced on wooden stands. Fires flamed beneath the cauldrons, and heavy steam rose into the arctic air. Simeon longed to be near that heat.

"We picked this one up on the road." The officer in charge of the lorry detail was speaking to a man with a clipboard. "Another Jew for you. What do you do, Jew?"

"I'm an engineer."

"Perfect." The Brigadeführer whispered something to the man with the list, who in turn looked straight at Simeon.

"Show me your arm."

The man pulled up his own sleeve and pointed at Simeon. "Arm!" he bellowed. Simeon rolled up his sleeve.

"No tattoo. So not from a camp. Name?" he shrieked in Simeon's ear.

"Karminsky," he found the strength to shout back. "I am Simeon Karminsky." It was suddenly important to be himself. If he had to die, he would die in his own skin. "Simeon Karminsky of Krustpils, Latvia."

"Occupation?"

"Lieutenant engineer third class, Peoples' Volunteers, the Red Army."

"Aha. Another one for you, Gunther," the man called across the heads of the soldiers towards the prisoners manning the cauldrons. "Another mouth for you to feed. He can take the place of that one." He pointed to a pile of rags heaped next to an old statue. "Take the clothes off that and put them on. Now. Before it freezes solid." The stick lashed at his back. Only then did Simeon realise that he was being told to undress a rigid corpse. Rigor mortis had already set in.

"Now." The stick fell again across his shoulders. He was conscious of the lines of prisoners staring at him. This was no time for modesty.

As he bent down to take off his wet trousers, he saw the other men either were barefooted or wore wooden clogs on their feet. The body had bare feet. Simeon put on the corpse's striped clothes without removing his boots. No one seemed to notice. With the stick digging between his shoulder blades, he was marched back towards the lines of men, now standing silently in pairs behind the cauldrons, holding their bowls in front of them. A very small person suddenly broke ranks and ran towards the steaming pots. A cry of despair erupted from his partner in the queue.

"Halt!" The order was sharp and clear. A single shot echoed across the silent space between the men and the cauldrons. Some of the soldiers started to laugh. The sticklike men stood in silence. One of the soldiers stepped forward and pointed his rifle at the man who'd been beside the child. "Pick it up!"

The man lifted the tiny body gently, hugging it close to him, kissing it. From where he stood, Simeon could see the child's face. The boy couldn't have been much more than eight years old.

"Father and son?" Simeon whispered to the man next to him. The man nodded. Simeon could see tears streaming down the father's face as he tossed the rag doll that had been his son into the well of the truck.

Someone thrust a tin bowl in his hands. The man he'd whispered to was short with deep brown eyes that were too big for his skinny face.

As the group of prisoners shuffled forward together, each received a single ladle of hot liquid from the cauldron and half a loaf of black bread. Simeon started to stuff the bread into his mouth. The man beside him whispered, "Don't eat it all. You might get nothing else today."

Simeon turned to him, but his face had disappeared inside his tin bowl. He was licking it clean with his tongue. *Like a dog,* thought Simeon. *We're all animals to them.*

"Where have you all come from?" Simeon whispered. "Who are you? What is this place? What are we doing here?"

45

"We're Jews. We were in a slave labour camp. Where have you come from? I don't recognise you from the camp."

"Simeon Karminsky. From Latvia, but lately of Leningrad. I'm an engineer."

"Dov Persky, from Vilna in Byelorussia." The man smiled. "You really don't know where you are? This is the Catherine Palace, home of the Amber Room. I'm an expert in Baltic amber." He put a warning finger to his lips and tucked what remained of his bread into his trousers as a guard walked up and down the line. The meal break was over. Simeon stood alongside Dov as they were marched into the building, across a black and white marble tiled entrance hall and up a grand staircase. What must once have been magnificent wrought-iron rails had been torn aside. The building was even colder inside than outside. They walked through four vast chambers, each larger than the last. All had been stripped back to bare brick. Most of the ceilings were gone, and large flakes of snow were falling through bare wooden rafters. Finally they had reached white double doors exquisitely decorated with gold ormolu embellishment. Were they, Simeon wondered, the gateway to heaven or hell?

Chapter 6

Hanna

HANNA WANDERED AIMLESSLY FOR WEEKS. NAZI UNIFORMS WERE everywhere, black ones, brown ones, men in grey overcoats, streams of tanks clogging roads. She took no care to hide herself. Nothing mattered without Nat and her boys. Even the Nazis seemed to ignore the dirty vagabond woman in her torn skirt and filthy blouse, her red curly hair tangled and unkempt. She had no roubles left, and shopkeepers seemed surprised when she opened her mouth to beg a crust, speaking like an educated woman rather than the gypsy she appeared. She watched other people going about their everyday lives, but she belonged to another species, a bereaved mother outside the human race. She was being punished, she thought, for leaving her babies. Mothers don't leave their children. Her babies were dead, and it was her fault. She was conscious of neither hunger nor thirst. A deep, dark pain gnawed at her guts and tore at her heart. She couldn't cry. Tears were a luxury reserved for normal caring mothers who protected their sons. Her tragedy was of her own making. Sometimes, when her normal need to nurture her body overcame her emotional void, she'd pick unripe fruit from trees to nibble on as she passed by gardens and orchards. Occasionally, she'd find herself by a market stall, where she would beg for, or steal, a piece of cheese. When her stomach reacted violently to her strange diet, she waited until the cramps and diarrhoea passed, and then she'd walk on again, to nowhere. She drank water from cool streams.

Once, in a town square, Hanna watched two young German soldiers beating up an old Jew, pulling at his beard and kicking him on the ground. To her shame, she cowered in a corner until the old man collapsed and the tormentors, their game over, walked away.

As summer turned to autumn and it rained, Hanna managed to find shelter in sheds or stables. At other times she curled up behind a bush or tree and slept with her head cushioned on a pile of damp leaves. She barely heard the birds' dawn chorus, nor was she aware of the insects that feasted on her bare skin. She scratched herself raw, but the soreness was almost a relief, physical pain overcoming mental torture. Her clothes ripped when she caught them on brambles. Nothing mattered. Every night, she relived the nightmare of finding her babies dead. She heard them crying as she closed her eyes. "Mama, Mama, where are you?" She'd awake, soaked with the sweat of their fear. Then she'd lie awake, wherever she was, with her hands resting behind her head, trying to recreate their fear in her mind. Sometimes she'd console herself that it must have been quick. *Bang, bang* and it was over. Had one brother watched the other die? Or had they been murdered simultaneously by two gunmen? She prayed it was the latter and that neither of them had seen his brother murdered. Sometimes she thought of her own brother. She tried to imagine how she might have felt at that age if she'd been forced to watch someone harm her own brother Simeon.

"Oh God! Simeon! Where are you? Where are you, Nat? The boys ... I need you both. Help me." Why had she been spared? To tell whom? Her mother always had said there was a purpose in everything. "So show me the purpose in this, Mama?" she called out aloud. "Come on. How can that be when I am living yet my poor babies are dead?"

When she heard the rumble of German cars or tanks rolling in convoy down the dusty roads, she was often tempted to stand in the middle of the road and shout at them: "Here I am, a Jewess who got away. Come on. Take me." Why couldn't she do it?

It was getting chilly at night. Hanna knew she was growing physically weaker through lack of proper nourishment, and yet her brain felt razor sharp, her thoughts and memories so clear and vivid that at times she thought other people must be aware of what she was thinking. She wondered if she could just lie down and wait for death to claim her. What was that thing deep inside her that made her go on and on?

Occasionally she attempted to clean herself up in streams, just for her own comfort, but the last time had been several days ago, and she knew she smelt. One morning, she awoke in a wood, shivering with cold and conscious of a terrible thirst. Unusually, she had not slept near a stream. As she walked down the dusty road, she could see a crowd of men ahead. Drawing closer, she saw it was a bar. Two men were sitting outside despite the chill and the early hour, playing some kind of board game. She could see a bottle of water in the middle of the table. So desperate was her thirst that she had to have it. Oblivious to how the rough-looking farmworkers, who had been laughing, talking, and drinking together moments earlier, fell silent as they caught sight of her, she picked up the bottle and swigged down the contents, stopping merely to catch her breath. It wasn't water, she realised, as the liquid burnt her gullet, but that didn't matter. One of the men caught her by the wrist.

"What do you think you're doing, little lady? That's our vodka," he shouted.

Her throat and chest were on fire. "A drink. For pity's sake, I need water. I can pay." She reached beneath the elastic on her skirt waistband to the secret pocket. The first thing that came to hand was her diamond ring, the ring Nat had bought for her when they were betrothed. Once it had been her most treasured possession. Now it had no value other than to buy the water she needed so desperately. She felt light-headed, but she had to have another drink. She held out the ring towards the heavily built man at the table while picking up a second bottle of the clear liquid. The man's chin bristled black, his large belly wobbling before her eyes. She drained the second bottle holding out the little diamond towards him.

He seemed to fade into the distance as she watched him hold the tiny precious stone towards the sun. She could see the light changing colour on its finely cut prisms. Someone put a third bottle in her hand. She swigged again, gasping as she lost her grasp on reality. The men's voices were fading now. She couldn't understand why she still felt so dreadfully thirsty. Something was pecking at her ankles. She looked down at her feet to see a number of chickens pecking, pecking.

"What are chickens doing here?" She heard her own voice. The laughter around her was louder. She defiantly shook her loose uncombed hair. Her head belonged to someone else. Her vision was blurred. There was something she wanted to say, but she couldn't think of the words. The man with the wobbly belly had become a triplet. She laughed to herself. His hand was under her skirt. She batted it off as though swatting a fly.

"Someone get her water." It was the voice of another man. She felt the patting again. Someone was violating her most private places. Again, she tried to push him away. The only man who could do such a thing to her was Nat, and Nat wasn't here. Perhaps if she peed on the hand it would go away. She needed a pee badly. She felt the warm urine against her legs and hit out at the clumsy hands that withdrew instantly as she relieved herself. She must have dropped the bottle. She heard it shatter. There was a howl of pain. She heaved herself up and vomited. She thought she heard someone shout: 'Serves him right, stupid bastard. It was Simeon's voice. She was sure of it. "Leave the poor woman alone," he yelled.

"Thank God you've come, Simeon. Thank you. I love you. Where are you? I can't see you."

"My name's not Simeon," came the reply. "I'm Sergei. Sergei Petrouishk."

Chapter 7

Simeon

SO, THIS WAS THE AMBER ROOM. HE'D HEARD OF THE GRAND AMBER ROOM in the Catherine Palace in Leningrad. Who in Russia hadn't? He'd seen photographs of it, a wondrous room composed of panels of exquisite amber mosaics. He vaguely remembered the story. A Prussian king had gifted it to Peter the Great in the early 1700s. He remembered part of the story from school. Hadn't Peter given the king some bizarre gifts in return for these amber panels, including fifty-five grenadiers for the king's regiment of giant soldiers, a lathe, and an ivory goblet he'd made himself? *What brought such strange facts to mind in such bizarre circumstances?* Simeon wondered.

"I've heard a rumour that we're about to dismantle this place," the man next to him whispered to him out of the corner of his mouth. "We'll be here for months."

They'd been ushered up a grand wrought-iron staircase and through the ruins of a number of vast chambers, empty of contents, their walls stripped back to bare brick. Intricate wooden floors had been torn up to become an obscene obstacle course. All ceilings and most of the roofing had vanished, leaving the once wonderful structure in skeletal ruins. As they'd trudged through the remains of four enormous chambers to reach their destination, snow had fallen on their bare heads and shivering shoulders. Most of the men shook it off like dogs. The room in which they now stood was about a hundred metres square, Simeon reckoned. The floor was intact, a parquet of fine woods laid in floral designs. He looked down at his feet and realised he was still wearing Valdis Berzin's filthy old boots. He felt as though he ought to remove them as a mark of respect for the beauty of this floor. The ceiling decorations showed bearded patriarchs protecting cherubs and angels in an exquisite fresco. The walls, by contrast, were covered by rough hessian. Where the hessian had been removed, there were a few white oak planks. Some of the planks had also been removed, and underneath were the most extraordinary wall decorations Simeon had ever seen. The entire room seemed to be constructed of panels of amber mosaics. In the centre of some were Florentine mirrors encased in amber mosaic frames. Powerful spotlights had been strategically placed to light the walls, which shone with a strangely muted golden glow. The shimmering amber had been dulled by a wash of something white so that instead of glowing gold as amber should, it appeared a flat, opaque yellow to the naked eye.

The prisoners were being pushed forward, further into the room, with guns at their backs. When they were all inside, the great white doors slammed shut so there was no escape.

An officer held up his hand to the silent ragged gathering. He was a tall man and sported an impressive array of medals on his grey greatcoat, all dwarfed by a large iron cross hanging from a red ribbon round his neck. On his head, he wore the black Waffen-SS field cap emblazoned with a gold motif. A shorter man in civilian dress stood beside him, wrapped in a heavy brown overcoat with thick leather gloves and a brown woollen scarf. He, too, wore a hat, a brown felt fedora, and small round eyeglasses that seemed to pinch his nose above a thin line of pallid pink lips. The same seven soldiers who'd travelled with Simeon in the lorry were now standing around the room brandishing both whips and guns.

The officer was speaking. "Heil Hitler. I am General Field Marshal Karl Rudolph Gert von Runstedt," he announced. Simeon's eyes were transfixed as he looked through the bare windows. Outside it was growing darker by the second. "Our Führer has charged me to oversee the dismantling of this room, intact. Each man here has been selected for his specialist knowledge and skills—all, that is, but one idle Jew we picked up on the road. He'll make up the one we were forced to dispense with a little earlier."

Simeon felt his face flush redder than his hair.

"Stand in groups of eight. You too, lying Jew." He felt the whip crack at his calves.

The man who'd stood beside Simeon in the food queue pulled Simeon towards him. "I was right. It is the Amber Room. It's as I suspected. We are to take it apart. What's your name?"

"Simeon Karminsky."

The field marshal obviously heard him and bellowed. "Shut up, Yid, or you'll enjoy the same treat as this idiot bugger." Simeon felt the whip slash at his ankles again, but they were so cold that he felt no pain. Turning to the entire group, the field marshal continued. "The task is to remove all the panels of amber mosaics and lay them in their numbered 'coffins'. There is one for each panel. There are separate containers for the mirrors in amber mosaic frames, as well as one crate for each of the large candelabra. The amber is fragile. The idiot Russians, in their haste to hide their treasure, used flour and water paste to cover the mosaics with cigarette papers to hold the amber pieces in place. We have no time to waste. You will lift the panels off the walls, working in teams of ten. Some morsels of amber may detach themselves. On the side of each crate you will see a large muslin pouch. Loose pieces must be placed in this pouch. As the crates are filled, they are to be covered with layers of soft cotton wool and gauze, then nailed down securely. Any of you bastards with ideas of preserving a small piece of mosaic for his own future enrichment will be caught and suitably punished. We will be watching *all* of you. We know you Jews. There is only one punishment for thieves: death."

He nodded to his left. "Now may I introduce Dr Alfred Rohde, an amber aficionado?"

Simeon was sure that if they stood still much longer, they would all freeze solid. The soldiers stationed around the room were stamping and wrapping their arms around themselves to keep warm. Von Rundstedt seemed unaffected. He spoke as though introducing a lecturer to a cognisant audience. Bizarrely, the small man in the brown fedora nodded in humble acknowledgement towards them. Rohde, short, slight and stooping, stepped forward. Coming from a man of such a physically delicate appearance, his booming voice surprised them. "Each of the twelve largest panels is approximately three and a half metres high. Ten smaller mosaic panels fill the space between the floor and larger panels as you can see. They have been supplemented by Florentine mirrors framed in amber mosaic frames."

The field marshal interjected. "The officers you see behind you have also been chosen for their skills. Their specialty, however, focuses on punishing insubordination. We want to ensure the Amber Room is restored to its full glory in its rightful home in Königsberg, with every part in place."

He nodded towards von Rundstedt, inviting him to conclude.

"You will be physically searched, now and at regular intervals throughout the dismantling process. Should any of the smallest pieces accidentally find their way into your clogs, your noses, or your arseholes as little 'souvenirs' of today, you will be suitably punished. We will be watching. Nor should you think of attempting to escape. Outside this palace, a battalion of armed guards are waiting to transport this amber back to its rightful home.

"Thirty-six hours from now, this room will appear as wrecked as the other rooms you passed through. The only covering this room will know is snow." The men were separated into their groups of ten, five on either side of each panel. Simeon, who was still standing beside Dov Persky, looked at him.

"You will work in silence. You will speak to your co-workers only in connection with the task at hand. Should you have a question concerning the amber or any aspect of this work, you will direct it to Herr Rohde through me by raising your hand."

Removing the panels from the walls was hard physical work. Although some of the mosaic pieces were stuck fast on their backings, others simply fell away as the panels were moved. After several hours without food or water a couple of the men collapsed, too weak to carry on. Finally, just as Simeon and the others in their detail were preparing to remove their third large panel, a short whistle blast called them to attention. It was followed by a single shot. Every eye was turned towards von Rundstedt. He shrieked: "See what happens to thieves who attempt to steal from the Third Reich? Your friend here obviously thought we wouldn't miss one little piece of amber. Maybe he thought it was an asset for his future. Well, now you can see his future for yourselves. I make no idle threats. He was trying to hide it in his ear. The same fate awaits any other aspiring amber owners among you."

Simeon and Dov exchanged looks. "He wanted to die. He's the father of the lad you saw shot as you arrived," Dov muttered under his breath. "He wanted them to see it. He wanted death."

Simeon was starving and desperately thirsty. As another shrill whistle startled them all to a halt, Simeon experienced the strangest taste of vodka on his tongue. He hadn't drunk vodka since the night after his meeting with Yuri Preditis in Factory 174. He felt light-headed, like he was drunk. He was surely hallucinating. His eyes wouldn't focus. It must be hunger.

The prisoners were ordered to form a line to collect a meal. With the barrels of guns manned by the seven "officiating" officers at their backs, they were moved forward a section at a time. They watched as the first men in the line were ordered to open their mouths. Two men in white coats they hadn't seen before appeared. One was examining inside their mouths with a torch and dental mirror. Simeon could feel beads of sweat breaking out on his forehead, although he had hidden nothing. The queue moved forward. The second man ordered them to bend forward and drop their trousers. Another two white-coated men walked along the line, poking some device on a stick up their backsides. Several of the men shat helplessly on the floor, the depth of their degradation evident in their red faces and sunken eyes. It was disgusting, the most demeaning act Simeon had ever seen. He prayed the stick wouldn't have the same effect on him.

Thankfully, both Simeon and Dov were declared clean. They received their portions of black bread and salt fish and their bowls of watery cabbage soup, which they gobbled in silence.

"They're not going to let any of us leave here alive, so we might as well die with full stomachs," Dov said.

Simeon spread his legs and leant back on his elbows. "You've changed your mind."

"We've seen too much. When the job's done, they'll shoot us. They won't want any witnesses."

"We could run for it when we get outside."

Dov looked at Simeon, his eyes full of pity. "How far do you think you'll get before they set their dogs on you? You're either target practice or dog food. Your choice."

"So why don't we end it now? Let them see us stealing a bit of their precious amber?"

"Because, my new friend, we need to believe that where there's life, there's hope."

The whistle blew again. The meal break was over. Simeon puzzled over his new friend's conundrum.

They had just started work again as a man on the other side of the room began shrieking, dancing like a wild animal caught in a trap, hitting out wildly with his arms and legs. That was when Simeon saw in the frenzy a little piece of honey-coloured amber in his own hand. He had been about to put it in the "cradle". It was the colour of his mother's chicken soup. His mouth watered. At its centre, he saw a single, minute fly, its legs caught forever in the resin trap. He put the amber in his mouth without thinking, wondering if there was any goodness in the old fly. As the screaming across the room went on, he dipped his fingers into the cradle, and his fingers closed around another piece. He glanced at it. It was the colour of treacle toffee. Now his mouth was filled with the taste of toffee sweetness. As the squealing from across the room continued, he dipped his fingers into the cradle a third time. The piece between his fingers was long, thin, and rounded at the end. Some kind of claw. It caught in his throat as he swallowed, causing him to cough.

⌁

Finally, it was done. The panels, the mirrors, the chandeliers, and the candle brackets were all neatly packed in their crates. The boxes were lowered to the waiting lorries using the glassless windows through a series of ropes and pulleys. The room was almost bare now, its beauty, its grandeur, its majesty ripped from its heart. The last panels had gone. Simeon watched through the window as the crates with their precious cargo were covered with tarpaulins. Snow fluttered in through the bare rafters as the men were lined up for the final walk down the once grand staircase. Precisely thirty-six hours after they had started dismantling the room, and as von Rundstedt had predicted, it was skimmed back to bare rafters and brickwork.

As he stood in line to board one of the open trucks, Simeon wondered briefly whether anyone involved in rebuilding the Amber Room in its new home, wherever that was, would ever realise that the three little pieces were missing from the cradle. He doubted it. And if they did, he had the satisfaction of knowing the he had challenged the Nazis, albeit unwittingly, and stolen the amber without getting caught. He had won.

Of the one hundred and fifty or so men who had been shepherded into the Catherine Palace when Simeon had arrived yesterday morning, there appeared to be fewer than eighty still alive. He looked around for Dov Persky but couldn't see him among the survivors.

The men were loaded into open lorries and driven out through the forest. The pine trees with their heavy covering of snow looked like those on pretty Christmas cards, but there was nothing pretty or Christmassy about the men's final destination. The lorries stopped suddenly beside an enormous deep black pit. Simeon could see the brown muddy walls at the sides, spattered with patches of snowflakes. The bottom was gleaming white with snow. They were offloaded in sixes and ordered to strip. The first six were told to stand on the pit edge, six rifle-wielding soldiers directly behind them. Simeon couldn't see their faces. He no longer cared about anything. Death would claim him very soon. The shots rang out. The first six men fell

56

downwards like rag dolls, arms and legs flailing. The next six were ordered to the pit edge. Dov had been right: there would be no one left to tell the tale. Simeon tried to hang back, his teeth chattering with the intense cold. The next six were shot, and the next. His mind felt crystal clear—as clear and clean as the snowflakes that were drifting all around them. He thought about Hanna. They had come into this world together. He counted the minutes between one set of shots and another, just as he'd been counting while he waited his turn. Six, five, four, three, two … He heard the shot and fell forward into the pit. He felt his limbs flying before he landed onto the bones of others. Despite the perishing cold, they still felt warm to his ice-cold body. He tried to roll against them to use what was left of their body heat. He heard more shots. Three, or was it four, lines of bodies had fallen on top of him, and he was conscious he hadn't counted them. He tried to breathe downwards so that the steam of his breath wouldn't alert those above that there was a survivor.

"Ist am Ende. Was sollen wir tun, während wir auf den Transport warten?" he heard one of the soldiers shout to the other. "Ist Kald. Wir can Fussball spielen."

With superhuman strength, Simeon managed to pull himself towards the edge of the pit to see the boy soldiers who'd shot at them. He saw their faces as they stooped just above him, collecting the prisoners' discarded pyjama rags and rolling them into a ball. They were children. There were ten of them left. They began to kick the makeshift ball about, right there beside the pit of death. One of them suddenly shrugged out of his heavy grey greatcoat.

"Ich bin heiss," he called to one of the others.

The coat fell within Simeon's reach. At that moment he wanted that coat more than he'd ever wanted anything in all his twenty-three years. *Dear God,* he prayed, *let him forget it.* Then he heard the sound of engines approaching in the distance. The covered transport lorries had come to collect the soldiers. Simeon watched the men's feet running towards it. The engines revved. He heard them calling to one another in youthful voices as they boarded. He was still too scared to move towards the coat. They might come back. He heard the lorry pull away.

He managed to haul himself out of the pit with the last vestiges of his strength, grab at the coat, and wrap it round himself. He heard the bones of those other men, dead and now frozen solid, crunch beneath his feet. He was aware of other arms pulling him over the edge of the pit until he was flat on the snowy ground. He lay in the snow, rolling the precious coat around him, breathing hard inside his "tent", hoping his breath would warm him. He closed his eyes. He was conscious that he was being dragged towards the trees, then stood upright supported by strong arms. Then everything went black.

He was lying somewhere comfortable, and he could see Hanna looking down at him. *Dearest sister, you didn't leave me after all. You were here all the time, waiting for me.* He had almost forgotten how this had started. Was his wife, his own darling Dora, somewhere nearby too, with their baby? But then he saw. The brown eyes weren't Dora's. Hanna's eyes were blue. Who was it? He felt something warm trickle down his throat. He put his hand to his neck. His throat felt terribly sore as though he'd scratched it with a bone.

"Come, take a little more. You must drink," the woman said. "Come on. Stay with us. Stay alive."

Chapter 8

Hanna

"**M**AX, SHMUELY." SHE HEARD HER OWN VOICE CALLING THEIR NAMES from a long way off. She opened her eyes briefly and closed them quickly. The light hurt. She was aware of a gentle touch on her arm, a soothing stroke, the kind of light, gentle stroke a mother uses on her sick child. She licked her dry lips. She was desperately thirsty again. A cup was held to her mouth; she felt its cool rim and gulped the contents, licking her lips again at the blessed taste of water. Her eyes opened cautiously again, testing the brightness of the light, and she saw an elderly woman, white hair escaping a black kerchief.

"So," said the old woman in the Byelorussian dialect. "The sleeping princess awakes." The words were spoken softly.

Hanna opened her eyes properly and saw she was lying on a high bed in a large room, the walls lime-washed white. A picture of the Blessed Mother and Christ Child faced her on the opposite wall, and under it hung a large ornate crucifix.

"Where am I? Who are you?"

"I should ask the same questions." The old woman sat down on the end of her bed. Hanna moved her legs over to make room for her and realised she was wearing a strange long white shift. The woman patted her hand.

"It's all right. Rest. You are safe. We won't harm you." She patted Hanna's hand again. "You are in our farmhouse. I live here with my son, Sergei. I am

Olga Petruishka. Sergei works in the bar some nights. You were lucky he was there last night. I hear you gave that lecherous old Vishnik what he has long deserved." She chuckled.

Hanna looked up and saw a peasant woman with clear blue eyes and rosy cheeks. She was dressed all in black apart from the vast white overall that covered her ample breasts and round stomach and was double knotted where her waist might once have been. Whatever she said, Hanna thought, she had nothing more to lose.

"I am Hanna, Madame. Hanna Abramskya."

"And if I am not mistaken, you are a Jewess?" As Hanna raised herself on her elbows in alarm, the old woman rested her soft hand on Hanna's shoulder again. "One of God's chosen people."

Hanna nodded. Suddenly awake, she felt round her waist. Olga saw her fumbling and handed her, her Mama Rachel's precious velvet bag with the few roubles she had left and the jewellery. It would look rude to peek inside as though she didn't trust the old woman.

"It's all there," Olga reassured her mind. Something else sparkled in the woman's hand: Hanna's betrothal ring. She handed Hanna the ring she had bartered for the vodka.

"Thieving bastards that lot are."

Hanna gazed at Olga, unable to find the right words of thanks. "You passed out in the bar," Olga explained. "You don't remember, huh? You drank a full bottle and a half of vodka. Like water, Sergei told me. That dirty old lecher Vishnik almost raped you for stealing his vodka. He took this in payment. However, I understand you gave as good as you got."

Hanna took the ring and caressed it before slipping it onto her finger as Olga continued: "He's a good boy, my Sergei. He knew you were no common drunk or prostitute, despite the state you were in. He shooed them away, those vile bastards who drink in that place. Threatened to call the police over their black market dealings if they so much as breathed a word of you to the Germans. When he'd frightened them away, he picked you up and brought you here. I will make you well. We're a good Christian family. Our Mary and Jesus were Jews. I don't understand why they persecute you. I will help you all I can, but I'm afraid you can't stay long."

"I understand."

The old woman felt into her pocket. "I have something else for you, but this time it's part of an exchange—an exchange to which I hope you will agree." Olga handed Hanna her own Star of David.

Hanna smiled, looking at it as it lay in the palm of her hand. "My grandmother bought this for me on the day I was born," she said. "She bought a slightly larger one for my twin brother."

"Oh! So you're a twin. It must be wonderful to have a twin."

"It was," Hanna whispered. "I don't know whether he's alive or dead."

"Let's pray he's alive. Now, give me your Star of David. Instead you will wear this." She handed Hanna a small gold cross on a chain. "It belonged to my daughter, Maria Petruishka. Wear my Maria's crucifix for your own safety. You are how old? Twenty-two, twenty-three perhaps? My Maria, she would be twenty-two now."

"I am twenty-three. My big boy, my Max, he would now be nearly five. He died in the forest. With Shmuely, Samuel, his little brother, who would be three in May."

"You were calling for your Max and your Samuel. And your twin brother, Simeon. I thought all three must be your children. I never thought you might be calling for your twin. My Maria was five when she died of measles."

Hanna lifted her hands in horror. "Measles. So dangerous. My little boy Max had measles. We kept him in a dark room and sponged him with cold water. And the cough! Terrible. Thank God, Shmuely didn't catch it. I think he was too young."

For a moment they were just two mothers discussing a killer childhood disease and they clung to each other, the round old peasant and the slender young Jewess.

Suddenly, Olga was practical again. "We must make some plans for you. Sergei will be home soon."

"Does Sergei know I'm Jewish?"

"Of course. He saw your little David Star." Hanna smiled to herself at the way Olga described her necklace. Olga brushed her own tears from her face with her sleeve and wiped Hanna's with the corner of her apron. She stood up.

"Tidy yourself up. There's a chamber pot under the bed and water on the washstand. I'll get you something light to eat." She brushed Hanna's shaking head. "You must take some soup. You'll do as you're told, young lady." It felt so comfortable to have an older, wiser woman to lean on. Hanna was happy to hand over all responsibility to somebody else and, just for a while, to feel like a child.

"In a few weeks, we will have you fit and strong again. Proper food and a lot of rest, time to heal—That's what you need." Olga smiled. "I think our God, the God who serves us both, meant us to meet. Jews are not too popular in this area now. So perhaps it would be a good idea if you were to take Maria's papers and her birth certificate, and from now on you will be Maria Petruishka, my daughter."

Olga lifted her hand gently and stroked Hanna's hair as though Hanna really was the beloved daughter she'd lost. It was a gesture of love and longing. "My Maria had blonde hair. Yours is red, of course, but if your identity papers were lost in a fire, then what? There are so many fires in the forest. Last month, we heard that when the Germans came, they torched the hotel not far from Vidzy at Inzkhaven because they believed the owner was either Jewish or harbouring Jews. If you had been working as a chambermaid in that hotel and you had run out and left your papers and your bag to be burnt to a cinder ... we can work out the details with Sergei. There's time."

Hanna laughed for the first time in more than three months. "You would make a great storyteller, Olga."

"My mama used to tell me I should have been a professional storyteller. I'm going to get that soup."

The two women hugged again, the differences in their age, their lives, their creeds and their loves dissolving in the common bond of bereavement.

Olga came back with a large white bowl of steaming liquid and sat herself on the bed next to Hanna as she drank the soup followed by several glasses of clear, cool water.

"Keep drinking, darling, and wash the liquor out of your system. Yes, you will be my daughter, Maria Petruishka. We are cut off here. We don't have too many curious neighbours. We've had a chat, Sergei and I. Get well first. Take your time. We think the best thing you could do then is go to Grodno. It's about an eight-hour walk from here. You might get a job in Grodno, possibly working with the Germans. In Grodno they are establishing two ghettos a couple of kilometres apart. Sergei says they are preparing them now. The first is about half a square kilometre around the main synagogue. God alone knows how many thousands of Jews will be crammed in there. We've heard gossip that it's for "productive" workers. The other will be on Slobodka Road, opposite the market square. There are railway lines there, and rumour has it that the "unproductive" Jews will be shipped east from there to camps they are setting up all over the country. Perhaps you could find work in the SS office on Hoovera Street to help your own people from the outside."

It was almost like listening to Simeon.

During the days that followed, Olga made Hanna rest, permitting her only to do the lightest tasks around the house. As she grew stronger, questions flooded her mind. "You are a Russian Orthodox Catholic, aren't you, Olga? I know nothing of the Catholic religion. How do I overcome that?"

Olga and Sergei had already worked that out, too. "Tomorrow is Sunday. I had already planned to take you to Mass with me. You will see what I do, and you will copy me. You will take Communion. After that, you will come with Sergei and me every Sunday until you leave here. You will come to early morning Mass with me during the week, too, if I go to give thanks for your 'safe escape'. That way, the liturgy will become familiar easily." Hanna said nothing. The old woman read the look dismay on her face as fear. "Don't worry," she told her. "You will pick it up fast enough. Father Peter is new here. He knows nothing about me. He doesn't know that my little girl died when she was five years old. I can say you've been working away for a long time. You tell them that you lost your papers in the fire as well as your job. You say your Mama can't afford to keep you here, so you are going to Grodno looking for work."

Hanna almost smiled again. "However, working in the hotel will have stood you in good stead to work as a housekeeper. Perhaps the good father in Grodno can help find you find such a housekeeping job? Alternatively, you might be able to apply for office work. Can you type? Have you ever done bookwork?"

"Yes, for my husband. I kept all the books and typed his letters to make them look professional. Nat is a carpenter. The best in Byelorussia."

It was Olga's turn to smile. "You love your husband as I loved mine," she said. "You will be together again one day. You'll see."

During the first week, Olga brought out a huge tin bath from a shed. She heated pan after pan of water and invited Hanna to step in. Hanna lay in the hot water, scented by lavender oil that the old woman had added, and it soothed her in a way nothing else had been able to for a very long time. Olga cut Hanna's hair and washed it, and when it was short she combed out the lice that had made her head itch unbearably.

"A minor problem. It happens to us all from time to time. Never mind. We'll soon get rid of them," Olga said as she cut hanks of curls from Hanna's wet hair. "It looks very pretty," Olga said as Hanna's newly shorn head dried into curls. "It's beautiful hair, and it will soon grow again."

"I'm afraid you can't stay forever," Sergei announced solemnly one evening as they sat round the farmhouse table, eating huge bowls of Olga's tasty vegetable soup with thick slices of home-made bread. "One of the villagers asked me who you were and I said you were my sister hoping to leave for Grodno to look for work. I'm sorry, 'Maria'." They had started to use Hanna's new pseudonym regularly so she would get used to it.

Hanna had mastered the basics of the Orthodox religion and knew her catechism as well as any Catholic woman might. Olga had washed and mended Hanna's clothes while she was still recuperating in bed. One night Sergei came home and brought some more clothes for her. "I got them from the barkeeper's wife. She's about the same size as Maria. I told her you were in desperate need of a few basics like a new skirt and blouse. She was glad of the cash I gave her."

Hanna immediately looked concerned. "How much do I owe you, Sergei?" she asked. "I have some. money."

"It's my gift to my 'sister'," he said. "It makes me happy to see you so much better. "You will take Maria's birth certificate. Most young people these days don't carry their birth certificates around of course, but if your identity papers were lost in a fire. Using the birth certificate, however, you can apply for new identity papers when you get to Grodno." Among the "new" clothes, Sergei had managed to find a warm green woollen coat for her.

The weather was turning colder by the day. The day before Hanna was due to leave was a Sunday. They went to Mass "en famille" for the last time. As Hanna took the wine and the water into her mouth, she thought not of the Catholic prayers, but of a prayer that was common to both faiths: "The Lord bless you and keep you. The Lord make his face to shine upon you and be merciful to you. The Lord lift up the face of his countenance to you and grant you peace." She looked over at Olga. Olga smiled at her. Hanna could see the love and the deep, heartbreaking longing in her eyes.

On Monday morning, Sergei left early. Hanna breakfasted at six thirty in the morning with him and kissed him goodbye. Olga helped her shrug into the warm green coat he'd found for her, covered her short red hair with her own blue wool shawl, and put an arm round her as they walked to the front gate. Both she and Olga were crying silently. She walked ahead but Olga called her back. "A word of advice, my dearest Maria. From a woman who would love you as much as she would love any daughter of her own, if only you could stay. If you live like your enemies and think like your enemies, they may become your friends and help you and all your people."

Chapter 9

Simeon

I T TOOK MORE THAN A WEEK FOR SIMEON TO RECOVER FROM HIS ORDEAL. FOR the first few days, the screams of the tortured men haunted him. He ran his tongue round his mouth and swallowed when he tasted something warm and slightly salty, but as he swallowed his throat was so painful that he thought it must have been torn in the pit. He tried to cough, but it hurt too much, and he couldn't ease the agony. Then he remembered: he'd been in the Amber Room. It was the last piece of amber he'd swallowed, a piece with a sharp edge. Had he dreamt that he'd been in a pit full of dead bodies? He faded in and out of consciousness, sometimes convinced that Hanna was there, holding a spoon to his mouth. She was hovering over his head, bending down, her long brown hair brushing his cheek, urging him to eat. He could feel a spoon on his tongue. She was trying to feed him, but swallowing hurt so much that he turned his head away. "Hanna," he urged in a rasping whisper, "no more. It hurts, Hanna. Stop it."

"Come on," a woman's voice soothed in Yiddish, but it wasn't Hanna's voice. Nor was it Dora's. "I'm not Hanna. I'm Rutti, Ruth. Another spoonful. You need strength." The stranger was coaxing him, encouraging him as though speaking to a child. He put his hand to his Adam's apple as he swallowed, but it didn't help the pain. His mind switched back to a vast chamber pared back to bare bricks. He shivered. He was falling. He could see the white broken bodies beneath him. He hadn't been shot. He had no wound. His fingers began to feel all over his body for the gunshot that wasn't there, only to find himself covered in some coarse woven garment. He screamed out. "Help me. Hanna, help me." Someone was wiping his forehead with a cool cloth, but it still wasn't Hanna. Perhaps it was Dora? Simeon could hear her voice, but he couldn't make out all the words. He was on a mattress—straw, he thought. He shook his head. He'd been looking for Dora, and now he'd found her. A gentle arm touched his shoulder. The voice of the woman Rutti. "It's all right. You're safe," she insisted.

Then the fever broke, and he woke up properly, but with a hacking cough. "Where am I?" He cocked his head to look towards the voice and fought to open his eyes. The face moved closer to his ear. He could see the long, dark hair, just like Dora's, that hung round her shoulders. Again she spoke in Yiddish. "Don't be afraid. Nite zayn moyre hobn. Du bist mit khavern zikh," telling him that he was among friends.

He tried to focus on her face. The woman sitting so patiently and spooning the warm liquid into his mouth had huge dark brown eyes similar to Dora's but her cheeks were hollow as though she was permanently hungry. She had a small nose streaked with dirt and pretty, bow-shaped pink lips. Her eyes were fringed with the longest, blackest lashes he'd ever seen. She stroked his shoulder gently.

"Come on. Take a little more. You're dehydrated. Drink a little, and soon you'll begin to feel better."

He opened his mouth obediently and sucked at the spoonful of soup that rested on his tongue. Every time he swallowed, it was as though his throat was being cut by a knife.

"Who are you? What's your name?" she asked.

"Simeon Karminsky. From Krustpils, in Latvia." He grunted hoarsely.

He started to look around. He was at ground level. The straw mattress upon which he was lying was on the floor in a long, dimly lit space. There was no natural light, but faint glimmers came from burning twigs stuck into the walls and a single oil lamp that hung from the low ceiling. He plucked at the coverings that had been heaped on him, his fingers anxiously feeling the heavy materials that must be his blankets. He couldn't see over the top of them and tried to lift his head.

"How long have I been here?"

"Three days." She pushed a hank of the long, dark hair off her forehead. She was crouching beside him, and he could see she was wearing a heavy jacket several sizes too large for her, the cuffs turned back halfway up the sleeve so that she could use her hands. The hand holding the spoon was covered by a frayed woollen mittens with holes at the fingertips.

"All you need to know for now is that you are safe."

He tried to prop himself up but instantly fell back, his head spinning.

"Slowly, slowly," she cautioned him. "We picked you up half-dead from exposure." He opened his eyes and looked at her quizzically. "You don't remember. You crawled out of a death pit. Somehow, you escaped being shot. You managed to wrap yourself in a coat discarded by one of the German soldiers. They were playing football. The coat probably saved your life. Our doctor thinks your survival in such circumstances is a miracle. Come on, just a little more soup."

"What doctor?"

"I ask the questions." It was a man's voice. "You need not worry, Simeon Karminsky. You are with the Ettinger partisans. We are a Jewish group and work with other partisans just outside Leningrad, under directions from the Russian army."

"Leave him for now, Mikhail." It was the young woman speaking. "He's caught a bad chill. He can barely talk. You can hear." She looked back to Simeon. "That was my brother. He is joint head of our group, with Oscar, my other brother. You will meet him later, when you are stronger. We have some honey for your sore throat. I'll make you a hot drink. Then you must sleep more."

"We don't normally give honey to adults," Mikhail told him brusquely. "Think yourself lucky. We only have one jar of honey. We keep such treats for children with measles or scarlet fever, not adults with sore throats, but you gave us a German greatcoat, so this is your reward."

Simeon had been with the Ettingers for almost a week before he was considered well enough to leave the straw mattress and sit beside the small stove inside the partisans' dugout hut.

"Our camp has fifteen of these Zemlyankas," Rutti told him. "Each one houses between twenty and twenty-five Jews. We've got a hospital hut, for people who arrive with infections like typhoid and typhus. Jews find their way to us from ghettos and from slave labour camps, and a few have even managed to escape from concentration camps."

"How did you know I was a Jew?"

Rutti laughed. "You didn't have too many clothes on when we rescued you, Simeon Karminsky, only the prized German greatcoat you wrapped yourself in. We were watching, you see, from the edge of the forest. We didn't know why the pit had been dug there or where you came from, but we witnessed everything that happened there."

"What did you see?" He needed to know how much he should share.

"We saw between eighty and ninety men being pulled from lorries, dragged to the edge of the pit, and shot. We don't know why they were being murdered, but we thought you'd all died. It's astonishing that you came out alive. Mikhail and Oscar, my brothers, brought you back here. A couple from our group stayed behind, hoping they'd find someone else alive."

Simeon looked up at her with hope. Rutti shook her head. "I'm sorry, Simeon," she said. "You were the only one. Can you tell us why you were there? Where had you come from? What were you doing that was so secret that they wanted no one left alive? Or was it just another massacre of Jews?"

Simeon took a deep breath, summoning the strength to tell them about the Jewish artisans who had been assembled to dismantle the Amber Room.

"And you were what? A jeweller?"

"No." Simeon told them how he'd gone to Leningrad to search for Dora, the baby, and his mother, how he'd written from the army back in March advising them to take a holiday in Leningrad. "I was very careful what I said in the letter. I thought Leningrad would be safe. First I went home to check. When they weren't there, I asked an old friend of my mama's, although she turned out to be a traitor. She told me I'd had a daughter but that all the Jews had been holed up in the old kosher abattoir before they were sent east. I didn't believe her. I travelled to Leningrad on the very last day the trains ran. She was right: they never arrived at my cousin's home. When I got to Leningrad, my cousin virtually threw me out. I got caught in the siege. My last hope was that the neighbour was still lying. Then it became obvious to me: my mama would have insisted on going to her daughter's, my twin sister's, in Vidzy, so I had to get to Vidzy. That's where my twin sister lives, with her family. The only way out of Leningrad, I'd heard, was across Lake Ladoga, but I was going the wrong way. The Germans picked me up along the road. That's how I ended up in the Catherine Palace in the Amber Room." He turned his head away of his tears.

Mikhail reached out a strong hand and rested it on his shoulder. "It's OK," he told him. "You can cry. Just this once."

Gradually, Simeon's strength returned. He'd been with the partisans more than ten days when he experienced severe stomach cramps.

"Dear God," he cried as he dashed to the buckets behind the curtain that served as lavatories in this freezing weather.

"It's not surprising," Rutti called after him. "After weeks of starvation, regular food, even potato soup, will give you diarrhoea."

His throat had healed, and he had almost forgotten about his amber "tablets" until he felt something solid tearing at his gut as he defecated. Only after the second solid mass had passed through, rapidly followed by the third, did he remember. The three pieces of amber sat on top of the mess in the bucket, almost winking at him.

He used dead leaves to clean himself, then took a handful to pick up the little amber pieces and carry them outside. He shimmied up the ladder with the amber in his hands and breathed the fresh air with relief. It was the first time he'd been outside since Mikhail's men had brought him here. In the fresh, ice-cold air, he looked around. Everyone else was huddling in the underground huts for warmth, except those out on operations, and he was alone. He took a deep breath and started to rub the small pieces of amber in the fresh snow that lay thickly around and over the hut. The sun was shining. As he held them in his hand, he felt strength, as though these small pieces of amber held some mystical power. His hands were numb, his fingers white with cold. The amber glowed at him. He remembered how he'd been mesmerised by that glow when he'd put them in his mouth. Now that the paste had been cleaned away by the snow, they were bright, almost translucent in the daylight. He slipped them into the pocket of the workman's dungarees they'd found for him. Back in the hut, he begged a cup of boiling snowmelt, "to ease my throat".

He took it to the bunk he'd been allocated, above the potato store that he shared with a young boy called Arieh, and washed them as best he could. They seemed to wink up at him. He felt they had life, that they were his friends. Only they knew the truth of what he'd been through. Only they had witnessed the miracle of his survival first-hand.

"You don't mind sharing a bunk with Arieh, do you?" Mikhail Ettinger had asked him when they'd moved him from his sickbed. It had been decided he would stay in Zemlyanka 1 with the Ettingers, the medic, and Arieh. "Poor boy has been badly traumatised. He won't speak. From what we can make out, he saw his parents killed. He's only about seven or eight years old. We're not sure exactly. Mikhail found him huddling under a pine tree in the forest late in September, clutching a beautiful concert violin and bow tightly to his chest. As he saw me approaching, he picked up the violin and to our amazement, he began to play Tchaikovsky's Sixth Symphony, the *Pathétique*. I recognised it. He grunted at me when I said hello. He hasn't spoken a word in two months. When he plays, though, it's as though he's trying to talk to us through his music. He wrote his name for us: Arieh Weinstein. From what we can make out, he was hidden in a cupboard when the Nazis came to 'liberate' the Jews from the ghetto he was in. He'd been stuffed in there with the violin. He escaped somehow and found himself in the forest.

"He sometimes sits for hours, shaking his head and rocking backwards and forwards on the floor, hugging the violin to his chest. The doctor says it's a reaction to his trauma. We know he hears well. He jumps like a crazy person if he hears a shot or even a surprising noise behind him, but he refuses to talk. The doctor said he's seen it before in traumatised children. They call it 'selective mutism'."

At first Arieh barely acknowledged his new bedfellow, not even with sign language, although he managed to have signed "conversations" with Rutti. Simeon tried talking to him about his violin as though he were a normal child. For the most part, Arieh ignored him. When Simeon asked him to play *Eine kleine Nachtmusik*, one of the few pieces Simeon knew could be played on a solo violin, Arieh stared at him scornfully, picked up the instrument, played it badly, put the violin back in its case, and looked at Simeon as though for praise or applause.

"I've heard you play better than that," Simeon said. "That sounded like a child playing. You're only a child, but I know you can like a man. Was your papa a violinist?"

The child nodded.

"What would he have thought if you played like that?"

Arieh shrugged.

"Not good enough." Simeon wanted to goad him into responding, and he could see by the boy's face that he was succeeding.

"Go on, Arieh. Play it again."

The child shook his head vehemently, lay down on his makeshift straw bed, tugged the rough brown woven blanket over his head, and feigned sleep. Simeon turned his back. He did as always and when he took his three little pieces of amber out of his pocket, unwrapped the rag in which he kept them, and stroked them lightly. Three odd little pieces of amber of no consequence or use to anyone but him. His secret. His talisman. He had come to believe that they understood one another, that they were somehow responsible for his survival. He tucked them back in his pocket and turned to lie down. Suddenly he was aware that a pair of childish brown eyes were leaning over him, watching him curiously.

"They're my secret," he told Arieh, as though speaking to a normal boy. "You mustn't tell anyone about them. Understand?"

The boy nodded. Simeon sensed that by sharing a secret, he seemed to have broken the ice.

Simeon spent the next few weeks recuperating. The need to fix broken weapons in the arsenal that grew with every successful sortie against the Nazis was essential, and Simeon's engineering background was proving extremely useful. "Here, Simeon. A couple of German guns for you to play around with," Oscar said, chucking an armoury of half a dozen former German infantrymen's rifles at him.

"We've got a couple of pistols here, but the barrels are sticking," Rutti told him, as she handed over the spoils of the latest sortie.

Their operational orders came directly from the Russian army headquarters based in Moscow and relayed by comrades in the partisan movement who had radio contact with the world outside. Thanks to friends within the local population, they had intelligence on German movements in the area, too, and although Simeon had no previous experience with setting explosives, he learnt fast about sabotage techniques. His skills were soon put to use.

"The old cart needs mending. With your engineering skills, couldn't you affix a motor to that instead of us having to exhaust the poor horse?" Mikhail joked. "Perhaps you could even build us a real tank if we're forced to stay here much longer."

"Bring me an old tank, and I'll do my best," Simeon replied seriously.

Often he would look up to see Arieh watching him. The boy had begun to follow him around like a little puppy. "Hand me that screwdriver, will you, boy?" he'd say, and Arieh would hand him the screwdriver, or a wrench, or whatever else he'd requested, with a grin on his little face that warmed Simeon's heart. Every night, they would admire Simeon's amber tablets together, until the night when, to Simeon's horror, he dug into his pocket to find them missing. He panicked. "Stay here," he ordered Arieh, before he ran back to the space in a corner of the Zemlyanka where he'd been working all day, fixing German pistols. He'd been hot and taken out the rag with his precious tablets inside to wipe his forehead. He breathed a huge sigh of relief to see the rag on the workbench he'd made for himself. He'd have to find another place to keep them safe.

It was Arieh who provided the first solution. Simeon had been given a flat cap. He wore it most days. Back in the hut, Arieh took the hat, unpicked a tiny portion of the lining, and showed Simeon how he could tuck the little pieces of amber into the hole before drawing the thread tight again.

"Clever boy," Simeon praised him, putting the cap back on his head.

In December, they had a Hanukah party to celebrate the Jewish Festival of Lights. In prewar days, it had been a time for celebration. They would light candles, one more each night for eight days, to celebrate the miracle of twenty-four hours' worth of oil that miraculously kept the everlasting light in the Temple burning for eight days until replacements could arrive. It was traditional at this time of year to give children gifts of money and small toys.

The first night of the holiday, Simeon sat on his bed as usual after a day's work, taking his little amber tablets out of their flat cap home. As usual, Arieh was watching him, reaching out with him to touch the little pieces of amber for luck. This time, however, Arieh picked up the honey-coloured piece, the first one Simeon had swallowed, with the fly at its centre.

"No," Simeon said more severely than he intended. "Don't touch. They're mine. Not toys. Not for you."

Arieh mouthed the word *me*, then said, "Give to me."

"No. They're mine. You can't have one."

He began to slide them back inside the hat when Arieh grinned at him and picked up his violin and bow. After a few seconds spent tuning it as he had obviously watched his beloved father do, he began to play *Eine kleine Nachtmusik* for Simeon, this time perfectly and without a single mistake. Simeon watched. Arieh was a small boy with a violin several sizes too big for him and with such little hands, and yet as he played, his long sensitive fingers seemed to grow and stretch. His little face relaxed and his eyes closed as his music-making took him to that place where he'd been safe and happy. So much emotion went into the boy's music that it brought tears to Simeon's eyes. As Arieh finished, there was a small burst of applause from others in the hut who'd heard the music and stopped in amazement. Arieh grinned and nodded his head in appreciation towards his audience in a suggestion of a bow.

Simeon took off his hat and removed the little piece of honey-coloured amber. It was Hanukah, a time for giving and a time for miracles. "Would you like to borrow 'Miss Honey' just for a little while, Arieh?" he asked, looking at the skinny, damaged child in front of him, a little boy made old by war—a child with nothing to his name but a violin, a worn bow, and an enormous talent. "You can borrow it if you promise to keep it safe and give it back whenever I ask for it."

The little boy smiled and nodded, stroking it gently. Then he threw his arms around Simeon's neck and hugged him. Simeon caressed the bony little back. His heart was filled with a new emotion, something he couldn't define. It was a need to take care of this child who'd suffered so much despite his young years. It was a wish to protect him, to cover him in a blanket of unconditional love. *That's what being a parent is,* he thought. He wondered if this was how it would feel to take a child of his own flesh and blood in his arms. He loved Arieh as he would have loved a son of his own. He knew that whatever happened, he would love Arieh for the rest of his life. He might never know a child of his flesh. He prayed he might one day meet his daughter, but common sense told him it was unlikely.

Chapter 10

Hanna

"IF YOU LIVE LIKE YOUR ENEMIES AND THINK LIKE YOUR ENEMIES, THEY MAY become your friends and saviours."

As Hanna walked away from the old farmhouse, it had begun to snow. She pulled the warm coat around her and wrapped the old woman's shawl around her head and shoulders. Olga's words echoed in her head: "If you live like your enemies ..."

"She didn't want to live like her enemies. The Nazis, the Latvians, the native Byelorussians—Jew-haters, child killers, bastards. Nor could she think of fighting them all single-handedly. She was a daughter, a wife, a mother, and a twin, yet she had no husband, no children, no parent, and no sibling. Try as hard as she could she was unable to sense Simeon as she so often had before in times of need. The space he'd usually occupied in her heart felt strangely empty. Was he dead too, she wondered? This old Christian woman, a total stranger until a few weeks ago, had become her friend and set her this enigmatic puzzle of uncovering a means of helping her own people. Yet she'd be damned if she'd live like those bastard Nazis, like the men who'd killed her precious children, even if it meant saving other Jewish lives. What sort of people murdered helpless innocent children, kicked and punched sick old men, and treated wizened, starved human beings worse than they'd treat a dog, for no better reason than that they practised other ways of worship? Live like her enemies? She'd rather be dead. Part of her wanted to die so badly, yet still she was fighting for survival.

As Olga had waved her goodbye, Hanna had thought of her mother, who had done just that every morning as she left for school. She looked down at her feet, shod in Olga's second-best lace-up shoes. Sergei had insisted on polishing them for her and then stuffing the toes with newspaper so they wouldn't slip. Her own fragile shoes had been beyond repair. She watched the shiny borrowed shoes moving as they marched one ahead of the other, left, right, left, right, almost independently of the rest of her. "Links, recht, links, recht." The Nazis' chant outside her own front door resounded in her head. Her emotions were as dead as her little boys. All she was capable of doing was watching the mechanical movements of the stranger's shoes that clad her feet. She wished she could cry, but grief stuck in her throat like a lump of lead that she couldn't swallow or spit out. Her eyes swept over roads and trees, houses and shops, but nothing registered in her mind. She was watching a bizarre play, and everyone else she came across was merely an actor. The difference was that she couldn't stand up and walk out of the theatre of this nightmare life. She tried so hard to conjure up the familiar beloved faces of her babies, but they evaded her, concealed behind a thick and dirty curtain that had descended on her memory. Nat's familiar and adored face was hidden behind that same impenetrable, filthy haze.

It was bitterly cold. At around midday, Hanna sat down by the roadside to rest for a while and eat some of the bread and cheese Olga had packed for her. She wasn't hungry, but she knew she had to eat. As she chewed, she fingered the strange little gold cross at her neck for comfort, just as she had used to caress her Star of David. After all, she reasoned, Olga Petruishka had been right about one thing: they were both symbols of worship to the same God. However, what could she, an isolated and lonely bereaved woman, possibly do in Grodno to aid Jews in a ghetto run by the mighty Nazi war machine? If Simeon was here, he'd know how to use this happenstance. She wondered whether Nat had survived. Supposing she found Nat and his mother in the Grodno Ghetto? She could imagine their comments: "What do you think you're doing with a crucifix around your neck and the Trilogy on your tongue? What did you do to your sons?"

Hanna stood up, brushed the crumbs off her skirt, and consulted Sergei's hand-drawn map. She could hear the sporadic gunfire behind her, and she ducked behind bushes as a Nazi motorcade lumbered past at only slightly faster than walking pace. Tanks, military vehicles, and motorbikes with sidecars were followed by a long line of miserable men and women, their heads fixed firmly downwards to the road. Soldiers were stationed at intervals alongside the lines, cracking whips round the bare legs of any stragglers. Hanna looked away as they lumbered past. Could it be that they were Jews being herded towards the Grodno Ghetto? Ought she to jump out and give herself up now? What good would that do, she wondered? She wanted Simeon's advice. She felt that without her sense of his twin-ness, she had lost part of herself. Why had he left her if he was still alive? She'd know if he was dead. Of that she was sure.

The sun had moved round in the sky, and it was getting even colder. Hanna pulled the warm woollen shawl Olga had given her tightly around her head and frame. Suddenly, her whole body began to shake. She looked up into the clouds and saw a vision of Simeon's face there. He appeared as white as the cloud, as pale as death. Her fingertips hurt as though they'd been scraping against something thick and muddy. She looked at her hands. To her amazement, thick mud appeared to be buried under the whites of her nails. She rubbed her hands together. They were white and bloodless. Suddenly she realised she must be feeling whatever Simeon was feeling. He was cold, dirty and hungry, but he was alive. She sensed he was in terrible danger. She had to start walking again. Grey clouds were gathering on the horizon. Perhaps it might begin to snow more heavily soon. She needed to get to Grodno and find somewhere to spend the night as fast as she could. She waited until the troops and their prisoners were out of sight before she followed their route. She heard other sounds behind her, and her heart began to pound wildly. They'd spotted her and were coming back for her! Then she saw a pigeon noisily flapping its wings as it hurled itself into the air from one tree to another. Another pigeon joined it, and the pair began to coo loudly. She started to laugh at herself. She was praying to die, yet now that she had the chance, she was dodging it. Who was this stranger inside her who wanted to go on living? It must be Maria Petruishka. It certainly wasn't Hanna Karminskya Abramskya.

Simeon was still there. He hadn't abandoned her. There was more scampering. She heard the movement of light paws rustling through fallen leaves followed by canine yaps. A pretty golden cocker spaniel darted past, hotly pursued by a boy aged about nine. The dog had frightened the pigeons. She heard the boy call, "Tommy, Tommy."

Hanna reached a tarmac road and consulted her map again. The land ahead was very flat, but she thought she could see a large pink and white building in the distance. *That must be the Orthodox Church of the Annunciation.* To her right was another large white church with green cupolas, far grander than the pink building. According to Sergei's instructions, the smaller church she sought was to the left of the large white one, only two streets back from the Neman River embankment. She must make her way towards the square and the pink church, then follow in a straight line until she almost reached the river. The light was fading fast now. It would be gone in a few more seconds. She must fix her hair. "Keep yourself tidy," Olga and Sergei had both urged her. She put her hand to her head, grateful that it was an easy task to comb her newly shorn hair. She looked in the tiny hand mirror Olga had included as part of her toilette and combed her short curls. The head lice had been a blessing. "It's as dangerous to look like a gypsy as to look like a Jew," Olga had warned her.

Hanna walked past the pink building and down a side street with a row of shuttered stores on both sides. In the gloom of early evening, the place appeared deserted. The clock on the church tower chimed four o'clock. It had taken her nine hours to get here. She kept close to the buildings, and through gaps in the houses she could see the river curling and twisting ahead of her.

Here it was. She stood in front of a sign pronouncing, "Orthodox Church of St Philip the Martyr. Pastor: Fr Dominic Chelbek. Services: Sunday, 6.30–10 and 11.30–1.30; weekdays, Mass at 7.15 a.m." She consulted Sergei's map again. Yes, this was it.

Hanna wondered if the place was locked and was surprised when she tugged at the right-hand oak door and found it gave easily. At least she'd found a dry place to sleep without needing to ask permission. Inside it was dark, but the glowing memorial candles at the altar offered a pale, flickering, almost eerie light. As she neared the altar, she saw the vast and elaborate gold crucifix above the high altar. Statuettes of gilded cherubs with gold-tipped wings appeared to be fluttering down towards her from the ceiling. The whole building, with its dark oaken pews, its hand-embroidered tapestry kneelers, and the beautiful marble statues of saints, all basked in the dim and dusty candlelight, which gave the church a quiet dignity.

Hanna's feet were sore and blistered from the ill-fitting shoes. She slipped out of Olga's overlarge footwear, and her stockinged toes relished the bliss of the icy stone floor. She massaged them, standing on one leg at a time as her eyes adjusted to the light. It was marginally warmer in here than it had been outside. The ceiling of this church was oak gabled, with heavy wooden struts supporting the eaves. Marble figures lined the sides of the church atop white marble tombs. The good and the faithful, untroubled in death. These sainted men and women were still honoured four and five hundred years after they'd left this life. Lucky them. She thought of her babies, buried in shallow unmarked graves by a lake, and hot tears fell as she pondered the unfairness of it all. The waters of the lake would lap at the edges of her babies' graves, and no one would ever know that two children were buried there. Suddenly, she felt as though the eyes of the old marble figures were following her. There was a live presence in this place.

The flames of the flickering candles drew her towards them. There were several unlit candles and a taper. Igniting the taper from one of the live candles, she lit two more, one for Max and one for Shmuel. She thought about adding a third for Nat, but then she thought hopefully that he was still alive. As she held the taper across the second candle, she whispered to herself, "Shema Yisroel Adoshem Elohainu Adoshem Echad" (Listen, oh Israel, the Lord our God, the Lord is One). *This is a place of prayer,* she thought. *God will accept prayers in any language.*

The prayer gripped her fiercely. When she had finished intoning it in a whisper, she became aware of the figure of a small man beside her. She turned her head and crossed herself quickly as Olga had taught her to do, head, chest, left, then right, and prayed she'd done it correctly. Thanks to Olga's repeated tuition, it came almost naturally. The voice that addressed her was old, crackly and very soft.

"Can I help you, my child?" He spoke in Byelorussian.

The elderly priest was a short man in a long black cassock and white dog collar, a fringe of white hair surrounding a practically bald pink pate. His skin looked as fragile as creased off-white crepe paper.

"You're a stranger in these parts, aren't you, my child?"

She extended her hand and hoped he hadn't noticed she was shaking. "Sir, I am Maria Petruishka. Are you Father Dominic?"

She stumbled over her new name slightly, but he seemed not to notice. Nevertheless, she felt uneasy.

"I found these boots by the font. Yours?" They both looked down at her stockinged feet and at the pair of now dusty shoes he held gingerly at the centre of their sides. She took them.

"Where have you come from then, little one?"

"Drushkininka, sir."

"Drushkininka, eh? How did you get here? Did you walk, or were you chauffeur driven? It's not exactly round the corner." The sarcasm grated. There was something about this old man's stare that made her uneasy.

"I came seeking you, sir, with a letter of introduction from my own priest, Fr Peter of Druskininka's Church of St Gabriel. He told me you might help me."

"So, you have a letter of introduction, do you? Not a runaway, then? Or a Jewess in hiding? Well, of course not. Mind you, I don't think many Jewish bitches have the brains to seek shelter in a church."

She was sure she was blushing. Her insides were churning as she tried frantically to recall the details of the story Olga Petruishka and Sergei had concocted for her. Should she spout it all out, or would that sound too rehearsed?

"Our family priest, Father Peter, told me you might be able to find me a job here in Grodno. As a housekeeper, perhaps. The hotel where I was working as a chambermaid in Inzkhaven was burnt out, you see. It was owned by Jews. I lost everything, including my papers."

"Father Peter, huh!" He stared at her thoughtfully for a moment then took the letter, opened it, and skimmed the contents before handing it back to her.

Not a muscle in his face moved. "So from the Church of St Gabriel" he said, naming the beautiful blue-painted church she had visited with Olga. "I'm not sure that I can help you, Maria ... what did you say your name was, Petruishka? However, it is getting late, and it's dark now. We have a six o'clock curfew for locals until seven tomorrow morning. Not that the Germans bother me. We get on well, you see. I understand them, and they seem to understand me. Do you have somewhere to stay the night?"

She shook her head.

"I cannot be un-Christian enough to abandon you here in the church, not in these temperatures. I think I remember Father Peter now. I couldn't leave one of Father Peter's flock without a meal and a place to sleep. So let us pray a little together first. Then you will come back to my home and we will talk. When was your last confession?"

"Last Sunday," she replied, truthfully remembering how she'd knelt in the confessional under Olga's guidance.

"We will say ten Hail Marys," he began. She wondered if this was his way of testing out her claims.

"Ave Maria, gratia plena, Dominus tecum. Benedicta tu in mulieribus, et benedictus fructus ventris tui, Jesus. Sancta Maria, Mater Dei, ora pro nobis peccatoribus, nunc, et in hora mortis nostrae. Amen."

She mumbled the unfamiliar Latin but managed it word-perfectly. Olga had taught her well. As the priest launched into another Latin prayer, Hanna knelt beside him, her eyes closed, moving backwards and forwards as though immersing her soul in prayer as he appeared to be doing. She watched him through slitted eyes, and when he'd finished, she helped him to his feet. He squinted and moved closer to her. There was a coldness in those eyes. He was clearly short-sighted, and the clouds across his pale blue eyeballs suggested cataracts. Close up, the smell of his unwashed body was masked only slightly by the warm aroma of pipe tobacco. He consulted his watch and tutted. "Frau Olzswelski, my housekeeper, expected me for dinner more than an hour ago," he said. "There's always plenty in my house, despite the rationing!" He put up his hand to cover his mouth. "It's just as well to keep in with the Germans, and I make it my business to do so. Do you speak German, by the way?"

"Fluently, sir."

"Good. I have made friends among some of the German bigwigs here in Grodno. They're not as bad as people make out, not if you know how to deal with them. We have developed, let us say, a little entente cordiale between us."

She nodded, not quite sure how to read this admittance of collaboration, possibly even of friendship. It put Olga's advice into sharp focus: "Live like your enemies and act like your enemies, and they may become your friends."

So, Hanna too must become a German collaborator if she was to accept this strange priest's hospitality. Had Olga remembered of such a thing? He patted her shoulder. "For tonight, you will stay in my guest room. I will ask around among my colleagues tomorrow to see if anyone is in need of a housekeeper. Do you have any other qualifications?"

"I am a proficient typist in both Byelorussian and German," she had her answer ready. "I can keep books." She thought how she'd produced their invoices for Nat's business on the ancient typewriter that constituted their "office" equipment.

"Excellent," he said, patting her hand. "In the meantime, Maria Petruishka, would you think it impertinent for me to ask to see your papers? You do have papers?"

Here was the moment she'd dreaded. "I lost my formal registration papers in the hotel fire," she said. She giggled nervously. "I carried everything in my handbag as most women do. When the hotel caught fire, I was upstairs cleaning bedrooms. We had to evacuate. My bag went. Everything went. That's why I went home to Drushkininka, to get my birth certificate from my mother."

He patted her shoulder, apparently satisfied. "Tomorrow, we will go to the Nebelstelle, as they call our old town hall. You are not the first person to lose your formal documents, and I don't suppose you'll be the last. Once we have 'legalised' you, as it were, I'll see what my colleagues say about needing housekeepers. Perhaps we can find you other work if you can typewrite. First thing tomorrow, I will personally escort you to get you properly registered." He cleared his throat with a loud harrumph. "I have a proposal. Until we get you settled, you can stay with me, and I'll tell people you're my niece. You could say your mother died but that you knew your aunt had your birth certificate. Oh, my poor sister, dying of tuberculosis. So sad. So young. You did say your mother died from consumption, didn't you?" She had just told him she'd come from her mother's house. He may be a priest, but he was a proficient liar.

"I have some black armbands. We will wear one each, you and I. Saying your mother - my younger sister - died means you can stay here without tongues wagging. You know how it is in small communities. Stay at the vicarage until we find a good job for you."

"That is very kind of you, but I cannot impose."

"I've taken quite a liking to you, little Maria ... how do you pronounce it ... Petruishka."

She was trapped, and she knew it.

Frau Olzswelski, the father's housekeeper, looked a sweet old woman. She was thin and petite with large, expressive blue eyes. "Come in, my dear. Happy to meet you. There's plenty to eat. I always cook too much. I never know who the dear father is going to bring home next, do I, sir?"

The meal was simple. Hanna presumed the thin slices of pink meat she was offered were ham, but she managed to swallow the forbidden pig meat without grimacing. Afterwards, Frau Olzswelski declined her offer to help clear the table and showed her up to a small whitewashed attic room.

"We always keep the bed made up." The old woman smiled as they climbed two flights of narrow stairs. "Help yourself to a bath if you wish, dear," she added, stopping outside the bathroom on the second floor. "There's plenty of hot water. Father Dominic told me you've had a long walk. I've put a towel on the bed and a clean nightie since you don't seem to have much luggage. Sleep well."

Hanna bathed, lay on the bed, and closed her eyes. Suddenly, she could hear her brother's voice for the first time in a very long while. It was loud, clear, and powerful. "Be strong, Hanna."

Father Dominic was already seated at the breakfast table and was finishing his coffee as Hanna appeared at 7.30 the next morning. She had awoken before dawn. "Here," said Father Dominic, obviously seeing her lick dry lips. "Take some coffee. It's real coffee. None of that chicory stuff here."

She poured herself a cup and sipped it gratefully.

"I telephoned ahead to the registration office, and we're expected at the Rathaus—sorry, Nebelstelle as they now call it—in an hour. "The ghetto administration is run from there. Ah! Good girl. I see you've brought your birth certificate down with you."

He handed her a black armband. "Put it on. I've told them about my 'dear sister's' death."

It was only a short walk to the Gestapo headquarters. Hanna shuddered involuntarily as she saw the huge red flags with the white circles at their centres and the hated black bent crosses in their centres, flapping in the breeze and marking the building out as the Nazi headquarters.

"Are you all right, my dear?" Father Dominic had noticed the shudder.

"Yes, fine. Thank you, sir."

"I saw you shiver."

"No. Just the cold." She must be careful not to give herself away.

He was obviously a well-known presence. The guards nodded them through the front door with a cursory glance at his papers and seemed to take it for granted that if she was with him, her presence must be acceptable. Inside, a receptionist was waiting to lead them down into a basement office. A tall, uniformed man came towards them. He nodded his head politely at Hanna.

"SS-Kriminalsekretar Heinrich Brandt at your service, Fräulein." He kissed her hand. "Father Dominic, always good to see you. Now how can we improve your sad situation. Let's get your paperwork completed."

She couldn't believe how easy it was to follow Father Dominic's story. The lies about the circumstances of tripped off her tongue, one following another. The story Olga and Sergei had concocted between them was gaining unexpected embellishment with every word Father Dominic spoke.

Brandt looked solemn. "You were so lucky to find your family still in Dominikankse. It's a long way from there to your uncle's, Father Dominic's, home, isn't it?" he remarked. "Your uncle's a good man. He seems to have had several nieces landing on his doorstep needing his hospitality in recent months."

"That's the way it is when one is one of eleven children," Father Dominic smiled benignly. "I had twenty-seven nieces and fourteen nephews at the last count."

There was no further comment on her family situation. SS-Kriminalsekretar led them back into a hall where a number of sad-looking men and women occupied metal seats. He jumped ahead of the queue, beckoning Hanna and Father Dominic to follow him to the registration desk where a thin-faced man with greased hair combed across his pink, balding scalp and heavy brown-framed glasses sat at the head of a number of rubber stamps on ink pads. Brandt whispered something to Father Dominic and stared at Hanna as she handed over Maria Petruishka's birth certificate. She noticed how his eyes behind the thick spectacles were hard and steely grey. The official gave the birth certificate no more than a cursory glance, looked back at Father Dominic, who nodded obligingly, wrote on a blank identity paper, and stamped it several times. "You will need a photograph," he said shortly. "We have a photographer on the premises. He works in that office over there." He pointed back along the corridor they'd just walked down. "Get the photograph taken and processed quickly. Tell them I said it's urgent. Then bring it back here.

"I hope you don't mind, but I have told the good Kriminalsekretar Brandt that you are currently looking for work and that you are an excellent little typist. They process the Jews, gypsies, and homosexuals from here, so there's a great deal of office work. The ghettos are really little more than holding stations. It's from the ghettos that we choose who will go straight to the camps and who will join the labour gangs or work in factories."

When the documentation was completed, Hanna was officially Maria Petruishka with perfectly valid documents that would pass even the closest examination.

"Thank you," she said meekly.

On the way back, Father Dominic chuckled, but there was a sinister edge to his laugh. "I will have to confess my little white lies to my own confessor sometime," he said. "It is, after all, only over the question of our relationship that I am 'bending' the truth."

The question of why rolled around in her head. It was only after she had helped Frau Olzswelski clear the table and wash the luncheon dishes that Father Dominic started to question her again.

"You mentioned your brother Sergei. Why isn't he away at the front, fighting for us?"

"He had tuberculosis as a child. Although he is cured, he was not passed as medically fit."

"How did the Jews behave towards you? Greedy lot aren't they, Jews? Did they pay you? Do you have any money?" he asked.

"A little." She thought of the roubles Olga had given her and of Rachel's jewellery in the little bag Olga had attached to a belt so she could wear it round her waist always, no matter which skirt she was wearing.

"Then Frau Olzswelski will take you shopping this afternoon. I have some spare clothing coupons that I won't use. What would a priest, a man of God, need smart new clothes for? After all, we can't have the priest's niece walking around looking shabby, now, can we?"

Hanna looked down at herself. She thought the clothes Olga had provided looked office smart. The priest clearly thought otherwise. "Maria" soon owned another good white blouse and a very serviceable dark grey skirt that they found in a second-hand shop in town. Thankfully, second-hand clothes needed no coupons. They bought another change of underwear and stockings, and when they found a pair of serviceable black shoes that fitted her properly, she was beginning to wonder if she was living in a bizarre dream. *I'm trapped in a web of deceit from which there can be no escape until the web is destroyed,* she thought. *Perhaps this is God's punishment for leaving my babies alone. Maybe it will never be over.*

That night as Hanna crawled into bed, marvelling despite herself at being able to rest between fresh clean sheets, she heard footsteps on the wooden stairs leading to her room. There was a gentle rap on the door. Father Dominic walked in before she had time to reply. He sat himself down heavily on the side of the bed. Hanna instinctively drew the covers up around her shoulders and moved as far as she could towards the wall. He stared at her for what seemed a very long moment, then leant towards her and pulled the sheet from her hands. He was murmuring to himself under his breath.

"Beautiful, quite beautiful. Such white skin. Such delicious curly copper-coloured hair. Why so short?" He ran his fingers lightly through her curls. "Such pretty freckles." He stroked his little finger across her cheek and down the length of her nose. "If it weren't for that red hair, I'd say you were as beautiful as some of the Jewesses in that place over there, although they generally wear their hair long." He was obviously becoming more confident with every word: "What do you think, little *Maria*?" He emphasised her name, as though by his insistence on using it, he might force her to reveal her identity and beg his protection. What a fool she'd been to think she'd be offered such hospitality for no reward. *My mama always said nothing's for nothing.* It made her think of Simeon. *Everything has a reason; every action, a consequence. Your life is only a little cog in that vast toothed wheel of life that makes it all go round.* Her heart was beating so fast that she was sure the priest could hear it. She knew she was breathing too rapidly. She should control herself, stay calm.

He said nothing, and she surmised he must have believed the change in her breathing was excitement. He was undressing himself with one hand, removing his cassock, pulling long grey underpants to his ankles, and all the while fondling her shoulders, his eyes never leaving her face. Of course he knew she was a Jewess. Why else would he dare do this? His vest was as discoloured as his long underpants. He smelt of stale urine. The nearer he moved towards her, the more he repulsed her.

"You're not frightened of me, are you, little *Maria?*" He emphasised her name again as though to prove its falseness. "What harm can an old man like me do to a beauty like you? I'm sure I'm not the first, am I, Maria? More than one man's been cosy up there in that little red pussy."

The meal she had eaten two hours ago rose in her throat. She swallowed to prevent herself from throwing up all over him. He was lying down next to her now, handling his floppy little cock and talking in a wheedling tone. The words came out as a high-pitched sing-song. "Even a priest like me needs a little comfort at times, as does my poor little johnny here." He lifted her hand and placed it on his flaccid member, rubbing it back and forth, showing her how he wanted her to masturbate him. She tried to hold her head away from his face. His breath stank of alcohol and stale tobacco. He was foul, but there was no escape. As she tried to move backwards, he shifted his own bottom further up the bed, closer to her, and wrapped his legs around her.

"We must discuss your future," he said. "Kriminalsekretar Brandt says he has found you the perfect job. You can work as a typist during the day at the Nebelstelle, making lists of all the Jews and homosexuals, and at night you will keep me company. So much more comfortable than searching for lodgings with people who might not treat you as well as I do. Food in your belly. Constant hot water to bathe in. All for the price of a little loving."

He gave her no time to answer, fixing his lips on hers. His hands were fondling her breasts, fumbling beneath the plain shift the housekeeper had given her. "Let's get this off," he said, unbuttoning it and lifting it over her head. "That's better. Now I can see you properly." He ran his fingers lightly around her breasts and down her ribcage, alighting on her pubic bone. There had only ever been one man near that place in all her life. She lay back and closed her eyes. "You're even enjoying it, aren't you? Don't deny it. I can see it in your face." She felt his cock stiffen slightly under her hand, and finally he was trying to enter her, but he wasn't hard enough.

"Rub it," he ordered. "Rub little johnny. Poor little johnny needs a little help, don't you, dear little johnny?"

She tried to remember Nat's gentle lovemaking, see his face, and smell his strength, the clean, fresh scent of an honest carpenter, instead of the stench of this vile man. She felt him jerk. Her hand was full of sticky wet muck: his ejaculate. He stood up, pulled up his underwear—which Hanna realised had still been round his ankles—and replaced his black cassock and white dog collar. Why?

As he let himself out of the door, he tapped his nose. "Our little secret. Our little secret!"

Chapter 11

Simeon and Arieh

"**W**HY DO YOU ALWAYS WEAR A HAT? YOU'RE NOT RELIGIOUS, ARE YOU?"

"No," Simeon retorted, laughing. "What makes you think that?"

"You never take that cap off. Arieh indicated you even sleep in it."

Mikhail, Rutti, and Simeon were sitting on tree stumps by the fire, coordinating ideas that Oscar was to take to the main committee meeting of local partisans during the next few days.

"Pure speculation." Simeon smiled. "Arieh may not speak much, but his lack of spoken words doesn't seem to have affected his communication skills."

It was true. At night, Simeon and Arieh had developed a ritual. Before they turned in, Simeon would release his two pieces of amber from his hat while Arieh would fetch little Miss Honey, as they had nicknamed the piece with the fly at its centre, from her new home inside Arieh's violin case. They would lay the pieces side by side, and the child would rest his head next to Simeon's shoulder as Simeon told him a 'fairy story'.

"These are very special pieces of amber. Once there was a queen called Catherine. She lived in a beautiful turquoise palace with her husband, King Peter, but it wasn't enough. She heard that fishermen trawling the Baltic Sea had found some wondrous jewels called amber. So she sent her servants fishing in the sea, and one day they came back to her with three special pieces." At this, Arieh ran his fingers lightly across the three little fragments of amber lying on the bed. "One was the colour of honeycomb."

At this, Arieh would pick up 'his' piece and clutch it tight to his chest. "Another was the colour of treacle toffee, and the third was carved into the shape of an eagle's talon. Do you know what that is, Arieh? It's the nail on the end of its foot. Some people call it a claw. Each of the pieces had a voice of its own. Miss Honey's voice was sweet as sugar candy. That's why the greedy little fly got caught inside. It told the other pieces: 'I like seeing people smile and keeping everyone happy. I will bring you joy and sweet things if you care for me.'

"The second piece was as dark as burnt treacle toffee. As you can see, it has five sides, and each side has a magic touch of its own and its own burnished voice. 'You can't eat me. I'm strong and tough, and if anyone tries to hurt the people I love, I will bring sticky situations upon them. That means they'll be in trouble they can't run away from,'" Simeon explained. At this Arieh's eyes would widen with wonder. As he stroked the toffee-coloured piece as if to tell it he'd always be kind to it. "The third piece was very strange," Simeon continued. "It didn't really talk. Not words like you and I understand. It gave long, eagle cries. 'Caw, caw,' it called. 'I want to fly.'

"'You're not big enough to have wings,' said the fisherman who found it on the seashore. 'But I will carve you into the shape of an eagle's talon. Then you can scratch and scratch and dig up worms. When winged birds see you pick up worms, they will come and take you in their mouths so you can soar higher and higher in the sky like a real eagle does and go anywhere you choose.'"

Arieh cocked his head and looked quizzical at this bit. "So you want to know where I'd fly to if I was the eagle's talon? I'd tell him to take me to Palestine. That's where I want to go when the war is over. But first I have to look for my wife and my little baby, and then we will go to Palestine together. Would you like to come?"

Arieh nodded frantically. Then he would lie down. Simeon would tuck the rough brown sacking that served as a blanket snugly around him and stroke his forehead until the child's eyes grew heavy. Only when Arieh was asleep would he try to sleep himself. *He acts like a grown-up in so many ways, but underneath he's just a little boy who needs a fairy story with a happy ending to believe in,* he thought.

Simeon had just dropped off to sleep one night in mid-January when he heard a piercing scream. He jumped up, sure someone had attacked the child beside him. "Arieh! What's the matter?"

The boy's eyes were still shut tight, tears escaping from beneath the long brown lashes. In the dim light he could see his face was contorted by pain. "Mama, don't go. Don't leave me. Papa, no. Papa, stay with me." It was the first time Simeon or any else had ever heard Arieh's voice.

"Shh, dear boy. Shh." Simeon stroked his skinny back gently. "It's a nightmare, Arieh. Wake up. You're safe." The boy opened his heavy eyes and looked around, confused. Simeon drew him close and cradled the small body bathed in sweat. "Don't leave me, Simeon. Mama and Papa went away. Even baby Bracha died. I wish I had died with her. You won't go away, will you, Simeon?"

"I'm not going anywhere. We're all staying here, Oscar, Mikhail, Rutti, and me. Do you want to tell me what happened to you?"

A small crowd had gathered round. "Is he all right, Simeon? What happened? Can we help?"

"A nightmare found his voice for him. Go. Go away. Leave us for the moment. Perhaps he will talk to me now. Will you, Arieh?"

The child nodded.

The gathering dispersed. Simeon held the trembling child tight. Arieh spoke slowly as he rediscovered his voice, unused for so long.

"The Germans came to Odessa and took Mama, Papa, baby—my little sister—and me. First they took us to the Nieśwież Ghetto and then to the Kovno Ghetto with lots of other people. It was horrible. We shared a room with two other families." His voice was growing stronger with every word. "We were always hungry. First baby Bracha—her name means 'blessing'—died because Mama didn't have enough milk for her. Then Mama died from crying. Losing Bracha meant she had a broken heart, so Papa said, but she'd made me eat her food. She said she wasn't hungry, but she was starving. I think I killed her because I ate her share. Papa kept the violin in the wardrobe. He used to play it with the Odessa Symphony Orchestra. He taught me to play on a little violin when I was two or three. In the bad days, he took me out with him and we played together in the streets to get food. At night we took the violins back to the apartment and put them in the cupboard. He told me, 'One day, Arieh, after all this, we will go to Palestine, me and you and our violins.' I loved to play the violin, and sometimes, for a treat, he let me play his instrument. It was my reward for doing my practice. He told me I must practise every single day. He told me that whatever happened, I must look after his violin." It was as though the floodgates of speech had reopened for Arieh; there could be no dam to stop the flow of words. "Then the Nazis came. I think it was in September, just before my birthday. I was six. I would be seven in October. When Papa heard them, he stuffed his violin into the wardrobe behind blankets and pushed me to the back as well. I was right beside Papa's violin. I hugged it tight. They opened the wardrobe, but I stuffed the coat in my mouth and stayed very quiet. They prodded me but didn't find me. I heard shouting and screaming. Then the cars and lorries drove away. I heard them. It got very quiet. There was some bread on the table. One of the other families had left it, so I took it and ate it. Later a big garbage van came to collect rubbish and bodies and things. I crept out with Papa's violin and crawled under the garbage and hugged the violin tight. It stank in there. They tipped the rubbish into a rubbish tip. When they drove away, the violin and I escaped. I walked and walked. Sometimes people gave me some food. Other times I stole it. I went into a forest and sat on a tree trunk. That's when Mikhail found me. I was doing what my papa had told me to do: practising my papa's violin. I was playing the *Pathétique*. It was the last piece Papa taught me."

Arieh stretched out his arms sleepily and wrapped them around Simeon's neck. Then he fell back into a sound and, Simeon hoped, untroubled sleep. Simeon lay awake for a while, thinking. He had a sudden dream himself. One day, when this was all over, he would find Dora and their child, and he would take them to Palestine. There they would meet up with Arieh again and become a proper family. By then, Palestine would be the promised state of Israel. It was only a dream but in this place, where almost every conversation was dominated by planning to risk life and limb to outwit the Nazis, dreaming was their only luxury.

A week later, Simeon had been struggling to put Valdis Berzin's exceedingly worn old boots on when he accidentally dropped the left one on the floor and the heel fell off. He picked it up and examined it. It was a solid block of wood with rusty nails protruding from the point where it had been joined to the upper. "Damn," he swore, limping with one boot on and one off across the floor of the Zemlyanka to where Rutti was sitting.

"Look," he said ruefully. "You don't know of a good cobbler round here, do you?"

"Our Ethan's fixed worse than that," she said. "My boots are more patch than boot. He's a wonder. He patches the patches on patches. He could make a fortune as an expert patcher after the war." Arieh followed close on Simeon's heels to the cobbler's shop, where old Ethan Solcowitz, too old at over eighty to go out on sorties, mended old boots and shoes and fashioned clogs from the only natural resource of which there was no shortage: wood.

"Your boots certainly could do with mending." Ethan grimaced, looking down at Valdis Berzin's ancient peasant boots. "You've had them built up. Are you crippled? I thought you were in the army. These aren't army boots."

"It's a long story," Simeon told him. "Just mend them as best you can without the built-up wedge."

"I can't guarantee they will be watertight, but they have to be an improvement on the way they are now. You're lucky the rusty nail didn't come all the way through to your foot and poison you."

Simeon took his cap off briefly and rubbed his forehead. Arieh pushed at Simeon's thigh, pointed to the hat. Simeon instantly understood and nodded at him.

"I need to hide something small securely," he said. "Can I trust you?"

Ethan looked puzzled. Then he saw that Simeon had removed his hat and was releasing the thread on the lining and pulling out the two small pieces of amber hidden inside it. "As you are building new heels for me, is there any way you could hide these inside them?"

Ethan scratched his head. "I won't ask why," he said kindly. "But it won't be easy. I'll have to hollow the heels out where they join the sole, cover them, and nail the heels onto the soles at the edges rather than in the centre. I don't have a glue strong enough to hold them in place here. Come back tonight. I'll see what I can do. The boots are pretty rotten, you know. Shall I patch them at the same time?"

Simeon nodded. "Please. But how will I go out without shoes? It's still snowing outside."

Ethan reached up, grabbed a pair of ancient old rubber boots, and threw them at Simeon.

"Thank you," said Simeon, "but I'd be grateful if you didn't tell anyone about this. It's a secret. The only person who knows about it is Arieh."

"I never talk about my work. I'm like a doctor. My lips are sealed." Ethan laughed.

Back in their bed-space, Arieh placed his little amber piece carefully in his violin case, cleared his throat, and took a long, deep breath. "Your brothers are safe," he told it, stroking it. "You will soon be near them again."

They had just returned to the Zemlyanka, when Rutti rushed in, red in the face and breathless.

"Arieh, there's a man here who wants to meet you. He's a very important man, and he says he has a job for you that only you can do. Come here. Let's clean your face." She dipped a rag in the water butt and Simeon laughed when Arieh flinched - in the way that small boys always do - as she attempted to clean his dirty face. "You need to come as well, Simeon. Arieh, bring your violin."

Rutti led the way back into the smallest Zemlyanka, which had now become an office and where they held the most important private meetings. Arieh looked around, obviously in awe. Marshal Merteskov held out his hand to the boy.

"So this is the young violinist of whom I've heard so much."

Arieh acknowledged the compliment by bowing his head. Simeon was still the only person to whom he would speak.

"Lieutenant Engineer Third Class, Comrade Simeon Karminsky, I believe." Simeon nodded, expecting to be arrested at any moment. Were Merteskov's heavies waiting outside? To his surprise, the general said nothing further on the subject of his army name, rank, or number.

"Please take a seat. This is important. We have intelligence that the Germans are planning a major offensive to take Leningrad and link up with the Fins in June or July," Merteskov told them. "A detachment of high ranking officers will be gathering in Shlisselburg shortly to finalise these plans. We have reason to believe they will be billeted at the old Shlisselburg fortress, but they will almost certainly go into town for their entertainment. We are asking for the assistance of all partisan groups in the area to cause as much mayhem as possible. However, what we need most is a 'spectacular'. We have been advised by other groups that spectaculars are the Ettingers' speciality."

"So you're asking us to herd a lot of Nazis into one place like a flock of sheep and blow them up en masse?" Simeon was joking. Merteskov's expression showed that that was exactly what he meant.

"How did you know? Has there been talk? Do we have a traitor in our midst?" The voice turned from friendly to menacing. "Lieutenant Karminsky, did you know of this in advance?"

"No, sir. It was supposed to be a joke, sir."

"In poor taste, sir."

Simeon blushed.

"That's exactly what we're asking of you, although hopefully if our plan works, no 'herding' will be necessary. Our little violinist here will draw them to one place in the centre of Shlisselburg entirely of their own volition, thanks to his music. We have to catch them unawares and all together."

"You mean you want Arieh here involved in all this? He's just a baby. He's only seven years old," Simeon protested.

Merteskov walked over to Arieh and placed a friendly hand on his shoulder. "We are hoping to use this young man's talent. Combined with his inability to talk, it will make him the perfect decoy." Arieh nodded and smiled broadly. This was all he had wanted, to do something positive to help win the war. Everyone who knew him knew how he felt. So far, his involvement with the partisans' real work had been minimal. He'd been allotted only what he considered "baby" tasks, such as setting bombs under railway lines where the gap between the line and the explosive device was too small for adult fingers.

"As I said, we know the Nazis are planning a meeting to iron out the details of this major offensive on Leningrad with the Fins. They have chosen Shlisselburg because of its proximity to Leningrad.

"As we understand it, they want to launch the assault before the bad weather sets in. There will be a short window when they are gathered together, before they put the plans into action.

"We will watch and wait to discern the Gestapo's favourite drinking hole in Shlisselburg. They usually suss out the local hostelries a week or two before their major 'conferences' begin and they always choose a beer cellar where the owner is, let us say, 'sympathetic' to their ambitions. The owner of one particular bar that we are sure use in Shlisselburg is well known to us as a German collaborator. We keep a close watch on him. It is for this reason we think they will choose that particular bar."

He looked straight at Simeon. "We know this young man finds conversation difficult, which is where we need your help, Lieutenant Karminsky Third Class with the Red Army People's Volunteers, or perhaps I should address you as Valdis Berzin, although I note you no longer limp." So the authorities knew who he was and where he was, and they probably knew what he'd done. He was living on borrowed time, whether he complied with their requests or not. The words, like the tone, were menacing.

"When we are sure of the chosen hostelry, you will dress the boy as a peasant child. Don't worry: we will supply his clothes."

Mikhail, Oscar, and Rutti were all staring at Simeon now and from Simeon to Arieh. Thank God he had told them the whole truth of his background. Simeon's response, they knew, posed a risk to Arieh. If he advised the boy to refuse to comply with the Red Army's request, they could quickly dispense with him. He could put the entire partisan band and their work in danger by speaking out of turn. So far, it was all very quiet and polite, but there was no reason to expect it to stay that way if Simeon did anything other than persuade Arieh to acquiesce to Merteskov's demands. And he knew as well as they did that what he was suggesting would be placing Arieh's life at risk.

Merteskov turned to Arieh. "You, young man, will just have to do the thing you like to do most. You will play your violin outside the hostelry with a little cap at your feet to collect small change. Do you read music?"

Arieh shook his head.

"We will supply him with music for the tunes we want him to play. Preferably it will be music we know the Germans enjoy. A little Beethoven, perhaps? Brahms? Wagner? Bach? Maybe a few hymns. You don't read music, young man, so we must arrange for someone to teach you the melodies. Do you play by ear?"

Arieh nodded.

Rutti had been biting her lip so hard that she had drawn blood. Suddenly, she could take no more. "This is too dangerous. I cannot permit it. He's only a little boy."

"I'm afraid, my dear, that you have no choice. That he will not speak is the biggest bonus for us. A dumb child is a child who cannot tell anyone what's happening, even under severe conditions."

Simeon knew he meant torture.

"He will go to stay with his 'aunt' across the road from the hostelry in early June. She will be one of us. The house will be a safe house. Each evening, he will take his little cap across the road and start to play—for the regulars, you understand. No danger there. After a few days, the host will almost certainly invite him inside and offer him food in return for playing. He might even pay him. Who knows?" Merteskov looked Simeon straight in the eye. There was no room for compromise. "He will learn the layout of the pub, looking for nooks and crevices where he will be able to start hiding gelignite sticks. Don't look so worried, Lieutenant Engineer Third Class. He will carry the gelignite in his violin case. There's no chance he will be detected. He will hide his violin in the crevices when he brings the case out at night, empty. Each day, the amount of hidden gelignite will increase considerably. By the time the Germans arrive, there should be enough to blow the place to kingdom come. Even then, though, we must be patient.

"At some time, one of the Berlin bigwigs will come down to see how it's all going—Goering, Himmler, one of Herr Hitler's top brass. That's when we will put the final part of the plan into action. Arieh will go 'to work' as usual the night the bigwigs arrive. We will send the order to light all the gelignite sticks that night. The fuses will be long enough to give him time to run out. Simeon Karminsky, you will be waiting on a fast horse to whisk him away before the fire takes hold. Inside, we will have massacred some of the Nazis' crème de la crème. Brilliant, isn't it?"

Simeon watched the visibly excited Merteskov patting himself on the back and waiting for applause at his own genius.

"When the Germans arrive for their conference, the boy will already be a fixture in this beer cellar. Between now and June, Arieh will be taught how to pack and plant gelignite. He will also have violin lessons and learn to read some music. We hope this young man may rid the world of some of Germany's most vicious vermin. Look what prestige there will be for you, Arieh, when you become the little boy responsible for blowing up men like Himmler or Goebbels. It will bring glory to the Ettinger partisans."

Simeon had been sitting white-faced and silent. He heard Hanna in his head and knew he had to stop this, even at the risk of his own life. What if it had been his own little nephews, Max or Shmuel, involved in such a plan?

"He's a little boy, a child who has been deeply traumatised, sir. With kindest respect, sir, would put your own son in such danger?"

Merteskov ignored him

"We are at war. It is the duty of every Russian citizen to serve the state, is it not?"

"But this is a child."

"He is a child citizen of the USSR. As such, he is required to do his duty. He will have time to prepare himself. We will keep in touch with you and with the boy. Understood?"

Rutti was shocked by what they were asking of Arieh. "What if something goes wrong?"

Merteskov turned his back, saluting smartly. "Then we may be forced to look into Lieutenant Engineer Third Class Simeon Karminsky's service record." He turned to address Simeon directly. "Nothing will go wrong, will it, Lieutenant Engineer Third Class Simeon Karminsky? The child's clothes will be delivered tomorrow. We will also send sheet music for the music the Germans enjoy. We know the child is a selective mute which will be very useful in this task."

So it was blackmail. Either Arieh did what they asked, or Simeon would be forcibly removed and, in all probability, shot. Arieh ran to Simeon's side and tucked himself against his trouser leg. He was nodding furiously.

That evening, Simeon returned alone to collect his newly soled boots, leaving Mikhail, Oscar, and Rutti to sort out the details of Arieh's planned mission.

Ethan showed Simeon how he'd hollowed out a space in the wood of each heel just large enough to accommodate one of the tiny amber pieces. "I wrapped each of them in my own shirt tails," he said, lifting his jacket. Look." Simeon saw he'd torn the two corners from his own shirt. "I laid each of them little parcels on a bed of dead leaves from the forest floor to cushion them and tucked straw all around them to hold them firm. Then I attached the heels back to the new soles with nails. It wasn't as difficult as I anticipated at all. Tell me, though, Simeon, what is the secret of those amber pieces? It seems they are such strange items for a big man like you to be attached to."

"I know you won't believe me, Ethan," Simeon replied, "but I'm pretty sure they saved my life. I swallowed them in a moment of madness and I'm sure I protected them from G-d-knows what fate. In return, I believe, they saved my life. But please, I beg you, don't tell anyone about them. I can't tell you where I was. Only Arieh knows. Arieh, me, and now you." Ethan smiled and patted Simeon on the shoulder.

That night, Simeon sat on the edge of his bed with Arieh. "I'm sorry, son," he said softly. "I wouldn't put your life at such risk for anything. It's my fault."

To his amazement, Arieh was beaming with excitement. "The general spoke to me himself," he said proudly. "He saw me as he was leaving. He said Mikhail will tell me about the music I must learn and explain exactly what I have to do and how to do it. We will spend some time together every day before we go. I will do anything to avenge those who murdered my parents and my sister. I am happy. You gave me Little Miss Honey. She will protect me. I know she will. You told me so." As the boy spoke, Simeon saw he was clutching the morsel of golden mosaic in his hand.

"I don't want you to take it with you," Simeon told him. "I only lent it to you. It will keep you safe, but only if it remains here. Otherwise I will take it back."

"Why?"

"Because I said so." Simeon couldn't offer him a valid reason. He could hear Hanna whispering.

What's wrong with you? It's a piece of resin. It gives the child confidence and comfort. Why not let him take it?

"I don't want him to take it," Simeon hissed back, as though Hanna were right there in the room. *I've told him, it's only on loan to him. It's mine.*

Perhaps he needs such a talisman at this time, came Hanna's reply in his head. *You shouldn't have told the child so many stories about its magic powers. He's seven years old. He needs a comfort blanket. He needs your piece of amber more than you do. Don't be so stubborn, Simeon Karminsky.*

Chapter 12

Hanna

BOTH THE WAFFEN-SS AND GESTAPO WERE FREQUENT AND WELCOME visitors to Father Dominic's house: members of the Nazi hierarchy were frequently invited in for drinks after dinner. Hanna usually managed to hide away from them by helping Frau Olzswelski in the kitchen or staying in her room when they had advance notice of such visitors. Sometimes on such evenings, and to her relief, Father Dominic would be too inebriated to remember to crawl into her bed. As yet, the job the priest had mentioned had failed to materialise she spent her days helping round the house.

"One of the bosses has promised to get me a nice tree this Christmas," Father Dominic told her as he disrobed one "bad" evening, lying his stinking body next to hers on the narrow bed. "Now come along, be a good girl, and help little johnny rise to his full glory. You know what I like. I've caught a couple of frauds out, especially boys who have no idea what they're doing, but I don't need to tell you."

She turned her face away from his to avoid the worst of his foul breath. She was under no illusion now that if she tried to escape, he would catch her and have her interred behind the two-metre-high barricades topped with barbed wire that ran through the back yards in Dominikanska Street. The worst that could happen was that they would hang her publicly in the square in front of the Great Synagogue. She'd seen a couple of such hangings, but she was beginning to believe that death of any kind would be preferable to this life as a priest's whore. Nothing more had been said about working at the Nebelstelle with Kriminalsekretär Heinrich Brandt, and Father Dominic had apparently forgotten his promise to speak to his "friends in high places" about finding her a job. Nor had she found any way to help her fellow Jews inside the ghetto. She often walked past the main entrance to Ghetto One in Zamkow Street, and on these walks, she had looked through the three layers of chicken wire that separated the ghetto's inhabitants from those on the streets outside. Even at a distance, the overcrowding and filth were visible. Every morning, long columns of workers were marched out of the ghetto to a factory where they were employed making weapons for the German Army. At night, they were marched back again. She'd seen the poor wretches, clothed in rags with wooden clogs on their feet, During the day their small children, some no older than her little Shmuely, were left alone. They often stood with dirty little fingers curled around the metal chicken wire, gazing out at the world beyond, waiting for parents to come back. Hanna longed to cut through the wire, lift them out of the squalor, take them back to the warmth of the presbytery, feed them, bathe them, hug them, and tell them she would rescue them and keep them safe. She thought of taking some sweets from the priest's house in her pocket and handing them to the starving children or throwing them over the fence, but large notices printed in red outside the ghetto wires and walls warned that any contact with, or help for, those inside would be instantly punished. She thought she would have welcomed an end to this pointless, wicked life, but supposing they shot the children as well as her? She knew from what she'd seen that German bullets didn't discriminate between young and old. She could do nothing. Instead, she stared at the children as she might have stared at caged animals in a zoo and prayed there would be an end to it soon.

On Hanna's fourth Saturday at the presbytery, she was sitting alone at the breakfast table, finishing her coffee, when the old-fashioned bell on the front door jangled noisily. Father Dominic was busy in his study preparing his Sunday morning sermon. Assuming that the housekeeper would take it, Hanna carried on sipping her coffee and didn't hear Father Dominic calling for her from his office.

"Answer the door, will you, Maria dear?" he shouted irritably the second time the doorbell jangled. She heard him stomp into the hallway. "It's Kriminalsekretär, Brandt with his big boss. Two bloody women in the house, and not one of you stupid bitches can answer the damned door. Do I have to do everything myself?"

He stood there, his face still red with fury, as Hanna rushed to open the door. She recognised Brandt from the meeting at the Nebelstelle when she'd got her papers. He greeted her politely, but when she looked up and saw the man standing next to him, she froze.

"Heil Hitler. Ah! So you're the little niece I've heard so much about."

It was *him*. Of that she had no doubt. She was paralysed, glued to the spot, unable to move, hardly able to breathe, let alone nod. Her throat was constricting so that when she spoke, no sound came out. She thought she might throw up there on the doorstep. Standing in front of her, clearly recognising her despite her shorter hairstyle, was the man who'd attempted to kick his way into her home in Vidzy, the same man who'd stood laughing as the younger soldiers had pushed her sons' little faces into the soup on the floor and kicked her poor mother-in-law out of her rocking chair. Hanna had tried to turn her face away, but it was too late. What the hell was he doing here? Those unforgettable, ice-cold, periwinkle-blue eyes stared into hers. She put her hands to her head instinctively, as though she could hide her hated red hair. After Olga's ministrations with her shearing scissors, it now formed tight curls all over her head. She was both sweating and shivering, praying she wouldn't collapse in front of him. Only when Brandt began to introduce her did she realise she was expected to speak to him. She had to answer his polite question, "Wie geht es Ihnen, Fräulein Petruishka?" He was asking how she was doing.

She didn't know how she managed to answer, but eventually she did, finally, and in a voice she barely recognized as her own she whispered:

"Danke. Sehr gut und Sie mein Herr?"

"Heil Hitler. Welcome. What a great honour to welcome you to my humble home, Oberst-Gruppenführer Schlossberg." Father Dominic had finally emerged from his office. "May I congratulate you on your promotion?" It appeared that she was momentarily forgotten. He was ushering them towards his study. She managed to take in a single breath when the Father turned to her, his temper tantrum thankfully forgotten. "Maria, dear, will you get these gentlemen some coffee and some of Frau Olzswelski's delicious Linzer torte?" Then he turned back to the officers. "Such cake you never have tasted, not even in Vienna," she heard him say as he closed the door.

Just as she thought she was safe, the newly promoted SS Oberst-Gruppenführer opened the door briefly and stared at her. "My apologies, Fräulein. You must consider me most discourteous for staring, but haven't we met somewhere before?" he asked.

Hanna took another deep breath and summoned the strength to reply. She shook her head. "Ich glaube nicht mien Herr", she murmured. She was shaking from head to toe. She prayed her legs would continue to hold her upright.

But he wasn't going to let it go. "It must have been here, of course. I've heard so many good things about you. You and your uncle are obviously close." He scratched his head thoughtfully. "Yes, of course, that's it. We must have met briefly when I visited here before."

She was conscious that her face was scarlet, a burning fire, right to the roots of her carrot-red hair. She tried to avoid his eyes but realised she must play along. If she was Father Dominic's niece, wasn't it plausible they'd met here before? What would Father Dominic say? Would he tell the SS Oberst-Gruppenführer that it was impossible because she'd never been here before? No. She was sure he wouldn't give the game away, not as long as he had a use for her—more than a use, a need. In her haste to respond rationally, she found herself tripping over her tongue. She shook her head.

Father Dominic was staring at her now, too. How could the Oberst-Gruppenführer remember her from among the thousands of people he must have rounded up as he stormed his way through Poland and Byelorussia? Of all the people, of all the places, of all the times in the whole world, how could it be that she had to meet him here and now? She decided to go into the kitchen to suggestion Frau Olzswelski help, sure that the offer would be turned down as it had been in the past and that she would be able to escape her room until the visit was over.

"He's not a nice man," Frau Olzswelski remarked to Hanna. "He's here every two or three weeks and seems to get on well with Father Dominic, but there's something about him I don't like."

I could tell you what it is you don't like, Hanna thought. *I could tell you so much.* Instead, she swallowed hard and nodded. As the older woman spoke, the bell on the board above the door rang, indicating that Father Dominic was requesting his housekeeper's presence in his study. She went out wiping her wet hands on her overall and returned a few minutes later, obviously cross.

"He's only gone and invited them to stay for lunch," she complained. "These bloody men! How do they expect a snack luncheon for three to materialise into a semiformal luncheon party for four on a wink and a nod? Does he think I've got a direct line to Jesus and he'll do the loaves and fishes trick? I don't know. No idea ..." She tutted. Hanna shook her head.

"Four?" Hanna questioned. "They've got another one joining them?"

"No! He's requested me to lay a place at the table for you. Apparently, you are to dine with them at the Oberst-Gruppenführer's express request. You are to sit next to him. To sit beside him is an honour."

"Oh, do I have to? I don't know how to speak to people like that." Hanna's face had turned from red to ashen at the thought of eating a meal sitting next to the man who had abused her and her darling family. She couldn't do it. It was more than she could bear. *Help me, dear God, help me. Simeon, for God's sake, can't you feel I'm in trouble—trouble like I've never known before in my life?*

"Frau Olzswelski, I don't feel very well. Can I go upstairs? Would you tell him?"

"Tell him what?"

To Hanna's horror, Father Dominic's head appeared round the kitchen door. "Where are you, girl? Come, don't be shy. And you, speaking such excellent German. You kept that quiet, didn't you? I want to introduce you properly to our revered Oberst-Gruppenführer. He has particularly asked to talk to you."

"Please, sir. I don't feel well. I was saying to Frau Olzswelski that I was going to my ..."

"I know all about you silly little girls and your faux period pains. The man's starving. He travelled all the way from Minsk overnight on ghetto business. He wishes to make your acquaintance properly, and you don't refuse men like the Oberst-Gruppenführer. You will do as he requested and join us for luncheon. I will take no excuses. He's been placed third in overall command of the ghettos in both Minsk and Grodno under General Commissar Wilhelm Kube. He understands the Jews, you see—knows all their little tricks." He was leering at her, making fun of her. She was sure of it. Had confided his suspicions that she was Jewish to the Kriminalsekretär? she wondered. Common sense told her he probably had not. As long as she could fulfil his perverted needs, he'd say nothing.

"Although he says he recognises you, he can't remember where. He thought a conversation might jog both your memories." He took her arm and guided her physically out to the hall, where the Oberst-Gruppenführer was waiting. He took her arm. "Maria, my dear, tell me something of yourself," said encouragingly.

"Sir ..."

"My dear, if we meet in the office, I will of course be addressed formally.

But I think within the privacy of your dear uncle's home, you must call me Friedrich ..."

"And, of course, you must address me as Heinrich although not in the office. Only in private, of course."

In the office? So had her job been finalised between them? "I haven't had a chance to tell her yet." Father Dominic simpered to his guests. "A dire dereliction of duty. I apologise, Maria. I meant to mention it to you the other day. Anyway it has now been confirmed that from Monday, you are to start work as personal assistant to Kriminalsekretär Heinrich Brandt here in Grodno. I had to boast about your amazing qualities to convince them and of course I mentioned how efficient you are and what an excellent little typist. Your late mother, God rest her dear soul, was so proud of you, and it's a pride I've had the joy to share. Avuncular pride is a wonderful thing to a man who will never know the joys of fatherhood."

Hanna winced.

"Danke," she murmured, nodding her head in what she hoped appeared a humble gesture, trying to hide her shock. How could the Father know what she could or couldn't do? They had never even discussed her typing abilities other than when she had confirmed that she could type.

"Aren't you based in Minsk, sir?" she asked.

"My promotion means I am responsible for both the Grodno and Minsk ghettos under the overall direction of General Commissar Wilhelm Kube," Schlossberg answered proudly. "I will be going to Berlin to have my promotion officially recognised. I am now Oberst-Gruppenführer der Waffen-SS Schlossberg, Still Frederick to my friends, of course. I hope that includes you now, my dear Maria?" He winked at her. She tried to smile but it was too much to manage. He didn't seem to notice. "I will be visiting Grodno regularly from now on, and I believe you are to start work there on Monday."

Hanna looked from one to the other in bewilderment. She could feel her face reddening again with a mixture of embarrassment and panic. Her hands were damp with fear. Schlossberg was staring at her so hard now that she was sure his eyes would bore a hole in her head. "Your face is so very familiar. Father Dominic was telling me how you were working in a hotel near Vidzy until a fire. I was in that area in June. Perhaps that's when we met?"

"I worked at the hotel by the lake at Inzkhaven as a chambermaid."

"Oh, that's right! But not in an office? That's interesting. I believe that's what you told me, Father Dominic."

She sighed with relief as he scratched his chin. Those evil ice-blue eyes of his were battering her very soul. "Yes, yes. The hotel. The one owned by the Jews. I was never a patron in that place, but I gather you lost everything. I'm sorry. Sometimes the only way to get these Jews to leave their filthy hovels is to burn them out. We will have to make it up to you, your loss of previous employment, that is. Since I was directly responsible for ordering the destruction of all such Jew-owned establishments, I suppose I am ultimately to blame for your displacement." The half-smile on his lips confirmed he was making a joke. "Did you know you were working for Jews?"

She swallowed hard. "A job is a job, sir. There wasn't much work in that area. Certainly little office work". She had decided to cover her tracks. "I went home to the family farm afterwards. The farm doesn't make enough money to keep me and my brother Sergei Petrouishk. Sergei works the land as well as taking on extra work in a local bar. Sergei suggested I might find work in Grodno," she improvised.

"Well, now," he said. They were seated side by side at the table, and Frau Olzswelski, having dismissed Hanna's attempts to help with a wave of her hand, proceeded to place plates of hot pea and ham soup in front of the four of them. "I was talking with your uncle, and as Kriminalsekretär Brandt told you, we'd like you to come and start work as Herr Brandt's Personal Assistant from Monday." He nodded at Brandt. "We do hope you'll accept the position."

She sipped at the soup with its forbidden pig meat and tried to push the small pieces of pink flesh to one side. Father Dominic noticed. "Eat up. Eat up, dear Maria. *All* of it," he emphasised. "You're far too skinny. You need building up. Ham is very good for you."

She felt sick and hoped it wouldn't show.

Father Dominic was displaying a grin of intense pleasure at his own private joke. She was sure he knew she was Jewish. He was setting her up to destroy herself. To him, it was the ultimate joke to watch a Jewess eat ham and to see her about to start work in the ghetto in a job that would inevitably make her complicit in the killing of her own people.

Finally, the meal was over. Hanna felt it had lasted for several hours, although when she looked at the clock on the wall, she could see they had been at the table for less than an hour. When the men adjourned for brandy and cigars, she helped Frau Olzswelski clear the table. As she dried the dishes, her thoughts were all of Simeon. She pleaded inside her head. *Help me. For God's sake, show me a way out of this.*

Olga's words echoed in her head: "Act like your enemies, and they may become your friends."

"He seemed quite taken with you, that big blond Nazi," the housekeeper said as she put the plates and dishes away.

"They have offered me a job as Kriminalsekretär Brandt's PA and I can hardly refuse it, can I?"

"Most certainly not. One doesn't refuse a job offer from men like them."

Hanna heard Father Dominic calling out to her from the hall just as she and Frau Olzswelski had put the last of the fine china away. Schlossberg and Brandt were leaving. She scurried from the kitchen, avoiding all their eyes. All three men were clearly drunk.

"Sush a shame we don't have time to get further acquainted now, Maria Petruishka. However, we will shee you in the offish on Monday morning." Brandt was slurring his words. "Eight o'clock prompt."

They bent, turn by turn, to kiss her right hand.

Her mind was whirring. "Think like your enemies ..." Olga's words were going round and round in her head. She longed to lie down and blot it all out. Schlossberg bowed politely, clicked a formal "Heil Hitler," and turned to Father Dominic. "Unfortunately, I can't make Mass tomorrow morning, Father. This was just a flying visit. I need to be back in Minsk by tomorrow afternoon."

"I will shee you on Monday at eight. Don't forget," Brandt said as he tottered into the chauffeur-driven car for the ride across the square to his lodgings. Schlossberg merely waved a hand in Hanna's direction.

She wondered whether Nat and Rachel were, or ever had been, inside the ghetto in Minsk. That's where the peasant Vladimir Zhurzavle had said he thought they'd been taken. Olga had believed that if Hanna came here, she might find a way to help her Jewish brothers and sisters inside the Grodno Ghetto. How could she do that from the office, she wondered? Would working in the Nebelstelle afford her the opportunity to do something positive to help her fellow Jews? Supposing being here in this place offered her a chance to save her own family? Was that what it was all about? Their faces flickered in front of her mind's eye. Her two precious sons, dead and buried in their lakeside graves. She felt their little arms reaching out to her for help, but she hadn't been there when they needed her most. Nat and his mother, her own mother, and maybe even Simeon and Dora were in that place. What would she say if she saw any or all of them? How could she ever face Nat again? What about Simeon? Supposing they were all in there and she could find no way to free them? Was that why she felt no response from her twin in her greatest time of need? If she must suffer to live and breathe this terrible lie, then at least let it be for a reason. Let her find a means of saving other Jews' lives.

Chapter 13

Simeon and Arieh

FOR SEVERAL WEEKS, THEY HEARD NOTHING. SIMEON WAS BEGINNING TO hope that Merteskov had forgotten the whole mad exercise. However, one day in May, Arieh received a parcel. He tugged eagerly at the string and brown paper to find some boys clothing and the sheet music General Merteskov had promised, together with a note. "To my young friend and future hero. Enjoy yourself learning this new music. I have sourced an excellent violin teacher for you in Shlisselburg. I hope you like your new wardrobe. I have faith in you." It was signed simply "Merteskov".

While Arieh ran off waving the sheet music excitedly – even though he couldn't read – Rutti examined the clothes, a set of worn peasant boy's brown-bibbed dungarees with a front chest pocket, a checked shirt, an almost new dark green sweater, a pair of boots, and heavy woollen socks. It also included a small brown checked flat cap, not dissimilar to the larger one Simeon wore and in which he'd initially kept his little pieces of amber, as well as a warm jacket. Arieh was delighted with his acquisitions.

"Who can read music here? Who can start to teach me?" he asked Simeon when they were alone. "Can you find someone to help me?"

Simeon was noncommittal. "I think the idea is that you will get lessons when you are staying with the lady who will be your 'aunt' for a few weeks, when we are preparing for the attack," he said. "I think you had better not talk to me too much or else you will forget you mustn't talk, and that will spoil the plan."

Later in the month, Simeon received word that a go-between, acting as Arieh's mother, would meet them at the logging cabin halfway between the encampment and Shlisselburg on the first day of June. Arieh needed to be ready for his first visit to his aunt Dasha's, where neighbours would be told he was spending the summer holidays. He was to dress in the clothes Merteskov had provided. The only other things he needed to take were his violin and bow.

You shouldn't let him go. As Simeon lay in bed, he heard Hanna's voice for the first time in weeks. *He's only a little boy. No good will come of it. Stop it, Simeon. Pretend he's ill. Pretend anything. Keep him safe.*

These days, he was never sure if he was hearing his twin sister's voice or if it was his own conscience telling him what to do. He wished he could differentiate between the two. Hanna had been the voice of his conscience for so long. If only he could see her and speak to her face-to-face. "Where are you, sister mine?" he whispered.

On the first of June they left as planned, Arieh riding up front between Simeon's legs for an hour until they reached the log cabin. The forest floor was thick with mud and a heavy covering of last year's leaves. The horse walked slowly, its hooves covered in rags to muffle the sound of its movement. The young woman pretending to be Arieh's mother was there waiting.

"I'm Amelie," she said, holding out her arms to help Arieh down. "Handsome little fellow, aren't you?" she said, taking his violin. He snatched it back instantly.

"Forgive him," Simeon told her. "He doesn't mean to be rude. He just won't let anyone else handle his precious violin."

Simeon patted him on the head and gave him a brief hug. "Be good," he said. "Do whatever they ask of you."

Arieh nodded.

Amelie chattered to him for the rest of the long walk as though she was expecting answers. Arieh nodded or shook his head when he thought it was appropriate. "As you are my pretend son, I will come into the house with you and stay a short while, just as if I was really visiting my sister. When I leave, I will come to the front door, and you will make a big play of kissing me goodbye on the doorstep so everyone can see. Can I see your violin?" He opened the case carefully, and she peeped inside. "It's a very beautiful instrument, and I know a good one when I see it. I used to play, but not on a wonderful example like this one." She handed him a small, brown cardboard suitcase. "The general sent you a gift. Inside you'll find another change of underwear, socks, and another sweater," she told him. "You need to look clean and smart at all times. By the way, you will be known as Ahlyeksyey while you are at Dasha's. Alex for short, perhaps. That suits a little fellow like you better, I think. The general has arranged some violin lessons for you too. You will be introduced to Dasha's friend who is a very good violinist, and she is going to help you learn some of your new music. You brought your new sheet music, didn't you? Well, of course you did."

It was almost four o'clock in the afternoon when they arrived at Arieh's "aunt" Dasha's Shlisselburg home. "I'm so happy you've come at last." Dasha greeted them with her arms open to hug them both as she opened the front door to the small, pink, terraced cottage with its freshly painted white windows. She was a short, neat woman with blonde curly hair pushed back behind her ears, full pink lips, and a smile that seemed to stretch from ear to ear. Arieh liked her instantly. He thought she was one of the prettiest women he'd ever seen.

"My goodness. You've grown, Alex," she said, hugging first him and then hugging her pretend sister profusely. "I've already told all the neighbours what a great little violinist you are. Everyone's longing to hear you play. Come in, come in. You must be so hungry after your long journey."

The three of them sat down round a table, and ate home-made bread and jam and drank tea. A little later, before Amelie left, they enjoyed another delicious meal, a chicken dinner the like of which Arieh could never remember. Anyone looking through the open window would have seen nothing more than a happily reunited family enjoying good food together.

"They all know you are a mute, so you won't have to answer any awkward questions," Dasha reassured him. "And I've booked a violin teacher to come in every day from tomorrow. Does that sound good?" He nodded vigorously.

They kissed and hugged goodbye on Dasha's doorstep. "If you don't become a violinist, I think you'll have a great career as an actor," Dasha told him softly, rustling his newly cropped hair just before she closed the door. The barber in the camp had cut his hair very short, his first haircut in more than a year.

The next morning they had breakfast early, boiled eggs that Dasha told him her chicken had laid. He had two of them all for himself and couldn't believe his luck. "I keep chickens," Dasha told him, "so we don't have to rely on rations. Vera is coming at 9.30 to give you your first lesson. She's been a professional for years. I don't know where General Merteskov found her, but she knows all about you and your violin."

Precisely at 9.30 the doorbell rang. Vera was a tall, handsome woman. Her black and grey salt-and-pepper hair was tied in a no-nonsense bun at the back of her head, anchored with brown hairpins. Arieh was fascinated by the way they seemed to be woven in and out of the bun to keep it in place. Her face was heavily lined, suggesting that she was no longer young, but she wore a yellow summer dress draped around the midriff that Arieh thought was the most elegant dress he'd ever seen, even though her bright red lipstick seemed to draw all the colour from her white face.

She was clearly a disciplinarian, and there was no preamble. "Let me hear you play something you know well," she instructed her pupil. He launched into *Eine kleine Nachtmusik* as he'd played it to Simeon.

"That's very much a beginner's piece. I think you can go for something a little more sophisticated. Beethoven. I believe you are familiar with Beethoven's Pastoral Symphony, or so your 'uncle' tells me." Arieh looked puzzled.

"I think she's referring to the general," Dasha translated. "We need to refer to him as your 'uncle' from now on."

"Do you have your music, the sheet music he sent you?"

Arieh opened the buff file containing all the music.

"Let's try 'Wir sind die Deutsche Soldaten'," she said. "Bear in mind this is a soldier's marching song."

Arieh shrugged and looked at her. "Ah, you can't read the music. OK. Let's read it together. Then I'll play it for you." She read out the names of every note, pointing to each one with a long stick and then making Arieh play it on his violin. "Each note with love," she insisted. "Play A again; now C. You need to be master of your instrument, not allow it to rule over you. Be brave with it. And watch your fingering. I know you only have little hands and they're negotiating quite a stretch on a full-sized instrument, but you can do it." He played it stanza by stanza, then all the way through, with Vera pointing each note out to him on the music as he played. "Now again, and this time listen to what you're doing. I know you're only seven years old, and I'm expecting a great deal from you, but according to your uncle, you are more than capable of doing it."

They worked through the first tune and were just launching into "Drei Lilien, Drei Lilien" when there was a knock on the door. It was one of Dasha's neighbours, Natalia Zarichnaka, curious to see the mystery nephew who had come to stay, since she couldn't recall Dasha mentioning him at all since she'd moved to the house back in February.

"Well, you are a little chap for a boy of seven," she said as she shook his hand on the doorstep. "You look more like a five-year-old to me, although I just heard you playing. You play like an adult. No, it's all right. I understand you can't speak, so I shan't ask you any questions. I'll ask your auntie instead." She giggled.

"Give the child a chance to settle down. He's just been having a lesson with my friend Vera here. He's tired. He needs a drink and some cake," Dasha said protectively. "He has to do another half-an-hour practice later. Come into the kitchen and we'll have some coffee. Now what's the news with Svetlana?" She ushered the neighbour out of the living room, but as she left, she turned back and explained to Arieh and Vera, the latter of whom was just taking her leave: 'That's her daughter; she's expecting a baby any minute. " But she was speaking to thin air. Arieh had picked up the violin again, and his full attention was focused on the new visitor. "Why don't you play something you know well for Madame Zarichnaka? How about the piece you've just learned?" Arieh grinned and launched into "Drei Lilien" without looking at the music that still stood on the music stand. He already knew it by heart.

"He's good, really good, especially for a child of that age. Malnourished, though," Natalia whispered to Dasha as she was preparing to leave. "Doesn't your sister feed him?"

Later that afternoon, Dasha suggested an outing. "We'll go to the fortress," she told Arieh. "You need to learn your way around Shlisselburg. And you need to practise again before dinner. I want you note-perfect by tomorrow."

By the end of the week, Arieh had grown quite fond of his new aunt. With the added delight of proper violin lessons, he'd almost forgotten about the real reason for his "holiday". He held Dasha's hand when they went out, just as he sometimes held Rutti's as they walked along in the camp—the way he had once held his mother's hand in Odessa when they went shopping. Dasha played with him. She taught him dominoes, and they played hide-and-seek in the back yard. "The bar they want you to play at is the Khroniki Bar in that building over there, the one with the yellow walls and red roof that goes round the V corner. The job you've come to do is of great importance, not only here in Shlisselburg but also to the whole world," she told him one night as she was tucking him into bed. He loved the routine of having a bath every Friday night before he went to bed. It was lovely to feel clean again, and it reminded him so much of the home he'd once had that some nights he sobbed into his pillow for his mama, his papa, and baby Bracha.

The weather grew warmer, and Dasha opened the windows whenever Arieh practised or had lessons so that everyone could hear. "Why don't you speak, Alex?" she asked. "Can't you try? Speak to me. I won't tell anyone."

He shook his head sadly. He wished with all his heart now that he could find the confidence to speak to someone other than Simeon, but it was impossible. There were no words in his mouth when he was with strangers.

At the beginning of July, German uniforms began appearing in the town. Dasha allowed Arieh out occasionally to play with local children so that the sight of him would become familiar to everyone, Germans and Russians alike. Rumour had it locally that the SS and the Wehrmacht were holding some kind of high-level meeting in the fortress, just as Merteskov had suspected.

"Arieh," Dasha told him one sunny morning, "I think you ought to get used to having an audience. After dinner this evening, I want you to go over the road and stand outside the bar with your violin and play. Play some of the new music Vera's been teaching you. You can open your violin case and leave it on the ground to catch any odd kopeks. And you can keep the money to buy chocolate if we can find any." "I'll watch you from the window to make sure you are safe. You won't come to any harm."

That first night, he played for just half an hour. Then, true to her word, Dasha came across the road to fetch him. "I think that's enough for the first night," she said, putting her arm around his shoulders. "Look at that. You've earned three roubles."

Two nights passed before Dasha suggested he could try again. This time, he went across the road at five o'clock. He'd been playing for just ten minutes when Vladimir Ivanovich, the barkeeper, came outside. "Come in," he invited, just as General Merteskov had predicted. "I've heard you playing inside Dasha's house when the windows have been open. You're her nephew, aren't you?"

Arieh nodded. Vladimir Ivanovich was a burly man with a vast stomach that he covered with an enormous white waist apron tied under his chest and a sparse grey beard that hid several of his chins.

"What's your name?"

Arieh put his finger to his mouth and shook his head. Then he mimed writing. Vladimir Ivanovich understood. Arieh took the piece of paper and wrote his assumed name, Ahlyeksyev, in Cyrillic script, just as he'd practiced with Simeon.

"Ahlyeksyev. I've heard them call you Alex."

Arieh nodded.

"Will you play for us inside? I will not only pay you, but also I'll give you some supper every night?"

Arieh shrugged.

"I'll ask your aunt and see what she says."

Arieh grinned.

That first evening, Vladimir Ivanovich showed Arieh round. He led him down some steep, narrow stone steps to a dark cellar. Arieh shivered as he followed him. Down at the bottom, Vladimir lit a kerosene lamp. They were in a vast room where huge barrels lined two walls. A third had bottle racks from floor to ceiling full of bottles of different-coloured liquids. Arieh was surprised that the cellar was exactly as the general had described it to him. One entire wall was bare, revealing loose bricks of uneven grey stone. On the far wall was a small door. "It leads to the outside lavatory," Vladimir Ivanovich explained.

He told Arieh to wait where he was. Arieh remembered his instructions. He used the few minutes alone to investigate the state of the stone wall. By the time Vladimir Ivanovich brought him down a thick cheese sandwich and a glass of soda, he had already worked out where to hide the first gelignite sticks he would be given.

The night was a triumph. First Arieh played his Beethoven, and then he played the piece about the brave soldiers. The two or three of the soldiers among the drinkers cheered and clapped for the tiny boy with the big violin. "Will you come another night this week?" the barkeeper asked when Dasha called for him at 8.30 p.m. Arieh shrugged. "Can he come, Dasha Toropova? How about Saturday night? Then again on Monday? We understand there will be more soldiers arriving on Monday afternoon. I think they'll love you. You're not frightened of the Germans, are you? I know a lot of Russian children are, but the German soldiers love little children, as long as they're not Jews. In fact, as a people they can be absolutely charming if they put their minds to it. Don't worry, little Alex." Arieh was petrified of the Germans but he refused to show it. He shook his head.

"Good lad. What's more, they can be very generous when they get merry, so you should do quite well out of it, aside from what I will pay you. You play the songs they like, and I'll feed you the food you like, and we'll all have fun and be merry."

During his meal breaks in the cellar during his initial visits, Arieh had managed to loosen two of the bricks and scraped out a space large enough to leave his violin. He knew that next time, or perhaps the time after that, he'd have to leave his precious violin here on its own while he carried the empty case home. He wondered what his papa would say if he knew. He felt in the bib pocket of his borrowed trousers where he had secretly concealed Miss Honey, despite Simeon's instructions to leave her back at the camp. If he didn't have his papa's violin, he had to have something else to keep him safe. He believed in the magic of Simeon's amber tablets. As long as he had Miss Honey and kept her close to his heart, he would be fine. Simeon had said so, hadn't he?

The Germans sitting in the bar enjoying their drinks, laughing raucously at their own jokes, and listening intently to Arieh's more serious music, seemed entirely different from the marauding Nazis who had killed his mama and baby sister and taken his papa away. He found the warm smells of beer and cigarette smoke comforting. The suppers he was given on each visit were delicious. There were generally sandwiches and sometimes chicken or sausage. Nadezhda Joffre, the boy who worked with Vladimir Ivanovich, greeted him every working evening and led him down to the cellar to eat before he began his set so he wouldn't be bothered by the customers as he devoured his supper.

He'd been "working" for two weeks when the first gelignite sticks were delivered to Dasha. He looked at them curiously: slim white cardboard tubes with string hanging from the bottom. Dasha showed him how he must hide them with their backs facing the wall and the strings hanging at the front. He must leave the tiniest part of the string hanging outside the brick, but it must be so small that nobody would notice it in the gloomy light of the kerosene lamp. They must be laid in straight rows, one behind each brick, so that on the night itself, he could run along the lines with a lit torch and then belt up the stairs to safety before the fuses blew. Dasha built a "wall" of similar bricks in his bedroom so that he could practise before they carry out the plan. There was no room for error.

The first night, Arieh hid the violin and walked out with the empty case, ready to accept its new cargo. He barely slept, thinking of his precious violin all alone in the cellar. When evening came, Dasha watched him cross the road as she always did.

"Good luck, my clever, brave boy," she whispered. "You can do it."

He usually carried his precious Miss Honey in the front patch pocket of his dungarees, but now he removed it and stroked it gently, just as he had done when he and Simeon had laid all three little amber pieces on their bed above the potato store. "Thank you for keeping me safe here," he whispered softly to it, without thinking.

Dasha turned, astounded, her usually genial face red with anger. "Did you speak, Alex? What did you say? Tell me?" Realising his mistake, he merely shook his head.

"I'm not deaf yet," Dasha insisted. "You spoke. I heard you. So you can speak? You just choose not to. Is that it? Or is this some part of the plot that I'm unaware of? Are you a spy? With the Germans, anything is possible. What's that in your hand? Here. Let me see."

Arieh reluctantly opened his clenched fist. His hand was wet with sweat. He had never seen Dasha angry before. Tears were coursing down his face. One silly little slip, and he'd ruined the whole plan. Dasha was a tall, strong woman. She towered over him now, and for the first time, the reality of what he was about to do hit him. He was trembling from top to toe, violently shaking his head.

"That's amber," she said. "It's been polished. And look, it was once attached to something else. I can see the little fixing. Where did you get such a thing?"

Arieh shook his head. The words had genuinely gone again. To his dismay, she put her hands on his shoulders and shook him. "Speak to me, you naughty child. Speak to me. You've had everyone believing you are dumb. Even Merteskov himself. Do you want me to tell him you're a liar? Do you?"

Arieh shook his head. "Look at me, Alex. What did you whisper? Who were you speaking to?" He shook his.

"You must not do it again. Understood?"

He nodded again, his little face rounder now than it had been three weeks ago but full of misery. People had been nagging him to speak for so long. Why had he done it unconsciously? He stood perfectly still.

"Go and find your violin. Shoo. Away with you. Go and practise the new pieces Vera taught you."

He looked up at her, his big brown eyes beseeching hers for forgiveness.

"It's all right," she continued. "Don't worry. I won't tell anyone. Not even Amelie. I understand she will be bringing the rest of the 'gifts' very soon."

Chapter 14

Hanna, December 1941–April 1942

W HEN HANNA ARRIVED AT THE NEBELSTELLE PROMPTLY AT EIGHT ON THE Monday morning, as requested, Heinrich Brandt was already waiting for her. He greeted her at the top of the grand marble staircase inside the entrance hall with the Nazi salute and a smart "Heil Hitler." She had no option but to reply accordingly.

"You are prompt. One minute early, in fact," he said, consulting his pocket watch. "Promptness is valued here."

He led her through the same impressive marble-columned black and white tiled entrance hall, followed down the iron-balustrade staircase, and turned right down the same long corridor she'd walked the day she'd registered her arrival here with Father Dominic. Windows overlooked a quadrangle garden to the right, in the style of an old abbey. The line of heavy oak doors broke the monotony of the walls, which were tiled dark green to waist level and then painted cream. Brass nameplates identified some of the offices as they walked past. Brandt spoke rapidly, turning towards her occasionally as they walked.

"The good SS Oberst-Gruppenführer Schlossberg was most impressed with you when you met at your uncle's place on Saturday," he said. "He's had a new addition to his duties. They've added Byelarus Ghetto to his portfolio. He's a very important gentleman now. He insisted I offer you more than a simple typist's job after we met at your uncle's house, and even without the typing test we usually ask all our employees to take. He admires your characteristic quietness—that you are a listener rather than a speaker. Not like so many of the girls today, including a number here, who think they know how to run this country so much better than the Führer, let alone my office. You are to work as my office manager."

He opened the first door on his left-hand side, which the brass plate on the door pronounced as The Secretariat, and as he did so, she heard the loud click-clacking of the busy typing pool. He stood in the doorway and held his hand up. The young women stopped typing almost instantly, although they had ostensibly been concentrating on their work, and looked up.

"May I introduce Fräulein Maria Petruishka, your new office manager? In future she will be in charge of distributing the work and checking to ensure that all that leaves this office is perfect—*perfect*," he repeated. "Fräulein Petruishka will answer directly to me."

He turned back to whisper to Hanna. "The last girl was entirely unsatisfactory," Brandt continued, "very disorganised. And then someone told us she was a quarter Jewess, so no wonder. Mother's mother, apparently. We had her arrested immediately, of course. She is currently in prison in the vaults here, awaiting further investigation. We need to know what information she has passed on and to whom. We don't understand how she got through our stringent checks." Hanna felt sick. If a woman was sent to a prison cell for no better reason than that she was a quarter Jewish, what would be her own fate be if her deceit were to be uncovered?

"Your uncle says you are a good, accurate typist."

She nodded. "I am not a touch typist, but yes, I can type." She was looking at the gleaming new Olympia sitting on her desk, a pile of clean white paper lay next to a pile of carbon paper for copies, and a notebook. Next to that sat several sharp pencils, a dip pen and ink, all neatly positioned. She decided to admit in advance to one area of skill she did not possess. "However, sir, I must admit that I don't do shorthand." She turned to him and tried to grin. "If you want to sack me now before I start, I'll understand."

"On the contrary, my dear, I admire your honesty. Just don't disappoint me." He was trying to return her feeble joke. "Now don't tell me you're half Jewish as well. That's all I ask."

She blushed deeply. "I'm not half Jewish. No, sir." That was true.

He appeared to see her answer as a retort to his joke. "Don't worry, my dear. Schlossberg has assured me you are entirely trustworthy. He can sniff out Jews from a hundred metres. They all stink. Whereas you, my dear, smell as sweet as a scented rose." They had reached his private office, the frosted glass window separating it from her desk and the main office beyond. He closed the door and indicated for her to take a seat, perching himself on the corner of the desk.

"There are one or two things you need to know," he said. "There is a large Jewish ghetto—actually there are two, Grodno One and Grodno Two, spaced two kilometres apart. I presume you know what a ghetto is. It's the place we keep the Jews before we 'resettle' them." He held up two fingers of each hand when he said the word *resettle* as though to make it clear it was a euphemism for something else. "Personally, I think it's ridiculous to keep them like that, even if Ghetto One does provide us with cheap labour before we ship them out. Those Jews taken to Ghetto Two are the weak ones. We ship them off for extermination. Frankly, I think they'd be better off building more proper gas chambers closer to this town to spare the expense of sending them off to Dachau or Auschwitz. It all costs money, you know. It's my opinion they should get rid of the lot of them, but I suppose they do provide a free work source for local factories. For the time being, our Führer in his wisdom believes the slave labour gangs are valuable to the German economy. And who are we to question the Führer's judgement?"

As he continued, Hanna was sitting forward, gripping the arms of the high-backed brown, leather chair so that her knuckles gleamed white. Her brother's face was swimming in front of her eyes. She could hear his voice. *Get a grip on yourself, Hanna. The way you're behaving, they will suss you out before you even start work. You've got an important job to do.*

Suddenly she shivered. Simeon himself was frightened, in some kind of danger. She felt that he, too, held the fate of others in his hands. But how was she to find a way to help the Jews inside the ghetto? That was what Olga had told her to do. Here she was being paid, although she had no idea how much, to work in a Nazi office next to ghettos containing thousands of her co-religionists, all doomed to the ultimate fate of death. What could she do to help them from here? Nat would expect her to turn the job to some advantage for them. What would Simeon insist she do if he knew where she was?

"Apart from requiring someone to oversee the work of the other typists out there, we need a reliable organiser," Brandt continued. He had been talking, she realised, all the way through her reverie. "You'll be working under me, but I report directly to the Oberst-Gruppenführer on his weekly visits here."

Hanna shook her head to stop herself fainting. She must show no weakness. He continued. "Apart from your work in the office, you will accompany me inside the ghetto from time to time to take notes when we meet with the Judenrat. That's the Jews' self-appointed governing body. They come to us with ridiculous demands. We're lucky; we have Jewish police here too, and they're always ready to tell on their own—anything to save their own skins and get a few more morsels of bread. They're called Kapo."

Hanna hardly heard the rest. She was to go inside the ghetto and be face-to-face with other Jews but must not be recognised as one. What if someone recognised her? How would she respond to the first person who called out, "What are you doing here, Hanna Karminsky Abramskya?" What if Nat was there? Or his mother? Or even Simeon?

"You know," he was saying, "The Oberst-Gruppenführer Schlossberg is still convinced you've met in the past. He never forgets a face. He'll remember where eventually."

And God have mercy on my soul when he does. He'll remember me and my poor old mother-in-law and my little sons licking soup off the floor, all of us with our bottoms in the air, being kicked in the backside by his henchmen. That's what he'll remember when something jogs his memory.

For the rest of the morning, Hanna familiarised herself with her desk and tested her skill with the German keyboard. Thankfully, her German and her typing were adequate for the task. She decided to walk along the lines of typists to introduce herself personally and familiarise herself with the young women and the work they were engaged in. They appeared overtly hostile, barely replying to polite requests for their names and particular specialities. Her appointment over their heads was clearly unwelcome.

In the early afternoon, Brandt called Hanna into his office. In his right hand he held a large sheaf of papers and three large, brown sealed envelopes. "Open them," he ordered.

She did so and saw long lists, name after Jewish surname. They had been listed alphabetically and included birth dates, ages, and occupations and were organised by the streets, villages, and towns the people originated from. However, Hanna noticed the oddest thing: all the men's first names were Israel, and the women were all listed as Sara.

She read through the first list: "Kropinia Village—Barzilia, Israel, 8.7.1937, child; Kurenets Village—Czapnick, Sara, 8.12.1919, housewife; Czapnick, Israel, 3.3.1938, child; Czapnick, Israel, 7.8.1939, child; Dvina

Village—Gluckstein, Sara, 5.12.1916, housewife; Gluckstein, Israel, 4.6.1914, doctor; Horowitz, Israel, 9.9.1885, schoolmaster ..."

Hanna could feel Brandt's eyes watching her as she read, although she hadn't looked up. *I must not react to what I see.* "Why are all the women called Sara and all the men Israel?" she asked eventually.

"Jews, my dear. Just our way of distinguishing their sex. My, you are a little ignoramus, Maria Petruishka. I need you to look through these lists and ring those with useful occupations. I want doctors, jewellers, engineers, nurses, and dentists primarily, the ones that can be useful to us. We are also on the lookout for specialist brick breakers. No, take no notice—my little joke. We need strong men to work in the quarries. When you have extracted what we need, you will place your list of those who may possibly be useful on my desk. Cross off the ones you've selected. Give the remainder to the girls in the pool to list again in alphabetical order. Two carbon copies. No typing errors, but then I don't need to tell you that. You will give the instructions and have the first ones back on my desk by this evening, please."

"Yes, sir."

Hopefully the conversation was now over; Hanna started to edge away.

"I must say you speak excellent German for a Byelorussian, Maria. Schlossberg said your father was German. From where?"

"Berlin, sir." So they had been talking about her.

"Never been there myself. I'm from Heidelberg." With that, he turned his back, and she took it as a signal to take up her position at her desk and start work.

After half an hour, Hanna looked up to see Brandt standing over her. "What happens to these people on my list?" The question was daring.

"The useful ones stay here in Ghetto One to care for one another and improve productivity. They all end up in the same place eventually, though."

She looked down the first list. She knew she couldn't save them all. Gluckstein, Israel, genuinely a doctor. She wrote his name down and blacked him off the list going to the typists. Czapnick, Sara. She did a double take. This woman shared Hanna's birthday. Her children were almost the same ages as Max and Shmuel. She crossed her out and added her to her own list, below the doctor, hoping she'd be able to keep the children with her. She gave her the occupation of nursing sister. Vishay, Israel. He sounded like a barber she used to know in Vidzy. He used his hands to work. Didn't that qualify him? She couldn't change too many to start with, or someone would get suspicious. "Electrician," she typed in the column beside his name.

Hanna handed the first list she'd completed to a young woman with bottle yellow hair and eyebrows the colour of ripe lemons. Elsa looked up at her briefly. "You heard what the boss said: no errors," she said firmly.

The young woman gave her a strange look.

When a couple of the typists queried alterations, Hanna simply took the list in question back to her desk, made a great show of checking it against the original, and handing it back, double ticked. Elsa, to her surprise, didn't question anything.

As Hanna became more confident with the new typewriter over the next few weeks, Brandt began delegating other duties to her. Her first meeting with the Judenrat, the committee of nine Jews under the direction of the former schoolmaster David Brawer, happened on Friday at the end of the third week. It was inside Ghetto One, in a hut the Judenrat used as their office. The smell as they entered the grounds, even in a car with the windows closed, was almost indescribable, a stench of unwashed bodies, garbage, and sewage. The few men and women they passed were huddled in ragged clothes. They barely looked up as the car passed, as though the effort of doing so would be a waste of essential calories. The room in which the meeting was held contained a long table with a bottle of water with glasses at its centre and a few folding chairs. Heinrich Brandt indicated for Hanna to take one of the chairs. He took another. The members of the Judenrat stood.

"What do you have to report?" There were no pleasantries to the conversation.

"We need an increase in the bread ration. We're all starving to death," David Brawer told Brandt. "You run Grodno on a shoestring and expect productive work from men and women who are ravenous." Hanna took minutes of the conversation as best she could, trying hard not to look up into Brawer's thin face. His cheekbones stood out behind saggy skin. His brown eyes had a haunted, hunted look. He wore an old flat cap that looked too large for his head.

Brandt stared at him. "The adult bread ration will be cut to half a loaf for every adult every two days. A quarter of a loaf for the children."

"Sir," Brawer attempted to protest.

"Too much. We're too generous. Oh, I understand," Brandt replied sourly. "Shall I cut it to quarter of a loaf for adults then? No. Perhaps I'll err on the side of generosity and leave it at half, for now at least."

Hanna looked round the room. Despair, fear, and hunger shone out of every one of the eyes of all ten wretched members of the Judenrat committee.

121

As the weeks went by, Hanna's duties became more onerous, but that equally afforded her more freedom to alter lists without Brandt staring over her shoulder, as he'd been in the habit of doing at the beginning. She typed all his private letters and was delegated responsibility for arranging both his and Schlossberg's accommodation at the elegant old Kronor Park Hotel whenever the latter was in town and they planned to have a meeting. Looking at the hotel brochure, Hanna thought the hotel looked idyllic, an elegant white mansion in a grand eighteenth-century French chateau style, surrounded by sunken terraces, manicured lawns, gardens, and low-cut privet hedges. It was Schlossberg's favourite, but despite its physical beauty and renowned cuisine, it was some way out of the centre of town. Hanna found it hard to understand why he insisted on staying there or indeed why he ordered separate accommodation for the two of them. "One day I will take you there and you will understand its attractions," he told her on the telephone when she was forced to inform him that one of the Gestapo generals from Berlin was visiting with a delegation and therefore only one single room was available—and that was at the back.

"I will take it, but you can tell that disloyal bastard proprietor Herr Lukashenko that I expect a greatly reduced rate for that cupboard he dares call a room? I stayed there once before under sufferance and vowed never again."

"Wouldn't you prefer a better room in a hotel in town?" she asked him. "The bishop often stays at a place in Kalinovskgog Street."

"Thank you, no. But tell Lukashenko I shall require services as usual." He didn't elaborate on what the "services" were.

Facing her fellow Jews at the Judenrat meetings without openly admitting her Jewishness was the most difficult challenge Hanna had faced so far. She longed to ask them whether they knew Nat or Rachel Abramskya or if they'd come across Dora and Rose Karminskya. She yearned to tell them she was Jewish too and that she was doing her best to help save some of them from whatever their fate would be after the ghetto. She had heard stories of concentration camps, of forced labour camps, and of death lorries, and each time one of her bosses boasted of a new way of eliminating Jews, the worse it became.

She thought of Olga and the promise she had made her. She thought of her mother and her husband and wondered what she would do if she ever came face-to-face with them or with her sister-in-law, Dora. Would they understand why she was working for Germans, what she was trying to do to help her fellow Jews? There was no confidante, only the voice in her head that was either her own conscience or Simeon's voice trying to advise her from afar. What would Simeon say to her if he knew where she was working and what she was doing? *He won't take any excuse,* she thought. *He'd murder me, twin or no twin. He would kill me for working with Nazis and colluding in sending my own brothers and sisters to their deaths. There is no excuse. None.* She lived every day in mortal fear of meeting somebody who knew her. She no longer feared Schlossberg as she had done at the beginning. She saw him as the one man who would put an end to her misery if he found out who she really was.

Hanna's second visit to the Judenrat involved a meeting with David Brawer and Ya'akov Efron, director of the ghetto's supply department. Again Heinrich Brandt invited her to sit down to take notes. He sat himself beside her. Although the table had been laid out neatly with notepads, glasses, and a jug of water for all of them, and although there was a chair for every person present, the Judenrat members were not invited to take their seats. Brandt turned first to Efron.

"We need thirty chairs and thirty white tablecloths immediately," he said. "You will provide cutlery for one hundred people, two dozen tables, and curtains, white if possible."

Efron Ya'akov shrugged his shoulders. "Everything we had of any worth was confiscated as we entered the ghetto," he said boldly. "Where are we supposed to source this stuff from?"

"Where are they supposed to get it from?" Hanna whispered to Elsa Muller, the typist with the bright yellow hair who had been invited to this meeting because she could take shorthand notes. "They bring stuff in with them and hide it to barter for their lives like this," Elsa whispered back. Hanna took a deep breath.

"Stop gossiping, you two," Brandt shouted across to them. "This is not a mothers' meeting."

He turned to David Brawer. "As already requested, I require one thousand people from Ghetto Two ready for moving to Lasosna tomorrow morning. Names checked in triplicate. March them to the station at 4 a.m. The train departs at 4.30 a.m. For each one missing, we will take a replacement from the street."

David Brawer handed a list to Hanna, and Hanna passed it to Brandt. "An additional two thousand from Ghetto Two will be transferred to Keilbasin." Again, she handed a carbon copy of the list of people to Brandt and kept one copy for her own files. Brawer produced a third list. "These people are strong, all artisans or professionals, and no longer in need of convalescence at Lasosna. Can we transfer them back from the hospital to Ghetto One?"

Brandt nodded. "Keilbasin might be better". Had Brawer just saved three hundred Jewish souls from certain death? She wasn't sure.

Rain was tipping in torrents as the chauffeur held a large umbrella and saw them into the Nebelstelle. Hanna had felt a strange emotion of relief mixed with shame as they had driven out through the ghetto gates, leaving the squalor and filth behind. Brandt continued to talk as they drove back into town. "We send the sick ones we think have a chance of recovery and therefore will become productive again to Laasona for feeding up. From there they go on to Keilbasin to labour. We think it's a good idea to get them fit for the journey. Then onto Auschwitz, where the strongest will be assigned the heaviest work."

"But I thought all those sent to Auschwitz would be spared," she said daringly.

"You're right. By the way, can you find me a doctor and a nurse to travel with the ones we're sending to Lasosna? The Jews stay calmer when they're being treated by their own" was all he would say.

Back in the office, there were several lists to be typed. Surely, he wouldn't notice a few minor alterations to the lists she had to make. Two names jumped into Hanna's mind: "Israel" Gluckstein and her "other twin", "Sara" Czapnick. She recalled them both from the very first list she'd every typed. Doctor Gluckstein was a medical man. "Sara" Czapnick shared Hanna's birthday. She would now become a qualified nurse. Hanna added the names of the two small children, making them older than they really were and suggesting that their mother needed their assistance to complete the task efficiently. She marched boldly into Brandt's office. "You wanted two people from Ghetto One to go with the Lasosna party, didn't you?" she said. "Here. I've found two from one of the first lists I typed: a doctor and a nurse. The nurse employs two young men who often help her. They know how she works, so I would suggest they go along with her for maximum efficiency."

"Sounds perfect. Thank you, my dear. I knew you were a well-organised lady the moment I set eyes on you." He simply signed the paper she handed him without even looking up.

Yet it was far from plain sailing. One afternoon when Hanna was in the lavatory, she heard a snatch of conversation between two of the typists. She recognised the voices. Sophia Warshawsky with her high-pitched whine and Elsa Muller, the young woman with lemon-yellow hair, discussing her.

"Bloody priest's niece," she heard Sophia say. "He seems to have rather a lot of them, don't you think?" Sophia was one of the typists Hanna liked least, always unpleasant, although she never dared be overtly rude. She was always looking for ways of shortcutting her work.

"Well, he is one of ten or eleven children, and you know what the Catholics are like. I shouldn't really say that as I'm one of them," was Elsa's reply, "but we do tend to breed like rabbits."

Hanna pulled the chain and emerged from the cubicle. "What is wrong with my uncle?" Hanna asked innocently, although she would have done almost anything to save herself from the indignity of his nightly assaults. "If you have something to say, please say it straight to my face, Sophia."

She caught what she thought was a strange half wink from Elsa. Perhaps Elsa knew something – or at least more than she was admitting.

"Kindly don't discuss my family in such tones again, Sophia, and you, Elsa. I may need to take action on your lackadaisical work and your general attitude." As Hanna stood looking in the mirror to reapply her lipstick, Sophia slammed out of the room. Now only she and Elsa remained. As Elsa turned to face Hanna, Hanna couldn't help but notice how dark the roots of the young woman's hair were against the rest of her hair and the bright yellow eyebrows that stood out starkly against her dark complexion. Her eyebrows, too, had been treated to a heavy dose of bleach.

⁂

Simeon was creeping into Hanna's dreams frequently now. Father Dominic's wretched assaults continued nightly, except for five blessed days each month when she had her period. After she'd ministered to his foul needs, she would fall into a trance-like sleep. Every night, her nightmare was the same: Simeon was chasing her round and round the garden on a very hot day. The pair of them were dripping in sweat. Then he caught her and hit her round the face again and again. "How could you collaborate?" he screamed at her. "How could you? You are a disgrace to our people."

"What more can I do?" she cried.

"Much more," came the reply. "Do more. Bloody well do more, you selfish bitch."

Her own cry woke her, but still his voice continued to taunt her, even in her half-wakeful state.

She looked down and saw that the fists she had felt beating her were her own fists. Simeon had never lifted a finger to her or used such language to

125

her in her life, yet now she could hear his voice as clearly as if he were there standing next to her.

She sobbed then into her pillow. "Simeon, oh Simeon. I'm sorry. I'll do more. I'll try harder."

Chapter 15

Arieh

IT WAS SEVERAL DAYS LATER THAT AMELIE ARRIVED TO VISIT HER "DEAR SON", carrying a large brown paper parcel in her shopping basket. "General Merteskov's instructions are to keep it under the bed, Dasha," she said. "Get rid of these this week, Arieh. Another batch should arrive on Sunday."

She took him out for the day. They were seen together arm in arm, Arieh bending his head towards her as she chattered in his ear, ostensibly mother and son. She even stopped at the Khroniki Bar to speak to the innkeeper. "I hope you don't mind if my Alex doesn't play tonight. I know you love to have him, but I am staying just one night, and I'd like to enjoy my son's company," she told him.

"Such a shame, but I suppose I understand. Where exactly do you live?" he asked her. She mumbled something Arieh couldn't hear, and the innkeeper grunted. He was obviously somewhat annoyed at losing his star performer, even for one single night.

Arieh slept on the settee that night whilst Amelie slept in his bed. The next morning, she showed him how to pack the first twelve tubes of gelignite inside the violin case and how to leave just the smallest part of the fuse showing through so that he would be able to set it easily without disturbing the bricks when the time came. "When we are sure you have enough gelignite to do the job, you will light the long fuses just by running backwards and forwards along the wall stacked in four or five layers. The detonators are extremely sensitive, so you will have to be quick. Then you will grab your violin, run upstairs, play the first four bars of *Die Soldaten* to let Simeon know you're ready, then run as fast as you can."

During the next four weeks, Arieh managed to plant between six and eight sticks on each occasion he went over to the bar at play. However, the danger of detection grew a little with every visit. Everyone involved, including Arieh, was afraid that the innkeeper might appear at the wrong moment or that he would light a cigarette and ignite the fuse before they were entirely ready, causing a premature explosion which would expose them all. The good news, however, was that once he'd got into a routine, Arieh was able to set the gelignite quickly and efficiently. Every night, to his consternation, he was forced to leave his precious violin behind. Day by day, more and more Germans arrived for the conferences in the fortress, and every evening the bar was crowded with inebriated Nazis.

For the following three weeks, Arieh managed to plant between twelve and fourteen gelignite-filled tubes on each visit. Several times, the innkeeper came downstairs before he'd finished, but each time, his footfall on the stone steps was enough to send Arieh scuttling back to his seat, ostensibly tucking into his supper. Twice, the boy was forced to carry several sticks of gelignite back to Dasha's house after having run out of planting time, but eventually the job was done.

It took until early July to plant all the sticks. It was an anonymous note through the door that alerted Dasha and Arieh to the arrival of the first high-ranking Germans for the meeting on 10 July 1942. There had been rumours that the Germans were threatening to use poisoned gas against the Russians. Dasha had a shortwave radio she kept under the bed and which she often used to listen in to the BBC Russian Services from London in the middle of the night. She woke Arieh to hear Winston Churchill's broadcast that evening. It had been two years since he'd taken over as British Prime Minister, and she wanted Arieh to be able to say he'd heard the historic broadcast, even though she knew he wouldn't understand a single word of it.

"We shall treat the unprovoked use of poison gas against our Russian allies exactly as if it were used against ourselves, and if we are satisfied that this new outrage has been committed by Hitler, we will use our great and growing air superiority in the West to bring gas warfare on the largest possible scale against military objectives in Germany."

The following day, they had news that the German high command were gathering, just as expected, at the fortress. The innkeeper's wife came rushing over the road to tell Dasha. "We don't know who is coming yet, but there's talk of important people. Someone suggested that even the Führer himself might turn up. Please make sure that young Alex here looks his very best. Tonight he will dine royally. We have prepared special food: pork belly with sauerkraut, bratwurst, and spaetzle. Have you ever eaten spaetzle, Alexi? Boy, you are in for a treat."

Behind her back, Arieh made a face. Whilst living with Dasha, he had eaten all kinds of foods forbidden to Jews, but the idea of pork belly turned his stomach.

"One more day," Dasha told him. "Tomorrow is Tuesday. The date 14 July 1942 will go down in history as the day the German hierarchy were destroyed by the hand of a seven-year-old Russian boy called Alexi, and your name will become famous all over the world."

The day dawned bright and warm and promised a beautiful and light summer's evening with a crescent of a yellow moon just visible high against the deep blue sky. At 17.25, Arieh left the house as usual, his violin in its case under his arm. Last night, for the first time in weeks, he had taken his instrument home. Tonight, alongside his violin lay a box of matches and a long taper. He had kissed Dasha goodbye warmly, and she watched him walk from the front door to the bar as she often did. However, both knew it was unlikely they would ever see one another again. When he'd gone inside the inn, she took a chair by the front window and sat with her sewing in hand to watch, all the while wondering how Arieh felt. She had grown fond of the boy and knew she would miss him, although it wasn't in her brief as a secret agent to show emotion. Nevertheless, and although he played his violin with a maturity way beyond his years, he was still only a little boy, a polite, delightful, attractive little boy who should be out playing football with his friends, not blowing up enemy installations. She knew she could cross the road, enter the bar, and order a vodka with tonic, and then she could keep an even closer watch over him, but it was more than she dared do. She had her orders. As soon as she heard the first explosion, she was set to leave as fast as she could through the back door. What Arieh was about to do could change the course of the Great Patriotic War. Indeed, it could change the course of the whole world war.

At 18.50, just as planned, Dasha heard the first haunting sounds of Arieh's violin playing the first few bars of *Die Soldaten* through the bar's open window. Hardly had he played the third note than explosions started to rent the air: one, four, ten—the whole place was exploding. As she ran, Dasha heard screams of pain, terror, surprise, confusion, and mayhem.

Simeon, realising the fuse had blown too early, covered his horse's eyes and led it as near to the inn as he could. He could see inside as sparks like fireworks shot through the wooden floor and smoke rose in thick black clouds from the cellar. Flames burst from beneath Arieh as blue and orange tongues of fire fuelled by barrels of alcohol spilled out. Simeon could suddenly see Arieh's silhouette, small and terrified, black against the background of orange flames. It seemed to Simeon that the bottom half of both his legs were on fire. Simeon tore off his jacket and rushed into the melee, grabbing the child and wrapping the jacket tightly round the lower half of his body to quench the flames. Then he threw him across the horse, jumped up behind him, and rode as fast as he dared, one hand gripping the reins, the other holding tight to the child's body. Once inside the forest, he stopped. Arieh was barely conscious and making no sound. Simeon grabbed the reins, and moved Arieh so that his back was resting against Simeon's chest, his legs still wrapped in the coat and stuck straight out in front of him. He could feel the child moaning as he galloped out of the melee, their ears filled with the sounds of screams, of crackling from the burning wood and the shattering of glass bottles. Once they were safely into the forest, Simeon slowed to unwrap his jacket from the boy's legs, hoping the cool air of the horse's movement would ease Arieh's agony. He took his water bottle and tried to drip small drops of water into the boy's mouth as they continued forward. He could see that the child's left leg was one enormous blister from toe to knee. The material of his right trouser leg appeared to have disappeared, melted into the skin or burnt away. Only as they reached the encampment did Simeon realise that despite it all, Arieh was still clutching his precious violin with all his might.

It took them almost an hour to reach the encampment. By then, Arieh's breathing was slow and shallow and his face was a frightening shade of grey. His skin felt cold to the touch, yet beads of sweat ran down his forehead and he was shaking uncontrollably. Simeon thought at first that he'd passed out from the pain. Then he heard a low moan.

"It's all right, Arieh. It's all right, boy. You're safe. You're with me. Your violin is safe too. Look." Simeon was desperately scared now. The child was making no noise. "Hang on, Arieh. Hang on. I've got you. You're safe." He tried to talk to Arieh to keep him awake. Yet even as he spoke the words, he had little faith that he could save the precious child's life.

"I should have listened to you, Hanna. I should have let Arieh take his amber tablet. Perhaps that could have saved him. Arieh. Dear Arieh. Don't die. Arieh, I love you. Keep breathing. We're there."

As they entered the camp, Simeon heard the boy whisper very faintly. "I want Mama and Papa. I must have my tablet." The voice was small and reedy thin.

Willing hands lifted the injured child down gently. "He's badly burnt. Get his legs into cold water," Simeon told those who crowded round.

"Get the doctor," Oscar ordered, taking the child's dead weight over his shoulder and running with him to the water butt. He dunked the boy's legs in cold water, supporting him under his arms, but clearly it was too late.

Arieh was shaking from head to foot. Mikhail tried to wrap the top half of the little boy's torso in blankets. The boy's breathing was growing shallower and shallower. From time to time, he made little noises, moans of exhausted pain.

"Does it hurt so much, darling?" Rutti soothed, holding his hand. He shook his head vehemently. "No. My tablet. I must have my tablet."

"We have to get him hydrated," she insisted forcing his mouth open and dripping cold water down his throat.

Suddenly, Simeon realised what he was calling for. "It's OK, Arieh. I've got tablets. Don't worry. You will have them soon." The words seemed to quieten Arieh a little. Their biggest fear was his uneven breathing.

"He's in shock," the doctor said.

"Keep dripping liquid into his mouth. Now lay him down. Gently. Keep cold cloths over his legs. You're safe, darling." Rutti continued to speak softly to him. Now it appeared he had passed out. He was still as a stone.

For the next weeks, Rutti and a team of young women she'd gathered together took turns sitting beside the desperately sick child, spooning water continually into his mouth, laying cool, clean boiled bandages over Arieh's burnt and blistered legs, trying to minimise the chance of infection. They had managed to cut away most of his bib trousers, but nevertheless, the child was running a high fever all the time and shook uncontrollably. Then he would lie still as death, unconscious, barely breathing. Simeon was sure he would die.

In moments of wakefulness he would cry out to his friend: "Simeon, I lost the tablet," he moaned.

For six weeks, Areih hovered between life and death. The doctor came two or three times a day to dress the raw flesh on both legs. The nursing "team" were excused from all other partisan duties. They felt a communal responsibility to save his life, with Simeon insisting on taking a turn to sit beside him some nights, stroking his hand gently as he slipped in and out of consciousness. Mikhail and Oscar made a daring visit into Leningrad itself, behind the lines, to secure specialist burn balm from the Erissmann Hospital. They refused to tell anyone how they got into or out of the besieged city.

They had no painkillers to ease the boy's anguish when they dressed the wounds. Someone found some brandy, and they tried dripping that onto his tongue, but he hated it and spat it out. Generally, he lay perfectly still during the procedures, his face white as he bit on a rag that Rutti gave him.

"What will we do if he dies?" Oscar whispered to Rutti when, despite all the precautions, the wounds became infected and Arieh suffered with yet another high fever.

"Mama," he called pitiably. "Mama, where are you? I want my mama." Alternately he would scream for Simeon: "Simeon, I'm sorry. I didn't mean it." His voice was barely audible, but Simeon heard and would rush to his bedside whenever he could to stroke his arms and bathe his face and body in cool water to lessen the fever. His presence, however, seemed to agitate the boy rather than calm him.

In the end, Dr Gottleib insisted Simeon must stay away. However, he also dictated that Arieh ought to be lifted upright into a chair each day to prevent pneumonia setting in. They would support him with piles of sacking and old clothes to hold him upright. "Pneumonia will kill him," the doctor stated. "We have to guard against it, especially as you have no access to oxygen here."

Arieh would sit in the makeshift chair bed, propped up by coats and rags, his heavily bandaged legs raised above hip level to increase the blood flow to help with healing. Occasionally he cried. Mostly he just sat staring blankly into space silently.

Simeon longed to take the sick and injured child in his arms, to soothe him, to show him how much he loved him, but Arieh pushed him away. He tried to reach out to reconnect with Hanna, to beg for her advice, but it was as though their unique twin bond had finally failed. *Help me, sister. I didn't listen to your advice, and it almost cost this child his life. How can I help him now? How can anyone help him?* But there was no response, no answer. He was sure that he would know if Hanna was dead. Could that be why he couldn't get an answer from her? The invisible line that had previously stretched between the two of them had disappeared. He'd ignored her advice and let Arieh take part in Merteskov's mad plan, and this was the result. He was being punished for his stupidity. At night, he slept with one boot in either hand, as close as he could get to his amber tablets. He wished he knew what had happened to the third one, Arieh's Little Miss Honey. Was that what Arieh had been crying for? He'd taken it with him, ignoring Simeon's advice. He'd lost it, and because he'd lost it, it had abandoned him.

Gradually, and against all the odds, Arieh began to recover. After he'd spent three months in the hospital wing, it was decided to move him back to the Zemlyanka during the day to try to lift his mood, although he must still return to the hospital at night for the wounds to be dressed. Finally, slowly, the left leg seemed to be healed, but a thick yellow crust had formed on Arieh's right calf. The leg was stiff and movement almost impossible. Dr Gottleib said that just before the war, surgeons had made great strides in skin grafting. "Arieh really needs skin grafts carried out in a proper hospital under sterile conditions by specialist surgeons. In these circumstances, there is no chance of such a thing. We must just be thankful that the child has survived."

"He doesn't think so." Simeon stayed close to him, but he had been forced to resume work. Every night, he took off his boots and let Arieh stroke them for a little while. Arieh refused to speak to him: it was as though he was punishing his mentor. However, winter was coming. It was getting colder and the doctor thought it was a good idea to let Arieh spend two or three nights a week in his own bed, beside Simeon. One magical night, and to Simeon's huge relief, he suddenly spoke normally. The voice was reedy and tinny, just as it had been when he'd first spoken. "I'm sorry I ignored you, Simeon. If I hadn't done that, maybe my legs wouldn't have been burnt. I thought Miss Honey would keep me safe, but I was wrong. Are you mad at me for losing her?"

"No. She did her job. She kept you safe. You live. Perhaps that is why she insisted you take her. Maybe without her you would have died."

Arieh grabbed the heels of the boots and pulled them onto his lap, where he hugged them.

"Oh, Simeon." The floodgates opened. "I was frightened. She made me feel safe, especially when I couldn't take my violin back to Dasha's house every night. The night of the accident, I had her in my bib pocket. She must have fallen out when I was running away from the flames. When I woke up here, I felt for her, but I didn't have my trousers anymore, and Miss Honey was gone."

"Your trousers were burnt. I think Rutti must have thrown them away."

"No! Simeon, I'm so sorry I lost your amber tablet. You told me not to take it with me, but I had to. She didn't work. I'll probably be a cripple all my life and all because I disobeyed you."

"Shh," said Simeon. "It did its job, Arieh. Little Miss Honey saved your life, and that's all that matters to me."

On Arieh's eighth birthday, 5th October 1943 a group of his friends got together to throw him a party. Ethan had fashioned a crude trolley on wheels so that as soon as he was well enough they could wheel him around the camp. The cooks had managed to make a cake for him, an unheard of luxury in the camp. And to everyone's amazement, he had an unexpected visitor.

"Look who's here, Arieh. General Merteskov has come personally to wish you happy birthday. He has told many people of your heroism," Simeon said.

Arieh looked up to see General Merteskov in full military attire with all his medals attached to his uniform. As he approached Arieh, he took a box from his pocket.

"I have a very special birthday present for you," he said. "Stalin himself has sent me to honour you for your patriotic service to our country." Arieh pulled himself up straight on his little trolley and saluted. "Did you know you were personally responsible for killing more than seventy Nazi officers with your courageous action that night?" he said. "It's a shame we went for it the day we did. The following day, Himmler would have been there. However, in recognition of your service to the Union of Soviet Socialist Republics, you are awarded the Order for Courage in the defence of the Soviet Union in war. This is one of the highest military honours ever to be awarded to a boy of your age, Arieh Weinstein. Your country is proud of you."

He leant down and pinned the five-pointed little bronze medal with its blue-edged, grey and white striped ribbon on Arieh's chest. Arieh accepted his honour with a small bow from his waist. He grinned up at the general, the first time anyone had seen him smile for a very long time. However, the general hadn't finished. "What is so incredible is that you won this amazing victory by using the most peaceful of all the weapons I've ever heard of: a violin," Merteskov continued. "Yet I have never heard you play. Will you play for me now, Arieh Weinstein? Play the piece you were playing when the inn went up. Or I believe you know another of my favourites. I've been told it's one of yours, too. Mozart's 'Papageno-Papagena' song from *The Magic Flute*. Not generally a violin piece, I know, but it's full of fun, isn't it?"

Arieh motioned to Rutti to pass his violin. It spent its days lying on his bed, and at night it stood propped up by a strut underneath the wooden potato store. He hadn't picked it up once since the fateful day of the explosion.

He started to tune it, but it was more difficult to do whilst sitting down. He handed it back to Rutti and began to push against the side of his chair with both hands to haul himself up to a standing position. There was a communal gasp of surprise and then a general intake of breath. Rutti rushed to help steady him on the right side when he attempted to stand for the second time. This time, Simeon supported him from behind, leaving his arms free. With the violin in his hands, Arieh's face seemed to change. It became instantly less haggard and more relaxed. It looked as though the violin itself was soothing away his pain. But as he started to tune up, there was a sharp *ping* sound followed by another. The A string had snapped, followed immediately by the G.

"Oh! Arieh."

"They must have been affected by the heat," Rutti said sadly.

General Merteskov said nothing. He patted Arieh's shoulder with a sad look on his face and walked away.

"I'm finished. Without my violin, I'm nothing," Arieh cried.

"It's impossible during wartime to find replacement strings for a violin," Simeon told him gently.

Arieh nodded again. "I can't walk, and now I can't even play the violin," he whispered. "What point is there in living?"

Chapter 16

Hanna

⟡

EARLY IN MARCH, HANNA DEVELOPED A COUGH AND A VERY SORE THROAT. There was a pharmacy on Zamkova Street on the edge of the ghetto that stayed open late. She decided to stop there on the way home from work for some throat sweets and cough medicine.

She walked towards the pharmacy, which bordered the ghetto, trying hard not to look at the wretched, ragged children whose fingers curled against the inner barbed wire behind the fencing. They were always there, it seemed. They had the wizened features of old people, drawn and careworn, which made them look like adult dwarves. She reached her destination and a strange phenomenon struck her. The front doors of some of the houses had back yards inside the ghetto. The wire that separated the ghetto from the rest of Grodno through the back yards. The front doors opened onto the main street. As she watched, she saw a tall, dark man open the door of one of the houses and step back quickly to let a woman inside. Hanna stepped into the shadows and watched. She could see that strands of brassy yellow hair were tumbling out of the woman's headscarf, onto her face. Hanna stood still and watched, hidden in the shadows. The woman came out a few minutes later, and Hanna recognised her for sure. It was Elsa, her colleague from work. Hanna thought she ought to wait, wondering if she dare approach Elsa and speak to her, but it was dark and cold and she felt so ill. She was shivery and feverish. Blowing her nose hard, she thought she must be hallucinating.

Back in the priest's house, she declined dinner and crawled straight into bed. Thankfully, Father Dominic was not at home.

"I'll bring you up a hot water bottle and some hot broth. You must try to sweat it out, and you must keep drinking," Frau Olzswelski had told her before she'd gone upstairs. Frau Olzswelski was the nearest thing to a friend Hanna had in this place. She had come to work for "the good Father", as Frau Olzswelski called him, when Grodno was Polish rather than Byelorussian.

Hanna's throat was so sore that she could barely whisper her thanks. Curling her shivering body around the hot stone, she finally slept, dreaming of Nat and her dead babies and of Simeon.

It was soon obvious that Hanna's sickness was far more than just a cold. Her cough deepened and rasped, and a concerned Frau Olzswelski insisted that Father Dominic should send for the doctor. "What would your poor sister say if she thought you weren't taking proper care of her precious daughter, Father?" she chided him. "And what about Hanna's bosses? They won't be too pleased if you lose her. I overheard someone saying she heard Brandt speaking to Schlossberg and your little Maria is one of the Oberst-Gruppenführer's favourites."

With a raging fever, Hanna was hallucinating. She saw her beloved children playing at the water's edge and rushed to chivvy them inside. "Quick, quick, do what I tell you," she screamed as she chased after them. She was following, and they were all in the water. She could feel herself sinking, choking for breath, heaving as she sank. Down, down, down. She awoke choking, tossing madly, and fighting the sweat-drenched sheets. The cool damp cloth Frau Olzswelski held against her forehead became icy drizzle falling from the colourless skies.

Sometimes, she was aware of her own voice calling to them. "Shush, boys. Shush. Mama's coming."

"You must be quiet, or you'll wake the father," Frau Olzswelski cautioned her.

Sometimes Hanna would be calling for her brother. "Simeon, I need you. Where are you hiding? Come out. I need you." Past and present were confused in her dreams. She would open her eyes and kick back the sheets, ready to run, but at such times, Frau Olzswelski would place a warning hand on her shoulder. "Maria. Be still, dear. You will have Father Dominic coming up here to see what all the fuss is about."

Hanna was wracked by guilt, praying every difficult breath would be her last. "Dear Lord, what have I done?" she cried pitifully.

Frau Olzswelski tried to soothe her. "Nothing, my dear. You've done nothing wrong."

As the fever abated, Hanna would watch like an onlooker at a play as Frau Olzswelski sponged her thin torso. Every breath was an effort. Once or twice, she tried to apologise to the housekeeper if she'd spoken out of turn in her fever. "Don't worry, pet," she reassured her. "All of us have our little secrets. I'm not one for telling stories." Then she stood abruptly, as though she had perhaps said too much. "Better get that old rogue his dinner."

For Hanna, the greatest benefit from her sickness was that the priest, fearful for his own health, left her alone. It was three weeks before the doctor pronounced her fit enough to come downstairs for just a few hours, and she was amused to see that when she was warming herself by the large fire, reading or knitting, he kept his distance, making excuses to spend time in his study or "visit the sick". Frau Olzswelski shared the joke with her.

"Visiting the sick he may be, but he's missing out on the delicious chicken and vegetable broth I prepared for his dinner. Never mind. We'll enjoy it together," she said, spooning a bowlful into Hanna's plate and sitting beside her at the large pine kitchen table to eat it companionably together.

It was April before Hanna was declared fit for work again. At first she came in only in the mornings, building up her hours gradually. The other young women there showed apparent concern for her and were more inclined to bring her an ersatz coffee when they made one for themselves. They were more respectful. Acknowledging her leadership these days, they tried to include her in their inane lunchtime chats, even gently teasing her at times about her bossiness. She took to handing any sheets she'd "altered" to keep people out of the now infamous Grodno Ghetto Two to Elsa, who never queried them.

"Hey there, little priest's niece," Frederika said, stopping by Hanna's desk one morning. "We're going out for a drink with the boys tonight. Why don't you come?"

"Thank you, but no. I have to get home to my uncle."

"Surely he won't mind, particularly as it's Brandt's and Schlossberg's party. To celebrate Schlossberg's latest promotion to Oberst-Gruppenführer. I was quite surprised to learn that the old man wasn't invited. He's quite friendly with them both, isn't he?"

Hanna looked up, surprised. "Schlossberg had been making regular enquiries to see how you were all the time you were ill," she continued. "You must be quite a pet of his."

The last thing Hanna wanted was to spend any length of time in Schlossberg's company, whatever his rank. The more time she spent with him, the more likely he was to remember where they'd met before. Supposing he suddenly remembered. Her hair had grown considerably, and she was thinking of having it cut short again. Her short hair had been almost a camouflage. Supposing he denounced her publicly. Would they torture her, too? She had heard the screams of people being tortured from the cells in the basement. Whippings. Starvation. Did it matter what they did to her? She'd be justly punished for leaving her darling sons alone to face their deaths.

"Oh yes. Our big boss is undoubtedly devoted to you. Do you know, he even misrouted his own calls to us every so often to ask after your progress? Said he couldn't get any sense out of your uncle. He's really sweet on you."

Elsa, who had been standing just behind them, ostensibly filing some papers in the huge wooden cabinet, rested the sheaf on the open drawer and drew closer to Hanna. She spoke in a semi-whisper. "He's quite a catch, our SS-Oberst-Gruppenführer Schlossberg. He is a rising star in the estimation of the Führer himself, they say. Hitler apparently thinks the world of him. They're all set to break the link between Grodno and Minsk. They're taking the Grodno Ghetto into the Bialystok region of Prussia and putting Brandt in total charge, with a promotion of course, while Freddy Schlossberg is to run the far more prestigious Minsk office. As it is, they say he rules it with a rod of iron." *Good news,* Hanna thought. If Minsk was cutting the tie with Grodno, she wouldn't be forced to see or speak to Schlossberg anymore. She could deal with SS Kriminalsekretar Heinrich Brandt. What's more, perhaps there would be a physical move. She'd be able to follow the office to wherever it was relocated and escape of the old priest's clutches.

Schlossberg! Her mind darted back to the kitchen in Vidzy and how he'd unpinned her hair, stared at her from the doorway, smashed Nat's Klezmer violin, watched as the younger men had laid into the women and two helpless little boys. A giant of a bully. She must stay clear of him.

"Have you got a man at home?"

"Sort of." Hanna spoke the words wistfully. Not a day went by when she didn't think of Nat, wondering where he was, praying that he was still alive. She thought a great deal about her twin brother, too. However far apart they were, their minds remained chained together by such a strong bond that Hanna was convinced that their love and special kinship could span the world if it had to. *The rules of my life may have changed, and the world might seem upside down,* she thought, *but the one thing I'm sure of is that Simeon and I will never lose the closeness of twin-ship that binds us.*

"I'd really rather not come," Hanna insisted. "I'm still not fully recovered." It was bad enough working with the bastards, let alone having to socialise with them. She would rather put up with the old priest's sexual perversions. However, Frederika in particular seemed determined that tonight's outing would include Hanna. Later, Hanna wondered whether Schlossberg had actually bribed her. As the others readied themselves for the party, she was forced to give in.

"All right. Give me a few moments to ring my uncle. Can I borrow some lipstick and powder from one of you?"

Frederika grinned. "That's the spirit," she said, as Hanna picked up the telephone. Thankfully, it was Frau Olzswelski who answered. "He's out, but I'll tell him you won't be in for dinner. Have a good time, dear. You deserve it."

As Hanna put the phone down, she felt something approaching lightheartedness, better in herself than she'd felt in months. Brushing her hair and applying some of Elsa's very red lipstick was almost fun. She was going out for a drink. Was that so terrible after all she'd been through? She didn't have to talk to *him* or even to Brandt. She could listen to the other women talking about the shortages of clothing coupons, about the difficulties of obtaining the food they liked. She could even join in, perhaps. Not going wouldn't bring her babies back, nor would it reunite her with Nat or rekindle a 'virtual' conversation with Simeon. But what harm was there in having an evening out with a group of women?

It was damp and chilly as they left the office. Hanna was grateful for her warm overcoat. The frost and biting cold of winter had finally given way to a muddy, wet spring.

"Easter in two weeks. Four whole days away from the office," Elsa announced happily as they walked arm in arm towards the bar.

Hanna had forgotten about Easter. If it was Easter, it must also be near Passover. Was it only twelve months ago that she and Rachel had been cleaning the whole house from top to bottom in preparation for the festival? Shmuely had been busy practising singing the Four Questions, tutored by big brother Max. "Why is this night different from all other nights?" he had chanted, with Max prompting him. "On all other nights we may eat either leavened or unleavened bread, but on this night, we must eat only unleavened bread?" She could hear his little-boy voice now. Ironic, she thought, as she walked to an inn for a drink with her new German "friends", that the tune was playing round her head: "Mah Nish ta'na, hallilah haze, miko-ol hal'lay lot. Miko-ol hal'lay lot ..."

She started to hum it very softly. The very thought of it made her want to cry. She was forced to fake a cough so she could mop at her nose, eyes, and mouth without causing suspicion. To her surprise, Elsa started to hum the same well-loved tunes as they walked in step. Hanna looked at her. The brown eyes gave nothing away, but Elsa nodded at her in response to the unanswered question.

Hanna nodded her head.

They had reached the bar. As the door opened, the pungent odour of smoke mingled with the heavy bouquet of alcohol. The stench of stale bodies leeched out to surround them. People were standing around the bar and sitting on low stools at little tables, drinking and smoking. The sound was a pleasant hum of shared enjoyment, interrupted only by guffaws of mirth from some of the patrons. Schlossberg and Brandt were already there, standing in a group with a number of other high-ranking Gestapo and SS, laughing loudly. Brandt's gaze seemed firmly fixed on the décolletage of one of the barmaids. Schlossberg, however, spotted them coming in and moved towards them—towards Hanna, in particular, to her dismay.

"Maria, my dear. How lovely to see you again." He was looking as smart and official as ever in his black uniform, although inside the bar he had removed his hat. The long blond hank of hair fell over his face as he spoke, and he habitually pushed it out of those bright pale blue eyes. She remembered how evil, how menacing, those same eyes had looked in Vidzy. Now they appeared very different—relaxed, softer, smiling even. Was he a schizophrenic? He put up his hand and stroked her hair, removing her headscarf gently. "Pretty, pretty hair," he remarked. "But, my dear, you are so frail. So thin. Come. Will you have a beer, or perhaps you prefer wine?" He took her arm and guided her away from the others towards a table in the corner. Hanna turned to her colleagues, hoping they would re-engage with her, pull her towards them, but all of them seemed to be involved in chatting with other men themselves. She had no choice but to follow. A glass of wine? She must be careful. Just sip at it. Guard her tongue. She was unused to drinking.

"Water would be fine," she murmured.

"Come, come," he insisted. "A glass of wine will do you good. Red wine, perhaps? Or would you prefer white? A Riesling. Slightly sweet? Light with a fruity nose." He waved at the waitress behind the bar and caught her eye over the melee.

"Another lager, and a glass a of Riesling for the lady," he ordered.

"Thank you," Hanna murmured.

"Now, Maria Petruishka," he said, "I hope you will permit us to get better acquainted. First I will tell you about myself. I am married, and I have two daughters, but Monika and I have our differences. She objects deeply to me working away from home yet refuses to move here with our daughters. She won't even visit me here. I suspect it may have something to do with her 'boyfriend'. It has come to my notice that she is 'seeing'—excuse the euphemism—our doctor rather more than necessary for medical reasons."

Hanna wondered why he was telling her this. It had nothing to do with her or with the job. As he spoke, he exhaled a mouthful of cigarette smoke towards her. It caught in her throat, and she began to cough. "I must get outside," she whispered through the coughing. "Sorry. I can't cope with the smoke."

The waitress had placed the wine on the table. "Here, drink some," he insisted, lifting it to her lips and almost feeding her. To her embarrassment, she spluttered as she tried to drink it. "There, there. Of course, my dear. I'm sorry." He stood up and stubbed out the cigarette as she made for the door. He followed her outside, leaving his drink untouched on the table with several Deutschmark notes.

"Come. Let me take you home. Just the two of us. I want to know whether you've heard about the Minsk and Grodno offices being split into different units."

"I only heard tonight," she said. "Elsa told me."

"Ah!" he said. "Little Elsa. A good worker, I hear. I have a proposition to put to you. I would like you to come and work for me in the Minsk office. Little Elsa can oversee the transfer of the Grodno ghettos to the Bialystok region with Kriminalsekretar Brandt. I'd welcome your services over in Minsk as I reorganise there. It's a much bigger ghetto—far more administrative problems. What do you think? You'd be my private secretary."

Hanna bit her lip. "I'm not sure I'm up to such a task, sir," she said. Dear God! Was there no let-up for her? Working for him full time would be worse than now. She'd have to see him every day. Although it would mean, she reasoned, that she wouldn't have to tolerate the stinking Father Dominic and his vile sexual games anymore.

"Oh!" She didn't know what else to say. "Um, I'm not sure what my uncle will think."

"Leave him to me. He should be proud that his niece has made such an impression on such a high ranking man as an SS-Oberst-Gruppenführer."

She nodded. "When do you propose I move?" He was handing her into the rear seat of his chauffeur-driven car and climbing in beside her.

"The parsonage, please," he directed the chauffeur. To her dismay, he took her hand in his. "Maria, I wish I could remember when and where we've met in the past. It's driving me mad."

She shook her head. She had no intention of sharing her memory with him.

"If something needs to be done, I'm a firm believer that it should be done at once. I would like you to pack up your possessions here this evening and tomorrow. Leave everything packed in the hallway at the priest's house. I will arrange for Anton, my driver, to pick your belongings up tomorrow afternoon. You will hand over to Elsa at the Grodno office tomorrow during the day and say your goodbyes to your colleagues. Kriminalsekretar Brandt will be moving to new offices in Bialystok in the next few weeks. It's his fault you're leaving, you know." He laughed. "He says you are the best PA he's ever had. Dear little Maria, don't mention what I've told you about Monika in the office. It could be embarrassing. You see, the truth is, Maria, I don't mind if she has a lover. It makes my situation so much easier." He picked up one of her curls and wound his fingers round it, just as he had done on that terrible day in Vidzy. "Oh Maria!" he murmured as the car drew to a halt in the road outside the parsonage. "I have to tell you, I've fallen in love again myself."

Thank God. He's fallen for somebody else. I don't have to worry. He pecked her cheek as a friend might. "Anton's driving me back now, overnight," he told her as they parted. "I'll give him a few hours to rest. Then he can come back and fetch you. Be ready to leave the office at about 4.30 tomorrow afternoon. He can drive you to Minsk overnight. You'll sleep in the car and wake up refreshed the morning after tomorrow. Until the day after tomorrow, then." He blew her a kiss as the car sped away.

Chapter 17

Simeon

THE ROLE OF THE ETTINGER PARTISANS HAD CHANGED DRAMATICALLY SINCE the Central Committee of the Communist Party and the Red Army had reorganised and banded together to form the Central Staff of the Partisan Movement at the end of May. General Leonid Govorov had established the Leningrad headquarters of the partisan movement in July, and he tasked his new committee with centralising all planning for, and control over, partisan warfare in the area.

"We've received orders to sabotage and destroy as many German garrisons as we can in the area," Mikhail announced at a meeting of Ettinger leaders. "We need to offer more support to the Red Army ground combat operations. I think we might be able to use Arieh again. After all, who will suspect a young boy in a wheelchair as a potential terrorist?"

"Don't you think the poor child's done enough?" Rutti was furious. "If we hadn't agreed to Merteskov's mad plan for the gelignite attack in the first place, he might be walking around fit and healthy now. As it is, he's been deeply traumatised for the second time in his short life. How much do you expect one little boy to take? You and my brothers tend to forget he is only a child. He should have been out playing with footballs, not gelignite."

"He wanted to do it," Simeon protested. "He's a brave little hero, a real Russian soldier. There's talk that after the war, he will be awarded another medal."

"He doesn't want medals. He wants a childhood, and it's been stolen from him by adults intent on murdering one another," she said shortly. "He's already lost his mama, his papa, a baby sister, his home, his legs, and some of his sanity. What else can you take from him, apart from his life?"

"It's a shame Himmler wasn't there. It was rumoured he was to visit on the day the explosion happened," Oscar remarked, lighting a cigarette.

"For God's sake." Rutti was fuming. "All you care about, Oscar Ettinger, is your bloody war. What happened to your humanity? Did you leave it on a battlefield somewhere? You're becoming as bad as the bloody Nazis."

She turned her back to walk away.

"Come back, Rutti. I'm sorry. You're right, but he really could be useful now. Did you know that all 'replacement' units in the German Army have been deployed as anti-partisan forces?" Mikhail said. "They're scared of us. That's what we like."

Many of the local Leningrad partisan groups had moved out of the immediate area to safety, but the Ettingers, who now had almost six hundred members, were too large to move en masse to a safer location. The logistics of physically relocating everyone without drawing attention to themselves were very complicated. However, the numbers were advantageous in that they had a huge resource of manpower with a wide range of skills to call on.

"We're growing stronger and more powerful every day," Mikhail said. "I've been approached by a number of non-Jewish groups in the area, asking if we can join forces for certain operations. Of course, I agreed. The city is in desperate straits. The constant heavy fighting in and around Leningrad and to the south around Demiansk has already forced the Germans' Army Group in the north to reduce the size and number of its rear-area security installations. The Red Army are planning to launch a second battle at Lake Ladoga in the second week of January. They will be mounting a massive assault by the Leningrad North-Western and Volkhov fronts. It goes without saying that we are involved. They're planning a forty-five-hundred-gun bombardment, followed by relentless attacks from the reconstituted Second Soviet Shock Army, the Sixty-Seventh Army, and us of course. They're relying on us as a third line of defence. If Leningrad isn't freed very soon, the city will cease to exist."

"You told me that the Germans failed to take Stalingrad. Are we winning at last?" Arieh smiled as Simeon relayed the news. "What can I do, Simeon? Tell them I want to do something. Don't make me useless just because I can't walk."

When Simeon relayed Arieh's message, Mikhail smiled. "Tell him we're going to plant him in the centre of Peterhof in his wheelchair with a few sticks of gelignite to throw into a bar," he joked.

"That's not funny," Simeon said, leaping to Arieh's defence.

The plans had clearly set Arieh thinking. "I heard you talking to Mikhail earlier about disrupting the railway connections again," the boy retorted. "If someone makes me another trolley like the one the boys made me after the accident, I could lay bombs or mortars under the lines at ground level and wheel myself away faster than any of you can run."

Oscar was delighted when Simeon relayed Arieh's suggestion. "The boy has a point," Oscar agreed. "Especially if our newest engineering member, Isaac—ooh I can't remember his name, but he got out of the Novogrodek Ghetto, and God alone knows how he arrived here. Anyway, he could construct a lever on a low wheel cart so that Arieh could propel himself by moving it rapidly backwards and forwards with his arms. Then the boy and his exceedingly nimble fingers could be very useful again.

"Merteskov said ..."

Rutti saw Arieh look from one to the other, his small face full of hope. She was having none of it. "Simeon, you're as bad as Oscar and Mikhail. Merteskov says this. Merteskov does that. Meanwhile, a young boy barely eats, doesn't sleep. Have you looked at the black rings round his eyes recently, Simeon? You and your brave fellow partisan 'soldiers' can be proud of what you've put him through, and now you want to put him through more. You have all turned a little boy into an old man. No more. Do you hear me?"

"He wants to do it!"

"You don't let children do what they want, no matter what the circumstances. Do you let children run to play in the middle of the road just because they want to?"

Simeon knew what she said was true. The child had lost everything. And only he knew that in the seven months since the "accident", as they all referred to it, he had lost more than his legs. He'd lost the "safety blanket" of Little Miss Honey. Simeon could hardly tell Rutti that Arieh was in mourning for the tiny piece of golden-coloured resin. Although his slight body appeared free from danger, and the skin on his poor burnt legs was slowly healing, the child's mind was in turmoil. He suffered night terrors, and his fear-filled screams would wake Simeon several times a night with his little body shaking as his subconscious mind relived the gelignite attack. Even more heartbreakingly, he would wake himself screaming for his mama and papa. Everyone in the Zemlyanka heard him, yet still the only person he would talk to properly was Simeon, and then only in private. As Simeon knew all too well, he had two massive burdens to bear.

"I want to play my papa's violin," Arieh cried pitifully as he and Simeon snuggled up together for warmth in bed. It was bitterly cold, even inside the Zemlyanka. "I can't play anymore now. I want to play again more than anything in the world, but God is punishing me. With the A string and with the G string gone too, Papa's violin is useless. He will be so angry with me when we meet again."

"No, Arieh, God wouldn't punish you, and neither would your papa. You are the bravest boy any of us know. God knows, you've got more courage in your little finger than most of us have in our whole bodies. If I knew where to get you spare strings, I would do so."

It was Oscar who found the solution to the damaged strings. The Ettingers had become very friendly with members of the Kuzim family, farmers who often supplemented the partisans' diet with an odd chicken or an old milk cow that had outlived her usefulness. In return, the partisans protected their farm, crops and animals.

"The Kuzims have a violin that they don't play. It's hanging on the wall for decoration. I think it belonged to a grandfather," Oscar remarked, as he and Simeon discussed how to to draw the boy out of his depression. It was Oscar who dealt most frequently in bartering with the farmers and peasants.

"Here," said Simeon, fiddling with the watch he always wore on his left arm. "Take this. My father gave it to me, but it will be worth parting with it if it can jolt Arieh out of his misery. We don't need the whole violin. Only the strings."

"These days, they don't need bribing. The Kuzims are with us. They know what happened to Arieh, and they know we are fighting to open Leningrad again. They will help us. We defend their farm from against marauders after all. But I'll take it anyway."

Oscar took the watch. When he came back with not only one A string and one G string but also two spares, Arieh was jubilant. Oscar, who had played the violin for pleasure in that other life they'd all once led, helped him restring the broken instrument.

"Where did you get four strings from?" Rutti asked.

"I took the A string and the G string and then asked what they planned to do with the other two," Oscar said cheekily. "I told them a violin with only two strings couldn't be played, so they gave me one and left one on their violin, just so it wasn't naked."

"Never was a gift so precious," Rutti whispered to herself as she watched Oscar restring the violin for Arieh, their heads close together, deep in thought. "Just look at his face. He's transformed. He's the Arieh we used to know."

"Almost. But now comes the test. Let him play it. It's more than six months since he played a note. Come on then, boy. Let's hear you."

Arieh threw his arms around Simeon and hugged him. He looked up into his mentor's eyes. "Only if I'm forgiven for losing little Miss Honey?" he whispered.

"Forgiven," Simeon whispered back.

To their joy, Arieh launched into his happy "Pappageno" song. Simeon stamped his feet to the music, or that's what everyone thought. Arieh, however, knew that by stamping, Simeon was reconnecting himself with the two precious nuggets of amber concealed in his boots: two pieces of amber with magic sealed inside their coats of resin, a pair of tiny bite-sized morsels from a long-gone dismantled mosaic that he felt sure would not only protect him but also change the course of their lives.

Chapter 18

Hanna, April 1942

HANNA ARRIVED AT THE OFFICE AT A FEW MINUTES BEFORE EIGHT THE NEXT morning to find her colleagues at their desks, all of them already aware of her proposed move.

As she walked between the rows of typists towards her own desk, she was greeted with pats on her arm and murmurs of "congratulations" and "well done". Heinrich Brandt came to the door of his office and motioned her in.

"Take a chair, my dear. We're all so proud of you, but with such a rapid move, there's much to be done and only a few hours to do it."

"Given the choice, I'd rather stay here. I'm happy working for you."

"But what a promotion. Private secretary to Oberst-Gruppenführer Schlossberg der Waffen-SS. He's obviously been impressed by what I've told him about you. You'll get a pay rise, for sure. You know he's sending the car for you later this afternoon. I believe he arranged it all with you last night."

"I believe I have to hand over to Elsa and that she will go with you to Byelorussia. Is that correct? I still have to clear my desk here. I can't just walk away. I left my bag already packed. I was told his chauffeur, Anton, will collect it from my uncle's house before he collects me."

"Now, please, show Elsa what she has to do. She has always seemed very efficient. If only she wouldn't dye her hair so ... so yellow. It's almost orange. That's by the way. Of course, it's none of my business, but there's something I have to ask you. Is the old priest really your uncle? You are so unalike."

149

She shrugged her shoulders. "I'm like my father's side of the family," she said.

While they'd been talking, Elsa had dashed out to the baker's shop around the corner. She had returned with fresh bread rolls and much-prized strawberry jam. How she'd done it without coupons, they had no idea. She and one of the other women made coffee. As Hanna and Brandt emerged from his office, the typists gathered round her, laughing and chattering. It could have been a leaving party for a member of staff in any office, anywhere, Hanna marvelled to herself, if it weren't for the dreadful undertones of their work and the heart-rending cries behind the ghetto's barbed wire. Yet, how the hell had she got herself into this, working under a flag she despised with all her heart, for monsters of men who treated her own kind with such hatred? There was so much evil in this place, so much that was wicked and unjust. She looked up at the picture of Hitler in his full Führer's uniform, a man with a clipped moustache, beady little eyes, and the blood of countless Jews, as well as gypsies, homosexuals, and cripples etched in his soul. *What have I become? I'm as bad as them. Why don't I just confess and kill myself? It would be so much easier than living this lie.*

Heinrich Brandt appeared at 3 p.m. precisely, with a number of glasses and a bottle of champagne. "It's a little early for alcohol, I know, but this is a special occasion," he announced. "The promotion of our own great Friedrich Schlossberg to the rank of Oberst-Gruppenführer der Waffen-SS and his new personal assistant, Maria Petruishka. Elsa, you have a hard act to follow." Elsa nodded and dared to lift her eyes to meet Hanna's. For a short moment, the two shared a mutual antipathy of their work.

Hanna had just finished going through the books with Elsa when the latter declared she must use the bathroom.

"All that coffee and champagne." She excused herself, looking directly at Hanna.

Hanna picked up the message. "I might as well come with you so we don't waste any more time," she said. They looked at one another, hoping that none of the others might decide that they, too, needed a bathroom break.

Brandt merely raised an eyebrow and smiled. "What is it with you ladies and your synchronised bladders?"

As they walked into the white-tiled lavatories, Elsa pushed Hanna ahead of her into a corner cubicle and then climbed onto the back of the seat herself, motioning Hanna to sit down normally so that only a single pair of legs might be visible to anyone coming in and curious enough to look.

Squatting above Hanna on the small stone platform underneath the heavy porcelain cistern, Elsa bent low and whispered in her ear. "You know and I know, we're born of similar parentage." Hanna felt herself shiver. Was this the final trap?

Elsa, reading her thoughts, bent her mouth into Hanna's ear. "We are both more used to Mah Nish Tana at this time of year than to Easter-egg hunts, eh? No one else in here knows of the boys eight or nine years old who, thanks to your efficiency, suddenly qualify as fifteen-year-old carpenters." She stopped to catch her breath. "But I know them. My sister's in that house in the ghetto where you saw me. I have to trust you. Quick. Pull the chain." Hanna flushed the toilet to mask their whispers. "There's much to be done in Minsk. Memorise this name." She handed Hanna a piece of paper on which was written a name: Joseph Gavi.

"He's only a little boy, but it means he's a brilliant 'runner', able to pass messages and sometimes papers without suspicion. He will find you. Trust me. Now flush it away. Stand up." As she stood up, Hanna heard someone else come into the room. She emerged from the cubicle quickly, leaving Elsa standing on the seat inside.

As Hanna washed her hands, she saw a pair of legs in a cubicle two doors up. Had she and Elsa been overheard? She was almost sure that whomever was in that cubicle had come in after they'd finished speaking. As she left the cloakroom, she heard two flushes, one after the other, then voices exchanging polite banter. She couldn't catch what they were saying.

Hanna showed Elsa the meticulous diaries, the way the lists were administered. Together, they looked through the minutes of previous Judenrat meetings. Where Hanna had altered or changed a name or an occupation, she signalled with a double bounce of her forefinger.

By the time Anton the chauffeur arrived at the office, precisely at four thirty that afternoon, Hanna was ready. Brandt appeared on the steps with a posy of flowers, which he presented to her with great aplomb. She wondered where on earth he'd found such flowers. Rosebuds clenched tight, the outer leaves the freshest, gentlest green. They certainly hadn't come from any garden or park in this area. Then he delivered another brief speech. "Good to have had you here ... so popular with colleagues ... will be much missed ... going on to greater things." Hanna kissed the other office workers on both cheeks, each in turn.

Brandt himself handed Hanna into the car, placing a packed lunch in a wicker basket beside her. "Herr Schlossberg himself ordered this to be prepared from the kitchens of the Grand Hotel this morning," he said, stooping to kiss her. She looked down at the simple packet of sandwiches Frau Olzswelski had sent, along with her possessions and a brief note from that kind woman: "Stay well, Maria, and may your God go with you." She already knew what she'd eat on the journey, if she ate anything at all.

To Hanna's amazement, she suddenly spotted Father Dominic. He had appeared from nowhere and stood beside Brandt, his face puce with anger. "I had to come and say a proper goodbye, my dear little niece, since you rather rudely didn't seek me out. What a pity, after all the hospitality I have afforded you. I suppose you've been far too busy to think of your old uncle. Remember to be careful what you say, young lady."

He bent towards her inside the car and pecked her politely on the cheek. She returned the peck, holding her own breath against the stench of him, and nodded goodbye as he walked away. She wondered what he'd say when she'd gone. Settling herself against the creased brown leather seat of the official black Citroën, with a blanket tucked cosily around her knees, she pondered on the last few hours. She didn't look back as the car drove off north-eastwards on Darvina Road towards Levanaberazhnaya, and from there to pick up the Minsk road. She and the driver had disliked one another on sight, and he obviously considered driving her back to Minsk a chore he could have lived without.

"How long is the journey?"

"Between eight and ten hours," he answered shortly. "Twice in forty-eight hours is really too much, but then who am I to step over so great a personage as the Oberst-Gruppenführer's orders? Depending on weather and traffic conditions of course. One never knows on the roads now. The partisans. Such damage; you can't imagine!"

He offered no further conversation, and she was glad. She sat snuggling into the rug, gazing out of the window at the flat uninteresting landscape, realising she hadn't left the town once since arriving here almost ten months ago. It had been more than a year since she'd lost her precious sons. It hardly seemed possible how much her life had changed. Eventually, the excitement of the day, the warm smell of the old leather and the movement of the car lulled her to sleep.

They arrived at the Nazi headquarters in Central Square in Minsk at six o'clock the next morning. Several red flags emblazoned with large black swastikas on a white background fluttered in the breeze above the central swing doors of the Minsk Nebelstelle, below the large Gothic windows on the second floor. At this hour, the streets were deserted. The chauffeur jumped out and ran up the steps, leaving Hanna alone in the back of the car. She had just enough time to register where they must be when he reappeared. Friedrich Schlossberg was following him down the steps and let himself into the back beside her while Anton cranked the starting handle noisily.

Schlossberg bestowed a gentle kiss of greeting on Hanna's cheek as, after a couple of false starts, the engine roared to life. The chauffeur turned left out of Ostrovskaya Street, then left again, and stopped in front of a low white detached building set in its own garden behind black railings. Hanna couldn't believe that they had driven such a short distance, just a few metres.

"We could have walked," she said.

"Why, when there's a car to carry us?" the Oberst-Gruppenführer replied, smiling. The chauffeur, obviously both tired and irritable, handed them both out, clearly disapproving.

Schlossberg ran ahead and up to the front door. The door opened, as though whoever was behind it had been expecting him. He greeted the elderly woman with a smart salute and a kiss on each cheek. An old friend? A tiny person with brown hair coiled around her head, she was wearing a long black skirt and a long-sleeved black blouse despite the glorious sunny day. Obviously a widow.

"Maria, dear. This is Madame Denicoloa, your new landlady. Several of the girls from the office already board here. I'm sure you will be happy."

Madame Denicoloa might have been any age between forty-five and sixty. Her forehead was wrinkled as though it had been deeply carved by worry.

"I don't have much luggage," Hanna tried to explain in response to their quizzical looks. "Never had the time or money for fancy clothes."

Madame Denicoloa chatted in broken German as she led the way. "You will share the bathroom with three other girls. Fräuleins Darja and Sonja, both local girls, live in a double room on the ground floor. Anastasia, who I believe came with General Commissar Wilhelm Kube - who is in charge of this place - came from Berlin and has her own room here, next to yours." They had walked up the wooden staircase while they were talking. "This is yours. I hope you will find it in order," she said, taking out a key and unlocking the heavy door. She held it open, indicating for both Hanna and Schlossberg to walk in ahead of her. She continued gossiping as they walked into the spacious room, so different from the small garret in the priest's house. Hanna noticed that apart from the traditional heavy wood-framed double bed, there was a matching oak armoire, a dresser with several drawers, and a stool so that she could undertake her toilette in comfort.

The landlady was about to start chattering again when Friedrich Schlossberg cut her short.

"If you will excuse me, Madame, I am a bit short of time, and there are several details of Miss Petruishka's new job I need to explain to her before she arrives in the office on Monday morning. I'm sure you understand."

The landlady was clearly a little upset to be so curtly dismissed. She turned to leave, calling over her shoulder as she went, "You are permitted two baths a week. You will find the rota on the bathroom wall. You have a time allocated to your toilette each morning. I believe yours is six thirty. Please ensure you are on time. You have a ten-minute time slot." They heard her steps on the bare wooden stairs fade as she reached the bottom.

The unlined curtains had been drawn against the sunshine, so Hanna had seen the room in a filtered semidarkness. It smelt musty and damp despite its size, as though it had been unused for some while. She walked across to the window, drew back the curtains, and threw open the window, desperate to let some fresh air into this gloomy place. To her horror, the first thing she saw, protruding above the rooftops of the building opposite, was high barbed-wire fencing. Spikes jutted above the fencing, and a watchtower with armed guards bearing guns across their shoulders faced her. She was sure they must be able to see into her room. Certainly they would do so with a light on and the drapes undrawn. What was it, some kind of a prison?

"What's that?" she turned to ask Schlossberg, who had come to stand behind her.

"Oh, that! Don't worry about that. That's just the ghetto. It's much larger than the one in Grodno." As he spoke, she could see he was furious. "I did ask that stupid woman to allocate you a room overlooking the gardens. I suppose there were none free. I will try to get you moved immediately." He turned towards the door, but she stopped him.

"It's all right, sir," she said. He put his arms on her shoulders and turned her so her back was to the window.

"Let's talk about you, about us, shall we, dear Maria?"

He spoke the words softly. She tried to detect a hint of sarcasm in his voice but could detect none.

Us. What is he talking about, us? "You are my boss. I am your secretary. That's 'us', I presume." So he'd been talking about her when he confessed there was someone he was in love with. Was that only two nights ago? Of course, she should have realised there would be a price to pay for escaping Father Dominic's perverted claws. On the journey, she had pondered on Schlossberg's motives for moving her to Minsk. She had felt relieved when Madame Denicoloa had indicated that she would be living alongside other workers from the same office.

"Maria, surely you must know. You must have seen it in my face. My dear Maria." He moved forward and fondled her hair as he had done on several occasions in the past. She'd never forget that first time in Vidzy. She tried not to shudder at the memory.

"I'm in love with you, Maria darling. There. I've said it. I vowed not to say anything for at least a few weeks, but Maria, I just can't keep it to myself anymore. I've been in love with you since the first moment I set eyes on you somewhere in the dim and distant past."

She pulled sharply back, her face white with fear.

"I'm sorry," he said swiftly, aghast at what he saw as her obvious shock. "That was insensitive of me. It was too quick. Too much after today, after your long journey and all you've been through. You must be exhausted."

"We only really met at the priest's house and only spoke properly for the first time when we had a drink in Grodno two days ago," she argued weakly. "How can you be so sure of such a thing? Besides, you're married. I don't date married men." She'd said the first thing that came into her head.

"I told you, Maria. Our paths have crossed in the past before that. Perhaps it was in heaven, when we were both angels. You may have been in your Orthodox heaven and I in my Protestant one, but maybe there's no difference in the life of angels."

He, who had done such heinous things in his life, spoke of angels. She thought she would be sick. *I wonder how passionate you'd be if you did remember where we'd met before. Simeon, I need you to help me. Tell me what to do now, how to respond.*

The voice in her head replied instantly, *Stay away. Run away. Get out. For God's sake, Hanna, run away.*

I can't, the voice she knew as her own answered.

Schlossberg shot her a puzzled look. To her horror, she realised she had been speaking out loud to herself. He sank down in the deep purple velvet bucket chair, drew his silver cigarette case out of an inside pocket of his uniform, and offered her a cigarette.

She had never smoked in her life and looked up at him, anxiously. "Go on," he urged. "Take one. They're good for your chest. Here." He had put two in his mouth, lit them both and handed her one. She looked at the alien little white tube resting between the first and second fingers of her left hand as though she were seeing a ghost and took a small puff. At this moment, she felt that it was probably the only thing that would calm her. She spat out the small, loose shreds of tobacco on her tongue. He took a deep draw himself and looked at her in amusement. "You are not exactly a habitual smoker then." He smiled a soft smile that changed his face. He was making fun of her, but kindly. He handed her a clean white handkerchief, and she used it to wipe her nose and eyes, glowing cigarette still in hand.

Hanna had to admit, against her will, that Friedrich Schlossberg was an attractive man. He was tall and slim with straight blond hair. Yet she couldn't forget how that same blond quiff had fallen over his eyes when he removed his cap as he'd entered her home that terrible day in Vidzy. He was close-shaven with a perfect unblemished complexion, just as he'd been then.. The very idea of any kind of personal relationship with him was abhorrent. It was ironic really. Had they met in a normal peacetime situation, at school or at a coffee house in Krustpils, she would never have considered dating him, even if they had both been single, which of course he wasn't.

"I've always been impulsive," he continued. "As you get to know me better, you will learn it is one of my biggest faults." She wished she could choke again, but the cigarette had burnt itself out and she had pinched it to a dead stub between her fingers. She blew her nose and realised her fingers smelt of stale tobacco.

"My doctor has assured me the feeling that you have met someone before sometimes happens when you were soulmates in a previous life. And that is why you are familiar to me. You are my other half. My missing half. I will give you all the time you need to learn to love me. I will care for you, cherish you, and make you happy when you are ready."

My missing half. You can't be that. Not even Nat could be my missing half. That honour belongs entirely to Simeon, my twin. "You're married," she managed to blurt out.

"I told you, Monika is having an affair. I hardly know my children. My daughters will feel no great loss at my absence. After the war, I will divorce Monika. I will, of course, be the guilty party to safeguard her reputation. One day, my dear Maria, we will marry and have children of our own. We will be happy together. I will see my girls from time to time, of course. Wanda and Helga will understand and come to love you, too, in time. No one could help but love you." He stood up and walked over to where she sat on the bed and lifted her chin with his little finger. "You will bear my son one day. A little boy with red hair like his mama."

Her eyes had no choice but to meet his. He ran his fingers gently across her forehead, stroking her hair.

"I may not be good at remembering faces. I meet so many people in a day. But I could never forget that exquisitely glorious crown of sun-blessed hair; hair so red that a golden halo shimmers around it in sunlight, hair so alive that it mimics a Mediterranean sun sinking to the horizon even on a snowy winter's day. It's the most beautiful hair, belonging to the most beautiful woman in all the world. Since that first day I saw you in that vile old man's vestry, I knew that hair belonged to the woman I intended to marry. There. I've shocked you again. I'm sorry." He sat down beside her on the big double bed, took her hand in his, and patted it firmly. "Don't fret, sweetheart. There's no rush. I'll give you all the time you need. I have to. You are the woman of my dreams."

She had no alternative but to play the game.

He kissed her lips then. To her own dismay, there was an instant when she almost wanted to kiss him back. She closed her eyes and imagined Nat's lips on hers. Then images of her mother-in-law and sons did a three-dimensional dance in front of her eyes, and she had a sudden violent urge to bite him. She wanted to see him bleed and hold his mouth in pain.

"There. Now you know my intentions are entirely honourable. Oh, my sweetheart! I'll leave you to settle down. Eat, sleep. I will see you in the office on Monday morning. No, wait a moment. I'll tell you what. Have dinner with me tomorrow night? You will meet little Sonja tomorrow during the day. I'll ask Madame Denicoloa to introduce you. As she, too, is Orthodox - I think - perhaps you can walk to church together on Sunday morning. Unfortunately I have to go back to Heidelberg on Sunday to see my girls. I promised. I haven't seen them since Christmas. I will collect you at seven forty-five prompt tomorrow evening." With that he was gone.

Hadn't Elsa warned Hanna that Frederick Schlossberg was sweet on her? God, was that only earlier this week? It felt like a lifetime ago. Dear God, he said he was in *love* with her. She gazed out of her bedroom window towards the ghetto walls. "So, Hashem, what other fine tricks do you have up your sleeve to throw at me?" she asked the sky.

Chapter 19

Simeon and Arieh

B Y EARLY 1943, AS THE RED ARMY MOUNTED MORE FRENZIED ATTACKS ON the German artillery, it became clear that the Germans on the Finnish border were losing the will to fight on. Everyone inside the partisan camp was still aware of the merciless nightly raids on Leningrad. Simeon was often out on duty, as were all the other able-bodied men and some of the boys, defending the outskirts of the city the best way they could. Arieh, who looked on enviously as boys only two years older than himself went out with the men, again sank into a deep depression. He couldn't go with them. He was only eight years old, and they all knew that it was impossible for a severely disabled child to be part of sorties. "Your job is to keep up morale," Simeon reassured him. "We battle the bloody Nazis all day and sometimes all night. When people come back from difficult operations, they need to relax. You can help them. We may not have much food for our bodies, but we need to feed our minds with pleasant sounds. Your music is one of the most pleasant sounds in all the world."

It was hard going. Many men and women were coming back to camp with serious injuries. There were some days when two or more of the "bosses" went out together, which generally indicated something major was afoot.

One evening in mid-April 1943, Simeon and Rutti called a general assembly for everyone in the camp. "You may have noticed that Mikhail and Oscar have been missing for the past few days." Simeon spoke into the loud hailer so all around could hear him. "They have been attending high-level talks with the command of the Fifth Partisan Brigade of the Red Army. Commissar Ivan Sergunin, Commander Colonel Konstantin Karitsky, and chairman of the Luga regional committee of the All-Union Communist Party Ivan Isakov have asked us to work hand in hand with them and with other partisans in the Leningrad oblast. They are opening a corridor into the city to allow food, fuel, medicines, and other essentials to reach the siege survivors and bring some relief from their misery. It is said that almost a million have died of starvation so far, and more are dying daily. The brothers will return in a few days with our new orders. Be prepared. The days ahead will not be easy, but you are all fighters."

A narrow corridor had been opened to allow small quantities of food and medical equipment into the city, but these weren't nearly enough. "Mikhail and Oscar have been in meetings with our old friend General Merteskov, and Merteskov, together with Govorov, has proposed an offensive to cut off, encircle, and destroy German forces in the Mga and Siniavino regions. Zhukov, another old friend of ours, has recommended that the Staka broaden the offensive to destroy Army Group North completely and liberate the entire Leningrad region. They're calling it Operation Polar Star. The North-Western Front is to attack from the Demiansk area through Dno and Luga to Pskov and Narva on the Gulf of Finland. Simultaneously, the Leningrad and Volkhov fronts are to attack the Eighteenth Army around Leningrad and ultimately link up with the North-Western Front's forces to encircle almost all of German Army Group North, south of Leningrad. Our part in this massive offensive against the enemy is to totally disrupt and disarm their communications without affecting our own. The offensive is to commence on the 8th of February. Are you ready?"

There was a simultaneous uplifting of rifles alongside joyous cries of "We're ready." Only one small person sat silently: Arieh.

"I want to be part of this. I deserve to be part of this," he whimpered.

"You will, but in ways that will ensure you stay safe."

Each evening before he went to bed, Arieh would bend down, pick up Simeon's smelly old boots, and talk to them softly. "I'm sorry your sister went missing," he would apologise, stroking the heels. "Wherever Little Miss Honey went, it still saved my life. That's what Simeon says. Please, let me be useful to the Ettingers again."

It seemed to Arieh that Simeon's boots were listening.

"The corridor is twelve kilometres wide into Leningrad, and you could help us if you're willing to," Simeon told Arieh just before they went to sleep on a freezing January night. "Drugs are desperately needed at the Erissmann Hospital on Apertesky Island right inside Leningrad. They have an outbreak of typhoid there, but no drugs. If I were to transport you and your little trolley there, you could wheel yourself up to the door with as many drugs as we can get our hands on, load them onto your trolley, drop them off, and come back to where I'll be waiting. No one will suspect a crippled boy. How do you feel about that?"

Ethan had adapted Arieh's trolley and affixed a chair to it so that he could sit higher to see where he was going. He'd added the handle so that Arieh could work it. It was a crude but efficient method of getting around.

"I worked there once, before I had the amber tablets, but I can't go back," Simeon explained. "But you can, Arieh. There is no reason why I can't transport you and your makeshift wheelchair to meet up with one of the trucks that is going through regularly now. They can take you in and drop you at the gates. You could take more drugs in than we can carry and hand them to the named doctor who will be waiting for you. Nobody will suspect a cripple of smuggling. They'll think you're going in for treatment."

"I hate the word *cripple*," Arieh protested. "Yes, I'll do it. Of course."

Twice Arieh ran the gauntlet. However, the nearer they seemed to complete liberation, the worse conditions seemed to get. When a man was gunned down at the gates of the Erissmann because he was believed to be carrying bread in for patients, it was decided they would take no more chances. The Red Army were, however, arming increasing numbers of partisans and taking them to fight at the front. "Every man, woman, boy, or girl over the age of twelve and under the age of eighty will be issued with a rifle and trained to use it," Rutti announced in March. "Those who do not bear arms will cut down telegraph poles to disrupt communications between the Germans. We must blow up specific railway lines we know they are using. This is the final push. We are the Red Army's Second Army. As such, we must work together, comrades, to cause as much chaos for our fleeing enemies as we can, while at the same time bringing relief to our besieged brothers and sisters not twenty kilometres away from here."

Suddenly Simeon thought of Hanna and wondered where she was and what she was doing to aid the fight against their enemies. If she were here, he was sure she would be the first to volunteer to use a rifle. She would see it as her duty to fight for Mother Russia. He hadn't thought of his sister in several weeks, yet suddenly he could see her in his mind's eye, dressed well, not as the partisan women here were dressed, most with filthy faces, greasy hair tied tightly in headscarves, coats belted with string to hold them closed, heavy socks, and thick boots, shouldering rifles and marching proudly to war against the Nazis. In the image that flitted across his mind, Hanna looked the way she'd always looked, neat and tidy, her hands soft and white, the nails neatly filed and shaped, her clothes clean and relatively fashionable, her red hair dressed in a pretty chignon, her blue eyes shining as they always shone when she saw him. He wondered whether she could see him now through that bond that drew them so close. Where was Hanna?

Arieh tugged at Simeon and pointed to himself. "I am eight years old now. I'm not a baby anymore. I'll be nine in October. I can shoot well, better than most twelve-year-olds. You've seen me practise shooting. Even sitting on my trolley, I'm a good shot. Without the chair on the trolley, I can get them straight in the balls."

Simeon laughed but wagged his finger sternly. He pulled his hands out as though holding a rifle. "No," he insisted. "It's too dangerous, Arieh. You'd be a sitting target."

It had been more than two years now since the "accident," yet the skin on Arieh's right leg was still pitted and often split open with weeping sores in places. It still needed dressing every day with clean boiled bandages. The bone was healing and growing back, but the muscle and tendons were so badly damaged that the leg was virtually useless. Arieh was using the crutches Ethan had made for him more frequently, but his armpits were raw and blistered despite the padding. He amused himself by sitting on his trolley for hours, playing his violin softly to himself.

"We've been asked to help rebuild the Shlisselburg–Poliany railroad. We'll be opening regular rail communication with the city and the rest of the Soviet Union soon," Simeon announced one morning in May. "Unfortunately, Mga station is still in enemy hands, and they've maintained a tough presence in the area, which means that it's carrying capacity is low. It's all heavy, dangerous work. Our people need to come home to an area that it is both as relaxed and as pleasant as we can make it. That's your job now, Arieh. We don't have any other musicians to play for our own brave heroes in the camp. Let them know that culture and civilisation still exist in this mad, war-torn world."

Simeon was on guard duty much of the time when he wasn't organising operations. Occasionally, he took Arieh with him, pulling his cart to maximise both silence and speed and to give his young friend the feeling of both participation and worth. It was on one such night that the pair's ears pricked as they heard movements in the undergrowth.

"Could be a bird, or even a fox," Arieh mouthed to Simeon.

They didn't need to wait long to find out the reason. Two men walked towards them, one tall and upright, his black hair slicked back neatly behind his ears. He was carrying the head end of a stretcher. The man carrying the foot was a stranger in the uniform of a senior sergeant with a thick red band running across his shoulder. He caught sight of Simeon and Arieh.

"Nikita Popov, Senior Sergeant First Class." Simeon saluted. Arieh copied his mentor.

"We bring you your comrade, Oscar Ettinger. He was shot in the foot during an engagement. We are fighting not far from here, near Lake Ladoga. The wound is healing, but we have another, more pressing need of you."

"Thank you for bringing Oscar home. What is it you want of us?"

They looked at the stretcher. Oscar was sitting up, his eyes moving from one to the other. Mikhail stepped forward. "I will go back with you, Sergeant Popov, as a replacement for my brother," he said, saluting smartly.

"You will do no such thing. You will remain here. You take his place, Lieutenant Engineer Third Class Simeon Karminsky. It is fortuitous that you are here, Lieutenant Engineer Karminsky. We need you. We constantly require running repairs in the field. There are battles raging on many fronts right now, and your professional training would be invaluable, particularly your experience with tanks."

Simeon nodded. "In the past, on the field of battle, I could do nothing with the tanks. You already know that. What use will I be now?"

"You have expanded your repertoire with the partisans. You are adept at fixing rifles that stick, at revitalising guns that refuse to shoot or that shoot too often."

Simeon shrugged. "I will go back to camp and collect my things."

"You will come now. The army will provide all you need. Comrade Ettinger, you will take this young man back to your encampment. Lieutenant Engineer Third Class Simeon Karminsky has been taken in place of Comrade Mikhail Ettinger to join the fight from the field headquarters."

Simeon made to appeal. Popov took out a gun. Simeon stamped his feet and saluted. Only Arieh and Simeon knew that the stamp had nothing to do with showing proper respect to the sergeant or the motherland. It was to connect Simeon with his boots and their tiny secret "passengers".

Oscar Ettinger placed a protective arm around Arieh as they waved goodbye to Simeon. Being an active participance and back in the army came almost as a relief to Simeon. Active service meant more than serving. It meant pride. For the most part, he sat in an armoury, repairing damaged instruments of war, while the Germans were inflicting heavy losses on the Russian partisans in retaliation for their own losses, only to discover that the tide had turned Russian citizens against them. The whole population, it seemed, had turned into partisans, working alongside the official partisan brigade to inflict damage on the interlopers. By mid-May 1943, the expanded partisan and underground structure was conducting a propaganda war against the invaders, publishing underground newspapers and pamphlets, and coordinating reconnaissance and diversionary movements in support of formal Red Army military operations. Simeon was at the heart of the planning, as well as operational in the battle.

"I was there. It was good. I got my own back on those bastards for ruining the lives of so many of our people. I just wish that I knew that my sister was somewhere safe," Simeon told the Ettingers on his return.

On 27 January 1944, Simeon, Oscar and Rutti gathered with the entire Ettinger partisan brigade, stood in the snowy forest to hear the momentous broadcast from Moscow over loudspeakers attached to the radio:

"The blockade of Leningrad, which has been besieged since German forces cut the land link to the city on 8 September 1941, is finally at an end. Soviet soldiers broke through the German line of defence at key points and recaptured hundreds of towns and villages in the region, according to a Russian communiqué issued by General Leonid Govorov, commander of the Leningrad front. It is believed that hundreds of thousands of Leningrad's population of two and a half million have died of starvation, exposure, disease, or enemy action since the 1st of September 1941. The German Army reached Leningrad soon after invading Russia on 22 June 1941 but stopped short of taking Russia's second city after facing fierce resistance and decided instead on a blockade. All land communication was cut off and the city subjected to air and artillery bombardment daily. The harshest winter in decades added to the suffering of Leningrad's starving inhabitants, but this was partially eased when Lake Ladoga froze, opening a truck route to bring in food and fuel over the ice.

"All able-bodied citizens did their bit to defend the city by working in munitions factories, digging defences, and serving in the front line. Now, one year after General Govorov managed to open a corridor into Leningrad, the blockade has been totally lifted. A task of historical importance has been completed', General Govorov announced. "The city of Leningrad has been completely freed of the enemy blockade and of the barbaric artillery shelling. I thank the troops of the Leningrad front and the sailors of the Red Banner Baltic Fleet and praise the citizens of the city for their heroic work and steel-like steadiness in enduring the siege that lasted for 872 days.'"

Loud cheers emanated from every corner of the camp. Finally, despite the bitter cold and the dire deprivations of camp life, it appeared that the worst was over.

Ethan had attached a crude but effective wooden calliper to Arieh's right boot. He'd made the boy a pair of boots from scraps of leather. The callipers reached to the thigh of Arieh's right leg, keeping it straight and allowing him to stand tall on both legs. The new boot to which the calliper was attached was heavily built up on the right side so that when he was upright, his legs were even in length. It was another of Ethan's marvels. The boy joined everyone else now, standing to cheer, waving his left arm in the air with excitement.

"Thank you, Papa, for trusting me with your violin," he called. The violin lay beside him. Suddenly, he knew what he had to do. He picked it up and began to play the opening notes of "Hatikvah"—a song whose title translated to mean "The Hope". It was already Jewish Palestine's anthem for the future. One day, thought Arieh, perhaps it might be the national anthem of the future state of Israel they all dreamt about. The voices of the 732 members of the Ettinger partisan brigade were raised in song to join the music of Arieh's violin:

"Kol ode belavoh, p'neimah ..." they sang in Hebrew. A few knew the Russian translation:

As long as within our hearts, the Jewish soul sings.
As long as forward to the east,
To Zion, looks the eye—
Our hope is not yet lost.
It is two thousand years old.
To be a free people in our land, the land of Zion and Jerusalem.

He finished playing. The entire crowd broke into wild applause.

"We have a surprise for everyone," Rutti announced. "In anticipation and celebration of the fantastic news, local farmers and growers who've been active alongside the partisans at this time are joining us tonight. They have kept us fed, even during the most difficult years. They have brought food for us to enjoy with them tonight. Many of them have relatives in the city. They say this is their way of thanking us for all we've done." The feast of roasted chicken and potatoes to feed more than seven hundred people was yet another miracle.

Suddenly, Oscar broke through the jolly crowd and whispered something in Simeon's ear. Simeon, in turn, whispered to Mikhail.

Simeon turned to Arieh and the rest of the Ettingers. "I'm sorry to break up the party, but Mikhail, Oscar and I have to go. Someone's ridden over from the Zelnick partisans. They need us. Can we have a dozen volunteers to come with us? The rest of you, carry on celebrating. Don't let us break up the party."

It was grim reminder amid the joviality that despite the triumph, they were still at war.

It was at one o'clock on Sunday morning that Rutti shook Arieh awake. "They've just brought Simeon back."

Arieh was instantly alert. "He's been shot," Rutti continued. "Hopefully the wound isn't deep, but he's bleeding a lot. And he's calling for you."

"I'm coming." She helped Arieh into his calliper boot. He picked up his crutches and followed Rutti to the hospital Zemlyanka. Simeon lay on a pallet, his face beneath the curly ginger beard a ghostly white. It seemed to Arieh that he was barely breathing.

"What happened?" Arieh asked urgently "Simeon, please don't die. I need you. I need you now more than ever."

Mikhail was standing just behind him. "You spoke. We heard your voice. Bravo." He put a firm arm on Arieh's shoulder. "He's not going to die," he reassured Arieh. "It's only superficial. We were on the way back from the meeting when somebody in the forest took a potshot at us. He caught Simeon's thigh. I think they must have hit an artery. We managed to halt the worst of the bleeding with a tourniquet. Between us, we managed to carry him back here, but there are lone Nazi gunmen out there, shooting blindly at anything that moves. They know they're beaten. They're just trying to disarm us. I have to leave now. Do what you can."

Rutti and Arieh stared at one another. Arieh was the first to speak. "First, we must hydrate you," he said firmly, remembering the words from his own sickbed. "Dr Gottleib will be here in a minute." He grabbed a spoon and a cup and began dripping small droplets gently onto Simeon's tongue, as he remembered Rutti had done for him.

"You're in capable hands, I see, Simeon. If I remember correctly," Rutti said, turning her attention to Arieh, "you were in an even worse state when we picked you up two years ago. With your nursing skills, he'll survive." Rutti was smiling down at him.

Simeon managed a weak smile in return.

"Let me get your boots off."

"No, no, no." Simeon lifted himself on his elbows with renewed strength. "Arieh, you take my boots off."

Arieh knew immediately what the problem was. Gently he removed Simeon's boots and handed them to him. As they lay on his chest, and with all his remaining strength, Simeon shook them. "Help me, amber tablets," Arieh heard him whisper under his breath. "Help me."

Chapter 20

Hanna

ANNA HAD BEEN FAST ASLEEP WHEN SHE WAS AWAKENED BY A SUDDEN sharp pain in her left thigh. She turned over and looked at her alarm clock. It was seven thirty in the morning. She had been awake on and off for hours and longed to sleep more. Her leg was really hurting. She looked down, and to her amazement she saw a little round hole in her thigh. It was oozing blood and hurt like hell. It couldn't be a bite? She wished she hadn't drunk so much alcohol last night.

Frederick Schlossberg had called for her on the dot of 7.45pm last night as he'd promised, with Anton at the wheel of the official black Citroën. As they drew up outside the Grand Hotel Excelsior, she fought to stop her jaw dropping. Never in all her life had she entered such an opulent place. Schlossberg took her arm and escorted her up the mottled brown marble steps into a reception area where dark oak-panelled walls were decorated with expensive-looking antique paintings and deer heads with staring eyes and complete with antlers. Young boys in smart dark green uniforms with little box caps manned the reception area. Plush plum velvet chairs were set in twos and fours around tiny marble coffee tables in the lounge. White-gloved waiters in smart black and white dinner suits served drinks to the exquisitely dressed clientele. It seemed to Hanna that this place was a film set, not the real shabby, dirty outside world of war. In her simple blue "best" dress, she felt shabby. She had no idea such wonderful clothes still existed, even during a war.

As they walked through, it was obvious Schlossberg was known here. "SS-Oberst-Gruppenführer Schlossberg, good evening. So nice to see you again. Congratulations on your promotion, sir."

The head waiter took Hanna's coat and handed them both large menus written in French. She noticed hers had no prices underneath the entrée listings. Schlossberg whispered something to the waiter that Hanna didn't catch. He held her hand, fondling it as the same waiter reappeared and served them with the drinks he'd ordered, a whisky sour for himself. He requested a long, orange-coloured drink with a red liquor at its base that he told her was called a tequila sunrise. It was delicious, but she could taste the alcohol. And knowing how unused to it she was, she declined a second.

The head waiter reappeared and took the food order. Hanna let "Frederick", as he insisted she should call him here, whilst he was off-duty, order for her. The penguin-suited waiter led them through a gangway between tables laid with crisp white damask cloths, gleaming silver cutlery, and fine polished crystal glasses. Men in evening suits or uniforms were accompanied by women in long evening gowns with elbow-length gloves. She had thought her Sunday-best dress with its draped body most elegant, but she felt decidedly the poor relation in this sophisticated and clearly moneyed company.

To her relief, their table had been reserved in a quiet corner. "I apologise. I am not correctly dressed," she whispered to Frederick. "I'm sorry, but I don't own a ballgown or even a cocktail dress."

"You look wonderful. Forget their fancy dresses, most of them entirely inappropriate for their ages." He smiled. "You are without doubt the most beautiful woman in the room." He produced a small box and placed it in front of her. "Go ahead. Open it."

Inside on a bed of blue velvet lay a pretty ring with a sapphire centre surrounded by tiny diamonds.

"Try it on?"

He took the ring out of the box and placed it on the middle finger of her right hand. It fitted perfectly.

"It's lovely," she said, holding her hand out to admire it. "I'm not sure what to say."

"Nothing for now, my dear. Just wear it and enjoy it."

Enjoy it. She thought of another ring, a ruby, also in a diamond setting, that Rachel had given her and which was now residing in the original black velvet bag in her underwear drawer. She looked at her hand again, wondering how one man could be so kind and generous in one set of circumstances yet so mean and utterly evil in another. The words fell from her mouth before she could stop them.

"Why do you hate the Jews so much, Frederick? What have they done to you?"

His face changed as though a mask had fallen across it. The benign smile vanished. His ice-blue eyes shot their frozen shards, his lips barely moved as he spat out the words: "They're vermin. Greedy, lying, filthy subhumans who thought they could rule the world."

"Even the children?" Now that she'd started, she couldn't stop herself.

"They'll grow up like their parents. Dirty, lying toads. Some have learnt how to steal already. We see children of six or seven escaping through holes in the wire, finding the markets and thieving. It's mostly food, although sometimes they steal clothes or things they can trade. It's inborn, this behaviour. Most of the adults were manipulating our money markets, running the media, pulling off illegal trade. I told you before. They would have been ruling the world if we hadn't stepped in to stop it. They have this foul stench. You can smell them a mile off. Their women breed like rabbits. I've heard they all have small bony protrusions in their skulls, the remnants of horns, although I've never seen them myself." He smiled with his mouth, but his eyes remained frost. "For one moment there, I thought you were going to tell me you are a secret Jewess, Maria."

Hanna fingered the little gold cross at her neck. "Hardly," she replied.

She looked down at the ring, sparkling as it reflected the chandelier above their heads. His eyes had reverted to a softer blue.

"No more talk of scum Jews," he said tersely, arranging his face back to a pleasanter smile. "So you like it? The ring?"

"How could I not? It's beautiful. Thank you." He was stroking her hand now. She wanted to snatch it away. How could one man be so two-faced? She knew now that it was inevitable she would have to sleep with him. The ring gleamed on her finger. She hated it. It was the colour of his eyes. The waiter removed the remains of their hors d'oeuvres.

"You didn't eat much. Didn't you like it?" Schlossberg asked as two large silver covered plates were brought to the table by two waiters, who lifted the lids together with a carefully choreographed flourish. "I ought to have asked you, I think, before ordering. But you'll enjoy the steak tartar, I'm sure."

Hanna looked at the raw meat on her plate. She hated the sight of bloody meat now more than ever, and the sight of it was too much. She took a tiny mouthful and managed to swallow it, but the texture of her second mouthful was too much. She felt herself choking. How could she sit here eating this exquisitely prepared meal and drinking fine red wine while her own people were dying of starvation not two kilometres from here? The food was coming back into her throat. She dashed out of the room with her napkin to her mouth, her exit followed by the curious stares of other diners.

Pull yourself together, she told herself as she finished vomiting into the toilet bowl and wiped her mouth. She emerged from the cubicle to see an older woman in a long lavender gown, her grey hair dressed in a pretty chignon held by a diamond clip, standing waiting patiently for her. "Are you all right, dear? Your boyfriend is most concerned."

"Something got stuck in my throat," she excused herself apologetically.

"Something got stuck in my throat," Hanna apologised to Frederick as she returned to the table. Thankfully, the meat had been removed.

"Take a little wine," he advised. She drained her glass.

"Dessert? Coffee?"

"Coffee would be lovely."

He ordered a crème caramel for himself. While she sipped her coffee, he offered her a taste, which she refused. She couldn't eat from the same plate as him, let alone from his spoon. He ordered brandy for himself. She declined any more alcohol. Afterwards, he'd taken her straight back to her lodgings, clearly concerned about her white face. He'd kissed her chastely on her forehead. She had let herself into the house and gone straight to bed without even removing her make-up. In her dreams, Nat and Simeon were disgracing her in public for consorting with Nazis.

That had been last night. Now the young woman who called herself Sonja, the one Frederick Schlossberg had said would go to church with Hanna, was standing right in front of her. She couldn't be older than seventeen, Hanna thought. She was a dainty figure with dark brown eyes that seemed too big for her face and with hair the colour of polished chestnuts, styled into a neat bob.

"Madame Denicoloa told me you were Orthodox and I wondered if you'd like to come to church with me this morning, Maria. I go to the Church of Simeon and Alena. We could meet downstairs in half an hour."

Hanna grunted and hoisted herself unwillingly onto one elbow. The Church of Simeon? That was a coincidence. She was unsure of Sonja or her motives, but if she had to go to church, where more apt than the Church of Simeon?

"OK," she replied. The door opened and closed shut, but when she pushed back the covers, Hanna saw Sonja was still standing there. She looked down at the makeshift tourniquet Hanna had tied round her leg.

"What the hell have you been doing to yourself?" she whispered. She put a finger to her lips. "You went out with our newly elevated Oberst-Gruppenführer last evening, I hear. Did he rape you? Surely not. He's a gentleman if nothing else. Here, let me see."

"No, of course not. I woke up with this mark on my leg this morning."

Sonja shrugged. "Are you really a practising Orthodox Christian?"

"Yes. Are you?" She could hardly believe she had dared to challenge her new friend.

"I am. Quick. Get dressed."

As they left the room, Hanna was limping. She picked up the little black hymn book Father Dominic had given her last Christmas.

"We'll grab a quick coffee and go. We'll talk on the way to church. Walls have ears in this place."

As they stepped outside the front door with Sonja leading the way, Hanna decided she must tell someone about last night. There was something about Sonja that made her instantly trust her.

"I've got a problem. The Oberst-Gruppenführer declared his undying love for me last night. I wouldn't call it passionate love or reciprocal. Do you still want to walk to church with me?" she asked, wincing. She was limping. Every step hurt.

"Well, you came here because of him. He took a special interest in seeing you settled, and everyone in the office knows he's paying your rent and that he took you on a date last night, even though you haven't even started work yet. However, one of the girls from the Grodno office already warned me that he thinks he knew you before Grodno. Is that true?"

"Yes. But I don't remember meeting him before." This was becoming a dangerous conversation. *There,* Hanna thought. *Even if he has sent Sonja as a spy, he'll learn nothing more.*

"Of course, you know he's married."

"He's told me that, too, but apparently he's going to divorce his wife after the war," she said carefully. "Naturally, he wants to remain in contact with his daughters."

"You don't believe that old line, do you?"

Hanna looked at Sonja. "You are very perceptive for one so young. How old are you?"

"Nineteen."

As they walked, Sonja spoke to Hanna in a low voice. "The thing is," she said, "despite the fact that you are Schlossberg's little pet, Joseph Gavi has told me you can be trusted. Have you spoken to Joseph yet?"

"No. I only arrived on Friday. I had the night out with Schlossberg on Saturday night, and now I'm with you."

"I'm taking a risk telling you all this. You might repeat it to your boyfriend, in which case I'll be shot. They'll make a great public show of it and hang me in the square. They are very good at staging the hanging of 'naughty girls'. They do it in the courtyard here by the cemetery gates so they don't have to carry the bodies too far. You can come and watch me swing if I've got it wrong, but Elsa in Grodno said you could be trusted.

"After the service, please follow me to the Confessional. There are a few people you must meet. No, don't question me now. You'll soon see."

Hanna nodded.

They both crossed themselves as they entered the church and remained silent as though in prayer throughout the service, kneeling side by side in a dark oak pew at the back. Hanna's leg was aching terribly. As they stood to join the back of the line to receive Communion, Hanna had a sudden moment of realisation. The injury on her leg hadn't been hers at all. It had been Simeon's. So had she imagined the blood and just felt as though she'd been wounded? He was hurt and there was nothing she could do to help him. Simeon had been shot in the thigh. He wanted to let her know what had happened.

Communion over, Sonja beckoned Hanna to follow her. "We must make our confessions," she said, slipping into the shadows at the side of the church, then through a small, narrow space behind the altar. A young man was waiting there for them.

"I'm Reuven," he introduced himself. "You're Maria, aren't you? Thank you for the clothes, Sonja. I don't know how you do it." She handed him a wad of notes. "It's for orphanage number two," she whispered. Then she turned to Hanna. "The Jews in the ghetto give us their clothes to sell, though God knows they have few enough themselves. Between all of us who are involved, we sell them and use the money to buy essentials for the upkeep of their children who are hidden in the Catholic orphanages. The Catholics care for young children in two orphanages here. The Russian Orthodox have two more, and the Communists have a fifth. They shelter between one hundred and fifty and two hundred children each, mostly Jewish children who might otherwise be in the ghetto awaiting deportation or death in other de … lightful ways. I presume you heard about the Purim Massacre?"

Reuven looked at Sonja. "Is it wise to tell her quite so much?" he whispered.

"She came from Grodno on Elsa's recommendation," Sonja replied. "If she lets us down, she knows she will have the death of several hundred children on her conscience now."

Hanna turned to Sonja. "What was the Purim Massacre?"

"Bastards set up a quicksand pit in the centre of the ghetto as a 'treat' for the children during the Feast of Esther festival. SS-Obersturmbannführer Adolf Eichmann, one of the architects of the policy against Jews, turned up. I understand it's customary to give the children sweets at this time of year. The wicked bastard threw loads and loads of sweets into the quicksand. The children jumped in after them and were dragged down to their deaths with their parents watching helplessly. The SS were all very pleased with themselves."

Reuven turned to Hanna. "We have important work for you to do here. Go into the confessional. Now." Sonja and Hanna watched the frail figure of an old woman leave the box and saw Reuven slip into the priest's side. Through the fretwork, Hanna could make out the outline of two men squashed closely together. "My friend, Father Francis," Reuven whispered through the panel between them.

"I will hear your confession now, my child." It was the Father's voice.

On instinct, Hanna stayed silent. "As Schlossberg's PA, you will have free access to both the ghetto and the major German organisations such as the factories and the Labour Exchange. We want you to act as a courier for the time being, Maria. A liaison. Nothing dangerous. Will you do it? Confess?"

"I confess."

"There's something else. We have a friend in the Labour Exchange who has access to the officers who issue the work permits. There are piles of them on their desks, all signed by the authoriser. But they need to be stamped. At lunchtimes, Wilhelm Kube's secretary goes out for an hour. For that hour, our contact has unchallenged access to that office. He takes the key to the safe where the stamps are kept, unlocks it, stamps a pile of permits, replaces the stamps, and locks them back where they belong. We need someone to bring these passes out to us."

Hanna thought for a moment and nodded. "We need weapons, too. Guns. They are the ghetto inhabitants' 'passports into one of the partisan brigades that operate outside this city. Every morning, the women working in the armaments factory are marched in to work. Once inside the factory, it's not hard for them to steal small parts that they can hide in their clothing. When their shifts end, they have to bring those parts back into the ghetto to be assembled. The trouble is that the workers are randomly searched both going in and coming out of the ghetto. Smuggling is a major crime punishable by death. You, however, can go in and out of the ghetto freely 'on business'". No one will search Oberst-Gruppenführer Schlossberg's 'little Maria'. All the inmates will soon get to know you, particularly with that red hair. We need you to ferry parts in and guns out."

Hanna's heart was beating hard; her hands were wet with icy sweat. She could hear Simeon yelling at her: *A reason. At last a reason for what has happened.*

"I will if I can."

"There is no 'if'. You can and you will, or you will be unmasked as a Jewish spy, and we wouldn't want that, would we? You'll soon get the knack of it. Just make sure you keep coming to church regularly to receive our orders. Keep that pretty little cross safely round your neck, 'Maria', and keep your boyfriend sweet. I think you know a lady called Hanna Karminskya Abramskya rather well, don't you?"

She nodded. *Dear God,* she thought. *Someone in the ghetto has recognised me.*

"Someone who knew you well in another life told me to ask you if you recognise the name Simeon Karminsky."

Here it comes, she thought.

"Simeon is here?" Was he was shot last night?" Maybe when they arrested him?" She rubbed at her thigh through her skirt. It was very painful. *He's so close that he could come and talk to me if he wanted to, but he's disowned me. Of course he won't talk to me if he thinks Schlossberg is my boyfriend. How could he know* she had come here specifically to help her own people?

"If you are to be of any use to us at all, you have to pay careful attention to what I'm saying. There are ten, twelve, maybe twenty people in the ghetto who may die if you fail. Tomorrow you will collect the first batch of passes and hand them over. You may not talk to the man who takes them from you. Not a word. He will show you a piece of paper with the word *Chavarim* written on it. It means 'friends'. You will say nothing. Just hand over the stamped passes. You will come to Mass with Sonja on Tuesday morning for your new orders."

"On the way here, Sonja told me that there will be a massacre next Friday. What good will six passes do?"

"You can get another six, possibly more on Tuesday, a few more on Wednesday, and finally as many as you can lay your hands on, on Thursday morning. You will leave the office for 'lunch' at midday on Thursday, and while you are out, there will be a 'break-in'. Everything will be in a mess. No one will know how many passes have been stolen, because somebody forgot to count them efficiently. Remember: every pass is a life. Don't question what you're doing. Just do it."

Chapter 21

Hanna

⁓✎✐⁓

"**T**HE BASTARD IS INSISTING THAT I HAVE TO MOVE IN WITH HIM BEFORE Christmas."

Hanna and Sonja were walking to church together as they did every Sunday, but today was different. Last night, when Hanna and Frederick Schlossberg dined out at the Grand Hotel as they now did most Saturday evenings when he was in Minsk, he had taken her hand in his, but more firmly than he had ever done in the past.

"This is a ridiculous situation," he'd insisted. "I live in a luxurious apartment with four rooms all to myself and two whole bathrooms, while you remain cramped in that bloody lodging house limited to two baths a week, ten minutes toilette time in the mornings, and second-rate rations when you could eat the finest food every day of the week. No, Maria. I'm putting my foot down. Either you move in with me, or we stop seeing one another. I'll find you a job somewhere else. This life is torture for me."

In early 1943, she moved into his luxurious, fourth-floor apartment in a new building. The apartment was centrally heated, and as winter approached, she had to concede it was bliss to move out of the dingy, cold lodgings with shabby linoleum-covered floors into the flat where the floor boasted a fine cream wool carpet and the salon furniture was the latest fashion: elegant curved armchairs and sofas covered in deeply etched patterned velvet and exquisite walnut dining furniture the likes of which she had never seen before.

"I don't know about working. I think I'll be spending all my time cleaning and washing," Hanna announced after seeing it for the first time. The bedroom boasted pure silk pale lavender sheets and pillows.

"My darling. You don't have to worry your head with such trivialities. You have cleaners from the ghetto who come in to see to those things daily. If one's not enough, you can have two maids. They're Jewish, of course, but they've been properly vetted, and it's more than their lives are worth to steal. The girl who comes here, Helga I think she's called, comes highly recommended by Wilhelm Kube's housekeeper."

When Hanna first met Helga Rothstein, she was concerned that the woman might also be working for the underground and would know Hanna's real role here. Hanna knew that if Frederick thought she was assisting Jews with even the smallest kindness, she would be putting her own life in danger, as well as the lives of all the others working for the underground cells.

"I've got more clothes than I can possibly wear," she'd told a puzzled Helga when she arrived one snowy morning, shivering in a thin ragged cotton dress. She'd handed over a warm coat, the one the priest had given her that first Christmas. When Helga appeared with bare legs and wearing wooden clogs, Hanna had given her a pair of boots and some socks.

"Helga, can you help me clear out my wardrobe?" she'd asked her one morning. She took out several skirts and warm jumpers and put them in a large paper bag. "Here. Don't tell anyone I gave you these," she'd said. "Share them with your friends, but say you stole them." Hanna only gave her things away, however, when she was sure that Frederick was either in Grodno for the day or in Berlin, never when he was in town or when there was any chance of interruption.

"No, ma'am," the cleaner had replied suspiciously. "I can't do that." Hanna could read her mind. Helga wondered whether she might then be "raided" on suspicion of theft and the clothes found and charges levelled against her.

"Well, could you take them downstairs for me and throw them in the dustbin, then? They're just clogging up my wardrobe," she said, tactfully. Given those instructions, she knew Helga would take them home.

When Hanna heard that Helga's children, the youngest only three years old, were sick and starving, she began buying extra groceries and giving Helga soup thickened with meat - but never with pig meat - saying she'd made too much "by mistake". "How can I let all this go to waste?".

Then she'd added, "By the way, there's no pig meat in it, Helga. I prefer beef stock."

⸎

The numbers interred in the ghetto were rising again. "We need another Aktion, and soon," Hanna overheard Schlossberg telling one of his staff in the office. "Otherwise we'll have to explain why the costs of feeding the buggers are rising so rapidly."

"The situation is explosive," Hanna warned Sonja that Sunday as they walked to church. "Kube called an office meeting on Friday and told all of us that they've decided to disband the Judenrat. They're replacing it with three 'trustees'. There's to be another massacre. I overheard Kube say they plan to liquidate the whole ghetto over the next few weeks."

"Oh my God."

"I'm going to tell Helga," she told Sonja. "Perhaps there's a way she could get her children out, even if she can't get out herself. If she tells anyone the news came from me and it gets back to Frederick, it will be the end for me, of course, but I don't care anymore."

"If you do that, you may be condemning hundreds of others to death."

"Whatever I do, it won't be enough. If I were Helga, I'd want someone to give my children a chance. Anyway, I've had enough. I want to be with Nat and my boys." It all sounded so simple that Hanna couldn't figure out why she hadn't thought of it before.

In July 1943, Hanna stood on the podium in the square alongside Schlossberg, Kube, and Anastasia, purportedly taking notes. "It was horrible," she told Sonja the next day. "Kube was shouting out his orders over the heads of the thousands of Jews. They'd all been forced to stand still for hours while they were counted and recounted. Every time someone fainted, the counting would go back to the beginning and start again. Then the random beatings began. Finally, they started shooting. I tried not to watch. I shielded my eyes with my hands, but Schlossberg put his arm around me and called me his 'little softie'.

"'They're only Jews,' he said. 'Untermenschen.' I lost control of my bladder as I watched the streams of blood run between the cobblestones. I don't think anybody noticed. They were all too busy watching the Jews. Then a young soldier appeared. 'I got him,' he squealed. He was waving Jewish identity papers. 'Moshe Yoffe, the Jews' leader. I got him. Here's the proof.'

178

"All Schlossberg could say to me was: 'Perhaps you ought to go home now.'"

"You did your best." Sonja tried to soothe her.

"I did nothing. I stood by and watched thousands of my brothers and sisters murdered in cold blood and did nothing at all."

As the summer progressed, the situation worsened. "There are about twenty-six people hiding in a tunnel under the Jewish cemetery," Sonja told Hanna. "They've disguised the entry and exit with planks, and a Byelorussian woman I know has been taking in food. They've somehow fed tin pipes in there to give them some air. Aaron Fiterson and Rosa Zuckerman, two of the bravest people I've ever met, are collaborating with one of the Byelorussian partisan groups to smuggle them out into the forest, one at a time. We need you to exchange clothes with Rosa. She is coming out of hiding today and going to the clothing factory where she used to work overnight. She will be coming in from the factory at exactly twelve noon today. She was on a night shift because that's the safest. She will pick some grass and tuck it behind her ear so you can identify her. Once she's inside, Maria, you must follow her and exchange clothes with her. She will walk out of the front gate, pretending to be you. Do you understand? She'll go back into hiding. At least she'll have some clean clothes. Later on, you will go into the old Judenrat building. Give Helga some clothes to hide there for you. Change back into your own clothes, and just go back to the apartment or the office or wherever."

"Is it fair to involve Helga?"

"You stupid cow. She knows you're one of us. Has done for ages."

"I'm a bloody coward. I admit it," Hanna said. Sonja, however, was in no mood for Hanna's fear.

"As Father Francis told you long ago, we have no place for cowards. You will do it. If you don't, one of the Führer's own bullets might find its way into your chest."

In the early morning of 24 September 1943, Schlossberg and Hanna were awakened by the phone ringing. Hanna looked at her bedside clock. It was barely six in the morning. She heard Schlossberg grunt a couple of times. He threw the phone's receiver down, threw his clothes on, and rushed out before Hanna could say a word.

When Hanna arrived in the office two hours later, people were standing around talking in whispers.

"I don't believe that you of all people haven't heard. It's Kube. He's been blown to smithereens in his own bed."

"How?" Hanna was in shock.

"We strongly suspect it was his housekeeper, Yelena Mozanik. We now know she's been working with one of the partisan groups. We think she put a bomb in his bed, inside his hot water bottle and timed it to go off while he was sleeping at around two thirty this morning. The Gestapo are already on the case. Schlossberg's in charge for the time being. Himmler has ordered mass execution of males in the ghetto today in retaliation. No male Jew is to go to work."

The numbers in the ghetto were diminishing daily. Two days after Kube's death and a day after a second massacre, Schlossberg left for yet another important meeting with Himmler in Berlin. He was back a day later. "I've got news for you," he said, balancing on the arm of the elegant sofa. "You remember the girl Elsa in Grodno? Yes, of course you do. It was you who suggested she should take your place in the Grodno office. I think at one time you were quite friendly. Turns out she's a Jewess. She had relatives in the Grodno Ghetto. Seems she was running in and out like she was visiting a holiday camp. Had to have her shot, of course. Made damned sure everyone in the ghetto watched, and we took along a few of the girls from the office, in case they had any ideas about 'assisting' Jew vermin. Heinrich Brandt is heartbroken. He trusted her." Hanna tried to focus on Schlossberg's face and found she couldn't.

Later that morning, he called her into his private office.

"Maria, darling. There is something I need you to do, and you are the only person I can trust to do it. I need some papers. They're in a file in the old Judenrat building. This is top secret. Don't tell anyone what you're doing. You know we're planning to liquidate the camp in the near future. I need these papers before I go back to Berlin tomorrow afternoon.

"Tomorrow I want you to go into the ghetto. I'll arrange for Anton to take you and wait for you."

"That man gives me the creeps," Hanna answered. "Don't leave him sitting around outside waiting for me."

"The ghetto is mostly empty now. There are very few inmates left inside, only two or three hundred at most. We've got most of those who survived the shooting now. We've sent them on a little walk. Well, a long walk actually. It's a drop-until-they're-dead march. Here's the list of what I need."

Helga arrived at eight o'clock as usual next morning, utterly distraught. "They've taken my parents and my children on some march," she cried. "I think my husband escaped. Madame, where are they taking them? Do you know? Can you tell me? Can I go to them, wherever they are? The little ones will be so frightened without me. They didn't take me only because I work here for you."

Helga was shaking. Hanna made her a coffee. She took some money out of her purse and gave it to her. "I don't know," Hanna said honestly. "They're walking, but I don't know where to. You're safer here for the moment than in the ghetto. It won't be long until it's all over from what I understand. Then you'll be able to go and look for them. It can't go on much longer."

The chauffeur called for Hanna two hours later as arranged and drove her straight to the now almost empty ghetto. No sooner had she entered the deserted Judenrat hut than she was conscious of a rattling coming from under the floorboards. *It must be rats or mice,* she thought. To her amazement, the lid of the stove in the corner lifted and Reuven's head emerged.

"It's my melina," he explained. "Most houses have 'melinas' or secret hiding places, and this is mine. That's how I keep in touch with what's going on everywhere. I heard you were coming. What are you doing?"

"I have to get some papers for him." They both knew to whom she was referring. "He's in Berlin for two days."

"Show me your list."

She showed him the list of documents Schlossberg required. "I only have an hour before Anton comes back for me."

"No problem. I know where all these are." He took several large files from the filing cabinet, extracted what she needed, laid those documents to one side, and then made a mess on the table so it looked as though she'd been rifling through looking what she'd been ordered to find.

"You need to come with me now. There are several people waiting to meet you," he insisted.

Please, please, dear God, don't let Simeon be among them, Hanna prayed as she followed Reuven out of the Judenrat building and through cobbled back allies, into a door marked with a huge red sign: *Private. Infectious Diseases Hospital: No Admittance.* He led her down steep steps and through a series of underground passages to a room where huge pipes gurgled and shuddered overhead. Although it was cool outside, it was terribly hot in here. The men who stood in front of her wore only thin vests or no vests at all. Sweat was pouring down their faces. As she walked in, a man stepped forward. She gasped.

"Hello, Maria," he said, "Or would you prefer I called you Hanna Karminskya Abramskya?"

She may not have recognised his face. He was painfully thin, his shoulder bones standing out, his cheeks sunken so that the skin on his face was taut, the cheekbones standing proud. His skin looked a greyish-yellow, and his chin sport a ragged beard. He looked like a walking corpse, but there was no doubting it: it was Hirschel Smolensky, an old friend of both Nat's and Simeon's. He'd known her since her childhood in Krustpils.

"Call me whatever you like," she said, bowing her head, her face pink with shame. "I'm doing my best to help you. I really am. Reuven will tell you. None of this is my fault. Please, please don't judge me. Don't tell Simeon."

"So living in luxury and sleeping with a Nazi just happened, did it? Living like a fine lady while we subsist like pigs isn't your fault? It just happened."

"How do you know all this?"

"We've been watching you for a very long time, Hanna. Almost a year, in fact. We know you lived with that vile old priest in Grodno until 'lover boy' brought you here. We know most things about our operatives. You've been working underground, firstly with Elsa and then with Sonja and Father Francis, as well as Reuven here, I believe."

She nodded.

"You might like to know that your dear Frederick hasn't gone to Berlin at all. He's busy moving his family to a safe house in the countryside outside Hanover. The Germans know they're beat, but Jewish lives are still in danger. The exterminations continue in the camps. The gas chambers are still echoing with the screams of dying Jews as the chimney continues to burn their remains. If you really want to help, there are important tasks for you to do still."

His brown eyes, staring unforgivingly into her blue ones were bright with emotion. "I suppose you know that Sonja's already left."

Hanna shook her head.

"She's be transferred and is staying with the Jewish Partisan Brigade in Polotsk, even though she's not Jewish. I believe you already know Elsa's fate. So, here's what we need you to do."

He rattled off what sounded like a never-ending list of errands that apparently were essential to the welfare and safety of those who still survived. "Security in the factory has become lax. There are only a few top-grade workers left in the ghetto now. They are escorted out to the gun assembly plant every morning and brought back in the evening. You need to go back on the gun run. You've done it before. Every weapon we can reassemble buys a Jewish life.

"Every evening, from now on, you will go into the ghetto and walk towards the Judenrat. You will meet up with a woman wearing a yellow scarf, not necessarily the same woman, but always wearing the same scarf. The dimwit Nazis won't suspect anything. She will brush past you and hand you a weapon. You will conceal it, in your brassiere, in your bag, in the top of your stockings. You will carry it out and back towards the office. A man with a red scarf will bump into you just outside the ghetto. You will give him the weapon. Conversely, if you can just happen to be outside the gates as they come home, either a woman with a yellow scarf or a man with a red one will feed you gun parts. You will take them back into the ghetto for reassembly. Do you understand?"

"Yes."

"We are also producing news sheets to distribute among those of us left. Believe it or not, there are only about 800 of us left now. You will be given the printer's address. You will collect the news sheets from the printer's address and take them to a number of different venues for distribution. They look innocuous but they contain coded information for those still in hiding. There are many important underground workers in sewers and tunnels. They need to know what's going on. We need to know we can trust you, Hanna. You need you to swear on your brother's life."

"I swear," she said. She looked up at her brother's old friend. "Is he still alive? Do you know?"

"We think so."

"We have something else here for you," he said, handing her two small capsules. "Rat poison. In two weeks' time, on a given day, you will make your beloved Schlossberg a celebration dinner. These innocent little pills are cyanide. You will incorporate them into a fancy dish. You are a good cook. You will make something you know he can't resist, something so tasty that he will scoff every last morsel. He will die a nasty death. Very painful for such a man. Very fitting too for such an evil person. You will pack a bag. Two changes of underwear for yourself, including a warm jumper and warm stockings or socks. You will find his gun. We believe he keeps a pistol next to his bed. You will be advised of the timings. Be ready. Someone will be waiting to take you into the forest to meet up with your friend Sonja. I will see you there, providing you have a weapon for us. The price for you is as high as the price for everyone else."

⁓⚓⁓

Schlossberg finally returned home two days later. "We know there are still one or two Jews hiding out in the sewers, but they'll have to come out sooner or later to get food, or else they'll starve. We'll get them then. We've got an idea of where they are. Meanwhile, there's a lot of tidying up to do. Our job's not quite finished."

Despite having completed all the tasks she'd been assigned, Hanna had a new worry. She had been so busy worrying about the fate of the Jews in Minsk that she hadn't realised that her period had failed to arrive. She was at least a month overdue. Her breasts had recently felt heavy and uncomfortable but she had ignored the discomfort as trivial. She ran a hand over her belly. Her skirts had been feeling tight, and now she realised why. Dear God. She was pregnant.

Chapter 22

Arieh and Rutti

THE SIEGE OF LENINGRAD MAY HAVE OFFICIALLY ENDED ON 21 JANUARY 1944, but the Great Patriotic War, alongside World War II, dragged on until April 1945.

In January, the partisans started to receive reports of atrocities against the Jews of Europe beyond any of their imaginations. The number of names of notorious concentration and death camps grew like a fast-spreading plague. The names became infamous: Auschwitz, Dachau, Bergen-Belsen, Treblinka, Bełżec, Ravensbrück, Mittelbau-Dora, Nordhausen, and Buchenwald. The list grew and grew as knowledge of the full extent of the way the Nazi Holocaust had stretched its grizzly tentacles across Europe became public. It seemed never ending.

"Mikhail and I have made up our minds. When this is finally over, we both want to go to Palestine. You'll come with us, won't you, Rutti? And you, Simeon and Arieh. We won't leave you behind."

"I've always wanted to go to America," Rutti declared. "I've dreamt for so long about the Goldene Medina, the golden land. Our cousin Lauren lives there, She used to be called Leah. We were little girls together in Kovno."

"You and Oscar were much younger than me. Go, if that's what you really want, but Oscar and I wish you'd stay with us. We want to go to Palestine and help build the new state of Israel. What about you, Simeon?"

"No. Not yet. First I have to go back to check if there is any news about my Dora and the family. Then I have to keep a promise I made to my cousin

Ivan. I'm sure they must have survived. His wife worked for the Ministry of Food Science. If anyone had enough to eat, it would have been them. I need to look for my sister, Hanna, too."

It had been many months since Simeon had had any feeling from Hanna. The last time was the day he'd received that gunshot in his thigh. He had felt her strength flowing through his body that day; felt her words of comfort urging him to keep strong. However, his connection to his sister seemed to have been severed ever since. Could it be that she was dead after all? Could she have died without him knowing it, feeling it?

"Maybe, when I've sorted myself out, I'll follow you."

Arieh had been listening intently to the conversation. "What's going to happen to me?" His large brown eyes met Simeon's blue ones. "I want to go with you, Simeon. You promised you'd never leave me. I want to go wherever you go. I can walk quite well now with my leg brace and my crutches. I won't hold you back. Please, let me come? Then you can help me look for my mama and papa."

"No, Arieh. You can't. Not yet. Not now. Maybe later." Simeon looked over, but Mikhail shook his head. They had no guarantees, even if they did manage to cross Europe and reach Italy, that they would find a boat to take them to Palestine.

"Do you have any family that you know of anywhere else in the world?"

"My mama's sister went to America, to a hot place called Miami, I think, before I was born."

Rutti put her arm around his shoulders. "In that case, Arieh, you will come with me. I'm not sure what you have to do to get into America, and I'm sure it's not easy. However, we will find a way. You will come with me to New York, and from there we will look for your aunt. We will tell everyone you are my nephew, my dead sister's son. That will explain the difference in our names."

"Mama used to tell me about my aunt Shayne. She was older than Mama. She left for America in 1931, before I was born, with her husband, Uncle Chaim. They wrote to one another. I saw a picture of her once, but I don't remember what she looked like. I think they had a son. She wanted Mama to come with my papa and bring my grandmother with them, but Papa thought it was a bad idea to pick an old lady up from her home and her friends. He didn't know if a musician could find work in America."

"I am going to write to my cousin in New York as soon as I can to ask her to invite us."

"America is a very big place, nearly as big as the Soviet Union," Arieh replied. "Supposing we don't find her? Then what will happen to me?"

Sometimes Rutti wondered where a little boy who'd never been to school and who had barely learnt to read had acquired his knowledge and common sense from. He was still only nine years old.

"I won't abandon you." Rutti laughed. You'll become the little nephew I've always wanted but haven't got.

"If I don't like it, can I come back to you?" Arieh looked up at Simeon with pleading big brown eyes.

"I love you, Arieh," Simeon said gently. "Probably. But it will be better for you to go with Rutti first of all. Your family may believe all traces of their flesh and blood have gone up the chimneys in the concentration camps. You must let them know you are alive and well. When I've found my family, then perhaps I'll send for you."

He knew that it was highly unlikely he would find any of his own loved ones alive. In his heart, he knew Dora was dead, but so far he had not permitted himself time or emotion to mourn for her. Or for their baby daughter, or for his mother. How could he tell a nine-year-old boy what he expected to find? With the optimism and innocence of youth, Arieh was dreaming of a future where he was with people who would love him and where his world would almost come right again. The child yearned to be part of a proper family. However, Simeon knew that apart from the practical difficulties of travelling with Arieh in his current physical state, his journey would almost certainly be a wild goose chase. "I can't take you, Arieh. Go with Rutti," he repeated. "Who knows? If I find my family, maybe I'll bring them to America. By then, you will have settled, and I will have somewhere to live. Then I can introduce you and say: 'This is Arieh, my surrogate son.'"

⚜

The Ettinger family finally left Leningrad in May 1945.

"Can I touch your boots for luck one last time?" Arieh asked Simeon on their last night together, sharing their straw mattress above the potato store.

Simeon nodded. "Here, you can sleep with one under your pillow just for tonight, and I'll sleep with the other one."

"Did you really mean what you said," Arieh asked him, "about always loving me?"

"Like the son I never had," he said, stroking Arieh's hair as he used to do

187

when he was younger. "I'm waiting to hear you play in America, Arieh. You will be a famous violinist, and you will fill all the most important concert halls in the world. You will go to London, to play at the Albert Hall. You will go to Carnegie Hall in New York and to the Olympia in Paris, and I will come to hear you. And I will tell everyone: 'You see that violinist there, the famous Arieh Weinstein? He's my surrogate son. We shared a mattress over a potato store during the Great Patriotic War.' The world will pay fortunes to enjoy Arieh Weinstein's music."

"You won't forget me, Simeon? You promise? Not ever."

"Not ever. I will be there to watch you. And however far away you go, my amber tablets will look out for you to keep you safe."

"Will they? I'm sorry I lost Miss Honey."

"It doesn't matter. Wherever she is, she's still looking after you. You know that. Perhaps you will find her, or something like her, one day. And when we meet again, you can give it back to me as a token. You know the bond I have with my twin sister. There's a bond between you and me with our amber tablets, Arieh. I told you a long time ago that they are magic. Nothing will break that magic, ever."

Eventually, Simeon, Rutti and Arieh left the forest together on 4 June 1945 to make for Leningrad. Whereas he went straight to the Vitebsk station, they made their way down towards the coast, looking for a guest house where they could tidy up, bathe properly, and sleep the night. Then they would find a ferry to Malmo. The Ettingers and Simeon split whatever money they had between them to allow for Rutti's additional expenses for Arieh. It was enough for them to afford to clean up and catch their breath, acquire clean clothes, and register as stateless persons before taking the ferry across to Sweden. In Malmo, they visited a Red Cross centre, where they were issued with the documents they needed. Half of Europe, it seemed, were refugees. What they needed next was a stable address, preferably a European one, in order to write to Rutti's American cousin to ask her to sponsor both Rutti and Arieh into the USA. Her cousin would have to guarantee to accept financial responsibility for them until they became financially independent.

"Can you call me Ruth now? It's more American," she asked a surprised Arieh.

"If that's what you want, although you'll always be Rutti to me." He smiled.

The story they agreed on was that Arieh Weinstein was the son of Ruth's dead sister, Lena Ettinger, and her husband, Simcha Weinstein. As Arieh had no idea where to find his mother's sister Shayne, other than that she had been somewhere in Miami when they'd last heard of her in 1940, it seemed a sensible story to stick to.

Their money wasn't lasting as long as they'd hoped. Although Ruth had enough to get herself to America on a third-class passage from Southampton, in England, the fare was not enough for the two of them, even in steerage.

It was Arieh who came up with the idea of asking their landlady if she knew anyone who might use some paid help. The landlady had a friend with a slightly larger guest house on the outskirts of the city offering dinners as well as bed and breakfast. She said she would be happy to employ Ruth as a chambermaid and after-breakfast washer-upper and cleaner. She would offer her and her "nephew" room and board if Arieh agreed to work in the kitchen, peeling vegetables and washing up, for a small wage. They could share a room in the attic. The arrangement suited them all admirably. She would pay them a combined wage each week, plus extra if Arieh agreed to entertain diners with his violin in the evening.

It was as they were unpacking in their new quarters that Arieh caught sight of a pale gold stone shining at him from the bottom of their shared suitcase. His heart skipped a beat. Surely it couldn't be. How could it? It was burnt and lost so long ago.

"What's that in your case, Rutti?" Arieh asked, picking it up and turning it over in his hand in wonder. It was a dull, yellow colour and looked as though it had been sprinkled with fine grey dust. As he held it, the edges became dust in his hand. He licked it. Suddenly, the dull dusty look gave way to a clear golden yellow. He could see a tiny insect frozen inside it. "Miss Honey," he shrieked in delight. "It's my Little Miss Honey. I must tell Simeon."

"Where did you get this, Rutti?" He held it out to her in the palm of his hand and looked up at her, his huge brown eyes wide open in surprise, astonishment, and near disbelief.

"Do you know what, Arieh? I forgot all about it. I found it in the top pocket of your bib trousers the day we had to cut your trousers off." She paused for a moment, thoughtful. "It was terrible that day. You were numb. Your poor legs! We cut off your trousers, but very gently. I remember we cut through the bib top to get them off with as little disturbance to the rest of you because of the terrible state you were in. As I cut through the pocket, this fell out. Something triggered me to pick it up—perhaps the thought that my brothers used to have lucky stones in their pockets when they were little boys. Anyway, I put it into my own pocket. It must have fallen out into the case as I packed." She giggled. "Not that either of us had much to pack when we left the camp." She looked up at his face. "What is it, Arieh? Is something wrong?"

"Simeon told me I'd find it. He told me on our last night that its power was still with me even though I'd lost it. He believed it had saved my life, just as he believed the three amber pieces altogether had saved his. Did you know there were originally three of them, Rutti? It just goes to prove what Simeon said: one day we will be together again, and I'll give it back to him. After all, he only lent it to me. Then the three of them will be reunited. " Tears were running down Arieh's face. It was the first time Ruth had ever seen him cry, it was a rare occurrence even when he was in pain. She put her arms around him and hugged him until the sobs subsided. Then he sat down on the edge of the bed, holding the stone gently in his hand as though he were holding the world's most precious diamond. Suddenly, he leapt up. "I'll have to go, Rutti. I must leave now. I will go to Krustpils where Simeon used to live, and if he's not there, I will go to Leningrad to look for him. He will be so happy when he knows."

Ruth looked at him. "I'm sorry, my dear," she said. "You can't. Apart from anything else, we have no idea where he's gone. Russia is a big country." She looked at the small piece of yellow resin in his hand, wondering how such a tiny imperfect piece of amber, its edges singed with fine grey ash, could mean so much. "This is the missing tablet you were calling for when they brought you back from Shlisselburg, isn't it? It had nothing to do with cyanide. I couldn't imagine Simeon, who loved you so much, giving you a cyanide pill."

Arieh nodded, but he closed his lips firmly. He took the little piece of amber and wrapped it carefully in the rag he used as a handkerchief. Every few minutes, Rutti saw him put his hand in his pocket to finger it, as though to make sure it was still there. "I thought it was gone forever," he whispered over and over. "I never thought I would ever see you again, Little Miss Honey, but you came back."

Ruth's cousin's address in New Jersey had been imprinted on Rutti's mind since they had corresponded as small children, always in their common language, Yiddish. She wrote the letter on behalf of herself and her "nephew" and sent it on a wing and a prayer that the family had remained at the same address throughout the war, or that whoever lived there now would have a forwarding address for them. Her joy knew no bounds when Lauren replied with a formal letter of invitation to them both. It arrived in Sweden in November.

"Look, Arieh, look." Ruth rushed into their room where Arieh was getting dressed, waving the fine blue airmail letter excitedly. "It's from Leah, or Lauren as she calls herself now.. She says she's delighted to sponsor us. She's gone along with the story that you are an Ettinger on your mother's side and says she's thrilled we're coming together. All we have to do is book a passage. It will have to be third class from Southampton, but it's only for six or seven days at sea."

Their third-class, six-day journey across the Atlantic was fairly unremarkable. They shared a cabin with another mother and son. The food was mostly inedible, but as the sea was rough, and they were both very sick, so it didn't really matter. They went up on deck for the last two days of the journey when the sea calmed, and the sky turned from ominous grey to a beautiful clear spring blue, and comforted themselves with the knowledge that they were almost there.

In New York, all the immigrants, most of them third-class passengers, disembarked onto the pier and were transported to Ellis Island for medicals and questioning. The Statue of Liberty stood, tantalising and teasing them in all her copper-green glory, her arm raised with the promise of a better life to come. As they underwent medical examinations to prove they weren't suffering from transmittable diseases such as TB, Ruth was frightened.

"It's my nephew," she told the mother of a thin and sickly looking young child, as they sat together in the medical queue. "His legs were badly burnt in an accident during the war. Surely they can't send him back? Not now."

"This is America. They can do whatever they like with us." The woman was exceedingly thin and appeared undernourished. "We came from the concentration camp at Majdanek. My boy had typhoid. He was so sick on the boat that he lost more weight. You? Where were you?"

"A partisan camp near Leningrad."

They waited several more hours in the queue in the vast reception hall, packed to the rafters with other hopeful immigrants, to have their letters of invitation scrutinised. They watched as several Italian men were put into a holding space to be returned to their place of embarkation.

"I'll die if they don't let me in," Arieh cried. "After all we've been through." Ruth noticed that he stood most of the time with his right hand in his pocket. She knew he was clutching his lucky fragment of amber.

"So, what will you say is your occupation? How do you intend on paying for your keep in the Golden Land?"

Arieh lifted up his violin. "I will tell them I am a professional violinist," he said proudly as he, unclipped his violin case and gently pulled out the instrument and bow. As the first notes of the *Pathétique* echoed round the vast hall, the chatter and babble of hundreds of anxious would-be immigrants, and even the immigration officers themselves, stilled to a hush. The beautiful music seemed to calm aggressive interrogators and troubled souls equally in a way no human voice could. Suddenly, Arieh found himself surrounded by men, women, and even children cheering and congratulating him in a babble of languages whose meaning was clear. They loved it.

Despite his scarred legs and his strange gait, Arieh passed the medical. Perhaps the pure music from his fingers paved his pathway. Both he and Rutti were pronounced healthy, recovered from the years of deprivation thanks to the good food they'd eaten in Sweden. As the Staten Island Ferry drew into the shore, Rutti began shrieking with excitement.

"Look, Arieh. I can see them. There's Lauren, the one in the red hat and coat over there. Look, she's seen us." As they stood to disembark and then took their first steps onto American soil, Ruth was holding tight to their shared brown cardboard suitcase with one hand and clutching Arieh's hand, curled round his crude crutch, with the other.

"Ruth, we've done it. We're here. We're finally here." Then Lauren's arms were round them both, exchanging hugs and kisses, covering them both in the soft blanket of warmth of a heartfelt welcome. Lauren grabbed the cardboard case and smiled.

Chapter 23

Simeon

EMOTION HAD BEEN A LUXURY FEW COULD AFFORD DURING THE GREAT Patriotic War, but Simeon found parting with the Ettingers much harder than he'd anticipated. They hugged and vowed to meet again in a new country with another life. They had shared so much, and inevitably there were tears. Hardest for Simeon was leaving Arieh. "I won't be a burden," the boy begged to the very last minute. "Let me come, Simeon. I will make money for us along the way, playing my violin. You'll see."

"I can't, Arieh," he'd tried to explain as they embraced. "I have so much travelling to do. You know that."

He boarded the train at Vitbesk and found a corner seat. As the journey slipped away, he sat quietly on the hard wooden bench, contemplating his boots. He longed to take them off to stretch his feet and feel the cold, hard wooden floor of the carriage under his toes, but he didn't dare. He thought about Hanna and then felt guilty for not thinking of Dora, Mama, and the baby. His daughter. He left the rattle at Ivan and Gilda's flat together with the tablecloth. What had Dora had called their little girl? He wondered if Hanna knew about Nat's death. Where was she? What about her small sons? He looked down at his feet and spoke to the two little pieces of amber mosaic hidden in the heels. He often talked to them. As the train huffed and puffed along the banks of the River Daugava, he read the watch of a man sitting opposite him. It was ten at night and pitch-black outside. A small child lay across his mother's lap, snoring lightly, his thumb in his mouth. He was about three or four, a similar age to Simeon's own little girl if she had survived. The train seemed to be slowing down, and he became impatient. He stamped his feet in exasperation, causing his snoozing fellow passengers to stir crossly.

"Some of us want to sleep," a large man in the corner muttered. *Army type, officer material.* It was something in the man's voice. *I must stop stamping my feet. It's not doing my little amber treasures much good.*

He jumped from the train at the old red cross "Halt" sign and was almost relieved to find himself the only disembarking passenger. Walking down Rigas Street, he thought it looked as though little had changed. The old street name clung to the wall of the first house on a single screw, like a drunken limpet. Flower heads genuflected in the breeze. The sweet-smelling stocks and patio roses blooming in wooden tubs at the sides of some of the houses were waving a scented greeting towards him. He had reached his parents' hardware store, their shop, his home. Unlike last time he'd seen it, the front door was closed. The window had been dressed with the familiar brushes, mops and buckets, pots and pans, and signs advertising string and glue. So the house and shop were occupied. Could it be that against all odds, his mother and Dora were in there? Was it possible that they'd reclaimed the business, tidied up the mess, and carried on as before? "Thank you, amber tablets," he breathed. Could Hanna be here too, safe with her little boys?

He started to cross the road towards the shop when he felt a tug on the collar of his jacket. Suddenly, the old fear overwhelmed him. He turned his head and almost put his hands together, expecting handcuffs. Had someone seen him murder Anna and Valdis Berzin four years ago? His hands remained free, but the dragging at the back of his collar intensified. He turned his head. Behind him, he saw the small wrinkled form of Eleyana Markovna Shoparivocha, one of his mother's regular non-Jewish acquaintances. She looked older than he remembered, her face thin and heavily lined, her hair whiter and sparser. Her blue eyes, once alive and alert, were clouded and full of alarm. She was tugging him backwards into her single-storey wooden cottage. She had a finger to her lips. Inside, dark, gloomy little shapes danced against the walls—shadows thrown by the light of a single oil lamp on the table. "Simeon Karminsky, as I live and breathe." She wheezed. "Quick, Simeon Karminsky, before you are seen. Everyone round here knows you are a traitor."

"Me? A traitor? No," he retorted, startled. "I've been fighting in the forest with partisans."

"The army came looking for the Jew soldier who went AWOL."

"They thought I was dead. I was knocked out on the battlefield. When I came to, I found myself with partisans. The army knew where I was. I worked with them. With generals and brigadiers."

"You won't find your family here," she said, ignoring what he'd said. She spoke the words with such authority that he knew his worst fears were confirmed. Her rheumy old eyes filled with tears. "The Nazis came in late August and marshalled all the Jews into the kosher abattoir. You had a daughter. Did you know? After they went in there, I never saw your mama or any of your family again. We heard everyone in there begging for help, but it was more than our lives were worth to try to save any of them. One man tried. Old Bariansky tried to creep up to the entrance and open the door. It was one in the morning. We all heard the shot. They blew his brains out. After that, we dared do nothing."

Simeon slumped down heavily. "I came back to find them in late August '41. They must still have been here. I heard people crying, but I thought they were animals." He sank his head into his knees and started to sob as he had never sobbed in his life. His frame shook, yet his eyes stayed dry. And then he yelled. It was the almighty wail of a mauled beast.

"Shh!" she insisted. "Shush ..." Only then did she lay an arm on his shoulder, drawing him close to her. "Your mother was a good woman, Simeon Karminsky. Your Dora was a kind girl. You chose well." She sat down next to him on a small stool. "I saw you come back," she whispered. "That day. I know what happened with the Berzins. No one else does. I never said a word, but I saw you standing at their door then pushing yourself inside. Two days later, they were discovered dead, rolled up in blankets. You can't stay here. The neighbours here hate the Jews. They blame them for all the evil that has overtaken this place. If they find you, they will lynch you just because you are a Jew."

"You haven't heard anything about my sister, Hanna, have you?"

She shook her head. "Stay here tonight, but tomorrow you must leave. There's an early train to Riga or Leningrad. I forget which. Leave while you can, Simeon Karminsky." She handed him a thin grey blanket. "Here. Sleep. When I awake in the morning, you must be gone."

He caught the first train back to Leningrad at six thirty the next morning. Emerging from the station, he stood blinking, his eyes readjusting from the gloom of the station to the bright sunlight.

Despite the terrible battering Leningrad had taken, the city had retained a certain elegance. Vestiges of her faded glory shone through the late spring sunlight. Here was a wounded beauty bearing testament to her suffering, yet still standing proudly defiant.

Simeon wondered whether he'd been a fool to come back. Perhaps he should have stayed with the Ettingers, who were so determined to get to Palestine. He might even have taken Arieh with him. Common sense told him, however, that such a thing would have been impossible. Anyway, a promise was a promise. His beloved cousin's bitch of a wife had been so cruel, yet he supposed he could understand. Her only child was being torn from her. True, the girl was one of thousands of other children from Leningrad, and it was for the child's own safety that she'd been removed. Mothers should have been grateful, but they weren't. They were losing their children. However upset Gilda was, it wouldn't have hurt her to have offered Simeon a bed for a couple of nights until he found his feet. He remembered back to Gilda and Ivan's wedding day, how she'd been at the centre of every photograph. It was all about Gilda. Ivan was merely a bystander. Simeon hadn't liked her then, and he'd liked her even less that day when he'd come back looking for their help. She was a cold, selfish woman. Now he stood looking up at the third-floor oriel window just as he'd done four years ago. This time, however, the window had no blackout tape, and he had no hope of finding a welcome. He wondered, had either of them survived?

The building stood almost intact, its pink facade pockmarked by strafing bullets and masonry that had scarred it from the next-door building as it dissolved into a pile of rubble under air bombardment. Simeon stamped his feet gently, slowly, deliberately. Left, right. *Tell me, amber tablets, can you see beyond the walls?* He started up the steps and noticed two large chunks of marble were missing from the second step. However, the name Solomon was still under the bell push for apartment number seven. As he laid his finger on the bell, the front door opened. The black and white checked floor was just as he remembered. He looked up to see a bent old hag huddled into a ragged brown shawl. She was barely as tall as his shoulder. He could see her skull, pink and shiny, through her thin brown strands of hair. Her cheeks were gaunt and hollow.

"What do you want?" she asked. She had a slight lisp, and he saw that two of her front teeth were missing. However, he'd recognise that voice anywhere. Gilda. Or perhaps it was her mother?

"Gilda?" he questioned.

She looked up into his face and gasped. "Simeon Karminsky?"

So, it was Gilda. How old could she be? Twenty-five, twenty-eight at most? She looked at least fifty-five, her back bent, her skin wrinkled, her eyes blank and dead.

"You'd better come in," she said. She led him up the three flights of stairs to their apartment. As he stepped inside the narrow hallway, he could see that the place had changed beyond recognition. The wooden panelling, the expensive red flock wall coverings, the fancy architraves round the doors, were all gone. The interior had been stripped back to bare grey plaster. The large old-fashioned black "candlestick" telephone that Gilda had been so proud of sat sadly on the bare cement floor, its unplugged wires snaking to nowhere. The elegant telephone table was gone. So was the parquet flooring. The apartment was grey and bare. There was no furniture. As she led him towards the kitchen, he looked through the door of the former grand salon where he'd spent that one uncomfortable night. The stylish Louis XVI furniture had been replaced by a jumble of stained mattresses covered with tangles of bedding and grubby clothes. The sour smell of sleep, of unwashed bodies and grubby bedclothes, wafted through into the hallway.

"You may well stare!" Gilda waved a shawled arm at the mess. "In case you are wondering, we broke all the furniture up and burnt it for fuel. The winter of '41 to '42 was the worst in living memory. The parquet flooring went the same way. It's more important to keep warm with hot water when you're starving to death. When the main supply fails, you boil snowmelt on a free-standing stove. We were lucky to have so much wood."

She put her hand against the bare wall. "And in case you are wondering, we soaked the paper off the walls, put it in buckets, skimmed off the paste, and drank it when it floated to the top. We boiled both Ivan's leather briefcase and mine for the protein in the cowhide, too. Someone in my office suggested that."

Of course, he thought. Inside information from the Ministry of Food Science. But had there been no black market? What about Ivan's Writers' Union subsidies? Surely, those reporting the news needed energy to work?

"We ate all the cats and dogs, all the rats and mice. And when there were none left, we ate soup made from joiners' glue. You wouldn't know about that."

And you don't care, he thought. How could she assume he hadn't suffered? He thought back to his own experiences, to his beating at the hands of the Nazis, to the brutality in the Amber Room. He stamped his feet, connecting with his little amber tablets. He thought of the death pit and then of Mikhail,

Oscar, Rutti, and Arieh. He thought of the other children who'd died fighting alongside adults in the forest.

"How do you know what happened to me?" His voice was tight as he fought to keep his temper.

"We heard all the rail links had been severed. Someone said they'd seen a man with red hair and a limp signing up for ambulance duties at the Military Hospital on Suvarov, so he went there looking for you. Someone else thought they'd seen you at the Erissmann during an air-raid but that the man they thought was you had gone off for a smoke and never came back. They presumed a bomb had got you. Life's very cheap during a siege, Simeon. Death no longer counts as a tragedy. They thought you were dead. I couldn't believe you'd survived when I saw you standing on the doorstep. I had envied you your death, just as I begrudged Ivan his."

"How did he die?"

"How did thousands die here? Starvation. The silly sod refused to eat the little titbits I managed to sneak out from work. I stole sugar for him, and fat. Risked my own life to bring him two hundred grams of proper bread made with pure flour, and I got hold of some horse meat sausages from the canteen. It was our job in the Ministry to keep the city's bellies from being entirely empty, so they made sure ours were filled. We were forbidden to take food out of the department, but we all did it anyway."

She almost spat with fury as she continued.

"Ivan the stupid insisted I must eat the extras I brought home for him to keep up my strength so I could go and look for Lena. He lay there on the old green sofa, his belly swollen like a ten-month pregnancy. He was bundled up in all the clothes and blankets we had, sipping boiling water. Then he refused even that. Said he'd be better off dead. So, he died ... It only took three weeks from beginning to end."

Simeon's voice was subdued. "I was very fond of Ivan. He was like my big brother."

"So he told me. He was very angry with me after we said our goodbyes to you, but I had only one concern: my Lena."

"Where is Lena? At school?"

Gilda sat down on the old green sofa and motioned for him to sit next to her. He felt trapped into complying. Her eyes were bright, tears gathering in the corners. "Lena never came home," she said in a choked voice. "None of them did. Remember the performance over the bloody porridge? You picked up her little toy, I think, and stuck it on her high chair as we went out of the door. I found it when we got home. I kept wondering if she'd have a tantrum when she discovered it wasn't in her bag. We left her at the bus station. All the Nursery 21 parents were ordered to leave to avoid 'scenes'." Gilda buried her head in her arms. Her speech came out in great hiccoughs, but Simeon could still understand. "They'd told us to make labels to hang round our children's necks, but when we checked them in, we were told we must remove strings from all the under-fives in case they strangled one another. The teachers wrote their names, dates of birth, and nursery school numbers on the palms of their hands with indelible pencils."

Gilda was sobbing now. Simeon suspected it was the first time she'd cried properly for her daughter. He knew how it felt to hold back your emotions until you thought you would burst with the pain trapped inside you.

"We understand the children were driven south-west from here, towards Dominikanse, where an old hospital had been prepared to receive them overnight," she continued. "However, on arrival the drivers were told they were driving straight into the Germans' path. So they fed all the children, except for a couple who'd been very travel-sick. They stayed behind and were reunited with their parents. The rest were reloaded onto the omnibuses and driven north-east, towards Siberia. One of the teachers who made it back later told us how they drove on for three whole days, almost without stopping. By then, the food had run out.

"She told us the two drivers who were taking it in shifts were both so exhausted that they were falling asleep at the wheel. The teachers were overtired too. The children were grizzling and crying. They were cold, wet, dirty, and hungry. The coaches stank of urine, faeces, and vomit. When they stopped, the adults opened the doors to air the bus despite the cold. Then they, too, fell asleep from total exhaustion. When they awoke, all but three of the children had vanished. No one knows what happened to them. The three children still in their seats were dead."

Simeon instinctively stretched out his arm to comfort her. To his surprise, she moved closer to him. He felt like an intruder into this raw grief. Her body against his was a bag of bones held together by loose, pale skin. If there had ever been anything attractive about Gilda, it had gone. Her thin shoulders, covered by the tattered shawl, were shaking. She pulled a dirty rag from a sleeve hidden somewhere under the shawl and blew her nose noisily. "None of the children on Lena's transport were ever found. All the surviving parents report to the Ministry for Evacuation every month. We used to go more frequently, but they told us we were making a nuisance of ourselves. They claim they are 'looking for them', but we think they stopped looking years ago."

She shook her head. Suddenly, she changed the subject. "I liked it when you put your arm around me, Simeon. It's been a long time since anyone touched me."

"It's been a long time since I touched a woman," he said softly.

Without warning, she pulled him towards her and kissed him. He was astounded. He felt no attraction towards her, yet he felt himself stiffening and tried to pull away.

"Don't stop," she said, sensing his intended withdrawal. "I need you, Simeon Karminsky." She began nibbling his ear and licking his neck, and then her lips softened as they met his. Her hand was on his manhood now. He couldn't hide his huge erection. She pulled his hand across her breast. He felt her nipples harden at his touch. Her breasts were small, shrunken. He cupped one in his hand and felt himself losing himself in her kiss.

She pulled away for a moment. "You are lonely, and so am I," she said. "No commitment. Just once. Please?"

To hell with it, he thought, as she led him towards the door of the small bedroom and closed it behind them. As they tore the clothes off one another, he was surprised to discover she wore no underwear.

"I don't have any," she answered, smiling. He thought it was the first time he'd ever seen her smile.

He dropped his trousers. Even within the privacy of the little room, with the door locked behind them, he would not remove his boots. He fell back on the little bed and pulled her down roughly on top of him. He was aware of her reaching above their heads and something small and light brushing his face as it landed on the floor. And then he was lost to her. She was ready for him, wet with longing. They came together, overwhelmed by physical need. When it was over, they turned on their sides to face one another.

"I'm sorry," he said. "I shouldn't have done that."

"Don't be. I asked for it." She stretched out an arm and picked up the fallen object. He saw it was a small white toy dog. He took it from her hands and turned it over. Its belly was embroidered in red thread: "To-To— property of Lena S."

Chapter 24

Hanna, November 1944

ALTHOUGH THE MINSK GHETTO WAS OFFICIALLY "EMPTY", A FEW OF THE underground Jews remained in the sewers to keep watch. Those above ground made sure they were fed. Hanna had taken to joining Sonja in the confessional early on Tuesday mornings as they awaited orders. Every visit, she prayed she'd receive the signal to use the cyanide. Since the ghetto had been emptied, the office had been working on a skeleton staff, and at home she was busy packing up the apartment in accordance with Schlossberg's orders. They were being moved to Heidelberg apparently. Surely the order to kill him must come soon.

On Tuesday, Hanna went to early morning mass as usual. She met Sonja there. After they'd taken Communion, they slid into the confessional. Only Father Francis sat inside. "We're set to remove the bastard Schlossberg and get you out on Thursday." He passed a tiny twisted paper through the fretwork to Hanna. "Extra cyanide capsules in case you need them. Have your bag packed and ready. You know what you need to take. We're short of shoes, so bring any spare shoes you can carry. Men's and women's. We know he probably keeps a gun by his bed, loaded. Look for any other guns or pistols. We are certain he will be out most of the day. When he arrives home, you will make a big fuss of him. Feed the Oberst-Gruppenführer Herr Schlossberg his last supper, his favourite meal and dessert. You will take out two bottles of his most favoured wine and make sure the table is beautifully laid. When he asks what the occasion is, you will tell him … what?"

Her voice fell. "That I'm pregnant."

"You're what?"

"Father Francis, I'm pregnant. Suddenly, I realised that I hadn't had a … menstrual period for two or three months. My skirts are getting tight. Dear Father, I don't know what to do."

"How far gone are you?"

"I tried to work it out. It's due in late June or early July. I want to get rid of it." She started to cry. "How can this same womb that carried my darling sons be carrying that bastard's baby?"

He shook his head. "You need to focus on my instructions now, Maria. Just listen. You will cook a good meal. You will work the contents of the cyanide capsules into his dessert. You have four capsules now. Be generous with the stuff they contain. He will suffer the death he deserves. As he is dying, you can do whatever you want to do to him, as long as you're done and ready to leave the apartment by 20.20.

"They say hearing is the last thing to go so say anything you like to him. A car will be waiting for you downstairs at 20.30. precisely to take you to a partisan camp in the forest for debriefing. Then a decision will be made regarding your future."

That night, and to her relief, Schlossberg rang Hanna to say he would be home a little early. When he returned at 18.15, the ham hock she had acquired was boiling merrily, the aroma of garlic and bay leaves filling the apartment.

"What's all this in aid of?" he asked, eyeing the beautifully laid table. She had folded the napkins into pleated cones as she'd seen in some of the smart restaurants where they'd dined and arranged flowers carefully in his silver rose bowl. A bottle of his favourite red wine sat breathing in the centre of the table.

"To say welcome home," she enthused. "You seem to have been preoccupied and distant recently, and I have some news I hope you will want to celebrate. You are going to be a daddy again."

He looked at her in astonishment, and then a grin spread across his face. He placed an arm around her waist. "You clever, clever girl." He picked her up and wheeled her around. "A son. At last a son. We will drink his health. When?"

"I'm not exactly sure. I haven't been to the doctor yet, but I think maybe in July."

She managed a sugar-sweet smile. The words stuck in the back of her throat and she began to cough. He handed her the whiskey he'd just poured, took another for himself, lit cigarettes for both of them, and inhaled deeply. He sat down at the table and pulled her onto his lap, rubbing her slightly rounded belly with his free hand. "So tomorrow I will arrange for you to fly to Berlin. You must be seen by a good doctor. The best. Nothing but the best for my son."

She sliced the ham as thinly as she could and served it with sauerkraut and sweet potato. They ate in silence. If the aroma of the ham cooking had been enticing, the strudel she had been baking smelt even more tempting. She had worked the fine filo pastry with care, pushing and pulling it to expand just as her mother had taught her years ago. She had laid it on a wet tea towel, rolled it out into thin slices, and spread it with jam, stewed apples, cinnamon, and currants, just as her mama had taught her. Despite all the wartime restrictions, the Schlossberg household had never had problems sourcing luxury foods. Then she had snapped open three of the four cyanide pods and sprinkled them on the first and second portions of the filling, rolled up the strudel, and decorated it with pastry leaves to mark the exact location of the cyanide. *I wonder what Mama would have thought of this little dish?* She giggled to herself as she carried the apparently beautiful strudel to the table. She saw he'd already opened and poured himself a third, or was it a fourth, glass from the second bottle of Spatburgunder..

Hanna cut Frederick his first slice of the strudel and watched him wolf it down so fast that she was sure he was barely tasting it. "This is gorgeous. What about you?" he asked, sucking greedily on the spoon.

"More?"

He nodded. She cut the second slice and placed it in front of him. She was sure all the contents of three of the four capsules had gone down. She fingered the fourth, still in her pocket. She'd kept it to one side in case the first three didn't work.

"You?"

"No, I'm too full. Maybe I'll have some a little later."

"You know, I thought you had put on a bit of weight. You sit there, sweetheart. I'll clear up tonight. Shame we don't have the maid. What's her name? Hey ..." He put his hand to his throat and began to struggle for breath. She watched him, smiling. His face turned puce. He stood up then crumpled to the floor. He was writhing and fitting. He seemed to be holding out a hand to her. She had waited for this moment, longed for it, prayed for it, every day for the past three years.

"Freddy." She laughed, using the short form of his name, which he hated. "You once suspected me of being a Jewess. Guess what? You were right. I'm not one quarter of a Jewess. Not even half a Jewess. I'm one hundred per cent Jewish. So there."

The body in front of her jerked and jumped. "So clever, but not quite clever enough, eh!" She kicked him in the balls and laughed at the surprised pain on his face. "Perhaps that will remind you how you and your bully boys kicked me, a red-haired Jewess, my mother-in-law, and my two innocent little sons in the backside with your boots in a little wooden house in Vidzy." She stamped on his nose and heard the bones snap. He cried out and began to shake his head violently. Had he heard? She kicked his crotch again. "That's for the way you made us lick soup from the floor. And this one is for all my brothers and sisters Jews whom you've tortured, and starved, and humiliated, and murdered. I hope you rot in hell!" She thought she saw a brief glimpse of comprehension in his eyes before they rolled to the back of his head and his throat gurgled. It was a loud death rattle. He was gone.

Hanna glanced quickly at her watch. Twenty-fifteen. She had just five minutes. She picked up the two uniforms and the bag with everything else in it including extra shoes and the pistol from beside his bed. She'd found two guns, one beside the bed and another in his bureau. She put on her warm blue coat, and turned to look at him one last time. "I beat you in the end, you bastard." She spat on him.

She let herself out quietly, running down four flights of stairs, hoping no one in the building would hear. The car drew up as she reached the front door. She hurled the uniforms, shoes and guns onto the back seat. As they drove out of Minsk, fires could be seen on the skyline to the north. They were heading north-west, towards the camp where Smolensky would be waiting for her.

Hanna was greeted with a mixed welcome in the partisans' encampment. She'd expected nothing less. Some knew how she'd risked her life on behalf of the ghetto Jews. Others were resentful that she'd lived a life of luxury as the Oberst-Gruppenführer's mistress whilst they starved and toiled in terrible conditions. They all knew she was pregnant through the grapevine, and there could be no doubt about the identity of the father. Hirschel Smolensky had made it clear she couldn't give birth in the forest. There was no point going back to Vidzy or Krustpils. She had thought about going back to Olga. After all, it was through Olga that she'd gone to Grodno and met Schlossberg again in the first place. She fingered the little gold cross round her neck. She could give it back and reclaim her own Star of David.

"Isn't it about time you took that bloody thing off?" Reuven had snapped at her whilst watching her playing with the little gold cross at her neck. He lunged forward and tore it off, breaking the chain.

"Now look what you've done." As she bent down awkwardly to pick it up, she murmured: "It's not even mine. It was given to me by a kind old woman. It was her daughter's. She saved my life and, through me, the lives of many more Jews."

She had picked up the cross, and now it was safe in her pocket, together with the broken chain.

⚓

Hanna had been at the partisans' camp for only three weeks, mainly helping Sonja with her orphans, when Hirsch Smolensky called her to a meeting. "We need to decide on your future," he said.

"I've been thinking," she told him. "If I can give birth in the hospital here, I can just send it to the orphanage to stay with the other children. If it dies, it dies. It's half a bloody Nazi anyway."

"Hanna!" Hirsch was shocked. "How can you say such a wicked thing?"

"I'm not wicked. The man who dumped this on me was the evil one."

"But you lost two children."

"That was his fault. That bastard Schlossberg. He was responsible for their deaths. Well, let him be responsible for the death of the son he wanted so much. The best thing I could do for this child is wring its neck at birth, or drown it. That's what they do with unwanted kittens."

"What would Nat or Simeon say if they heard you speak like that?"

"They'd be as disgusted with me as I am with myself," she replied, reddening. "Simeon would never talk to me again if he knew I was pregnant with that man's bastard."

"I think he would tell you that they were circumstances beyond your control. I knew Nat well enough to know he was a decent human being, and he would appreciate the risks you took to save other Jewish lives. You are this baby's mother, whether you like it or not. And whatever your thoughts about it, it will be a Jewish child. Jewish children inherit their Judaism from their mothers, not their sires, as you well know."

"I want rid of the bloody thing," she persisted angrily. "Don't you understand? I won't be able to look at it without thinking of *him* and what he did." The truth was, she was suffering horrible nightmares in which the

205

child was born with a quiff of long blond hair and a swastika tattooed on its chest. She would awake, screaming in mental agony and slapping her swelling belly hard, hoping the pain of it could reach the child inside her.

One morning in early May, Hirschel Smolensky called her in again. "Hanna. I've been discussing your plight with Sonja and a couple of the others. Whether you want this child or not, you're stuck with it. You can't have it here. However, Johanna Spitz is travelling to Bergen-Belsen, the former concentration camp that was liberated last month. I understand the British who liberated that place are setting up a displaced persons camp there under the auspices of the United Nations Relief and Rescue Administration. It's the only one of its kind that accepts only Jews. We think you should travel with Johanna while you still can. If you give birth there, the child may even be a British citizen as of right. That will give it some kind of a start in life, even if you decide not to keep it. Things can be worked out from there. Nobody ever needs to know the baby's paternity. I won't tell anyone; I give you my word."

"Who is this Johanna?"

"She came to Minsk in late 1939 from London to help care for children in one of the many Jewish schools in the Minsk area. She spoke fluent Yiddish and took a job teaching eleven- and twelve-year-olds English. She's blonde and blue-eyed, and with her British passport, she appeared to be safe. However, when the school and its pupils were herded into the ghetto, there was nothing in her passport to suggest she was a Jew. Initially, the Germans were prepared to put her in a POW camp for the duration. However, before they had a chance, she was put in touch with Sonja. And because of her experience with children, she volunteered to help in the orphanages. She's a very brave lady. Now it's over and she wants to go home to the UK."

Hanna nervously pulled at threads on the hem of her over-tight dress. It didn't seem as though she had much choice.

"No one will check on you," Smolensky told her. "Maybe they'll even be able to help you find Simeon."

"How long did you say the journey to this place will take?" Hanna looked anxiously at her bump.

"Probably about twenty-four hours. The town of Celle, where Bergen-Belsen is situated, is near Hanover. We'll find you both overnight accommodation in Warsaw to break up your journey and arrange for a guide to meet you at your lodgings after an overnight rest, to see you onto the right train. You'll be met at the other end."

Hanna made a face.

"You don't have a choice, Hanna."

"You hated what I did, Hirschel. Why have you decided to help me now?"

"Because you did whatever we asked of you, even when it imperilled you personally. Helga told me how you secretly helped her and her family survive. Did you know she died a few weeks ago, just before the final liquidation of the camp?" he said. I think the children are OK, though. I offer you help because you are Simeon Karminsky's sister and Nat Abramskya's wife and because Maria Petruishka saved many hundreds of lives. The coaches to Warsaw leave on Fridays, Saturdays, and Sundays. We'll get your tickets."

Chapter 25

Simeon

IT WAS OBVIOUS THAT SIMEON COULDN'T STAY IN GILDA'S APARTMENT, EVEN IF there had been a place for him to sleep. He wasn't registered in Leningrad. If he was reported for staying in her flat without temporary residency, the price would be her job. She suggested he should make his way to a nearby hostel.

He wandered down the narrow street, Kadetskiy Perenlok, and found himself in front of an austere grey stone building that looked as though it was barely able to stand upright. It was shortly after 17.50 according to the clock he could see through the clear glass panel in the black door. A note was taped to the door advising that the place would be open for registration from 18.00 to 19.30 tonight. He could see the janitor lolling on an ancient chair inside, unshaven and unkempt, lazily scratching at his balls. Simeon rapped on the door to catch his attention. The man looked up briefly and pointed to the clock on the wall. Finally, at 17.59, he got up.

"A bed for tonight?" Simeon asked.

"Unlikely," the janitor said. "Most are regulars. How long do you want it for?"

Simeon hadn't thought further than tonight. "Tonight, and possibly tomorrow." He dug into his pockets, found a couple of roubles, and tucked them into the man's hand. "Please," he said. "I came to Leningrad to see if my cousin had survived. He didn't. I want to pay my respects to his widow."

"If I find you a bed, you have to be out by 7 a.m."

"It says 7.30a.m. on the notice."

"Seven in the morning," the man repeated. "Residency papers?"

Simeon shrugged. "Only army papers. If I stay beyond tonight, I will register tomorrow."

It was one minute after six o'clock. A queue had formed behind Simeon. The janitor opened the door and let Simeon in, then shut the door firmly behind him and led him down a half-tiled green and white corridor that stank of urine and up a flight of stairs. There were open doors on either side, and Simeon could see that each contained several iron beds squeezed so tightly together that a man must climb up over the bottom of the bed to get into or out of it. They stopped at the last dormitory at the far end of the corridor. The janitor led Simeon to the third bed on the right-hand side. It was a crude iron army-issue frame with a coarse blanket thrown over rusty springs. There was no mattress. Another blanket, which he suspected was probably alive with lice and fleas, was folded at the bottom of the bed. There were about twenty such beds in the room, all with folded blankets at the bottom. Simeon marvelled that the blankets appeared to stay still when they were clearly alive, harbouring thousands of parasites within their wefts and weaves. He would go back to Gilda's tomorrow, in the hope that she would let him bathe and delouse himself properly before he travelled onwards. His biggest concern was how to guard his precious boots through the night. Sharing a dormitory with nineteen other men, he could hardly sleep in them.

Although it was so early, he felt exhausted. He'd eaten, so there was nothing to stop him from going to bed now, before other men came in.

He nodded his thanks to the janitor, who repeated, "Remember, out by seven in the morning."

There was nobody else in sight, so Simeon bent down, undid his laces, and took his boots off for the first time since he'd left the forest. He folded the grey blanket round them and used that as a pillow, and then he covered himself in his heavy old coat. He was ready to close his eyes when a fat, unshaven man appeared at the end of the neighbouring bed to his left. "I can see you're familiar with the score," he said. "Leave your boots on the floor, and sure as eggs is eggs, someone will steal them. Sleeping in one of these hostels is an art form. They'll steal the teeth out of your mouth if you yawn." He sucked his own bare gums and laughed.

Simeon was awake at four the next morning. He had to think carefully about his next move. He wanted to search for Hanna. He was sure she must still be alive. Was it worth travelling to Vidzy to see if, by some miracle, she and her boys had gone back there? He'd go back to Gilda's at dawn to take his farewells, then start the journey to Vidzy at last.

As Simeon walked down Tiffliskya Prospect, he was drawn by the aroma of baking bread. It was still too early to knock on Gilda's door, so when he saw a small queue standing outside the bakery, he decided to join the line. He would present himself at Gilda's front door holding a fresh crusty white loaf as a parting gift.

"No coupons?" the baker said, holding out his hand.

Simeon was ready. He handed the man a two-rouble note, more than six times the cost of the loaf. The man nodded. It was a luxurious breakfast indeed.

Simeon rang the apartment bell soon after eight thirty, and when Gilda came to the door, he handed her the bread, still warm from the oven. She looked at him in amazement.

"To repay you for the meal I had with you yesterday."

"You bought this without coupons?"

"I thought I ought to say au-revoir properly." He was smiling shyly.

"Ooh, that smells so good. Well, well. I have a little butter and some conserves. We will breakfast like kings. Come in."

They ate breakfast in a comfortable silence. "Help yourself to a bath or shower," she said between mouthfuls, licking her lips with pleasure. "All Ivan's old shaving stuff is still in the bathroom."

"The chance to shave and feel clean would be very welcome." He laughed. "I'm afraid I am rather dirty. And this beard doesn't do too much for my looks."

She blushed. "I don't want you to think ...?" she started.

"I don't think anything, Gilda. It was just once. For old time's sake. Now I need to get going. I've decided to go to Vidzy to look for Hanna."

She sucked in her already converse cheeks and bit her lip. "I've had an idea. You're an engineer, aren't you?"-

"Yes. So?"

"One of the workers in my office owes me a big favour. His wife is in quite a high position at the Leningrad Kirov Tank Factory. As you know, Leningrad was a hub of military factories and plants before and during the war, and they've been looking for recruits to undertake research."

He stopped chewing and looked up at her. "I am a tank expert."

"Why don't you go to the city hall today and register for a temporary permit, using this as your current address?"

"I thought you didn't have room for me. Thank you." As he spoke, she was scribbling the full address for him on a piece of paper.

"You can sleep on the floor of my room if necessary, but you must have temporary registration if you want to stay here for even a few days. After yesterday, how can I pretend shame? While you're out, I'll contact my colleague. I may have some news for you by the time you return."

This was a new side to Gilda, a soft, giving side Simeon had never seen before. *Sometimes, white bread is a better aphrodisiac than champagne.*

They left together and she pointed him in the direction of the city hall, where he registered as a former resident of Krustpils now seeking temporary residency in Leningrad. On his way out, he saw a sign pointing to the United Nations Relief and Rescue Administration office. He knocked on the door.

"Can you help me?" he asked the young woman at the desk. "I'm looking for my twin sister. I have no idea where she and her two little boys might be."

"You need to post an appeal for her, or anyone who has any knowledge of her, to contact you. We work by regions."

"Would you know if she's been looking for me through your organisation?"

"We work in conjunction with the Red Cross. Some of our lists are a little out of date. As you can imagine, the Nazis have caused the displacement of millions of people, and it's chaos, but we've had some measured success already in reuniting families. Fill this in."

She handed him a piece of paper. He went across to a wooden counter, where he found a pencil attached to the surface by string. He read the form through before filling in his own personal information and the last-known details of Hanna and her family: "Simeon Karminsky, formerly of Krustpils, Latvia, seeks news of sister, Hanna Karminsky Abramskya, and family, last heard of in Vidzy, Byelorussia. Also mother, Rose Karminskya, and wife, Dora Karminskya, last known address 81 Rigas Street, Krustpils."

Simeon turned to the young woman. "Do I use this office as my contact?"

"You need a post office box number address."

"I don't have one in Leningrad."

"I'll arrange it. Where are you staying?"

He handed her the paper with Gilda's address on it. "I am staying with my cousin temporarily. These are my temporary details, just until I get settled."

He returned to the empty flat before Gilda did. He had treated himself to a copy of the Leningrad *Izvestia*. Having bathed, shaved, and once again dressed in some of Ivan's old clothes, he crept into Gilda's room and sat quietly on the bed, absorbing every word of propaganda in the news sheet. He dozed for a while. Gilda reappeared soon after two, bubbling with excitement.

"Guess what?" she said. "I think I've arranged a job interview for you."

"That's amazing."

"Svetlana Orlova Petrvoicha tells me they are looking to employ engineers with special knowledge of tanks in the Kirov factory. When I told her my cousin is staying here, saying that you have a degree in engineering from the University of Riga and that you've worked at a tank factory near Riga, she said they might consider you. I told her you were anxious not to be out of work. She made a couple of phone calls and said to tell you to be at the Kirov Institute at eight on Monday morning for an interview with Professor Leonid Dzernov who is head of the Institute." She stopped to catch her breath. "You will need residency papers. Did you get them?"

"I did. I have a one-month visa. They had an UNRRA office too, so I registered a search for Hanna, Dora and Mama there. I told them you are my cousin and gave this as my temporary address. I also have a PO box number now—5189—so I can collect my post from the local post office."

"Well done," she said. She had prepared a meal of beetroot borscht and herring. As they sat side by side on the old green sofa to eat, she looked at him.

"You can't turn up for an interview dressed like that. I see you helped yourself to Ivan's old clothes."

He started to protest. "Don't worry," Gilda said kindly. "You needed clean clothes. Ivan certainly doesn't need them now, and I think he'd be happy to know you had a use for them. You look much younger now that you've shaved. But have you any money?"

He nodded. "A little."

"Today is Saturday. The Udenlaya flea market stays open late. We could go now, if we hurry and get you some proper, decent clothes. They ate a quick snack, just bread and cheese. As the other residents of the apartment returned from work, Gilda introduced Simeon as "my husband's cousin who is staying for just a few days." Then they set off for the market, giggling like two excited children.

Finding a dark navy suit, however, was not as difficult as he'd expected. It was of no consequence that the sleeves of the shiny navy jacket came over his wrists or that the waistband on the trousers was so wide that it needed to be held in place by a belt. Gilda assured him she could alter it. They found a white shirt easily enough, and although the collar and cuffs were frayed, it was a good fit. Gilda picked out a blue knitted cotton tie to complete the outfit.

"The good news is that the trousers are so long, they'll hide my boots," he joked.

But Gilda wasn't finished. She was already scouting around a shoe stall and swooped upon a pair of black brogues with navy laces. "Look," she said. "These are smart and about your size. Try them on?"

"My boots are comfortable," he insisted. "I will dye them navy to match the suit. No one will notice."

The thought of removing his precious boots with their hidden talisman in the middle of a crowded market scared him.

"No. Stop being childish."

He could hardly refuse. He took the boots off one at a time and stretched out his right arm to hand them to her. "Hold them, please?"

She held them at arm's length. "For goodness's sake, they stink. I'm not spending a second longer than I have to holding these revolting things," she protested.

He tried to make a joke. "You'd stink too if you'd been worn every day for four years."

She was far from amused. "Throw the bloody things away. You're not taking them back to my apartment!"

This was more like the Gilda he remembered: feisty and furious.

"Either you hold them, or I put them back on and leave. I didn't ask you to get me a job interview," he spat.

She glared at him fixedly and held the boots while he tried on the shoes. They were slightly too large, but nothing he couldn't fix by stuffing the toes with old newspaper. He turned to the trader. "I'll take them. Five roubles, you said. I'll give you three." He fumbled for the money in his pocket.

"I'll get rid of those for you, Comrade," the trader said, looking at Gilda, who was standing behind Simeon, still holding the boots. He snatched them from her and threw them on a pile in a corner. "Unsaleable, those. Even to a tramp."

"Give them back. They're mine." Simeon panicked. All else was forgotten as he thought of his amber tablets. He jumped across the trader's counter and began searching for his precious boots and their hidden secrets.

"I gave you a special price on the new shoes. If you take your old boots back, it's two more roubles."

Simeon had retrieved his boots. He held them close to his chest and rattled them reassuringly to assure his amber tablets they were safe again. Then he kicked off the "new" shoes and slipped the old boots back on his feet. "New?" he said, handing the shoes back to the trader. "Perhaps they were new ten years ago." He was stamping his feet in his habitual manner, left, right, left, to let the amber tablets know they were again in his care.

Gilda, obviously embarrassed, was trying to placate him. "For God's sake, Simeon, stop making such a spectacle of yourself." To the trader, she said, "I'll take the black shoes."

"They're twelve roubles now."

"Five or nothing." Gilda was screaming above the noise of the ever-growing crowd. "Take this," she said, thrusting six roubles at the stall holder. "Give them to me. Thank you." She placed the shoes in her capacious shopping bag, alongside the suit, shirt, and tie. Simeon had already walked away in the opposite direction.

"If you want the job, you know where your interview clothes are," she called after him.

He had walked round in circles for almost two hours, thinking. Nobody, not even Gilda, would part him from his boots and their secrets. In retrospect, he had to concede she was right. He couldn't turn up for a job interview at the Kirov factory dressed as he was. He would have to apologise. She wondered whether she might still alter the suit if he spoke to her nicely. He could imagine her scoffing at his obstinacy. However, with his amber tablets under threat, he'd had no choice. If he got the job, he could rent half a room of his own somewhere else and be independent.

On his way back to the flat, he found an old woman selling flowers. He bought a pretty bunch of chrysanthemums with money he could barely afford in order to mollify Gilda. He hoped she liked flowers. The odds were that a woman like her hated them.

Gilda opened the door. "I thought you'd change your mind." Simeon bowed his head.

"Take those filthy old boots off and leave them outside the door."

"I'll leave them just inside the door, tucked in the corner."

She nodded, accepting the compromise. Then she took the flowers and sniffed at them.

"I'm only doing this for Ivan's sake, you know," she said shortly. "Do you know, in the five years we were married, he never once said he loved me. He never bought me flowers. He would say he was fond of me or occasionally that I looked nice. But love was never in the equation." Simeon looked at her quizzically. "Oh, we had sex, of course. Otherwise there would have been no Lena. You and I had sex. It wasn't 'making love'."

He said nothing. There had been both passion and fulfilment in a time of need. Nothing more.

Gilda measured him. She shortened the trousers and the jacket sleeves and stitched a large tuck in the waistband so that it fitted him more or less. "I knew you couldn't afford to miss such a chance" was all she said, handing him a hand-stitched brown felt bag. "Here. Put those disgusting old things in that. You can hide them at the back of my old wardrobe if you like."

On Monday morning, Simeon was up at five thirty. Before he took the neatly pressed and altered suit out of the wardrobe, he bent down and grabbed at the felt bag. "Listen," he whispered into the heels of his old boots, "I can't take you with me, but be with me in spirit." It seemed to him that the pieces of amber grinned their reply at the join where the heels and sole met at the back.

He left the apartment by seven in order to arrive at the Kirov plant by eight. Gilda had prepared some bread and cheese for breakfast and then waited to say "goodbye" and "good luck". "Bonne chance is what the French would say," she said, standing on tiptoe to wish him well. Then she looked him straight in the eye. "You're hiding something inside those boots, aren't you, Simeon? Something that's important to you. That's why the filthy old things are so important to you?"

He merely shrugged and left.

Chapter 26

Hanna

I T WASN'T A PARTICULARLY COMFORTABLE JOURNEY, BUT HANNA AND JOHANNA finally reached the displaced persons (DP) centre near Hanover on 23 June 1945. Hanna looked down at her bump and addressed it for the first time ever. "You and I won't be together much longer," she told it. "It's not your fault you exist. I hope you have a good life. I'm sorry for you."

After a thorough medical, she was immediately admitted to the Glyn-Hughes hospital to rest. Her tiny daughter was delivered at eight in the morning on 20 July 1945, weighing barely two kilos. She slipped out easily after a three-hour labour. Hanna refused to even look at the new-born infant.

"You've got a beautiful little girl, but she's very small," Dr Hadassah Bimkow, who delivered the baby, told her. Hanna turned her head. "Take it away," she ordered the young nurse who tried to place the infant beside her. "I don't want it."

"She needs you," Dr Bimkow coaxed.

"I don't need *it*. I never wanted it." Hanna was adamant.

"You're sure about that? It's your child, Hanna. Your daughter. Do you have any idea how many thousands of women have lost their babies during this terrible war?"

"I lost two sons. I don't want this … this thing. Give it to one of them. Let one of them adopt it."

"It happens to be a little girl," Hadassah Bimkow said firmly. "She belongs to you. You can't throw the poor little mite away like an unwanted kitten."

"Oh, I can."

"Presumably her father was a Nazi on the run."

"You could say that."

Hadassah Bimkow picked up the tiny, now swaddled parcel of a baby, turned her back on Hanna, and walked away. Hanna buried her head in her pillow and wept. She was thinking not of this child but of two other precious souls who had inhabited her womb—two much-loved little boys who would never live or breathe again.

The ward was crammed full of pre- and postnatal women, but Hanna didn't want to talk to either of the women on each side of her. She refused lunch at midday. By six in the evening, her breasts were becoming increasingly uncomfortable. She called the nurse. "Have you got anything to relieve the tenderness?" she asked. "Perhaps you could bind them so the milk doesn't come in." The nurses ignored her and continued bringing other babies from the nursery to be fed. At nine o'clock, Hadassah Bimkow appeared. She was carrying a heavily swaddled infant, who was mewling loudly.

"What's the problem?" Hanna attempted to sit herself up for the first time since the birth.

"Here. Take it. You've got plenty of milk, and it's hungry. Its mother won't feed, and as you've got so much milk, it's a shame to let it go to waste. It will put you both out of your misery." Hadassah Bimkow thrust the child into her arms. "Feed it," she ordered.

Hanna took the baby. Her breasts had leaked all over the hospital gown. As she held the child against her, the baby, desperate for food, began to root around for the breast and, once latched on, began to suckle loudly.

As the child relaxed in her arms, Hanna looked at it. She saw the new-born's tiny fist had removed itself from its bondage and was caressing the breast that was feeding it. A sudden sensation of warmth shot through her body. As she moved the child to her other breast, the baby looked up at her. There was something very familiar about the blue eyes that were fighting to focus on her face.

"Whose is it? Did its mother die?"

"In a way." Hadassah Bimkow looked down on the now contented baby who had burped obligingly and was snuggling to sleep. "Undo the shawl, Hanna Abramskya. Take a good look at her."

To her own surprise, Hanna found herself obeying, doing what she'd done with her first two babies, counting the baby's tiny fingers and miniature toes, marvelling at the perfectly formed hands and feet. "Is it a girl or a boy?" she asked as a shot of pure maternal love flooded through her.

"A girl."

"Who does she belong too?" Hanna asked curiously.

"You, of course."

Hanna thought for a moment. She opened the blanket again. The baby had the same colouring as Shmuel, fair skin, and a light sandy-red down covering her tiny head.

"I'll name her for her brothers," she said quietly. "She will be Maxine for Max and Shoshana for Shmuel."

"Good names. Strong names. Let's have no more talk of the man who fathered her. Babies can't choose their parents." The child's eyes seemed to be studying her mother's face seriously.

"Will I do, little one?" she asked softly as she caressed the baby's fingers with their minute nails. "I didn't want you, but you're here, and it looks like we're stuck with one another. Your biological father was the vilest creature ever born. Thank God he's dead. I killed him. At least I know he can never come looking for you. I will never talk to you about him again, little Maxine. I promise."

During the next few days, Hanna became friendly with Lottie, the Hungarian woman who was in the next bed. Her baby son, Harry, had been born the day before Maxine. She and her husband had been taken to Auschwitz from Budapest, but then, five months pregnant, she'd been moved to Ravensbrück, the Nazi death camp for women and then on from there to the Bergen-Belsen death camp. It was amazing that her son had survived and had been born healthy. The two new mothers spent ten days convalescing on the postnatal unit before they were moved together to share a double room in a converted former officers' barracks. They became close friends.

It was a large room with two beds, two cots, a sink, and an electric hotplate on which the women could heat a kettle and small amounts of food for themselves and their babies. They ate most of their meals in the canteen. Like so many others in the camp, they conversed in their common language, Yiddish. Lottie was as unwilling as Hanna to talk about her wartime experiences. It was over. At first, Johanna was a frequent visitor, but then she was repatriated to London, and Lottie and Hanna became closer than ever.

Hanna knew Lottie was looking for her husband, Harry's father. The last she had heard of her husband had been in November 1944, just after she had discovered she was pregnant.

"I'm sure there must be some organisation in place for helping Jews reunite with family," Lottie said as they sat chatting late one evening while their babies slept soundly in their cots.

"I was wondering the same thing. I need to find my husband, Nat, and my twin brother, Simeon," Hanna replied.

They decided that Lottie would go to the United Nations Relief and Rescue Administration office that had been set up in Celle near Hohne. Transport had been laid on between the main camp where they lived and the UNRRA office which ran in synchrony with the Red Cross and the British Army, They agreed that Hanna would babysit the two children while Lottie went to the office in Celle to find out what was required of them. She came back with forms in her hand, but only for herself.

"The people in the office gave me forms but they're all in English. Look Hanna. There's an English captain there who speaks perfect Yiddish and perfect English. Apparently you have to schedule meetings with him individually. I've got an appointment for tomorrow morning with Harry. Why don't you come too, with Maxine. You could make your own arrangements, then.

Why not?

The next morning, Hanna rose early and they walked to the bus station. They knocked on the UNRRA office door. It was opened by a stern-looking woman in a British Army uniform.

"Can I help you?"

"I have an appointment," Lottie said in broken English. The woman looked down a list and nodded. "Charlotte Jachmann. To find my husband Arthur."

"Und Sie?"

The woman nodded at Hanna. Relieved to speak in German, Hanna replied: 'I need to find my husband, my mother, and my brother. I understand you can help."

"Wait here." The woman indicated a chair, and Hanna sat on the edge of it, her fingers twitching nervously. Another woman appeared to take Lottie into another office.

"May I help you?" The man spoke first in English. Hanna shrugged. "Mamaluschen?" he asked in Yiddish. "The mother tongue?"

Hanna nodded. "I need to find my husband and my twin brother," she said. "I'm sure my twin survived."

"Come into my office. Your name, Madame?"

"Hanna Karminskya Abramskya. My husband is Nathaniel Karminsky.

219

I know he and his mother were put on a train to Auschwitz in late June or early July 1941. We had been living in Vidzy, Byelorussia. My brother was serving in the Red Army."

He was writing as fast as she spoke. "What makes you so sure that your brother survived?" he asked.

"We're twins. I can feel him around me. I'm sure I'd know if he was dead."

"What about other relatives?"

"My mother, Rosa Karminskya, and my mother-in-law, Rachel Abramskya. I don't expect either of them will have survived. I have a sister-in-law, too: Simeon's wife, Dora Levy Karminskya. She was pregnant in June 1941, so her baby would be four years old now."

"Well, let me introduce myself. My name is Eric Rosenberg. I am British, and I was here at the liberation of the Bergen-Belsen concentration camp, working alongside the Reverend Leslie Hardman, the British Jewish chaplain. I'm Jewish, and because I speak Yiddish, they asked me to stay on at the DP camp to help people like you. As you know, there are only Jews in this camp, and everyone has lost touch with their families." He held out his right hand to her.

Hanna nodded her head and shook his hand. He was slim, of medium height, with short, wavy brown hair, fair skin, a balding head and thick spectacles. When he removed them to wipe his brow, she saw he had light brown eyes and freckles scattered across his nose. He wasn't exactly handsome but had what her own mother would have described as a "choochie face", round and smiley with a strong, square jaw, in contrast to his slight build and curly fair hair.

"Are you here alone?"

"I gave birth to my daughter here six and a half weeks ago. Her name is Maxine Shoshana Abramskya," she said proudly.

"Very pretty name," he said. "The forms are all in English, but don't worry. I'll help you fill them in."

They went through the routine questions: name, age, date of birth, place of residence, place of last residence prewar, and so on. "Since you originated in Russia, your message will be posted on our noticeboards all over Russia and across Europe. We telegraph them. Modern technology is wonderful. Now, as for your appeal for contact, you must give me names and places of origin of the people you are looking for, together with last known addresses. Can you keep the message to one hundred words?"

She dictated. "Hanna Karminskya Abramskya seeks mother, Rosa Levy Karminskya, and sister-in-law, Dora Levy Karminskya. Last known address: 81 Rigas Street, Krustpils, Latvia. Also twin brother, Simeon Karminsky, at the same address, last heard of Lieutenant Third Class, the People's Volunteers, the Red Army. Anyone knowing the whereabouts of any of the above, please contact via ... What do I put there?"

"Leave that to us. We'll make sure they will be able to find you."

Eric looked at his watch and then back at her. "Would you like a cup of coffee, proper coffee in the officers' canteen, Mrs Abramskya?"

"That sounds very nice, but..." she looked at the baby sleeping contentedly in her arms. "She will wake soon for a feed. I must feed and change her."

"There's a quiet office here, unoccupied at present. Do what you need to do. I will meet you here in half an hour."

Hanna attended to the baby's needs, then joined Captain Rosenberg. Over coffee, she told him about Nat, Max, Shmuely and the forest hideout.

"What a pretty baby," he said when Maxine awoke, opened her huge summer-sky blue eyes, and regarded him seriously. "She will be a little redhead like her mama."

The baby obligingly showed off her latest trick, a beautiful wide gummy grin.

"Have you got any children?" she asked.

"Not yet, but that's probably just as well as I don't have a wife either." He laughed. "I hope when I do one day that she'll be as gorgeous as this one."

Chapter 27

Simeon

⸺⁘⁘⁘⸻

As he walked up the main white marble steps of the vast Kirov factory at five minutes before eight on Monday morning, his back straight, his red curly hair brushed as flat as he could make it with oil he'd found in Gilda's bathroom, Simeon felt confident. He wasn't "wearing" the amber tablets on his feet as he usually did, but he was aware of their presence, just as he always knew Hanna was with him in his head, her mind tuned to his. He could feel her wishing him luck, telling him he would be fine.

He was obviously expected. The receptionist at the front desk glanced at her list, nodded, and led him along a series of corridors until they reached one with the nameplate "Professor L. Dzernov". The receptionist rapped. A secretary with glasses perched on the end of her nose opened the door, nodded a greeting to the receptionist, and led Simeon in.

"Mr Simeon Karminsky has an appointment with the professor."

The secretary rapped lightly on the door of the inner office and indicated for Simeon to stand behind her. The heavy oak inner door was opened by a tall gentleman in a well-cut navy suit with a grey-white goatee beard and thick white hair. He wore rimless spectacles, from behind which a pair of pale brown eyes stared out, seemingly X-raying Simeon through to the bone.

He held out his hand, "Professor Leonid Dzernov. So, you are Simeon Karminsky? Come in, come in. Take a seat." He gestured to the brown bucket chair in front of the large desk with its green, gold-tooled writing panel on which sat a large notepad covered in blue-ink notes and a fountain pen. There was no preamble. "So, Mr Karminsky, I see you served your country well in the Red Army and latterly in the partisans near Leningrad through the Great Patriotic War. What can you offer me?"

As he spoke, the telephone rang.

He got up, opened the door, and barked at the secretary. "I told you to hold all calls for thirty minutes."

"Excuse me, sir. I apologise," Simeon heard her say. While the professor was otherwise engaged, Simeon took the chance to look around and saw that the bookshelves were filled with dark bindings, all technical textbooks by the professor himself. Models of various tanks, armoured trucks, and heavy four-wheel-drive transporters the professor had been credited with authorising or working on were displayed behind glass in a wooden showcase.

The professor was back. "Stupid bloody woman," he muttered. "Ah! I see you are looking at my models. Some of them are prototypes still under manufacture. Others are older tanks that have been designed in this factory. In case you're wondering, the portraits looking down upon us are those of our faculty founders: Petrov, V. L. Kyrpychov, A. A. Radtsig, I. I. Ivanov, and L. Z. Ratnovsky."

"So, Mr Karminsky, I note you graduated from Riga University and worked prewar at Factory 174 in Jekabpils. What can you offer me?"

Simeon spoke about his dissertation on the practicality of tank warfare in 20th Century battles, his work in Factory 174, and his experiences as a partisan. He failed to mention the Battle of Raseiniai or his unofficial exit. Nor did he speak of his experiences in the Amber Room. The professor seemed unfazed that Simeon said nothing more of his army experience.

"Tell me about the tanks you worked on in the battlefield. The old ones, of course."

"T-34s mostly," Simeon replied. "Older—the T-28s—occasionally. Mostly I was adapting old tanks for modern warfare."

"What do you know about the T-54s?"

"Nothing, sir. That was after my time."

"They are being developed right now at our Nihzny Tagil plant. That's in the Sverdlovsk oblast, out east. However, we are working on components of the prototype right here at the Kirov plant. Would you be prepared to offer your expertise to such a developments? Of course, you realise I am entrusting you with state secrets. I am already treating you as a member of an exclusive team."

Simeon's eyes were alight with enthusiasm.

"I believe you were a favoured engineer in Factory 174," the professor went on. "I spoke to Comrade Yuri Preditis yesterday. He recommended you very highly. Said you were the best graduate they ever had. You were personally chosen by Colonel Berlovsky, I believe, to join the army as a lieutenant engineer third class in December 1940."

Simeon's mind was in turmoil. In the two days between Gilda's friend asking if there was a position and the granting of the interview, the professor had done his homework. What else did they know about him? Given that the appointment had been made on Friday and today was only Monday, quite a lot, he supposed.

"The Ettinger partisans were admired for their war work by the Red Army," the professor continued. "I believe you served as a leading light with them. What has happened to the other leaders?"

"I'm not sure, sir." It was the truth. Simeon was too terrified to say anything more about Rutti, Mikhail, Oscar, or even Arieh.

"Would you be interested in joining us? There is much scope for research within the arms industry, right now in Leningrad. This city has an excellent reputation as a manufacturer and supplier of arms to our great and glorious Red Army." He didn't wait for Simeon's reply but he held out his hand. "Of course you will join us. So, welcome, Comrade Karminsky. You are, I hope, about to join the Party here in Leningrad. I believe Gilda Solomon, your cousin - or to be accurate your late cousin's wife - is an active party worker in her department."

"Thank you, Sir," Simeon replied earnestly. He felt his heels tapping nervously on the floor as he spoke, feeling for the strength of the amber tablets. He was speaking to them in his head as he always did when an important decision was at hand. They may not have been with him physically at that moment, but they were with him yet. He was aware that the interview was drawing to a close.

"I hope you will be happy with us here at the Kirov plant," Professor Dzernov said finally, standing up and extending his hand. How Simeon wished he could feel Hanna. He had a sudden need of her reassurance, but she had never had any input into the professional side of his life. She didn't understand engineering. As Simeon got to the door, he suddenly realised he had forgotten a vital question. "Excuse me, sir, but we didn't discuss salary," he said.

Dzernov laughed. "Of course, you will be paid on the lowest salary scale for a Senior worker to start with." He smiled. Simeon bowed his head humbly and took a step to go, but Dzernov called him back. "I understand a man has to eat. The salary scale will rise fast as we judge your worth. You won't be on the breadline for long. Coincidentally, I notice you are smartly dressed. We appreciate our staff looking good. You have impressed me, Karminsky. You have a week to prepare yourself. Catch up on some reading. You may use our library if you wish to come up to speed with my own work. I believe you are currently staying with Gilda Solomon. We will send a pass to her home to give you access to this building starting tomorrow. We start work at eight in the morning. You will report here, and I will personally take you over to the factory tomorrow to introduce you to your new colleagues and then escort you to the library myself."

As he strode back along the Neva embankment, Simeon felt proud of himself. He had been in Leningrad for just three days and already he had a job, thanks to Gilda's introduction, although it was he himself who had impressed the famous professor. With a job, he could apply for a six-month residency permit, and when he had that he could look to rent a room of his own.

He made his way back to Gilda's as there was nowhere else to go.

"You have a job, I understand," she said as she walked through the door, denying him the pleasure of announcing his good news. "It would appear that Professor Dzernov was most impressed by you. Knowledgeable but humble. Well-mannered but not pushy. 'Unusual in a Jew,' he told my colleague. Did he question you about being Jewish?"

"He never said a word. You were right about the suit and the polished shoes," he said, offering her credit where he felt it was due. It was almost an apology for the way he had behaved in the flea market. "The professor seemed to know a great deal about me already. Where did he get such knowledge? He is going to take me to meet colleagues, and he's getting me a library pass. Now I need to find somewhere to sleep."

"I've already arranged that."

Was there anything this woman didn't know or hadn't done in advance of his requests?

"I've told the Markovs that they have to make room on one of their many mattresses for the oldest son. At present, he's sleeping on the green settee," she continued.

He thought of the green settee. He was nearly 1.9 metres tall. He wondered how long it would be before his neck began to ache from lying curled on the ancient two-seater on which Igor had died.

Next day, as planned, he met the professor who true to his word took

Simeon to meet his new colleagues and then led him over to the factory library. Aware what was expected of him, he took care to study the Professor's work although he soon realised he'd covered much of it years ago, at university

For the first two weeks, the work he was given, suggesting updates to old plans in the main studio was boring. "It could be done by a bright ten-year-old," he told Gilda. When the professor called him to his office, Simeon was worried. Had he made a stupid mistake? He was conscious that the eyes of everyone else in the laboratory followed him to the professor's door. The professor, not the secretary, opened the door and invited him in. He wasted no time in getting to the point. "You have pleased me by your efficiency," Dzernov said. "We have, as you have realised, had you working on old material. Now we would like to offer you promotion to senior design engineer. By the way, the factory is a closed shop. Have you joined the Party yet?"

"Not here in Leningrad, sir. I haven't had time but I will this week, of course."

"Well, Comrade-to-be Karminsky." The Professor smiled. "I am an official at the local level, and I know my fellow comrades will be delighted to welcome you. I will make the necessary arrangements. Please be sure to attend party meetings regularly. There's one in this office this evening."

Simeon loved the work, and although he thought that at first he detected a certain reticence among his colleagues, they mellowed when they discovered he was happy to be "one of the boys".

"Come and have a drink with us before you go home," Anatoly Popov invited him one Friday, about six months after he'd started work.

Why not? he thought to himself. Then he realised it was a test. "Jews don't drink much and never go out on Friday nights," he'd overheard Anatoly telling another colleague. "If he refuses, we'll know the rumour's true."

So they'd discovered he was a Jew. He was being tested. "I'd love to," he replied.

Through the autumn and winter, Simeon and Gilda settled into a cosy routine. They were both out at work all day. In the evenings, Gilda prepared a meal that they ate together. He insisted on paying her rent now that he was earning a salary.

As spring approached, they started meeting after work to attend classical concerts together. They shared a mutual love of Shostakovich, Beethoven, and Rachmaninov. When they went to a Tchaikovsky concert which included the *Pathétique*, he told her for the first time about Arieh. "I wonder if he's still with Rutti? He should be having proper violin lessons now. He has too great a talent to waste. Most importantly, is he happy?"

"Maybe one day you'll be in touch again," she soothed. He dared not tell her how often he thought of his surrogate son when he saw other boys around Arieh's age playing in the street. He wished he had a way of communicating with him.

To his surprise, he and Gilda were becoming close friends as the weeks rolled on. It was, he told himself, inevitable. She had done so much to help him. He often asked himself why. At the weekends, they would sometimes pack a picnic. The mother of one of his colleagues loved to conjure fancy cakes from the few ingredients available, and sometimes he would order one and hand it with pride to a smiling Gilda on a Friday evening. Because she was cooking for him, she was eating regularly herself. Her sunken face had begun to fill out. He insisted she use the rent he gave her to get her teeth fixed, and the dentist fitted her with a bridge.

When they were sure that they were alone in the apartment, they would go into her room for sex. Their sex satisfied a hunger, just as food satisfied them when their stomachs were empty. It was sex born not of love but of physical need. Simeon enjoyed the simple domesticity of their life after the theatre of war. The only connection he had with that life before he joined the partisans was his boots and their amber secrets. He sneaked a peep at them every day, usually in the morning while Gilda was in the bathroom, as though to remind them he was still there, standing guard over them just as they had protected him. Sometimes when Gilda was out, he would go to her room and remove the boots from their rough felt bag. He would sit on the floor cross-legged with them on his lap, stroking the heels and holding them against his ears, urging the two little pieces of carved amber inside to infuse him with the mental strength he needed. He vowed he would never leave his amber tablets. He truly believed their magical powers had somehow saved his life.

One Tuesday evening when Gilda got home an hour earlier than expected, she caught him sitting on the floor, cradling the boots, and talking to them as though they were people who could give him the answers to the questions he yearned to ask. Had Dora, his mama, and the baby all really died in the abattoir? Had their cries been among those cries he'd heard that fateful day when he went back to Krustpils? Was there no way they might have escaped?

It had crossed Simeon's mind that he should propose to Gilda, make an honest woman of her. However, how could he when he had no proper proof that Dora had died?

He was so deep in thought, almost in prayer, that he didn't hear Gilda enter the room. He was utterly oblivious of her as she stood over him. Suddenly, she broke the spell.

"What is it with those filthy old things?" she asked. "Why don't you just throw them away and be free of whatever treasure you're hiding in the heels? You have hidden something in the heels, haven't you? You don't need that old rubbish anymore. You have two decent pairs of shoes now. Throw them out."

She had picked one up and was holding it up above her head. He stood up quickly and reached for it.

"Leave them alone. They're none of your business."

"For God's sake, Simeon." Instead of handing it back, she hid the boot behind her back.

"Come on, Gilda. Give it to me."

She was juggling with it now, throwing it into the air. Finally she fell onto the bed giggling, and he wrested one boot from her, but it went flying, hitting the green glass lampshade that covered the single lamp in the centre of the small room. There was a smash of glass, and they watched in horror as the shade shattered, sending shards across the bed in what appeared slow motion. Sole and heel had parted company. Amid the dust of brown leaves scattered over the bedding lay a tiny parcel wrapped in the remnants of Ethan's old shirt.

"Dear God, woman, what have you done?"

She looked at the hollowed-out heel in her hand and went to pick up the tiny parcel on the bed. "Take your hands off that!" he shouted sharply. "It's mine."

"What is it?"

"None of your bloody business."

"Then tell me what the secret is."

They both looked up and saw it at the same moment: a little black microphone attached to the lighting wire, previously covered by the smashed green shade.

"Bloody hell," he breathed. "We're being bugged. By your place or mine?"

"Both, I suspect."

"Let's get out."

"Let's clear up first."

"No. Out. Now." He picked up the tiny parcel, wrapped in a rag from

Ethan's shirt. He didn't know which of his amber tablets it was yet but he slipped it into his pocket.

"Where are we going?"

"It's too hot indoors" was his only reply.

They walked downstairs side by side, crossed the road, rounded a corner, and made their way towards the Neva embankment, glancing behind themselves frequently to make sure they weren't being followed.

"I think you like me. Or is it just that you like our sex together, Gilda?" Even as he spoke, he wondered where those words were coming from. They were not words he'd planned to say.

"The answer is yes. To both." She giggled.

"Then perhaps it is time to become more to one another than flatmates. We could become a partnership. Together, perhaps, we could even find a more suitable place to live, a flat of our own. After all, we are both in positions of power and trust, or they wouldn't think it worth bugging us."

"What are you asking, Simeon?"

He was gazing into her eyes. "Dora was only a child when we married, Gilda. Only seventeen. You are a woman. I need a woman to care for and who will care for me. Marry me, Gilda. I promised Ivan I'd look after you. So I'll be keeping my promise." He realised suddenly that he had not yet used the word *love*.

She pursed her lips and looked at him seriously for a moment.

"Let's go and sit down in the park and talk."

The grassy parkland beckoned ahead of them. They found a comfortable spot under a shady tree where last year's leaf drop provided a natural cushion. As they settled themselves, he saw that someone had left an old Leningrad *Izvestia* newspaper right beside them.

Simeon glanced at it, and a headline caught his eye. Gilda was trying to snuggle against him.

He sat up straight. "Just a minute."

"What?"

It was a single column in small print. Three words, *Amber Room Mystery*, jumped out at him. Looking over his shoulder, Gilda read the date on the top.

"Simeon, this paper's more than a week old."

He ignored her and sat staring at it.

> The Amber Room, looted by the Nazis from the Catherine Palace in Tsarskoye Selo in November 1941, has been officially designated a missing art treasure. Allegedly dismantled

by seven German officers in a thirty-six-hour period in November 1941, it was on public display in Königsberg Castle until April 1945. When the Red Army recaptured the castle, however, there was no trace of the Amber Room. Professor Alexander Brusov has been appointed to lead a full enquiry into the mysterious disappearance of this priceless work of art. The only remaining original pieces of the amber mosaics that made the room world-famous remain in vaults at the Hermitage Museum. They were undergoing restoration by master craftsmen at the time the Amber Room was looted.

As he read, he forgot Gilda. He forgot where he was or what he'd been doing. Every hair on his neck stood up straight, and shivers gripped him as he recalled every detail of those two terrible days in November 1941: the child shot for being hungry; the prisoner killed for trying to secrete a single piece of amber in his shoe; the madman who had danced his way to certain death; Dov Persky. Simeon recalled the seconds when he had swallowed his amber tablets. He rubbed his throat. He could feel them again passing down his gullet like unchewed, hard-boiled candy. He recalled how it felt when nature had expelled them more than a week later. Suddenly, he was aware of Gilda looking over his shoulder, her hands on his neck. "Simeon. Are you all right? You've gone very pale."

"Oh!" He jumped. "I forgot you were there."

"Thank you." She grinned. "Nice to feel loved and wanted. One minute you are proposing marriage to me, the next you forget I exist." She picked up the paper. "What does this Amber Room have to do with you, Simeon? Is that where the little parcel that fell out of the shoe came from?"

His face reddened. "My God. You were there, weren't you?" He shook his head, no. His rapid, vehement denial belied his words.

"You do know something about it. A reward might help us finance a home."

"I don't think so. I was there when the Amber Room was dismantled, but not when it was stolen. Let's leave it at that." He dug into his pocket, pulled out the little parcel again and undid it. It was his eagle's talon.

"This is my eagle's claw, but you never saw it, right? *Never.*" He reached out and held her by her shoulders so that he was staring straight into her brown eyes. "Promise."

"Promise." She spoke the word softly, a vow solemnly given. Then he laughed. Gilda was bright. He could read her mind. They were both wondering. She knew now that the "secret" inside the other boot must also be a fragment of amber, but could the two little pieces of amber in his keeping be all that remained of the world-famous wonder? He'd believed nothing would persuade him to part with them for any money, not even a million roubles. However, was he currently in possession of part of Russia's precious heritage? This was not a free country. It was Stalin's Russia. The Stasi was over every shoulder. Proof of that was the little bug they'd just discovered in their room. If his two remaining amber tablets were really all that was left of the Amber Room, would they possess magic beyond any he could imagine and grant him a place in history? He tore the small story out of the paper, wrapped it around the eagle's talon, and stuffed it back into his pocket.

"Come on," he said. "I presume the answer to my earlier question about getting married is "yes" so let's go out for a drink and celebrate our engagement."

"First let's go back to the apartment. I need a jacket."

The air was cooling. Simeon moved closer to Gilda and put his arm around her shoulders. He could feel her shoulder bones through the fine cotton material of her summer frock. Back in the apartment, he waited until she visited the bathroom, then took the ragged newspaper and tucked it into the toe of the remaining whole boot. He put the eagle's talon, still wrapped in the remains of Ethan's ragged shirt, into an almost empty cigarette pack in his top pocket. Once certain the eagle's tiny talon was safe, he began clearing up the mess, pulling the edges of the eiderdown, onto which most of the glass had fallen, together so that the shards pooled in the centre, then taking the whole thing downstairs and shaking it straight into the communal garbage can as best he could.

Back in the flat, he found Gilda sweeping the worn brown linoleum with a dustpan and brush, then pulling fresh sheets and her winter eiderdown from the cupboard and changing the small single bed. "You'd better not walk on the linoleum without shoes," she warned. "I'm not sure that I've got it all."

Somewhere, in the back of his mind, Simeon felt a little uneasy about having proposed to Gilda so hastily. What if, by some twist of fate, Dora and the baby had survived? If he married Gilda, he'd be a bigamist. But Eleanor had been adamant that they had all died in the abattoir. Anyone who'd escaped had been shipped to Auschwitz. Still, he had no proof that she was dead. As for Hanna? Gilda had never questioned whether he'd heard any more about Hanna's survival. But he had. Only two days ago he'd heard to his joy that Hanna had survived. She'd sent him a note to say she was living at a DP Camp in Celle in Germany and she wanted to be with him. As yet, he hadn't had the courage to tell Gilda that his sister wanted to return to Russia. He had to reply, of course, although he'd received a veiled warning from his boss. "I understand you've heard from you sister," Dzernov had said casually. "I think perhaps that you must reply to say you are glad she is alive. Point out that you cannot write again and you would appreciate it if she didn't try to correspond with you. Your work is in a protected field. It is highly secretive work you do, Simeon Karminsky."

Chapter 28

Hanna

"**L**EAVE IT FOUR OR FIVE WEEKS BEFORE YOU START CHECKING THE noticeboards for news of your brother," Eric Rosenberg advised Hanna. "With so many people displaced, it could take months or even years before we get any news of loved ones. It's a difficult fact to have to tell people, but that's the way it is."

Everyone in the DP camp was expected to work once they were fit. Hanna had been allocated a job in the nursery, caring not just for her own daughter but also for other people's babies and young children. A school had opened for older children. Cooks were at work almost twenty-four hours a day running the canteens, while laundries and shops had sprung up in the camp. The authorities were trying their best to rehabilitate people whose civilised lives had all but disappeared.

Lottie worked at the feeding centre where some six hundred displaced and orphaned school-aged children received meals three times a day. Many had suffered in internment and concentration camps, and had witnessed scenes of such violence and cruelty that their lives would be tainted by the experiences forever, but few spoke about them.

During the fourth week after she'd first met with Eric, Hanna began checking the noticeboards daily, then weekly. Finally, after six months—when there were no messages, she left it a week between visits. Then once a month.

The babies were nine months old when Lottie came flying into their shared room one evening, frantically waving a brown envelope.

"Look, Hanna, look! Don't you bother to check the noticeboards anymore? You've got a letter." Hanna stared at the envelope with its official stamps.

"For God's sake woman! Open it."

"Suppose it's bad news?"

"Suppose it's good news? How do you know until you open it?"

Hanna slit the envelope and drew out a piece of formal paper.

Dearest Hanna,

I received your message. I'm so happy. We both survived. I wish I could hug you. I was in a partisan camp in the forests just outside Leningrad through the war. I went back to Krustpils to learn that Mama and Dora had been taken to Auschwitz with our newly born daughter in July 1941. I believe they are all dead. I don't know if you are aware that Nat also died. I am living in Leningrad with Cousin Ivan's widow, Gilda. Ivan died of starvation during the Siege. There is no room for you here. Please don't write again but I will always love you.

Simeon

"He survived. I knew it. My brother's alive and in Leningrad. He says I cannot go to him. He tells me not to write any more. No. He can't mean that. This letter isn't from my brother Simeon. It can't be. Simeon would never cut me off. Never!" She stood, holding the letter, white-faced. "I will write back. I will challenge whoever wrote this nonsense to explain. He can't mean it. My brother Simeon would never say such a thing."

Eric had become a regular visitor to the quarters Hanna and Lottie shared with their babies, often knocking on their door with little treats—a bar of chocolate, a tin of peaches from America, a tiny dress for Maxine, a pair of trousers for Harry.

"He's really sweet on you," Lottie told Hanna one day, smiling up at her from the second-hand sofa they'd been given. The latter was busy applying red lipstick for a date to the cinema with Eric. He always paid Lottie for babysitting Maxie with a bar of Lottie's favourite candy, Cadbury's dairy milk chocolate or Hershey's bars he'd scrounged from the Americans.

"I'm more than happy to sit and read and listen to the radio with a lovely bar of chocolate to keep me company," Lottie told Hanna. "I'm so happy. My Arthur has been found in an army hospital near Nancy in France. I don't know how he got there, but he's recovering. And as soon as he's well enough, we will be together."

Sometimes British celebrities like Vera Lynn or Tommy Trinder and Charlie Chester paid surprise visits to the camp to entertain the troops, and whilst the boys and girls in khaki clamoured for them, Eric always managed to get an extra ticket for Hanna.

"He's a good friend," she admitted to Lottie.

"Surely he's more than just a friend. Anyone can see that by the way he puts his arm around you when he comes to collect you. I've seen the look on his face. When he kisses you goodnight, it's more than the kiss of a 'friend'."

"I bet it's just because I'm here and available. I'm sure he has a girl waiting for him back in London. Of course, I think he's attractive, if you look beneath the spectacles. And he's such a clever man. He's going to study law when he goes home. I don't believe he doesn't have a girlfriend at home."

The thought had frequently crossed Hanna's mind. She was growing fonder of Eric than she had ever intended. Although Eric had reassured her that there was no one else waiting for him back home, she remained unconvinced.

"I've heard from my brother," Hanna told Eric as she answered the door that evening, her eyes rimmed red from crying. "Mama is dead. So is my husband. I expected as much. However, my twin is alive. He has told me he is living with our cousin's widow. She had a huge flat, three whole rooms with a kitchen and a bathroom all to themselves. But he's told me not to write any more. Why? I don't understand."

As they walked towards the officers' mess, Eric put his arm around her. She felt some comfort for the first time in years.

"I have to reply, whatever he says," she told him.

"I understand," Eric told her, but conditions in the East are bad. "He must have had a very good reason for asking you not to contact him again. Be careful Hanna. You are dealing with a strict, dictatorial regime. We don't know the repercussions of disobeying it, from Simeon's side. If you write your letter, be very careful what you say. I am sure all the post to the East is being censored."

Dearest Simeon,

I am so sorry that Mama is gone and that you lost Dora too. She was so lovely. I am also heartbroken that Nat died, although I think I already knew in my heart that he hadn't survived. Both my boys were killed too. We were hiding in the forest. When Nat didn't come, I left them asleep to go to look for food. When I returned, they had both been shot through the head.

As she wrote, tears fell on the paper, blotting her ink. She dried them with her sleeve and continued.

I am so happy and grateful that you survived. I am living in the DP camp at the former Bergen-Belsen concentration camp, which is under the control of the British. I have nothing and no-one but you. I had hoped I could come to live with you. My dearest wish is to be with you again. Please send Gilda my condolences on the loss of Ivan. Haven't they got a little girl? I wish you both only happiness.

With much love, your twin sister,

Hanna

"I will post it for you," Eric told her. "It can go in one of the Forces' bags—but don't tell anyone. I understand that otherwise, letters can take as long as six months to reach the Soviet Union from here.

It was three long months before Hanna did receive a reply, just in time for Maxine's first birthday. Eric brought the letter with him when he arrived to take her out one evening. Hanna opened it as she stood leaning against the door, staring at her brother's familiar handwriting on the airmail envelope. Eric saw her hands trembling as she read, saw her face changed from excited anticipation to total despair. Her left arm dropped to her side, still clutching the flimsy blue paper. She stood staring into space, white-faced and too shocked to cry.

"So it isn't good news?" When she looked up, he could see her usually red-blonde lashes were dark with tears.

"He doesn't want me," she whispered. "He says conditions in Gilda's apartment are difficult. I remember the apartment being huge, but he says they have only one small room. There are seven of them living there now, and no place for me."

She looked back down at the letter in Cyrillic script back.

"Read it to me," he said.

7 April 1947
PO Box 5189, Leningrad

Dearest Hanna,

We are all grieving for our losses, but you cannot come here
and I beg you, don't write again.

I share one small room in Gilda's apartment. Six others
now live in the flat that was once rented to her and Ivan
alone. Their daughter, Lena, was evacuated in September
1941 and never came home. We plan to marry. I have a job
in a factory. I am forbidden to correspond with anyone in
the West, even you. I was given special permission to reply
to you this time but I implore you. Please, do not write
again. I hope you will soon find another place to call home.

My love to you, xxxx

Simeon

"It doesn't make any sense," Hanna said. "First my brother tells me he is well and happy. He's planning to marry that woman. I remember her as a cold bitch. He tells me he is forbidden to correspond with me." She fell backwards onto the chair behind her. "Finally he sends love and signs it 'Simeon'. I never liked that woman. This is not my brother writing. It's her. Now where will Maxine and I go? What will we do?"

"You have me."

She looked up at him, her eyes wide open and questioning.

"You know I said I had something I wanted to discuss with you, after you'd heard from your brother. Well, here goes." He bent down on one knee.

"Hanna Karminskya Abramskya, will you and *Maxine Shoshana Abramskya* take me as your husband and father? Will you marry me and give me a beautiful daughter?"

"You can't take both of us on. Where will we live?" She gasped.

"In England. We will move to England as soon as my duty here is finished in three months' time. I will make arrangements. Please say yes?"

He fumbled in his pocket and pulled out a little ring box. Lying in the centre was a solitaire diamond ring. He took it out and put it on the fourth finger of her left hand. Then, as if that weren't enough, he fished into the pocket again and came out with a tiny little silver bracelet with the name *Maxine* etched into the front. "Come home to England with me, Hanna? Be my wife? Pretty, sweet, clever little baby Maxine. I want you to be my daughter, and I will be the best daddy you could ever want. I promise you. If you say no, I can't marry your mama."

The small girl looked at her mama, who was nodding. She put out her chubby little arms towards Eric, and he took her, complete with a heavy wet nappy, and cuddled her. The three of them laughed as her damp bottom left a wet mark on his uniform sleeve. Then he handed her back to her mother. "I supposed I'll have to learn to change nappies now. I've loved you both since the first day I set eyes on you in my office." He turned to look at Hanna hopefully. "Perhaps you won't love me yet as you loved your Nat. Maybe in time you will learn to love me a little. I want to go home and take up the offer of a place to read law at Oxford University that I was offered before the war. We will live with my parents to start with, and they will adore their new granddaughter."

"You know her natural father was a Nazi soldier who raped me."

"I wouldn't care if she'd been sired by a Martian with green skin and cauliflower ears. Have you never heard of nurture over nature?" Eric laughed. "Maxine will grow up with me as the only daddy she will ever know or need. I can't change her genes, but I can give her a good life as a little English girl." He looked at his watch and tapped it with frustration. "Come on, Hanna. I need to get you home."

Hanna looked at the ring on her finger and remembered two other rings that stayed safe in the little velvet bag beside her bed. She would sell the rings Schlossberg had given her and the jewellery she' had from Nat and from Rachel when they got to England. Then she would put the money into a savings account for Maxine.

"I hope you said yes," Lottie said when Hanna told her. "What an opportunity for you both."

Hanna looked at her. "I did." She held out her newly ringed finger. "He's a good man. He will be a good papa. We will get married after his next leave. I suppose I must be grateful." She handed Lottie Simeon's letter. Lottie shrugged. "At least you know where you're going now. Harry and I are still waiting. Arthur's progress is very slow. I wonder whether we'll ever have a normal family life, ever again."

Chapter 29

Arieh - Summer 1947

W HENEVER HE WAS FEELING HOMESICK, ARIEH WOULD TAKE HIS PRECIOUS morsel of amber out of his pocket and talk softly to it. "Please, Little Miss Honey, help me find Simeon. I need him so much. I miss him so badly."

He was almost twelve years old now, and as much as he loved Ruth, and despite all that Ruth's cousin Lauren and her husband, Blake were doing for him, he missed Simeon as much as he missed his parents.

He knew he was lucky to sleep between clean white sheets in a proper bed in a room that they called "Arieh's room", yet he longed for the physical presence of the man in whose arms he'd curled on a mattress of straw almost every night for four years. He missed how Simeon had brushed his fingers through his hair and called him son. He longed for the warmth and familiarity of the large man with his untamed red curls and heavy patched farmers' boots who believed in the magic of the amber tablets.

Blake was doing his best to fulfil the role of father figure. He'd enrolled Arieh in a local school where most of the children were Jewish, and he was paying for him to have proper violin lessons. They had had his violin restrung professionally. Arieh loved them for all of it. Lauren had arranged for both Ruth and Arieh to go to an English-language school set up by the Joint Jewish Distribution Committee, known locally as "the Joint", where they were learning not only English but also the new way of life in their adopted homeland.

All this, and yet ... Arieh looked at Little Miss Honey and wished with all his heart that she could help him contact Simeon again.

Winter had been cold and hard, but no worse than they were used to in Leningrad. But now Arieh was properly dressed, and Lauren and Blake's spacious apartment was toasty warm with central heating radiators in every room.

They had taken him to a doctor who had arranged for him to have physical therapy to encourage his muscles to grow in his damaged right leg. He had been seen by a plastic surgeon but sadly, it was too late now to think of skin grafts. The wounds were too deep. He had creams and ointments to soothe the pain and a proper bone doctor and a physical therapist had ensured he had a proper iron and leather calliper built around a custom made boot that he had to strap on every morning. It was a heavy, cumbersome thing but it had vastly improved his ability to walk with only a cane to support him. Blake had taken him shopping and bought him American-style clothes, long trousers that covered the hated calliper, and T-shirts and sweatshirts like the other boys at school wore. Life was quiet; it had a regular rhythm in a way Arieh hadn't experienced since his childhood in Odessa. When spring arrived, to Arieh's surprise, the trees in Central Park were gowned in the same fresh green garments as those he'd come to love in the forest, heralding the beginning of better weather. New York was very different in so many ways from the place he thought of as home, yet Arieh found it a great comfort that at least the trees looked the same.

He could hold a conversation with real Americans now. The best part of his new life was that every day of the week, he and his adopted family did whatever they had to do, but on Shabbat, from sundown on Friday night until the first three stars appeared on Saturday night, they rested. This was a traditional Jewish home, just as he remembered from when he was a little boy in Odessa. They went to the synagogue. At home, Lauren and Ruth lit the candles and Blake blessed him, just as his father had done. On Saturday morning, they worshipped together in the Synagogue where Arieh sat next to Blake downstairs while the "girls" sat in the gallery. The tunes were the familiar tunes Arieh remembered from home. It was a real day of rest. Arieh loved the Sabbath and vowed that when he was grown up, he would keep it properly, too.

They were sitting round the lunch table one Sabbath afternoon in late May when Arieh suddenly said, "You have been very kind to me, Blake and Lauren, but I think the time has come that I should look for my aunt."

Blake pushed his chair back sharply from the table. "I consider you as part of our family," he said.

241

Lauren looked at the serious young boy. He was still only eleven years old, yet he sometimes spoke and acted like a much older young man.

"You said you think that your mother's sister lives in Miami, didn't you? First, I think we ought to check with UNRRA and the Red Cross to see if she's registered her search for you with them. If she has, that makes tracing her easy."

"If she knows my parents are dead, she'll expect that my sister and I died with them."

"You think she's in Miami, so we could put an advert in the *Florida Sun*," Blake suggested. "I was speaking to one of my colleagues whose relatives escaped from Germany just before the war, and she found her family through a newspaper ad."

Immediately after the Sabbath ended, Lauren took out a pencil and a piece of paper. "You don't have to do this, Arieh. We love you very much. However, it's right that you look for your mother's sister and at least let her know you've survived. You're welcome to stay even if you do find her. You are part of our family now. Anyway we'd love you to ..." She looked at Blake before she continued, and he nodded at her as though giving his assent. "We would love you to be a big brother to our baby who is going to join us in October, just in time for your 12th birthday."

In the ensuring excitement, Arieh's family was forgotten. "How wonderful. That's so exciting." Ruth hugged her cousin.

"Then you'll need my room for the baby." Arieh giggled. "Such great news. I've chosen a good time to go, haven't I?"

"You'll always have a home here with us," Blake said warmly. "We don't want to lose you, Arieh. I can't believe it's nearly a year since you arrived. It feels like you've been here forever."

Lauren took her pen and began to scribble on the back of an envelope quickly. "What do you think of this? Listen: 'Arieh Weinstein, aged eleven, formerly of Odessa in Byelorussia, seeks Aunt Shayne Goldmeyer, also formerly of Odessa, Byelorussia, now believed to be residing in the Miami area with husband, Hyman, and son, Yehuda Goldmeyer. Please write care of Ruth Ettinger, Box 91748, New York.'"

"That's great, but how do we know they'll see it?"

"We don't," Lauren said practically. "However, it's worth a try."

"Do you think my aunt will want me?" Arieh asked. "After all, we've never met. You didn't tell her I'm a cripple, did you?" He blushed. "I mean, shouldn't you warn her?"

"Why?" Lauren answered. "Anyone would be proud to claim a handsome, talented boy like you as a nephew. I am."

"I can't walk far," Arieh said. He was fingering the precious piece of amber in his pocket.

"True, but nobody chooses their relatives according to whether they can run a marathon or not. Just wait until they hear you play the violin."

⚜

"Sharon. Have you seen this?"

"Who has time to read the newspaper?" Sharon Gold swept past her husband Howie as she prepared pancakes and bacon for Saturday brunch, whilst he sat in his vest, his elbows resting on the table, the *Florida Sun* propped against a coffee cup.

"Some people prepare breakfast, put on the wash, clean the house, cook lunch, do the ironing, and go to the supermarket on a Saturday morning. Others sit around stuffing their faces, reading the newspaper, while waiting for their breakfast to be served. Then they take a long bath and go to a ball game. What am I looking at?"

"Other people don't start work at 3 a.m. every other day of the week," he countered.

"Anyway, look here!" He pointed dramatically with his finger. "This advert. Could this be your sister Zelda's son?"

Sharon read it, then looked up at him. "They all perished in the Kovno Ghetto. That's what the Jewish Agency told us. Give it here …" She snatched the paper from his hands.

Such advertisements had been common in the Miami press since the end of the Second World War. Holocaust survivors frequently advertised for relatives. But this was different. Someone was looking for them by their old names.

"You never met this child?"

"He was born in October '35, after we left Odessa."

"Sharon, we have to ignore it. We barely earn enough to feed ourselves. We can't take on responsibility for another child."

Hyman, or Howie as he now called himself, stood up and stomped off heavily to shower. Sharon, however, in a rare moment of standing up for herself, was equally firm. "My sister's child survived. I can't ignore it." She pointed at the mound of food on the table. "I haven't noted you going hungry recently. Supposing this boy is Zelda's son? He'd be about twelve years old now." Her face was pink with excitement.

"No breakfast today then, Ma?"

The interruption came from their own fourteen-year-old son, Jerry, who stood at the kitchen door, wearing only a singlet like his father and pyjama trousers. A hank of greasy blond hair tumbled over his spotty face. He was a lanky, sullen youth and the untidy beginnings of a beard who worked alongside his father in the kosher-style bakery on Lincoln Road from Sunday morning through to lunchtime on Friday. The family's only concession to the Sabbath was the plaited challah bread they ate on Friday nights and Saturday mornings.

She pointed at the mound of pancakes and the grilled crispy bacon on the table.

Jerry began piling up his plate. "No eggs, then, Mother? I heard you talking just now. If this kid comes to stay, there will be even less for us."

"Don't worry. You'll still get breakfast and a seat at the ball game with Pops on a Saturday afternoon."

"Come on, Jerry. We'll be late. The game starts at 2.30 p.m., and it's nearly one o'clock now—and you ain't washed or dressed yet." For once, Sharon thought, Howie was laying the law down to their spoilt son.

She put a piece of bacon into her own mouth, chewed it, and spat it out when she thought Howie wasn't looking. Suddenly, she wished it was a Shabbat morning like she remembered from the old days, a proper day of rest. Breakfast then had been freshly baked challah spread with butter and with fruit on the side, or sometimes cake so Papa didn't need to make blessings over a meal before he left for synagogue.

Even after living in Miami for fourteen years with Howie and Jerry, Americanising all their names, and changing their lifestyle, Sharon still found it hard to share their enthusiasm over the blatant nonobservance of the Sabbath and their new-found culinary "freedom". She no longer ate kosher or kept a kosher home. At first, it had been a game, trying all the forbidden foods, but she felt ill at ease with every mouthful.

When she was sure they were both out of sight, she threw the remains of her brunch into the garbage can, ate a piece of buttered challah bread, and drank some coffee. She didn't know why she'd given up the fight for the old life. It had left her with a feeling of emptiness where her connection to her God and her community had once been.

"It's a new country, a new way of life," the reinvented Howie had enthused, putting his black yarmulke in a drawer. You're not religious Shayne from Odessa anymore. You don't need to hide your own hair behind some hot, cheap nylon wig or under a scarf that makes you look bald. Stop being a Jewess. Be a woman."

She'd been slim and attractive when they first arrived here in 1932. Now she was shapeless and ugly. Eating bacon, pork, prawns, crabs with mounds of fries, and vast quantities of ice cream had done nothing for her figure. The rules she'd followed all her life were irrelevant now. She had no beliefs to lean on when she felt lonely, no community to rally round her to help her adjust. They had joined Temple Beth El, a Reform synagogue in Hialeah, where many of the members were the descendants of the first German refugees who'd arrived here in the 1870s, and a large proportion were converts. She found the addition of an organ to the traditional Shabbat and holiday tunes very strange. Her husband insisted he needed the car on Saturday afternoons to get to his beloved ball game, so she couldn't stay for the after-service kiddush, a get-together where she might have made friends, so she gave up attending at all and remained friendless. It was worse than mere loneliness. It all felt so pointless. There was no joy to her existence anymore.

"What do you need friends for?" Howie had questioned her. "You don't have time for friends. You've got work and us."

She'd hoped at first that her mama might come to join them here in Miami. She had wondered how Mama would adapt to the new ways. But it soon became clear that Mama didn't want to uproot herself to leave the place where she'd been born, married, and had her children. In her heart, Shayne didn't blame her, and in her letters home, Sharon "forgot" to mention how they had new names, new identities, new ways of life. The Goldmeyers from Odessa were now the Golds of Hialeah. Howie Gold no longer practised as a committed Jew. When Sharon had dared to point out to him that their son was almost thirteen years old and needed to study for a bar mitzvah, a Jewish boy's ritual coming of age, Howie had laughed in her face. "Bar mitzvah, shmar mitzvah," he'd jibed. "Just an excuse for an expensive party for people we don't know, spending money we don't have on something we don't believe in anymore. You keep telling me you have no friends, so whom did you plan to invite, anyway?"

"We're off." The front door slammed. Sharon turned up Stravinsky's new Symphony in Three Movements being played by the New York Philharmonic orchestra on her radio. She swayed to the mournful tune as she began to write:

June 20, 1947

Dear Ruth Ettinger and Arieh,

I think I may be the aunt Arieh Weinstein is looking for. I was Shayna Goldmeyer when I arrived in the USA with my husband, Hyman, now known as Howie, in 1932. My sister was Zelda Weinstein, the wife of Simcha Weinstein, who played first violin in the Odessa Philharmonic Orchestra before the war. We had been advised by the United Nations Relief and Rescue Administration, who were working with the Red Cross, that the whole family perished in the Kovno Ghetto. Can you send me further details, please, of the boy you know as Arieh? Where was he born? Has he any brothers or sisters? Can he remember the name of his maternal grandmother? We would like to be sure that this boy in your care is my sister Zelda's son before we agree to go further. I pray that your Arieh and my nephew are one and the same. If he is indeed my nephew, then my arms and my heart are open to welcome him as soon as possible.

I would love to know how he survived, and I wish to thank you most sincerely for looking for us and for caring for this boy.

With warmest good wishes,

Sharon Gold, formerly Shayne Goldmeyer of Odessa

A while later, there came the reply:

7 June 1948
4 Stuyvesant Oval, Apartment 21B
Lower East Side, Manhattan

Dear Mrs Gold,

Thank you so much for your letter. I understand the need for your questions, and we will answer as best we can. Arieh

Weinstein was a traumatised six-year-old who could barely speak when my brothers, Mikhail and Oscar Ettinger, came upon him sitting on a tree stump in a forest not far from Leningrad. Leningrad was under siege at that time, and we have no idea how he got there. He was playing a beautiful old violin with a maturity and knowledge way beyond his years.

Arieh told us he was born on the fourth day of Succoth, corresponding with 5 October 1935. His maternal grandmother was Abigail Chaia-Zipporah. We don't know how he remembers that so clearly, only that he knows his *zaida*, his grandfather, had recently died. They all lived together at 121 Shvygina Street in Odessa, and his father played first violin with the Odessa Symphony Orchestra. His mama, Zelda, was a housewife, and he had a baby sister, Bracha.

When the Germans arrived in Odessa in 1941, they rounded up all the Jews. First everyone was taken to the Bogdanovka concentration camp, but then they were moved on to the Kovno Ghetto. Arieh's mama and the baby died. When the Germans came, his papa pushed him into a wardrobe behind some blankets and told him to care for his papa's violin. Arieh told us that when the Germans had gone, he hid in a garbage truck. He can't remember how he survived, only that he was very hungry. Nor does he know how he got to a forest some twenty-five kilometres outside Leningrad, where my brothers, Oscar and Mikhail Ettinger, found him sitting on a tree stump playing the violin in the late autumn of 1941. He was starving, very cold, very thin, and totally mute, although we all knew he could hear. As he began to trust us, we realised he had been deeply traumatised by his experiences. He became a great favourite among our partisan group and is particularly fond of Simeon Karminsky, with whom he shared a straw mattress bed on boards above a potato store.

Arieh proved himself to be a valuable member of the Ettinger partisans. In late 1943, he was instrumental, quite literally, in using his violin to kill more than seventy

German officers in a daring raid on a bar. Sadly, he was badly injured and suffered severe burns to his right leg. He is currently forced to wear a calliper on his right leg, but his courage, his natural talent, and his violin saved many hundreds of Jewish lives. He was awarded a medal as a hero of the Soviet Union in recognition of his courage.

Arieh and I are currently living with my cousin Lauren here in New York. Lauren kindly sponsored both of us into the USA through Ellis Island with the help of the Hebrew Immigrant Aid Society and the American Jewish Joint.

Arieh was very excited when we told him we thought we had found his mama's sister. He can't wait to meet you. Lauren has suggested that if you believe he's "your" Arieh, I could put him on a Greyhound bus all the way to Miami, where you could meet him at the bus station. He is a very talented boy who has known much hardship in his young life, but he responds to affection and is generous in giving his love as well as gratefully receiving all that is offered to him.

With best wishes, and warm, excited hugs and kisses from Arieh,

Ruth Ettinger

Not too long after Ruth had written that, they received a reply:

Miami
July 2, 1947

Dear Ruth Ettinger,

Thank you for your letter. It is clear that Arieh is indeed my nephew, the little boy I believed had died in the Kovno Ghetto. I am most grateful to you and your brothers for caring for him through the war and now escorting him safely to America. I can't wait to meet him. It will be great for our son, Jerry, to have a younger "brother". I am sending you a timetable for Greyhound buses from Central Station, New York, to the central bus station in Miami, as well as a little money towards his fare and food for the journey. It will take two days from New York to Miami with comfort stops. Perhaps you will be kind enough to write to let us know when we might expect him. Thank you for all the care you've shown our nephew.

Sincerely yours,

Sharon Gold

Two ten-dollar bills dropped out of the folded letter. Lauren, to whom Ruth passed the letter wordlessly, opened her purse and took out another $10, putting her finger to her lips.

"Look, Arieh. Your aunt is so excited, she has sent thirty dollars to pay for your fare and food en route. She's written such a lovely letter. She can't wait to see you. Now we have to start to make your travel plans."

Arieh looked up and smiled, but there was sadness in his big brown eyes.

"I still wish I didn't have to leave y'all," he said. They laughed at his attempt at the colloquialism. Arieh had taken the little piece of amber from his pocket and was rubbing it gently.

"Tell me," Ruth said, suddenly changing the subject, "what is so special about that little piece of amber, Arieh? Why won't you tell me its secret?"

"It's not my story to tell," Arieh replied softly, putting his precious amber back into his pocket. "Oh, Rutti." He cried softly, reverting to her familiar name. "I miss Simeon so much. I wish I could tell him I had Little Miss Honey."

"I'm sure he misses you, too," Rutti murmured softly. "You will. One day."

Chapter 30

Hanna, June 1948

TINY MAXINE SHOSHANA ABRAMSKYA DANCED WITH DELIGHT AS SHE JUMPED up, trying to reach the little cream silk frock that hung beside her mother's long dress of the same material on the front of the wardrobe door.

"My dress," the almost three-year-old lisped in her slightly accented, high-pitched little-girl English. "My wedding dress."

Hanna Karminsky Abramskya gathered her toddler daughter in her arms and whirled her around the room, smiling. She put her down on her plump legs, ruffling her short red-gold curls.

"Not *your* wedding, my darling. *My* wedding. You will be Mama's flower girl when Uncle Eric becomes your papa."

Maxine toddled off, satisfied in the way of easily diverted almost-three year-olds to play with her most precious possession, the rag doll with the multicoloured checked skirt and black wooden dreadlocks she had named Erica, because Eric's parents had generously sent it to their new granddaughter, all the way from England.

England, a land of peace, the place of their dreams. Once they were married, Eric had promised, they would be able to apply for the papers that would allow Hanna and Maxine into that country as his wife and prospective adopted daughter respectively. Tomorrow, their worlds would change, their whole future remapped by the love and kindness of this man who would become Hanna's husband and Maxine's daddy.

It was Captain Eric who had arranged that he and Hanna would be

250

married under a proper wedding canopy in the small rededicated synagogue in Celle where the Sefer Torah (Book of the Law) imported from England lived inside a salvaged kitchen cupboard. They would be married by an English clergyman, the Reverend Leslie Hardman, who had been the Jewish chaplain at the time of the liberation of the Bergen-Belsen concentration camp. He had been with the British troops when the gates to that world of horror had opened to reveal the whole ghastly truth of the Nazis unspeakable war crimes. Eric had managed to arrange it all. "Tomorrow you will have a new papa. He will be a proper daddy like all little English girls have," Hanna told her daughter.

Tomorrow, as a bride for the second time in her life, Hanna would wear the lovely long cream gown fashioned from parachute silk rescued from a German prisoner as she stood beside her groom, Captain Eric Rosenberg, of the British Eleventh Armoured Division. The whole division had been called to the camp following the liberation of Bergen-Belsen in April 1945. She had only one more wish for tomorrow, she thought, as she arranged the pretty posy of pink and white roses Lottie had sent her from the new home in Belgium. She had been reunited with her husband almost a year ago. She would carry her roses down the aisle with her. There was only one person's presence who could change Hanna Karminsky Abramskya's wedding day from a special day to a totally perfect one. However, it was the one thing beyond even her fiancé's, seemingly endless powers. He could find no way for Simeon, to join them. He had made inquiries and discovered that Simeon and his wife Gilda now lived in a communal flat in Leningrad, much more comfortable than the cramped space they'd shared in her former home. Eric had made representations through the Russian Consulate, but the Russians had refused to grant him a temporary exit visa, even for an occasion such as this.

"Oh Simeon," she whispered under her breath, bending down to her little girl and nuzzling her baby's neck. "I wonder where you are. What are you doing that is so secret that the Russians won't let you leave for a few days to attend your twin sister's wedding?"

Recently, Hanna had told Eric that she had been raped by a German officer in Minsk and that her daughter was the result. Throughout all those years in the ghettos from 1941 until the present day, her biggest fear had been that someone would recognise her for herself and tell her former lover Schlossberg that she was not Maria Petruishka after all. Schlossberg was dead, but since the liberation, she had lived in constant terror of someone recognising Hanna Karminskya Abramskya as Maria Petruishka, SS Oberst-Gruppenführer Frederick Schlossberg's mistress. In England she would be able to relax at last. The name Hanna Rosenberg had a nice English ring to it, she thought. Hanna Rosenberg would be safe. She would never hear the words she'd dreaded these past four years. Neither would her new husband or her darling daughter. She'd be starting a whole new fear-free life.

She'd known there must be a good reason why Simeon had begged her not to write to him again. However, she was getting married. What harm could there possibly be in sending her twin brother an invitation to her wedding? When Eric had proposed in March, Hanna had written to Simeon straightaway, hoping and praying he would receive her letter. She'd read the letter to Eric before she sent it.

> Dearest Brother,
>
> I am marrying English Army captain Eric Rosenberg here at the DP camp in Celle on 24 August this year, and I am so hoping you will be permitted to attend. Eric proposed to me when you wrote saying there was no room for me to join you in Leningrad. Now we are getting married and planning to go to England with our little girl, Maxine Shoshana. She is a beautiful little girl with the Karminsky red hair. I know you will love her. You did ask me not to write again, but I am hoping that an invitation to your twin sister's wedding will be a permitted exception.
>
> Forever your loving sister,
>
> Hanna

"Are you sure you are doing the right thing, sending this?" he had questioned.

"Maybe things aren't so bad as they were. Perhaps the authorities will take a compassionate look at permitting a twin to attend his sister's wedding."

She'd tucked a small black-and-white snapshot of Eric holding Maxine in his arms into the invitation. It had been taken several months prior, and Maxine still looked like a little baby, rather than the toddler she had become.

Hanna had received Simeon's response in April. It was entirely as Eric had expected it.

Dearest Sister,

I thank you for your invitation. Life in Leningrad is very hard. I am working. I'm afraid I have been refused a visa to attend your wedding. Gilda and I send you love and our warm good wishes for a happy life and a kiss to my niece. Letters from outside the USSR are not welcome. I beg you, please don't write again. Be happy in your new marriage and in your future with your husband and daughter. Gilda sends warm wishes.

Affectionately,

Simeon

It had cleared the censors without mark, apparently, but the message was clear to Eric. "The Soviets have tightened their grip on the Soviet sector of Berlin since the reparation agreements broke down last year. You must have heard of the 'Cold War'. Simeon can't get out. You will love England. I will make you happy in our new home. Don't let this ruin our day. I don't have sisters or brothers, but my parents will love you. I will make you happy."

He took her hand in his and kissed it gently, stroking her arm. "She began to calm down, her breathing slowly returning to normal. As they moved together, their lips touched and the embrace became more passionate. He still held Maxine in his arms. Hanna knew there was indeed true love in his kiss. There was tenderness in his touch, and kindness shone in his eyes behind those old-fashioned spectacles. She knew that she might never again know the chance of such happiness as he was offering her and her daughter, and she felt she ought to be more grateful for it.

It hadn't been perfect for Eric, either. They needed to be married before he left Germany in September at the end of his tour of duty in order to fulfil entry permit requirements for both Hanna and Maxine, who were listed as stateless persons. He had hoped to stand under the wedding canopy with his parents at his side. However, given that his parents were both in their mid-fifties, they felt unable to undertake the long and difficult journey to Celle. Travelling wasn't easy in postwar Europe.

"We have our whole future to look forward to," Eric said. "I will do my best to give you both a good life. You mustn't look back, Hanna. The past is done and gone."

Hanna had asked Dr Hadassah Bimkow and her new husband, Joseph Rosensaft, to stand under the canopy in place of her parents. Joseph had worked closely with Eric founding the Central Committee for Liberated Jews at the Camp and was a close friend. Dr Hadassah was credited with saving hundreds, if not thousands, of Jewish lives at Auschwitz during the reign of terror of Josef Mengele, who had conducted notorious experiments on women and children during the war, particularly twins. It was Hadassah who had brought Maxine into the world. "Your parents would be so proud of you," Joseph Rosensaft whispered in Hanna's ear as he took her arm, waiting for the synagogue doors to open. Maxine stood in front of her mama, holding a basket of rose petals to scatter. A friend of Hanna's was holding the toddler's other hand lightly.

The choir began to sing "Baruch Haba", the traditional welcome to a bride and groom approaching the marriage canopy. The congregation rose to greet them in a single movement. Maxine shrugged off her protector, clutched her basket tight, and confidently scattered petals in front of her mother and new step-father until they reached the canopy. The simple unadorned room seemed to fill with light and happiness. Eric glanced back to see her. Hanna thought that in full dress uniform he looked taller, prouder, and more distinguished than she'd ever seen him before. Standing on his left were his senior officer, Major General George Roberts, and his wife Hilary, who had agreed to stand beside him in place of his parents. Reverend Hardman had insisted that the only requirement was a married couple. Their faith was unimportant. The wonderful Reverend, had gone out of his way to make the Robertses, who were not Jewish, feel welcome.

"It would be an honour for us indeed," the Major General had told Eric when he'd put in his request. "It'll be the first Jewish wedding we've ever attended. We will be happy to give you and your beautiful bride wine to drink at the appropriate time, as long as my colleague Reverend Hardman gives us the nod as to when and how." George Roberts smiled. Welsh-born Reverend Leslie Hardman, the first Jewish chaplain to enter the camp at the liberation of Bergen-Belsen, and the major general, Eric's commander, were great friends. The major general had sent Eric and Hanna an extraordinarily generous wedding gift of £10, a huge sum of money, to help them buy something for the new home they would build together. It would all have been perfect if only …

A tear fell down her cheek as Hanna walked towards her groom. She remembered her first wedding, to Nat. Her parents had both been there, and Simeon too, of course. She could see him winking at her. She watched now as her friend whisked Maxine into a pew in the front row, sat her on her lap, and began shushing her with bribes of sweets. Maxine's freckled nose wrinkled with pleasure at the treat as Hanna began to circle her bridegroom seven times to signify that they would be building a home together and that, henceforth, Eric would be at the centre of his bride's life.

Eric sipped the wine Joseph offered him. Hilary lifted Hanna's veil, and she drank from the same cup as was traditional. Eric placed a plain gold band on the first finger of Hanna's right hand, and in time-honoured fashion, she heard the reverend asking Eric to repeat the ancient mantra after him, two words at a time—*Haray at m'kudeshet li b'aba 'at zo k'dat Moshe v'Yisrael* (Behold, you are dedicated to me according to the Laws of Moses and of Israel). A glass was placed on the floor ahead of Eric. He stamped hard on it. As it shattered, everyone shouted, "Mazel tov!" and "Good luck!"

Hanna caught sight of her young daughter, sitting quietly, picking the remaining petals in her basket, and scattering them. She looked at the tall, upright, bearded figure of Reverend Hardman at her side and at Eric, her new husband, resplendent in his uniform, his shoulders covered by a traditional prayer shawl, beside her. Someone grabbed her arm and they started dancing, right there, under the canopy. "Chatan, callah, mazel tov" (Bride and groom, good luck), everyone sang. *Eric's right,* Hanna thought as she joined the merriment of the moment. *We've got the rest of our lives to live. I mustn't look back.*

Chapter 31

Arieh

ARIEH BOARDED THE BUS AT THE CENTRAL BUS STATION ON THE CORNER OF West Thirty-Fourth Street and Eighth Avenue at 5.45 on the morning of Wednesday, 8 August 1948. He was not quite thirteen years old, but for the rest of his existence, he'd remember it as a pivotal day in his life.

Ruth, Lauren, and Blake had all come to wish him bon voyage. Lauren had offered to buy him a new suitcase of his own, but he had asked Ruth a special favour. He wanted to take the little brown cardboard case which he and Ruth had shared to bring all their possessions to America. Now he watched it being thrown into the luggage compartment at the base of the bus. It was filled with only his clothes. Thanks to Lauren and Blake's generosity, he had acquired a full wardrobe: two smart pairs of long trousers, the shorts he was wearing and another pair for hot weather, several changes of underwear and socks, two new shirts, and two new T-shirts. He felt smart, almost rich, and confident that but for the calliper on his leg and his walking cane, he looked like any other American boy of his age. At least the calliper he wore these days was made of strong leather and metal and was affixed to a proper custom-made built-up shoe. He wore a matching brown boot on his left leg. He wished he could wear sneakers like the other boys, but at least he could walk without too much of a limp and needed only a walking stick to steady himself, rather than a crutch. He insisted on carrying his violin case onto the bus with him. Lauren and Blake had bought him a brand-new one. The bus driver helped him up and into the right-hand aisle seat, then handed him the case, which he placed across his lap. Arieh's face was red with repressed emotion, but he was determined not to cry as Ruth followed him up and hugged him one last time.

"I love you" was all he managed to say.

"We've been through a lot together, Arieh. I will always love you. Come back and see us soon. Remember, if things don't work out for you in Miami, you will always have a home with us."

"Your sister?" asked the large man who had wedged himself into the window seat, his thigh overhanging onto Arieh's side. Having elicited no reply, he repeated the question. "Were they your sisters and brother seeing you off? Don't cry. I'm sure you'll see them soon. Going to Miami for a holiday, are you?"

Arieh nodded, not really wanting to engage in a conversation with a total stranger. He spoke good English now, thanks to the regular classes he'd attended, and he knew the man was only trying to be kind, but he couldn't find the right words to reply.

He turned his head away and tried to read his English book. It was *The Wind in the Willows*, a fantasy about creatures like frogs and toads, but the movement of the bus made him feel sick, so he closed his eyes and pretended to sleep instead. When they made their first comfort stop, Arieh got out, bought some cold water, and ate the chicken sandwich Lauren had prepared.

The bus finally reached Miami thirty hours later. The temperature was in the high eighties Fahrenheit, and Arieh felt sticky, dirty, and desperate for a cool shower. He wondered how he'd survived in the forest for so long without such a luxury. He was first off the bus with the driver's help, but then he had to wait for his luggage. As he stood waiting, clutching his violin, he realised he had no idea what his aunt looked like. He imagined her to be a mirror image of his mama, but the memory of his mama was fading fast.

It wasn't until almost everyone else had gone that he noticed a very fat woman wearing what appeared to be a black tent approaching him. His mama had been short and slim and wore a wig in accordance with the Orthodox Jewish way of life. This woman was short too, but she wobbled towards him, her breasts dancing freely under the loose tent, her hair dyed the colour of overripe strawberries. And she was breathing hard.

"Arieh Weinstein?" she asked as she neared him.

He nodded. "Are you my aunt Shayne?"

"Sharon, please. Not Shayne. Shayne stayed in Russia. We are in America and it's a new life."

He looked closely at her. Beneath the layers of fat and under several chins, he couldn't see where her jaw ended and her neck began. Her bloated cheeks seemed to rise above her eye sockets, and heavy black eyebrows lined the area above them. Her eyes seemed almost reduced to slits. He tried to study them and saw they were exactly the same pale brown as his mother's had been, just like his. She was sizing him up, staring at the leg iron, noticing the walking cane and the fact that he couldn't pick up his suitcase and carry his violin at the same time.

"I see you are quite severely crippled?"

The last word hit him like a gunshot. *Crippled.* But that's what he was. "It was an accident."

"I know. Your friend Ruth wrote to me."

She had picked up the brown suitcase and was waddling slowly towards a small black Ford 10.

"Medical treatment is expensive here in the States. Is that why they wanted to get rid of you? We are poor people."

"They didn't want to get rid of me. They begged me to stay. I wanted to be with my mother's sister."

"Of course, since you are Zelda's son, we'll do our best for you, but ..."

He had been desperate to hear if her voice resembled his mama's. The intonation was the same, but he knew that no matter how poor they had been, his mama would have been kind to her nephew. The only part of this woman that vaguely resembled his mama was the intonation in her speech when she spoke in Russian. Suddenly, he needed his own mama as he hadn't needed her since she'd died in Kovno. He held his father's violin tight to him now, just as he had hugged it inside the wardrobe. He could hear Rutti and Lauren telling him he could go back at any time. He could write to them, tell them his aunt didn't want a "cripple". Arieh often thought of his papa whenever he picked up his violin, but his mama had somehow faded in his memory. His aunt threw his baggage into the trunk of the car, came round to the passenger door, and opened it for him. As she did so, she drew him close to her enormous bosom and hugged him. He tried to close his nose. She smelt of stale sweat. His mama never smelt like that, not even in the ghetto. "I wish my mama were here with us," he sobbed as she held him.

"So do I."

The *cripple* word wasn't mentioned again. Sharon chattered all the way back to Hialeah. "Uncle Howie couldn't come with me today. He had to go to work. He's a baker, and on Fridays, he starts baking challah at three in the morning. As it's a kosher bakery, he finishes at one thirty, lunchtime, on Fridays. It's a long shift, but then he has the rest of Friday and all day Saturday free.

"I can't believe you survived. What happened? When the Germans came and took your mama, your Tatti, and the baby? They all died, didn't they?"

He nodded.

"Tell me about you?"

"Can I tell you another day, Tante Shayne? I'm tired."

"I'm sure you are, Arieh. I told you, I'm Sharon now. Your uncle used to be Hyman; now he's Howie. It's more American. Yehuda is Jerry. So perhaps you'll be more American too. You could be Al."

"I'm Arieh," he said firmly. "I wish to stay Arieh Weinstein, if you please."

"You're twelve, aren't you?" his aunt asked as they drew up at the house. "So we'll enrol you at Miami Dade County High School for this coming year. Hopefully they'll take you, even with that bad leg. That was your cousin Jerry's school. At least you speak English. That's a bonus, I suppose."

"I'm eleven. I will be twelve in October. October fifth."

Even in the camp, Arieh's leg had never been an issue. There had always been a way to overcome it. In New York, they had done everything they could to overcome his disability. He wondered why it was suddenly such a big deal here, in this place where life was so comparatively easy and there were no battles to fight and no major obstacles to overcome as there had been in the forest.

"I should be bar-mitzvahed in October next year," Arieh said, trying to make conversation. "Blake paid for me to have Hebrew lessons, Aunt Sharon. I know what my portion of the Law is."

"We don't do religion, Arieh. We didn't make a bar-mitzvah for Jerry. He's just three years or so older than you. So we won't be doing one you, for sure. I thought you might be able to work after school to earn your keep, but you'll never get a job with that thing on your leg. The truth is, son, I work five days a week as a seamstress at the Burlington Coat Factory. Uncle Howie and Jerry work at the bakery on Collins every day. It's twenty minutes by car from here, although it takes more than an hour on the bus. We need every penny just to eat, never mind financing bar-mitzvahs! What happens if you take that thing off? At least your handicap wouldn't be so noticeable!"

Arieh stared at her. "I can't walk," he replied shortly. "My right leg is several inches shorter than the left one; It won't support my weight."

"Oh."

Even as the car pulled into the driveway of the shabby, one-storey pink board house the Gold family rented on Northwest Ninety-Eighth Avenue, Arieh realised life here was vastly different from the American "good life" he'd experienced in New York. The house stood on piles in the centre of a barren yard, as though it was only ever intended as a temporary structure. As his aunt opened the front door, he gasped with shock. The place was a pigsty. Even the primitive Zemlyanka, for all its lack of a proper structure or hygiene, had been kept as tidy and clean as was possible for an underground mud hut. His mother had kept an immaculate home in Odessa. Even in the ghetto, they'd done their best. The front door of this dwelling opened straight into a living room where pegs on the wall held piles of coats, some of which had fallen on top of a jumble of shoes that stuck out from beneath them, littering the floor. Piles of newspapers and magazines were heaped in one corner. He could see no books or bookshelves. A large TV screen dominated the room. Through a door on the right-hand side, he saw the kitchen. Dirty dishes and pans were piled high in the sink. Behind the kitchen was a living space with a wooden gate-leg table covered in papers, two worn leather armchairs, and a matching leather settee. The whole place had an undefinable smell of dirt and neglect.

"Come into the kitchen, honey. Let me fix you something to eat." Her tone had become friendly. Perhaps she'd been brusque because she'd had a shock when she'd first seen him. "You must be hungry. Pancakes? Do you like American pancakes?" Sharon seemed to have overcome her initial reaction to his physical disability and was trying to treat him "normally". He nodded wordlessly. He had been starving, but his appetite had suddenly deserted him. His aunt saw him looking round. "I didn't have time to get the place cleaned up this morning," she apologised. "Oh, you need a bathroom? It's there, behind the kitchen."

He used the bathroom, which was as filthy as the kitchen. He looked in dismay at the squalid shower stall. He was stuck here. When he returned to the kitchen, his hands dripping because he could find no towel, he found his aunt busy beating the pancake mix with eggs and milk in a glass bowl and frying what he assumed to be bacon on the grill.

"Sorry, Aunt Sharon. I don't eat bacon."

She nodded. "I see. Well, I'm afraid we don't keep kosher here. If you don't eat what we eat, you're going to be hungry."

Arieh ate a pancake and watched her devour the pile of bacon she'd cooked.

"Let me show you your room."

It was a tiny room, just big enough for a bed, a small wardrobe, and a three-drawer chest. The window, he saw, looked to the front yard. A pile of grubby sports gear was piled under the window.

"That's Jerry's stuff. I'll ask him to move it when he gets home. Hey, do you play that fiddle?"

"I play the violin, yes. Lauren and Blake paid for me to have lessons," he said, looking at her, without hope.

"No free lessons here. We just have enough to eat. I already told you. You want violin lessons, you'll have to go out and earn them. You're like your Tatti, huh? A musician. Play something for me then?"

He put the violin case carefully on the bed and removed his violin. He tuned it gently, then started to play *Für Elise*.

"That's lovely," she said. "Play something else."

He began playing his favourite Bruch, Violin Concerto no. 1. That was the last tune he'd been learning with his New York teacher. As he played, he looked up at her face. Aunt Sharon's features had softened. She opened her eyes wide in an expression that suddenly reminded him very much of his mama. It was as though his music had lifted a burden from her shoulders. "Will you play for me sometimes?" she asked. "When we're alone, just the two of us?"

"Yes," he whispered.

All of a sudden, there was a loud *ping*. A string had popped. Arieh looked at it in horror, and then at his aunt. "Do you know where I can get it mended? I have a little money," he said. She shook her head sadly. "Someone in town is bound to do it."

"May I take a shower and change, please?"

She handed him a thin towel. "Don't use too much hot water. Uncle Howie will be home soon. He likes his shower hot."

Arieh disliked his uncle Howie on sight. Like Sharon, he was grossly obese, his belly hanging loosely over the top of his trousers. He was unshaven and smelt of yeast. The hand he extended to Arieh was still covered in dough. "Welcome," he said. Arieh felt the insincerity in the word. His cousin Jerry was just behind him.

"Oh dear. He's a poor little cripple," the spotty youth teased. "Well, that puts you out of joining our ball game. Bet you can't even play that thing," he said, indicating the violin.

"He just played for me. He plays beautifully."

Arieh blinked. Sharon was actually standing up for him against her own son. He vowed to himself that he would never tell any of them about his second most precious possession, his amber tablet.

Every morning, Arieh tucked the piece of amber into his violin case before he left for the school bus. He was scared that his aunt or Jerry might be tempted to go through his things. Every evening, after he'd showered, he took it out, and he slept with it clutched in his hand under his pillow. Sometimes he spoke to it, just as if he were talking to Simeon.

"Little Miss Honey. Help me out of this foul place. I hate it here. It's not fair to go back to Lauren and Blake now that they're expecting a baby." Sometimes the amber felt warm in his hand, as though it had understood his misery, as though it sensed its connection to Simeon and Simeon's other amber tablets.

At night, Arieh would sit on his bed, fingering his broken violin. He wrote to Ruth, Lauren, and Blake. When they had a little girl, he bought a small gift from the change he had hoarded from his journey and sent it with love. On his bar-mitzvah weekend, they wrote congratulating him. "Congratulations. We wish we were there." They sent money as a gift. It took all his courage to be honest and tell them there had been no Bar-mitzvah.

"My uncle and aunt can't afford it now, and we are a long way from the synagogue," he wrote.

He'd cleaned his little room as best he could. He washed his own clothes in the bath, hung them on the washing line outside to dry, and borrowed his aunt's iron to press them. He was determined to stay neat but not to be a nuisance. The weekend that should have been full of celebration was the most miserable he could remember. He sat in his room and cried.

Arieh had hoped to go up to New York to visit Ruth, Blake and Lauren in the summer and meet the new baby but his uncle refused to allow him to take a holiday from work. The week he celebrated his fourteenth birthday, on 5 October 1949, he said polite goodbyes to his schoolteachers and thanked them all for their help. He'd been an "A" student. One of his teachers brought a chocolate cake in for the whole class to celebrate with him. On Wednesday, 6 October, he rose at three thirty in the morning and left home, sitting on the back seat of the Ford, with Jerry and Uncle Howie in the front. That day, he started work alongside them full time, weighing flour, adding yeast and water, and putting the bread to prove. There was no time to think about his broken violin.

On Friday afternoons, the shop shut at one thirty. Arieh often took the bus across to South Beach after work on Fridays. He loved walking along Ocean Drive, sometimes crossing the green parkland, taking off his left boot and sock and letting his bare left foot wriggle freely in the hot white sands. Sometimes, he would treat himself to a Coke or an ice cream and wander along Lincoln Road, exploring the backstreets of the Spanish District. He wrote bright letters to Ruth, Lauren, Blake, and baby Abigail saying he was well and working hard. They'd sent him photographs of the baby with Lauren and Ruth. She had fine dark hair and rosy full cheeks and wore pretty frocks. How he wished he could cuddle her. She reminded him of his own sister, Bracha.

On a pleasant afternoon in late November 1949, a month after Arieh's fourteenth birthday, he came across a tiny half shop just off Espanola Way. The inside of the shop was obscured by a blue curtain. The only object in the window was a single violin. He stared at it for a long time. A notice on the door proclaimed: "All string instruments restrung. Repairs by expert string player. No job too large or too small." On two subsequent Fridays, he stood outside the shop staring at the notice. However, he knew he couldn't get an estimate without the repairer seeing the instrument. On the third Friday, he smuggled his violin into the car and hid it under the back seat so Uncle Howie wouldn't spot it if he looked in his rear-view mirror. At the bakery, Arieh sneaked it out under his arm and hid it behind a pile of flour sacks in the yard.

"Don't wait for me this afternoon, Uncle Howie," he called after work. "I'll get a bus back."

"Don't be late," his uncle called. "You know your aunt likes you home before she lights the Sabbath candles."

Their lifestyle was bizarre, Arieh thought. They ate pig meat and shellfish. They ate ice cream after chicken. Nothing in the house was kosher. Yet every Friday night, without fail, Sharon lit the Sabbath candles and Uncle Howie made the traditional Friday night blessings over wine and bread.

"I know the bus times," Arieh called back. "I won't be late."

Señor Pedro Diaz saw the young man walking towards the shop window and recognised him as the boy who had been staring at the single violin and blue curtain for the last two weeks. He had noticed the boy was disabled and wondered if he was thinking of applying for a job. This time, however, he was carrying a violin.

The shop door jangled as Arieh pushed it. Suddenly, his stomach rose in his throat. He was taking a chance. He looked at the dark haired, black-eyed

Spaniard as he took the old violin carefully out of its case. The man took it carefully and began to examine it. "This was once a beautiful instrument," he said, noting where the polish had worn off, taking the instrument almost back to bare wood where it had been exposed to the elements. He noted the broken string.

"Where did you get it? It's a beautiful instrument, Austrian or possibly German. The name Hermann Wagner springs to mind, but it looks as though it's had a hard life."

Arieh shrugged. "It belonged to my papa. It lived with us through two ghettos," he said. "My papa used to play with the Odessa Symphony Orchestra. The violin and I were in a partisan camp together."

"Where is your papa?"

"He died in the Holocaust. I took the violin with me when I escaped from the ghetto and played it for my friends in the forest where I lived." His own dark brown eyes met those of the man. "It helped me kill seventy German officers," he said proudly. "That's how I got this." He pointed to his leg iron.

"My name is Señor Pedro Diaz," the shop owner said, holding out his hand.

"I'm Arieh Weinstein." Arieh propped himself up against the counter, leaned forward, and shook Diaz's hand, just as he'd seen other men do. "Simeon got replacement strings for me from a farmer who had a violin that no one played. Then Lauren and Blake had it properly done for me in New York."

"So is this man Simeon here with you in Miami?" "No, sir. He's in Russia. He went home to look for his family." He bit hard on his lip to stop himself crying.

"I have met others who survived this terrible thing. You want me to restore this violin?"

"I don't have enough money to get it restored, but I've been saving. I've got enough to have it restrung. Look."

He tipped $24.15 onto the counter. He was paid $8 a week at the bakery and gave $6 to his aunt for his bed and board. He had spent hardly any of the money Ruth and Lauren had sent, except for the present he'd bought the baby, Abbie, and had managed to save an additional $17. As he pulled the money out of his pocket, he felt like a millionaire. The little piece of amber came out with it and sat winking at him as sunlight poured through the small window at the top of the door. Arieh picked up his amber quickly and was about to return it to his pocket when Pedro Diaz stopped him.

"What's that?"

"It's amber. It's my lucky charm."

To his surprise, Señor Diaz didn't laugh. Instead, he picked up the little amber piece and examined it. "My boy also had lucky stones," he said. Arieh noticed he was wiping a tear from the corner of his own eye.

"Does your son play the violin, too?"

"He used to play the cello."

"He doesn't play anymore?"

"He was killed. In Europe. On D-Day, June 6, 1944." He held out his hand to Arieh.

"Show me your lucky stone. Do you realise that fly is thousands of years old?

"Tell you what. I'll charge you twenty dollars to fix your violin and re-hair the bow. Plus you give me your piece of amber. That should leave you with enough to buy some cookies and candy."

"No!" Arieh snatched back Little Miss Honey and replaced her in his pocket. "I work in a bakery. I don't need cookies. The amber was only lent to me."

Señor Diaz had stared at him as Arieh tucked the small piece of amber back into his handkerchief and stuffed it into his top shirt pocket.

"OK. Twenty dollars, and you keep the amber. Do you want to pay me in advance?"

A warning sounded in Arieh's head. He remembered his father saying, "When somebody does a job for you, don't pay them all in advance." He could see his father's face reflected on the violin's wooden face. Señor Diaz read his mind. "Give me five dollars to buy the materials, the rest when it's finished. You're a smart boy, Arieh Weinstein. Come back next week, and it will be ready." They shook hands, like men, to seal the deal.

As Arieh and his violin were parted for the first time since he'd fled the ghetto with it in 1941, he thought his heart would break.

"You will take care of it, won't you?" he said, turning back. "It's all I have left of my papa."

All the way back to Hialeah on the bus, he kept his hand in his pocket, guarding his precious amber tablet. It was his private piece of magic, his only connection to Simeon. He thought he'd look down and see his fingers missing or see his heart beating outside his chest wall. He got off the bus and limped back to the little pink board house, where he washed, changed his shirt, and prepared to go downstairs for the Sabbath meal that wasn't a Sabbath meal at all.

When Arieh returned to the violin shop a week later, he scarcely recognised the instrument Señor Diaz handed him. He looked at the familiar fine grain of the wood, now restored to a glorious rich golden brown. It seemed to be smiling at him. "You restored it and polished it," he said, astounded. "It's like new. Like the way Papa kept it. But I'll never be able to pay you for all this work." He ran his fingers lovingly over the exquisite revived wood, then picked up the violin, tucked it under his chin, and let his fingers drum on the fingerboard, feeling the new strings as he plucked each one gently, his sore, chapped hands momentarily forgotten in the sheer joy of holding his most precious possession in the world, again.

"This is just how it was when Papa played it in the Odessa Symphony Orchestra," he said. "I couldn't look after it in the forest. It wasn't my fault. But my papa, he would be so happy. Thank you."

Señor Diaz handed him his bow furnished with new hairs. "Play," the Spaniard ordered. "Let me hear you."

Arieh put down his cane, leant back against the counter for support, fingered the strings of his violin, and tuned it carefully.

"I will play you the Bruch, the last piece I learned when I had lessons in New York." he said.

Señor Diaz walked around to the front of the counter with his stool in his hand. "Perch on this, Arieh. I didn't ask, what happened to your legs?"

Arieh told few people the cause for his need for the calliper and cane, but he suddenly trusted this man. He told Señor Diaz his story, as briefly as he could: Mikhail finding him in the forest; Simeon; setting the gelignite and his violin's part in the plot; the fire and the months of suffering. As he tucked his violin under the left side of his chin, he sensed its intimacy. It felt as though he was holding his papa's hand. As he played, all the pain in his fingers and in his heart disappeared. Suddenly, Arieh was with his mama and papa in the old apartment in Odessa. His mama was baking for the Sabbath. Baby Bracha was lying in her crib in the kitchen, playing with her hands. He could smell the apple cake for tonight's dessert wafting through the apartment. He was six years old again, and his small fingers had to stretch. The violin was almost bigger than he was, but he stood in the living room with his father's fingers over his, showing him where to put them, practising these same notes on this very violin.

Then came the *Pathétique*, and there was Mikhail, plucking him from the tree stump and taking him back to the Zemlyanka. He allowed his arm to brush his breast pocket, and as he felt the small nodule inside his shirt, his amber tablet, he could feel Simeon's presence. When he finished, there was a moment of complete silence. He laid down the bow, placing the violin carefully back in its case on the counter. Señor Diaz stood back and applauded, and suddenly Arieh was aware of more applause. Two other people had entered the shop as he'd been playing and had been standing, listening intently. They were clapping too.

"You play beautifully, young man. What's your name?"

"Arieh. Arieh Weinstein."

"My name is David Lawrence. My wife here is Eve. We loved what we heard. Where do you take lessons?"

"No. I don't take lessons. I used to when I lived in New York, but my aunt doesn't have enough money to pay for lessons. I live with my uncle and aunt in Hialeah." He turned to the shop owner. "Señor Diaz, speaking of money, how much do I owe you? I think I will have to pay in instalments."

Before Señor Diaz could speak, David Lawrence jumped in. "Young man, you must let me settle your bill."

Arieh began to shake his head violently, but the man put a calming hand on his shoulder. "I think you were not born in America, young man. Where do you come from? You obviously love your violin. It's a wonderful violin. You are a very lucky young man to own such a marvellous instrument. Let's go and drink some coffee together. We've come to collect Eve's instrument, Pablo, but tomorrow will do. Let's all go for coffee. Then you can tell us more about yourself."

Arieh looked at the clock on the wall. It was almost three thirty. "I haven't got time. I need to be back in Hialeah by six fifteen." The bus journey would take him at least an hour, and he'd missed the three fifteen already. He dared not be late.

"We'll take you back in our car, Arieh. We must talk. I think you are a Jewish boy. We are Jewish too. Where did you come from?"

In the car, a white Cadillac convertible, the three adults sat on the red bench seat in front. David Lawrence had first lifted Arieh onto the long seat in the rear with the violin in its case tucked safely on the floor. They stopped outside a cafe on Ocean Boulevard. The three of them got out, and David Lawrence put out his arms to lift Arieh down. Of course, the boy insisted on taking his violin.

267

They ordered coffees for themselves and the largest chocolate milkshake Arieh had ever seen covered in a swirl of thick cream. With his precious violin tucked between his feet, and in the company of these strangers, he was suddenly happy. They talked, initially about his mama and his papa and Arieh's wartime experiences. He told them how he'd come to America with Ruth and how he'd had lessons once a week thanks to Blake and Lauren.

"Play the violin for us again," Eve requested.

He picked up his violin, ran his hand over his breast pocket to draw both strength and comfort from his amber tablet, and began to play the *Pathétique*. Then he followed with the Bruch. He lost himself in his music as he always did. When he had finished, and to his amazement, everyone in the cafe applauded wildly.

"Would you like to take violin lessons again?"

Arieh's eyes filled with tears. He nodded. "But it's impossible. My uncle and aunt are very poor."

"Nothing's impossible." David Lawrence looked at him and stroked his own dark blond moustache. He was having a private conversation with Eve, their eyes sharing silent thoughts, although not a word had passed between them. Then he spread his large, well-manicured hands flat on the table and opened his mouth to speak. Suddenly Arieh spotted the ring on the fourth finger of his right hand, and it hit him. It was a beautiful gold ring with two wide flanks holding at its centre a sparkling diamond about the same size as Little Miss Honey. He felt in his pocket. His amber tablet was there. "Listen, Arieh. We don't have children ..." Even though he knew it was rude, Arieh couldn't help himself. He jumped in. "Can you tell me, sir, where did you buy your ring?"

They all looked at him quizzically. "I didn't buy it. I made it. I'm a jeweller. Now about your music lessons."

Arieh took the small piece of amber from his pocket.

"Excuse me, sir. I need this to be put in a ring. As you've so kindly paid for my violin to be restored, and since you're taking me home, which means I don't need my bus fare, would twenty-three dollars be enough to make me a ring like yours, but with this at the centre? It doesn't have to be gold," he added quickly. "It could just be silver or some other metal. Just make it so I could wear it on my finger instead of keeping it in my pocket. It's not really mine. My friend Simeon lent it to me when we lived in the forest. I lost it once, but then my friend Ruth, who bought me to America, found it. If I could wear it, I would never lose it again. Then I will be sure to be able to give it back to Simeon next time I see him. It's one of his lucky amber tablets, you see."

David Lawrence took the piece of amber, fidgeted in his pocket, and brought out an eyeglass to examine it. "It's beautiful-quality amber, but it's been burnt at the edges. It was affixed to something solid, but the fixing wore loose. Yes, I think I could do that." Suddenly he realised that Arieh wouldn't accept his ring as a gift. The boy was sitting, his back straight and proud. David could read his mind from his stance.

"Let's say fifteen dollars. That should cover it. Would you like a receipt?" Arieh nodded and grinned. "Yes, please." Finally, he was being treated like a grown man.

David Lawrence scribbled on a paper napkin: "Received, one piece of amber, the size of a large pea, from Arieh Weinstein. To set in gold ring, fee as agreed, fifteen dollars." He took another piece of paper napkin, tore it, and wound it round Arieh's finger. "Just to ensure I make the right size." He smiled. "Now let's get back to the conversation about your violin lessons. Sadly we don't have a family of our own, but we love music. Eve used to play the violin professionally, didn't you, dear?"

She nodded.

"So, we would be honoured if you would let us sponsor you through music school, Arieh. What do you say? Of course, we would discuss it all with your aunt first."

Arieh looked around him. They were sitting under a sunshade to protect themselves from the fierce heat of a Miami afternoon. The tiny piece of amber sat on a paper napkin on the table, a pebble of shimmering gold reflecting the sun's glorious rays. He stared at it, and the tiny fly seemed to wink at him. Violin lessons? "Is this your doing?" he whispered at it. "Or am I dreaming?"

"Will the teacher help me read and write music properly?" Arieh asked, stroking the little piece of amber in his hand.

"Yes," Eve Lawrence answered. "If you are serious about your lessons."

"I would love that. More than anything in the world." He was beaming so hard he thought his face might split. "I will learn to write down the piece of music I've got in my head. It's been there for years, just waiting to come out. I will call it the *Amber Concerto*, and I will dedicate it to my best friend, Simeon Karminsky."

Bibliography

Ales Adamovich and Daniel Granin translated by Dr Clare Burstall and Dr Vladimir Kisselnikov *Leningrad Under Siege* Pen and Sword Military 2007

Barkan, Menachem, ed., *Extermination of the Jews in Latvia, 1941–1945: Series of Lectures* (Riga, Latvia, 2009). ed Sceptre paperback 2009

Benioff, David, *City of Thieves*. Viking Press - 2008

Glanz David M, *The Siege of Leningrad 1941-1944* (Cassell Military Paperback edition) 2004

Epstein, Barbara, *The Minsk Ghetto 1941–1943*. University of California Press 2008

Gilbert, Martin, *The Routledge Atlas of the Holocaust*. - ed 4 Routledge 2009

Inber, Vera, *Leningrad Diary*, tr. Serge M. Wolff and Rachel Grieve Hutchinson & Co 1971

Plaude, Victoria, *The Amber Room*, tr. Valery Fateyev (official guide of the Amber Room).

Salisbury, Harrison E., *The 900 Days: The Siege of Leningrad*. ed 2000 Pan Books

Scott-Clark, Catherine, and Adrian Levy, *The Amber Room*. Atlantic Books, London 2004

Lightning Source UK Ltd.
Milton Keynes UK
UKHW040922131119
353452UK00002B/248/P